Praise for CAROLYN HART
and her latest Henrie O mystery
DEATH ON THE RIVER WALK

"Carolyn Hart is one of the most popular
practitioners of the traditional mystery."
Cleveland Plain Dealer

"Fun . . . intriguing . . . absorbing . . . entertaining . . .
It keeps the reader guessing . . . Once again,
Hart transports the reader to a picturesque locale . . .
Henrie O is an endearing female sleuth."
Los Angeles Times

"Hart is an expert at seamless storytelling . . .
Henrie O is a senior citizen who refreshingly fits
no stereotype, a woman who is as independent,
confident, and capable as anyone half her age."
Ft. Lauderdale Sun-Sentinel

"Carolyn Hart serves up another frothy brew with her series
character Henrie O . . . The spry sleuth triumphs with wry
wit and grit . . . Hart lovingly describes San Antonio's
famed River Walk . . . She also builds
an inspiring portrait of a Latino matriarch."
Chicago Sun-Times

"Cheers for Henrie O, an intelligent, engaging sleuth!"
Mary Higgins Clark

Books by Carolyn Hart

Henrie O

DEAD MAN'S ISLAND
SCANDAL IN FAIR HAVEN
DEATH IN LOVERS' LANE
DEATH IN PARADISE
DEATH ON THE RIVER WALK
RESORT TO MURDER

Death on Demand

DEATH ON DEMAND
DESIGN FOR MURDER
SOMETHING WICKED
HONEYMOON WITH MURDER
A LITTLE CLASS ON MURDER
DEADLY VALENTINE
THE CHRISTIE CAPER
SOUTHERN GHOST
MINT JULEP MURDER
YANKEE DOODLE DEAD
WHITE ELEPHANT DEAD
SUGARPLUM DEAD
APRIL FOOL DEAD

And in Hardcover

ENGAGED TO DIE

CAROLYN HART

DEATH ON THE RIVER WALK

A HENRIE O MYSTERY

AVON BOOKS
An Imprint of HarperCollins*Publishers*

This is a work of fiction. Names, characters, places, and incidents are products of the author's imagination or are used fictitiously and are not to be construed as real. Any resemblance to actual events, locales, organizations, or persons, living or dead, is entirely coincidental.

AVON BOOKS
An Imprint of HarperCollins*Publishers*
10 East 53rd Street
New York, New York 10022-5299

Copyright © 1999 by Carolyn Hart
Excerpt from *Estate of Mind* copyright © 1999 by Tamar Myers
Excerpt from *Creeps Suzette* copyright © 2000 by Mary Daheim
Excerpt from *Death on the River Walk* copyright © 1999 by Carolyn Hart
Excerpt from *Liberty Falling* copyright © 1999 by Nevada Barr
Excerpt from *A Simple Shaker Murder* copyright © 2000 by Deborah Woodworth
Excerpt from *In the Still of the Night* copyright © 2000 by The Janice Young Brooks Trust
Excerpt from *Murder Shoots the Bull* copyright © 1999 by Anne George
Inside cover author photo by David G. Fitzgerald
Library of Congress Catalog Card Number: 98-46962
ISBN: 0-380-79005-X
www.avonbooks.com

First Avon Books paperback printing: February 2000
First Avon Books hardcover printing: April 1999

Avon Trademark Reg. U.S. Pat. Off. and in Other Countries, Marca Registrada, Hecho en U.S.A.
HarperCollins® is a trademark of HarperCollins Publishers Inc.

Printed in the U.S.A.

10 9 8 7 6 5 4

In loving memory of Philip
December 22, 1960–February 21, 1998
Someday upon a far distant, sunnier shore...
——Mother

Acknowledgments

I am especially grateful to Patsy Garza Asher, owner of San Antonio's superb mystery bookstore, Remember the Alibi. Patsy welcomed me to her hometown, willingly served as a cheerful guide, and was extraordinarily helpful in finding excellent books about San Antonio.

I am also grateful to Spanish scholar Dr. Judith LeBlanc Flores for her translations of materials from Mexico City's National Museum of Anthropology.

It was a great pleasure to visit San Antonio, explore its unique and lovely River Walk, and learn more about Hispanic art, which has made and is making a vital contribution to the wonderful cultural mosaic that is the United States.

prologue

ALFONSO scrabbled every day to survive. He'd been on the streets since he was seven. He knew no other life. He cadged food from the garbage bins behind fine restaurants, flashed smiles at norteamericanos and offered information they liked, where to find women and drugs and hotels that catered to guests with peculiar tastes. His English was not grammatical, but he spoke it well enough. In the summers, he wandered Chapultepec Park, Mexico City's oasis of loveliness amid the stinging brownish smog that dimmed the porcelain-fine sky and tainted lungs. It was only at night that the air freshened. Alfonso especially enjoyed prowling in the darkness from his hidden nesting place in a clump of willows behind the National Museum.

Alfonso was as attuned to his surroundings as a cougar alert for a meal. He first noticed the big blond norteamericano late on a moonlit August night, slipping from shadow to shadow behind the museum. Alfonso watched and wondered. The man came a second night. The next morning, he was in a crowd waiting for tickets. There was a grand exhibit at the museum, drawing visitors from around the world. When the man came again late that night, Alfonso called out, "Señor, if you are looking for anything, I can help."

I

The man jerked toward him.

Alfonso tensed his muscles, ready to run. He wasn't afraid. And he had a knife in his pocket.

"So what do you sell?" The big man's Spanish was accented, but he spoke it with ease.

Alfonso felt a stab of disappointment. He'd wasted a lot of time tracking this man. No one who spoke Spanish that well needed help to find whatever the city had to offer. But Alfonso slipped into his usual patter. "Girls? I can take you to a special place . . ." But not even the mention of drugs or gambling evoked a response in the alert eyes that watched him so closely.

Instead, the man's big head tilted back and he laughed. "How to Skin a Gringo in One Easy Lesson."

Alfonso was turning away when the man said, "Wait. Wait a minute. I've got a job for you. If you've got the guts."

Alfonso swung back. And listened. When the man finished, Alfonso rocked back on his heels and gave him a cocky grin. "Sure." He spoke in English. "No problem." He held out his hand. They haggled, but Alfonso walked away with a third of the money he'd been promised.

The next night, Alfonso slipped down a quiet street outside the park. He carried a pop bottle. The liquid inside sloshed as he walked. The rag stuffed in the mouth of the bottle was moist and the smell of gasoline made his nose wrinkle. When he reached the tall fence, he used a wax match, lit the rag, and threw. The simple bomb exploded and huge flashes marked the destruction of the electrical transformers serving this portion of Mexico City.

In the National Museum, the lights went off. As did the alarm system. Alfonso's employer, dressed in black sweater and slacks, slipped from the cover of a clump of willows and ran lightly toward the back of the museum. He flung high a rope ladder, pulled to make sure its hooks held snugly, and climbed swiftly. He pulled the ladder up with him and moved purposefully toward the front of the museum, the small knapsack on his back bouncing with every step. His heart thudded and he felt the sweet, sharp elixir of adrenaline.

one

I glanced at the computer printout that rested on the passenger seat of the rental car, a casual picture of a grandmother and granddaughter, arms linked, faces aglow with laughter and love. The bright photograph had been scanned into a computer half a world away and the resulting crisp picture that had issued from my daughter's computer was one of the small miracles that no one remarks in today's technological wonderland. The grandmother, Gina Wilson, was one of my oldest friends, a shining memory from the happiest years of my life. The granddaughter, Iris Chavez, was a child I'd come to know because she spent much of her growing up time with Gina. Iris was near in age to my own granddaughter, Diana.

The faces in the photograph were sharply different, despite their laughter on the day the picture was snapped on a sunny summer afternoon at Laguna. It wasn't simply a matter of age. Gina's short-cropped white hair and Dresden china pale skin and Iris's richly raven curls and creamily dusky complexion made a lovely contrast. Gina's sharply planed features were arresting, her light green eyes curious and skeptical, her smile amused yet with a sardonic undercurrent, as befitted a woman who'd been one of the cleverest political reporters of her time. Iris's face was cherubic, still so young there were no lines. Her eyes were also green, but there was no challenge in Iris's gaze. Instead eagerness vied with uncertainty. Iris's bow of a mouth was marked with brilliantly red lipstick, but the vivid color couldn't hide vulnerability.

The two sets of green eyes were the only real resemblance in the photograph. What had Gina once told me? She'd looked out the window at Iris playing in the yard and smilingly observed, "Iris is the image of her father, except for her eyes."

Iris. The name brought to my mind the vision of a slim blonde with startlingly blue eyes. But not this Iris. Not Iris Chavez, whom I remembered as a giggling little girl with a mop of curly black hair and later as a plump, eager-to-please teenager. A sweet, bouncy, cheerful girl. I'd not seen Iris or Gina in several years. Yet when the phone rang yesterday at my daughter's home in east Texas, I'd immediately recognized Gina's voice and just as swiftly known there was trouble. Or, to be precise, realized immediately that Gina was terribly afraid.

I hoped that soon, very soon, I could call Gina and say everything was okay. I slowed for a red light, checked my map. Although San Antonio streets often change names, I was finding my way without difficulty. Gina's directions had been clear and careful. Almost there.

Gina hated to ask for help, but there is nothing you won't do, no mile you won't walk, no mountain you won't climb, no effort you won't make for a grandchild. I understand that. I have two grandchildren of my own.

I didn't blame Gina for being frightened. Even though Gina was half a world away, Gina in Majorca,

Iris in San Antonio, they kept in close touch by E-mail. At least once or twice a week, they exchanged messages. It was their custom to chat on Saturday morning Iris's time, Saturday afternoon Gina's time in Majorca.

"Nothing, Henrie O, nothing since last Wednesday. And Iris never misses E-mailing on Saturday mornings without telling me in advance that she will skip. I've sent message after message. I've called and called. There's no answer. I thought of contacting the police. But what could I tell them? That I haven't received an E-mail? That I can't get her on the phone? That's not enough to report her as missing." She paused. "And maybe she's just out of town with a friend. Oh, there could be many reasons. I don't want to embarrass her. But I can't wait any longer." Gina's voice quavered.

E-mail. It links us to the world no matter where we live. It was through a casual E-mail that Gina knew I was visiting my daughter, Emily, and that I was only a three-hour drive from San Antonio, where Iris lived. And yes, my days were free. I was no longer teaching, though I'd decided to keep my home in the Missouri college town where I'd been on the journalism faculty for several years. And yes, I could easily go to San Antonio and yes, I would do that for my frightened friend.

I'd received Gina's call early this morning. Now, the answer was near. Perhaps I would find Iris at her apartment. If I didn't find her, I would go to the store where she worked and perhaps we'd both laugh and—after she'd called her grandmother, assured her she was fine—Iris would offer to buy me a cold raspa, the shaved-ice confection so dear to San Antonians, and I would stay a few days in this lovely city—what better place to do some early Christmas shopping?—then resume my visit at my daughter's.

I turned to my left, my right, and found the apartment house at the end of the street. I locked my car and stood in the shadow of a palm tree. I hated leaving the windows up. September marks fall in the north. In San Antonio, sunny warm days continue. Oh, an occasional cold front will drop the temperature into the low eighties. Sweat beaded my face. My soft cotton dress clung to me. I took a deep breath of moist air softer than skin lotion.

The two-story stuccoed apartment building, La Casita, was bordered by dusty flower beds with a few stalks of parched impatiens. A narrow parking lot abutted the building. I stepped into the lot, shaded my eyes. I spotted Iris's car immediately. A fifteen-year-old coupe with a battered left fender and one headlight lower than the other. Gina had described the car perfectly. "A rattletrap, but that's all she can afford. She had it painted pink and green, said it made the car laugh. Oh, Henrie O, I can see her now, giggling and pointing to the car. She gave the car a name, too— Whiffle." That's when Gina choked back a sob.

It was easy to see the car. Not only was it spectacularly, jauntily painted in swirls, bright even by San Antonio standards, it was one of only three cars in the small lot. I walked to the car. The windows were down. Was Iris habitually careless? Had she parked the car expecting to return shortly? Or did she figure nobody would steal a dilapidated old car painted in pink and green swirls? A candy striped beach towel was crumpled in the front seat. A couple of paperback books were on the floor, the latest by Nora Roberts and Merline Lovelace. On a pink sheet, oversize printing reminded: "Cinnamon rolls, eggs, rum. Pick up cleaning. Buy sugar for pralines."

I hoped the sudden constriction in my chest was nothing more than the press of heat and humidity. The car worried me. I'd called Iris's apartment before I left Emily's house, called again on my cell phone when I reached the outskirts of San Antonio. No answer. Sighting Iris's car, after my last fruitless phone call, worried me. If her car was in the lot, why didn't she answer her phone?

The neighborhood was quiet, somnolent. An ordinary, unremarkable, pleasant Sunday in a modest neighborhood off Broadway, not far from Incarnate Word College.

I stepped through an archway, welcoming the shade. The apartment house was built around a bricked courtyard. Once there had been a central fountain. No water pulsed now. The tiles were chipped, some were missing. But a huge magnolia flourished, dappling benches on either side of the fountain with shade. Glossy leaves had drifted into the fountain. The ground floor apartment doors opened to the courtyard. On the second floor, they opened to a narrow exposed corridor.

On the second-floor corridor, an elderly man shuffled to an end apartment, unlocked the door, closed it behind him. Otherwise, there was no one about. A wooden arrow with faded red letters—"Manager"—pointed toward the back of the courtyard.

I walked up the stairs. Apartment 26 was halfway up the corridor. Two windows looked out to the courtyard. The slatted blinds were closed. I knocked sharply. The sound was loud in the Sunday quiet. Behind me, the magnolia leaves suddenly rustled. A crow erupted into flight, his strident caw startling.

I knocked again, bent my head to listen. No sound.

No movement. I rattled the knob. I stepped to the nearest window, gave a tug. It didn't budge. Iris might be casual about her car, but as a young woman living alone she wasn't foolish enough to leave her windows unlocked. A little thing. It made me feel better. There could be a dozen reasons why her car was in the lot. Maybe the battery was dead. Maybe she was out with a friend.

Anything was possible. But that, of course, was why I had come. Please, God, let it simply be thoughtlessness, an energetic girl too consumed in living to remember that her grandmother looked forward to cheerful E-mail messages and waited expectantly every Saturday for a connection to bring them close despite the thousands of miles that separated them.

Please, God. This was a child dear to me and a child beloved to Gina. Gina, my dear friend, my old friend, the kind of friend you make when life is full of promise and the future is greater than the past. No matter how often or how rarely you meet, there is a bond that defies time and age. And Iris—I remembered a visit years ago, oh, she couldn't have been more than ten or twelve—her cheeks flushed with excitement, her eyes sparkling, Iris had bustled about Gina's small apartment, setting a table for tea, bringing us dainty finger sandwiches of peanut butter and jelly and pimiento and pound cake cut in slices and waiting eagerly to hear our cries of delight. A girl who always tried hard to please.

This morning, I'd reassured Gina that she was too quick to worry, that there could be many reasons why Iris hadn't E-mailed on schedule. Gina said, "I know. I know, but . . ." I heard her sudden quick breath and knew the fears she didn't want to voice. Gina and I had both spent many years as reporters. We learned that all things were possible, and some of them were ugly indeed.

I gave one final demanding knock on the scuffed wooden door, then swung around, walked swiftly to the stairs and down. Brown-edged magnolia leaves crunched underfoot as I crossed the courtyard. When I reached the door marked "Manager," I heard the tinny sound of television. This time my knock was answered.

"Yes?" An imposing woman in a green-striped smock and black slacks looked at me without interest. She looked to be in her fifties, with dark salt-and-pepper hair and a stoic expression, a woman who no longer had great expectations of life.

"I hope you can help me." One advantage of age is the projection of a non-threatening image. My dark hair is streaked with silver. I hope the lines in my face reflect reason and good humor. "I'm Henrietta Collins. I haven't been able to reach Iris Chavez in Apartment 26. I knocked on her door, but there was no answer even though her car is in the parking lot. Iris is the granddaughter of a close friend."

A thin black-and-gray striped cat edged inside the open door. The manager gave an exclamation of annoyance and waved her hand, shooing it back into the courtyard. "These cats. People leave them and think the good Lord will provide." But her dark eyes studied me.

"Iris's grandmother has been trying to get in touch with her for almost a week. She's concerned that Iris might be ill and I promised to check on her. May I come in?" I moved forward.

She hesitated, then stepped back to let me enter. The window air conditioner scarcely cooled the tiny apartment. Bright shawls draped two easy chairs. A silver-flecked German shepherd was splayed on the tiled floor. The dog's cool eyes watched me carefully. The television shared a corner with a shrine to Mary.

The manager looked me over, from my short-cropped hair, a new style, to my navy blue dress, comfortable for travel, to my well-worn but well-made leather purse, to my sensible navy flats.

She lifted her big shoulders in a shrug. "The rent has not been paid. It is due this morning."

I flipped open my purse, pulled out my checkbook. "How much is the rent?"

"Three hundred and twenty-five dollars."

I wrote the check, handed it to her.

She studied the check, then frowned, her face heavy and questioning. "You do not live here. I need a local address."

"I'm not sure where I'll be staying. You can get in touch with me through the store where Iris works." I was presuming, but that was my next stop. "Tesoros. On the River Walk."

She didn't write the name down. Perhaps she already knew where Iris worked. Or perhaps she had a good memory. Her glance had moved past me, to the television set and the drama unfolding on its small screen.

"When did you last see Iris?"

Her shrug was dismissive, uninterested. "I don't know. Some days ago. She was leaving."

"What time of day?"

On the screen, a woman sobbed, pushed away from the smoothly handsome man. An ad flashed.

The manager flicked an irritated look at me. "People come and go. I pay no attention. What does it matter to me? Oh, I think it was afternoon. Maybe Wednesday, maybe Thursday. She's a silly girl, always smiling and walking so fast."

I held out my hand. "I'd like a key to the apartment."

She glanced at the check in her hand, then moved heavily to a desk near the door. She opened a drawer, pulled out a ring of keys, thumbed through them, detached one.

"Thank you." I glanced back as I stepped out the door. I wished I could read the look on her face. Was it suspicion? Curiosity? Or something more? A quiet calculation, a conclusion?

I didn't like that last look she'd given me. But I was in a hurry to get into Iris's apartment. I was walking swiftly up the second floor corridor when I realized that she had not asked me to return the key. Did that indicate a knowledge that Iris would not return and therefore would not protest this invasion of her privacy, or did it simply indicate indifference?

When I reached the door, I knocked one more time, waited, then shoved the key quickly into the lock, turned the knob. As the door swung open, relief washed over me. The air in this small, scantily furnished apartment was hot, stale, and slightly sour, but there was no stomach-turning stench. Iris, dead or alive, was not here.

But I doubted Iris's apartment customarily looked this way. Books were tumbled out of their orange crate cases. The pink throw that no doubt usually covered the dingy mustard-yellow sofa straggled over one end. Sofa cushions were bunched on the floor, their covers unzipped, tufts of foam rubber protruding. Near the single closet, shoes and clothes were humped in an uneven mound. A black vinyl wheeled suitcase lay on its side, every zipper undone, exposing empty compartments. The dresser drawers had been dumped too, the drawers upended, their contents—lingerie, cotton tops, shorts—spilled onto the floor. The single bed along the back wall was askew. The mattress, stripped of sheets, lay on the floor. The box springs leaned against the metal frame. In the small bathroom, towels and washcloths made another untidy heap near the open cabinet. In the tiny kitchenette, cabinet doors were flung wide.

I stepped inside, closed the door. Skirting the helter-skelter piles, I crossed to the window air conditioner and turned it on. It would take a while, longer probably than I would be here, for the room to cool. And that was all there was, the one room, now littered with the bits and pieces of Iris's life.

I stood with my back to the air conditioner, welcoming the waft of chill air, and surveyed the chaos. Chaos but no destruction. This was not wanton vandalism. Moreover, there were odd exceptions to the disorder. Spices sat in order in a spice rack. Photographs on a pine end table appeared undisturbed. A thick swath of paper with a half-finished watercolor was clipped to an artist's easel. The box of watercolors was closed. Nearby, a small oil painting was propped in a wooden chair. When I walked close to the easel, I saw that Iris was copying the painting, a common-place exercise for budding artists.

What is the children's game? Smaller than a bread box, bigger than an orange?

The searcher hadn't been looking for tiny items—witness the undisturbed spices—or for pieces of paper that could be hidden, for example, behind a picture in a frame, or for anything larger than a suitcase might contain.

I studied the open suitcase. A box, say, could be a

maximum of four inches deep, twelve inches wide, eighteen inches across. A box or an object. Or objects.

This was not the work of an ordinary thief. Such a thief, looking for items easy to pawn or sell, might have passed up the small oil painting even though it appeared to me to be out of the ordinary. But a thief would have taken the television set on a stand across from the sofa, the headset lying on the kitchen table, the mobile telephone, the computer on a card table. Or, for that matter, the answering machine. The red light winked on the answering machine. Fifteen recorded calls.

When I punched "rewind" and listened, I recognized Gina's voice on seven of the calls, but every so often there was a call and no voice; nothing, simply silence. Of course, it isn't unusual for people to call and decide not to leave a message. But that many? Was someone calling to see if Iris had returned? I glanced around the room. There was only the one telephone and the inexpensive recorder. But no caller ID. How nice that would have been.

I reached out, then let my hand fall. I must call Gina. But not yet. The news I could offer would only frighten her more. All I could say was that I'd not found Iris and her apartment showed the effects of a hurried but thorough search.

There was one last hope. A slender hope, but it staved off the moment when I must place a call to Majorca. I found the telephone directory, looked up a number, dialed.

"Tesoros. How may I help you?" It was a young man's voice, well educated and pleasant.

"May I speak to Iris Chavez, please."

It is well to listen to silences as well as speech. The

pause pulsed with tension. I realized abruptly I should not have called first.

His answer was stiff. "I'm sorry. She doesn't work here anymore. Sorry I can't help you."

The line went dead.

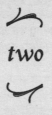

two

SAN Antonio's River Walk is a place where dreams have been made and broken. It would be easy to dismiss today's River Walk as a commercial lure, but the river, sweet product of artesian springs, made life possible ten thousand years ago, when the land knew the occasional nomadic Indian, and the water still makes life possible, though its function is as different now as a present day shopkeeper from a hunter and gatherer. Today's River Walk, the creation of visionary architect Robert Hugman, hosts lodging, shops, restaurants and romance, drawing an unceasing flow of visitors who seek a glamorous respite from the everyday world.

If any city represents the glory of Texas, it is San Antonio, where Spaniards, Indians, cowboys, and European immigrants created a multilayered culture unlike that of any other city. The mission San Antonio de Valero was founded May 1, 1718, the result of a missionary journey made by Father Antonio de San Buenaventura Olivares in 1709. Fifteen Spanish families from the Canary Islands arrived in 1731 to establish near the mission the town of San Fernando de Béxar, which became the town of San Antonio. In 1794, the mission was turned into a fort staffed by a

Spanish cavalry company named for the town from which it came, San José y Santiago del Alamo. The fort became known by the cavalry name, shortened to Alamo. After Mexico achieved independence from Spain, Mexican armies and Texas colonists struggled for control of Texas. In a passage of arms celebrated forever in Texas, the 180 defenders of the Alamo refused to surrender and died to a man after a thirteen-day siege that ended March 6, 1836. Eventually, San Antonio, the heart of Texas, became a part of the United States and the lovely city by the river drew immigrants from Europe, especially Germans. San Antonio remains unlike any other American city. Some cities have elements of San Antonio's intertwined culture, but none match it for sheer exuberance and colorful individuality, permeated by Hispanic grace, German industry, and Southern gentility.

The River Walk is modern San Antonio's heart, attracting well over a million visitors a year, just as the flowing waters in earlier years attracted, in turn, nomadic Indians, Spanish friars, and German immigrants.

I sat at an outside table and sipped iced tea and looked across the placid green water, water that once ran red with blood. In the aftermath of the battle for the Alamo, Mayor Ruiz burned the bodies of the defenders. Charged with interring the bodies of Santa Ana's slain, the mayor buried as many as he could and dumped the rest into the river.

Today a barge glided past, the passengers smiling, taking pictures, welcoming the brief escape from the sun as they passed beneath the occasional arched stone bridges. I shaded my eyes. In a moment, I would cross the near bridge, my goal the three-story stucco building directly opposite. The river is bordered by wide sidewalks. Stone walls serve as the river's banks as it meanders through the city. The restaurants and shops on the River Walk are the first floor of buildings that open to the downtown streets on their second floor.

The breeze rustled tall cottonwoods. Sunlight striking through shifting leaves made filigree patterns on the buildings and the stone walk. Some of the buildings looked very old and some startlingly modern. The stuccoed structure directly opposite was old, the walls probably a foot or so thick. But the curved glass windows that provided a magnificent display area were a renovation. The shining shop windows contrasted oddly with the ornate iron grillwork of the second-floor balconies, each with blue pots holding bright red canna lilies. A white wooden sign hung from an iron post. Gilt letters announced simply: "Tesoros." At one corner of the building hung another sign: "La Mariposa." An arrow pointed up the stone stairs. A glistening monarch butterfly was painted hovering above the arrow. Gilt letters beneath proclaimed: "The River Walk's Oldest Bed & Breakfast."

A silver bell rang a sweet clear tone whenever the ornate carved green door of Tesoros opened. Customers were casually but expensively dressed. As I watched, a young man appeared in one of the windows, arranging a display of pottery. I caught quick glimpses of him, his face in shadow—shining dark hair, a fashionable goatee perfectly trimmed, deft movements. An older man walked slowly around the corner of the building, carrying a pail and a squeegee. His shoulders were bowed, his eyes downcast. The windows looked quite clean, but he walked at a deliberate pace to the near window, carefully put down his pail, then slowly began to wash the sparkling glass.

I spent half an hour at the café, taking the time to consider how I should approach the store. Sometimes frankness can be effective. Sometimes it can be foolish. I knew nothing about Tesoros, about the people who owned it, about Iris Chavez's job there. In the years when I was a reporter, I prepared exhaustively for interviews, reading every bit of material I could discover about my subject. But I'd had no idea when I drove toward San Antonio that I would have any need for knowledge about the store where Gina's granddaughter worked, other than its location. But when I telephoned and asked for Iris Chavez, the connection was broken. That was surely odd. Yet, during this short observation, I'd seen nothing remarkable about the store or its clientele, nothing that could even hint at why one of its employees had disappeared. If she had.

I finished my tea, left a bill on the table, and strolled to the bridge. I stopped at the top of the bridge and looked at the green water and at the occasional palms and lacy ferns and bright flowers that promised a never-ending summer. The river curved lazily around a bend, creating an intimate pocket of stores and people enjoying a lovely Sunday afternoon in September. It was hard to connect this holiday picture with the shabby little apartment and Iris's disarranged belongings and the blinking red light on the telephone answering machine, signaling calls for reassurance and calls where no one spoke.

When I reached the front of the store, I glanced in the first window, the window even now being meticulously scrubbed by the stooped man who seemed oblivious both to its cleanliness and to the constant mill of pedestrians behind him.

I've looked in many shop windows in far distant countries. I'm not a shopper. I have no desire to own treasures of any kind. But I appreciate beauty, even beauty priced beyond the reach of most and certainly beyond my reach.

A magnificent glazed pottery jar dominated the display. Stylized birds, flowers and palms in gold and black glistened against a finely hatched background. Two glazed plates were to the left of the jar. One featured a woman villager, her hat filled with fruit, and the second a man gathering up the fruits of harvest while his donkey rested. On the right of the jar were two dramatic dinner plates with greenish and gold peacocks and flower motifs against a tomato-red background.

A card announced in calligraphic script: "Tlaquepaque style, glazed pottery from the state of Jalisco."

The other window was as bright with color as a field of Texas wildflowers. The young man, arms folded, studied his arrangement of a dozen or so clay banks. The banks were created to hold coins, but now it would take a fistful of dollars to buy them. I especially liked the orange lion and pink polka-dotted pig.

This card announced: "Santa Cruz de las Huertas, 1920–1930."

The silvery bell sang as I opened the door. I still wasn't sure how to proceed, whether to be direct or oblique. Whatever I did, I hoped I made the right choice. I'd found nothing in Iris's apartment to lead me to her. This store was my last hope. I stepped inside to coolness and quiet, to a sense of serenity. Classical guitar music played softly. The wall on my right held a striking Rivera mural, a surging crowd, yet each face distinct, the whole vibrating with passion, protest, and pride.

I saw only one customer, a slim blonde with ash-fine hair drawn back in a chignon, who waited by the front counter. The woman behind the cash register was ringing up the purchase, a wooden bas-relief of a farmer leading a donkey laden with corn-filled baskets.

I wandered among the display islands, slabs cut from big tree trunks that had been dried and glazed. The shiny, rocklike platforms sat on wrought-iron supports. Spotlights inset in the ceiling highlighted each display. There was a glorious diversity: three-dimensional clay figures including a set of Mexican presidents by the celebrated Panduro family, Talavera tiles, flower-decorated bowls by Enrique Ventosa. Several wall cabinets held ornate silver pieces, trays, candlesticks, pitchers. A bookcase contained Day of the Dead representations, including a skeleton poking his head out of a rocket ship. I wandered among the islands and knew that I was indeed in the presence of treasures. It was the same sensation I felt on a visit to a grand museum. It would take weeks to appreciate the collection here, a lifetime to understand the many kinds of art.

I paused at a display of carved wooden animals from Oaxaca. If I were a tourist, here for pleasure, these works would tempt me. The brightly colored animal figures—pink giraffes, spotted rhinos, lemon tigers—spoke of a world of unleashed imagination, the artist's ebullient recognition that the pulse of life is more than is ever seen by the eye alone, that the spirit of joy colors every reality.

The flip of that coin reminded me that behind light there is dark, that I could not accept the serenity and beauty of this room as the totality of this place.

I reached the back of the long, wide room and turned to face the entrance. The young man still worked in the display window. The woman behind the main counter finished ringing up the sale. "We'll be happy to ship the panel. Please put your address on this card—" Her voice had the liquid grace of a speaker who also speaks Spanish. It is a melodious cadence familiar in San Antonio. The blonde gave a languid thank you and drifted toward the door. The woman at the cash desk glanced toward me.

I had a sense of energy and vigor barely contained. Lustrous black hair streaked with silver poufed from a broad curved forehead. Deep set dark eyes glittered with restless intelligence. Her skin was smooth and creamy, her lips scarlet as a tanager's wing. She wore a crisp white blouse embroidered with a peacock, its tail spread in iridescent glory. She might have been stunningly attractive, but deep lines bracketed her mouth, and her eyes were pools of sullen fire. One hand moved abruptly, rattling the silver bracelets on her arm.

"May I help you?" It was a polite query, spoken with a perfect intonation for this expensive shop, a gentle offer but unobtrusive, undemanding. And, I would guess, at odds with this woman's questing, rebellious nature.

"Yes. May I speak with Iris Chavez?"

Just for an instant, I thought her eyes flared in shock. Was she surprised? Alarmed? Angry? The fleeting expression came and went so quickly, I was unsure of its meaning. But I certainly read the meaning of the frown that pulled her dark brows into a straight hard line. "That girl! I'd like to talk to her, too." Her voice was no longer melodious. It bristled with disgust. "Gone off without a word to anybody. No sense of responsibility. I thought she'd at least show up this weekend. She knows the weekend is our busiest time. And we're in the middle of preparing for the auction. Well, she needn't think she can come to work here only when it suits her fancy."

"It's important that I contact her." I spoke sharply. "When was she last here?"

She looked at me icily. "Who are you?" The demand was just this side of rude.

"Henrietta Collins. Iris's grandmother, Gina Wilson, is a close friend of mine. Iris customarily gets in touch with her grandmother every Saturday. But Gina heard nothing from her this Saturday. Moreover, Gina has heard nothing from Iris since last Wednesday. Gina is very concerned and I promised her I would find Iris." I spoke pleasantly, but with intensity because I, too, was increasingly concerned. No answer at Iris's apartment. The apartment searched. And now, a girl who had left her job unexpectedly.

"Oh." The irritation seeped out of the woman's strong face, replaced by uncertainty. She lifted a hand to smooth her unruly hair and the bracelets jingled, silver on silver. "I called her apartment Friday. And again Saturday morning. There was no answer either time. I didn't try again."

The front door opened.

A middle-aged couple in polo shirts and Bermuda shorts entered. The woman made a soft cooing sound. "Oh, that air-conditioning. It feels wonderful." I placed her accent somewhere near Montreal.

The woman at the cash desk glanced toward the couple, then her hand moved swiftly. Faintly I heard a buzzer. She looked past me at the newcomers. "Hello." A swift smile. "Bienvenidos a Tesoros. May I help you?"

"Thanks. We'll just look around." The woman smiled. She stepped past us, then stopped with a delighted exclamation. "Oh, Johnny, look." The woman grabbed his arm. "Those candlesticks are just what we need." She pointed at a pair of cobalt-blue Talavera candlesticks.

A brown door, almost indistinguishable from the wall, opened at the back of the store. The man who strode through, head high, dark eyes flashing, knew that he was handsome. Bold dark eyes dominated a long face that could have stared out commandingly from a thirteenth-century Spanish tapestry, almost oval, with a high-bridged nose and sharp chin with a deep cleft. But there was no gloom here, no somber soldier marching in a Crusade. His broad mouth stretched in a merry smile. He knew women responded to him, knew he was a hell of a guy. I'm not ordinarily impressed with cocky men, yet my mouth curved in an answering smile. Yes, he was cocky, but he brought with him an energy and enthusiasm that immediately charmed.

He came right up to the cash desk, gripped my hand. "Hi. I'm Tony Garza." His voice exuded good humor, eagerness.

"Hello." I was still smiling. "Henrietta Collins."

The woman behind the cash desk apparently wasn't charmed. Her voice was dry. "Tony, this is a friend of Iris's grandmother. She wants to know when Iris was last here. If you'll take over, I'll check the time sheets."

"Iris?" His dark eyebrows rose. "Isn't she around?" He glanced toward the front of the store.

"Tony"—now her tone was long-suffering—"I told you she skipped out on Thursday. Well, she hasn't come back. Her grandmother's worried and asked Mrs. Collins to check on her."

His face immediately became serious, but it was obviously an unaccustomed look. "Oh, hey, that's too bad. Well, anything we can do to help, you just let us know." He squeezed my hands again, let them drop. Then he shrugged and his smile was rueful. "You know these kids, here today, gone tomorrow. But"—and he shed the concern like a stripper tossing off a garter—"I'm sure she'll be back and sorry she's worried anyone. Iris is a sweetheart. Okay, Susana, check the times and see if you can help this lady."

She nodded, but there was no smile on her face as she stepped out from behind the counter. She started toward the back of the store.

I was right behind her.

She stopped at the brown door. "It may take me a few minutes. There's a love seat in that alcove." She pointed toward a cozy nook with a tile-topped table and an array of art magazines.

"Thanks, but I'd like to come with you. It will give me a better picture of Iris's job here—to see the storeroom and offices."

Her hand, smooth, large and heavily ringed, tightened on the door handle. For an instant, I thought she was going to refuse me entry. But she shrugged, pushed through the door. We stepped into a bare but well-lit corridor. Three doors opened on the left, one double door on the right. A circular iron staircase curved at the end of the hall.

She gestured to her left. "Our offices. The receiving area is to the right." Her brightly patterned skirt swished as she walked.

"Does Iris work back here sometimes?" Our shoes clicked on bare cement.

She opened the middle door, stood aside for me to enter. "Sometimes she helped Rick with the unpacking."

"Rick?"

"My nephew. He's in charge of tagging every item with a price."

The office was small and jammed, a desk overflowing with catalogs, a full in-box, a pile of unopened correspondence, a telephone with caller ID. A computer terminal sat on a side desk, the printer on the floor. The stucco finish of the walls had aged to a light coffee color. A Fiesta calendar and a bulletin board with pinned notes hung behind the desk. A gilt baroque mirror filled the wall opposite the desk. The glass was so dark and warped, we shimmered like silver ghosts as we moved.

She slipped into the desk chair, punched on the computer. She clicked the mouse a half dozen times, then swung to face me. "Iris punched the time clock at ten A.M. Thursday. She didn't punch out." She spoke evenly, but I heard a tight echo of anger.

I leaned forward, placed my hands palms-down on the desk, held her gaze. "So you don't know if she ever left the store?"

Her face flushed. "That's absurd. She's a thoughtless girl who walked out without speaking to anyone. I found the door to the storeroom open. A fortune in art works with no one in attendance. Where did she go? Not that we care." She stood, stared at me haughtily.

I rose and our gazes were level. "Did you look for her?"

She threw her hands up and the bracelets jangled. "Everywhere. Here. In the storeroom. Upstairs in the bed-and-breakfast. No, she is not on our premises. She disappeared Thursday afternoon without a trace. Where she went or why, I have no idea." She spoke with utter assurance. "You must look elsewhere." She fingered the shiny gold beads of a long looping necklace, beads intermixed with gold coins, gold jaguars, and gold parrots, ending with a filigree butterfly. "You are here to find her." It was almost an accusation. Her dark eyes watched me intently. "Who are her friends? Surely someone knows where she is."

"I hope someone does. But I'm from out of town. I need help. Do you know anything about Iris's friends? Can you tell me anyone she knew, anyone I can talk to?"

Her slender fingers, the nails glossy red, twirled the beads and the tiny clicks seemed loud in the silence between us. I knew she didn't hear the sound, that this was a familiar, automatic action that accompanied thought. Her face was composed, but her eyes narrowed in concentration. Abruptly, she nodded.

She reached down to the desk, pressed a button on an intercom. "Tony, send Rick here." She clicked off the machine. No please or thank you, nor even a wait for confirmation.

As we waited, I asked, "Let me see. Iris started working for you—" I hesitated.

"In April." She was watching the door.

"And in all that time, did she ever miss work? Leave without explanation?"

"Of course not." It was almost a hiss. "I don't put up with any nonsense, I can tell you that. I didn't want to hire her. I was against it from the first. Believe me, she did everything right. I insisted on it." Resentment glistened in her eyes, thinned her bright lips.

I wondered if she realized how at odds that answer was with her immediate assumption that Iris was simply a thoughtless girl who'd walked out of the store without a word.

The door swung open, and the young man who'd been at work in the front window ducked his head to enter. There was a strong family resemblance to the older man, Tony, who'd taken Susana's place at the cash desk: the same tight dark curly hair, aquiline nose, and deep-set dark eyes. Rick, too, was tall and husky with an athlete's build. A small, fashionable goatee and crisp mustache framed a poet's mouth, sensuous and sensitive.

He looked from me to his aunt. Although his glance was pleasant, I sensed a tension, an uneasiness, almost a flash of fear.

His aunt nodded toward me. "This is Mrs. Collins. She's looking for Iris, wants to know who her friends are, where she might be." The woman's hand tightly clasped her necklace.

His face turned cold and haughty. "I already told you, Susana, I don't know where she is. And I don't care where she is. If she wants to go off with some guy, that's her business. Just leave me the hell out of it." And he turned and was through the door, slamming it behind him.

Uh-oh, a lovers' quarrel. That was not pleasant, but it was certainly better than some of the possibilities I'd begun to consider. I didn't hesitate. I darted to the door and yanked it open. My shoes clattered on the cement flooring. I hurried up the hall to the back entrance to the showroom.

"Rick. Rick, wait!" I caught up with him in the middle of the store. He stopped beside a huge pottery lion, faced me, his back against the pottery.

I stared into wary dark eyes. Why was this young man so tense? He looked past me, watched his aunt approach.

I spoke quickly. "Rick, either you talk to me, or you can talk to the police."

"For heaven's sake, Rick." His aunt tossed her head

and that mass of dark hair quivered. "What's gotten into you? If you know who that girl's friends are, tell this woman. We certainly don't want the police coming around here."

"The police." His eyes flickered between us. "You don't need to go to the police. Iris—" He took a quick, sharp breath. "She's just off on a trip." He tried to laugh. "Sorry. I didn't mean to get upset. But"—he clasped his big hands together, twisted them—"I guess I took too much for granted. I thought Iris liked me. And then Thursday, she told me she was going to Padre with a guy she met last weekend."

"What guy? What's his name?" I opened my purse, pulled out a pen and small notepad.

Those big hands twisted again. It took him a long time to answer and when he did, the name came in a spurt. "Jack. Jack Smith."

"Where did she meet him?" I tried to hold his gaze, but his eyes shifted away from me.

"I don't know." Now his voice was defensive, irritated. "I mean, God, she didn't tell me."

"Okay, Rick. Let me get it straight." I spoke quietly. "You and Iris have been dating—"

He threw out his hands. "Not exactly dating. Kind of hanging out together. Nothing serious."

"Sure. Nothing serious. But friends. Right?"

"Yeah. Friends." He took a deep breath.

The wooden floor creaked as his aunt stepped closer. But I didn't take my eyes off his sullen face. "Okay, you've hung out, gone places. Where did you usually go?"

He shifted from one foot to the other. "Oh, well, sometimes Mi Tierra. And there's a coffeehouse in Monte Vista—"

I held out the notepad to him. "Please. Write them down."

He took the pad and pen, stared down at it, and scrawled some names, then thrust the pad at me.

"How about women friends?" I wished now I'd looked through Iris's apartment for an address book. Did anyone her age keep an address book? I didn't know. But I'd look hard when I returned to her apartment.

His almond-shaped eyes blinked. Some of the tension eased out of his body. "Oh, yeah, well, she used to go shopping with Shandy Valdez. But Shandy's just moved. To Dallas."

"Do you have her address in Dallas?"

He looked relieved. "No. She's going to write and tell us when she finds a place."

"I see. All right, Rick."

His relief was almost embarrassing.

I smiled. "In case I need to talk to you, what is your phone number?"

He rattled it off. Interesting. That was information he didn't mind giving.

"And you are Rick Garza?"

He looked surprised. "No. No, I'm Rick Reyes." His eyes narrowed.

Did he think I should have known his name if I was close to Iris? Maybe so. But I couldn't guess which questions might excite suspicion. And these were answers I had to have.

I slipped the pad and pen into my purse. "Thank you for helping me. And Rick." I looked at him, then at his aunt. "Please, if you hear from Iris, ask her to call her Grandmother Wilson. Tell Iris her grandmother is terribly worried about her."

I walked to the door, then looked back.

Two faces watched me, the woman's hard and thoughtful, the young man's tense and wary.

"Mrs. Garza." My tone was tentative, but I guessed Tony Garza was her husband.

She smoothed her stiff hair.

I had a strong sense that we were adversaries, though her face remained composed, polite.

"This is a family store, isn't it?"

"Yes." There was a proud toss of her head. "Yes, the Garza family has been here since 1960. My husband's mother, Maria Elena, opened it when no one cared about the River Walk, when they laughed at its future."

"You. And your husband? Is Tony your husband?"

She nodded. So my guess was correct.

"And Rick." I glanced at him and knew he wanted desperately to get away from me. "Who else works here?"

Susana Garza spoke quickly, almost too fast for me to understand. "My husband's sisters, Celestina and Magda. And Tony's brother Frank runs La Mariposa. Our hotel. Along with his wife, Isabel."

"You said you didn't hire Iris. Who did?"

Her sullen eyes flashed with resentment. "Maria Elena does all the hiring. I told her we shouldn't have this girl. But she wouldn't listen."

"Is your mother-in-law here? I'd like to talk to her." Why had Maria Elena Garza hired Iris? It might have nothing to do with her disappearance, but there had to be a reason. And I wanted to talk to everyone connected with this store.

"I'm afraid that won't be possible. She's not been feeling well recently."

"I'm so sorry," I said quickly. "Nothing serious, I

hope. Rick"—I shot the question at him—"what is wrong with your grandmother?"

Rick's mouth opened, closed. He looked at his aunt, stuttered, "Well, I think she's had the flu. Yes, the flu."

Susana's face didn't change, but her hands clenched into fists.

"I hope she's feeling much better soon. Perhaps I can meet her another time. When I return." I said the last with emphasis.

The front door's silver bell sang as I left.

I stopped beside the window cleaner. The swipe of the squeegee made a faint moist sound.

"The window is very beautiful." I spoke softly.

He ducked his head, peered at the ground. His eyes edged toward me, shyly, timid as a startled fawn. I saw the family resemblance, dark ringlets, these frosted by gray, the long, oval face, the indented chin, and glowing dark eyes.

I was startled by his eyes. They were soft and kind, filled with a yearning and a guilelessness that touched my heart.

I smiled, a genuine smile this time, not calculated to impress or disarm.

"Hello."

He didn't speak, but his eyes spoke for him.

"I'm Henrie O."

He lifted a hand, pointed at himself.

"Hello," I said again.

It was the right answer. His mouth curved in a gentle smile.

"Do you know Iris?" I don't know why I asked. I already knew he couldn't answer.

He clapped his hands once. Then he looked at the window, moved carefully to a spot bathed in sunlight, and held up both hands. He moved his hands in swift gestures and shadows moved on the window. I glimpsed flowers, then a darting bird, a bird that bobbed against the glass, a happy, saucy bird. Almost a silly bird.

His hands moved faster and his features drew down in a worried frown.

The shadow bird flew to the right, to the left, then streaked away.

"Yes," I said slowly, "Iris has gone away. I'm trying to find her."

His head bobbed. He gestured with his hands, the immemorial movement that signals, "Come. Come here."

"Yes. I'll bring her back. If I can."

As I walked away, I looked back. He was once again cleaning the shiny window.

I walked with foreboding. That simple man knew something. It worried him. And whatever he knew about Iris could only be connected to Tesoros.

three

I knew what I was going to do, what I had to do. But I wanted Gina's approval. The pay phone was in the vestibule of the main entrance to the police department. As I made the call, I looked through smudged glass doors at the central reception desk. The second doorway to the right led to a counter for the sex crimes and homicide units. I hoped I'd never have to walk through those doors in my search for Gina's granddaughter.

When I was a young reporter, I spent a few years on a small Kansas daily and I covered everything from fires to murders to bank robberies. I always remembered that little town's police chief with respect. At the time, he'd terrified me. Over six feet tall, he was rangy and muscular like John Wayne, with a weathered face and a harsh voice. But he cared about his town and its people and once I'd seen tears in his eyes when they found a missing schoolgirl raped and beaten and dead. The case wasn't solved while I lived there. I heard later, years later, that he'd finally found the killer. He never gave up. He'd told me once, "Keep asking questions. Liars always make a mistake." I followed his advice then and I follow it now. It works for reporters as well as cops.

The phone was answered midway into the second ring. It was late in Majorca, but I wasn't surprised when Gina answered on the first ring, her voice tight with anxiety. As I finished speaking, Gina gave a low moan. It started deep in her throat, came from her heart. I could picture her on the other end of the line. I knew fear glazed the bright green eyes I'd so often seen dancing with joy or sharp with inquiry or soft with compassion. Gina and her husband Kent had been very good friends to my husband Richard and to me when we lived in Mexico City. She was a correspondent for a Los Angeles daily, Richard was with a wire service, and I was freelancing. Her husband, Kent, was a historian, his specialty the Mexican Revolution, the sea change that created pride in all things Mexican. Kent was working then on his biography of General Alvaro Obregon, the hero of the Revolution who was later President of Mexico. As families we'd picnicked in Chapultepec Park, wandered through country markets, enjoyed fiestas, embraced a country and people who, despite a society often in turmoil and plagued by poverty, celebrated life with vigor and enormous creativity. Those happy years in Mexico seemed a lifetime ago. Now we both were widows and Gina was in Majorca doing a nonfiction book on the prehistoric remains, especially the chambered stone towers called talayots. Always interested in everything about her, she'd sent me a cheerful postcard about the abandoned monastery at Valldemosa which had counted among its famous guests Frédéric Chopin and George Sand.

Now there was no reason for cheer. I spoke gently. "I'm calling from a pay phone at the police station."

A wavering breath. "Yes. That's next. Has to be next. Oh, Henrie O—"

"Gina, it's odd and scary, but there was no trace

of"—I didn't want to say blood—"no trace of a struggle in Iris's apartment. And the boy, Rick, claims she's gone to Padre Island with a guy." I wanted to hear Gina's response to Rick's declaration.

"No. God, I wish it were so. Not that it wouldn't be like Iris to meet someone and be immediately infatuated." Her tone was rueful. "Iris, to put it kindly, is something of a fool, especially where men are concerned. But she'd tell me all about him, burble with her news, declare her love from a mountaintop. In fact, that's exactly how she's sounded about this Rick ever since she started working there. Every E-mail begins with Rick this, Rick that . . . Iris is constant in her fashion. Her love affairs always last at least six months. Henrie O"—her voice was suddenly cool and crisp—"I think this Rick is lying."

I thought so, too.

"All right, Gina. I'll make a formal report to the police. And, Gina, don't give up hope. There could be a dozen reasons why she's gone off. A quarrel with Rick. A new boyfriend. Just for the hell of it. Maybe it's nothing more than that."

"Please, God," she said softly.

"I'll call after I talk to Missing Persons."

Missing Persons turned out to be handled within Youth Services, no matter the age of the vanished person.

Detective Investigator June Hess waved me to a seat in front of her gray metal desk. She was fortyish, trim, almost muscular. Smooth brown hair cupped a pale, composed face with aloof blue eyes and a firm, colorless mouth.

I gave her high marks as a listener. Her eyes left my face only when they dropped to the pad where she made brief notes. Or when she gave an occasional glance at the computer-printout photograph of Iris and Gina.

When I finished, she turned to her computer screen. It took her only a moment to scroll down the homicides reported since Thursday morning.

"No young women. The only unidentified body is that of a white male approximately forty to fifty years old. Killed in a knife fight." She clicked close. "What's the grandmother's phone number?"

She punched the numbers on her speakerphone. I listened to Gina's weary voice as she answered the detective's precise questions. Detective Hess's fingers flew on her computer keyboard.

I watched the fuzzy green screen of the monitor as she keystroked entries into the missing-persons form, distilling the substance of Gina's replies.

Name—Iris Constance Chavez
Date of birth—April 3, 1979
Marriage status—single
Social security number—826-00-9358
Address—La Casita Apartments, No. 26.
Physical description—Five feet five inches tall, 118 pounds, black hair, green eyes, nose straight, clear complexion, small ears. Identifying marks, small quarter-moon-shaped scar on the left earlobe caused by an infection from earpiercing, appendectomy scar; nail missing on the second digit of the right foot.
Health—Excellent. No history of mental instability. No history of drug use.
Personality—Energetic, enthusiastic, happy-go-lucky. Dependable and responsible, but easily

influenced by friends. Attracted to opposite sex, sometimes unwisely.

Resident—*Lived in San Antonio since April. Previously attended Long Beach City College in Long Beach, Ca., average student. Grew up in various California communities, mother a nightclub singer/hostess with erratic employment. Iris often spent time with widowed grandmother in northern California, now living in Majorca.*

Family—*Maternal grandmother Gina Wilson. Mother Connie Anderson, entertainer on a cruise ship presently in the Caribbean. Mother married three times, presently single. Father Arturo Chavez, an artist, believed deceased. A native of San Antonio, he was reported to have returned to San Antonio after divorce from Iris's mother. No contact since then. Recent information indicates he died in a car wreck in San Antonio. Location paternal grandparents unknown. Two married half-sisters, Janice Frank, Albuquerque, New Mexico, and Nancy Toland, Minneapolis, Minnesota. Neither in close touch with Iris, both deny having heard from her within last month.*

Friends—*Rick Reyes, assistant manager Tesoros art gallery on the River Walk. Shandy Valdez, recently moved to Dallas, address unknown. Grandmother uncertain of names and addresses of friends in San Antonio or elsewhere.*

Job history—*Employed at Tesoros in San Antonio since late April. In Long Beach most recently worked in an antique store. Also has worked as a waitress, lifeguard, and as a clerk in an art-supply store.*

Church affiliation—Methodist, inactive.

*Interests—art, antiques, Rollerblading, surfing.
Since childhood spent every free moment
drawing, sketching, painting, always seeking
information about the artist father she never
knew. Fascinated by the colors and spirit of
straw mosaics, the intricately wrought artworks created by an artist applying a design
to plywood, coating it with beeswax, then laying colored straw onto the beeswax. She didn't
grow up speaking Spanish but studied the lan-
guage in middle school and always made A's,
the only A's in her school years.*

Detective Hess's hands dropped to her desk. She
looked at the speakerphone. "I haven't been to your
granddaughter's apartment yet, Mrs. Wilson. Mrs. Collins informs me it appears to have been searched. Do
you know if there is anything of value that Miss
Chavez possessed, something"—she looked at me for
confirmation—"about the size of an attaché case or
anything of value that would fit in an attaché case?"

I nodded.

"No." Gina sounded puzzled. "I can't imagine. Iris
doesn't have any money. She just scrapes by. But she
never asks for help. She's determined to make her own
way. She worked two jobs to earn enough money to
go to San Antonio. Oh"—Gina's voice trembled—"I
told her not to go there. I knew she shouldn't."

"Why?" The detective's voice was sharp.

"It isn't good to go into the past. But she was determined. I understand why she went. She wants to
know about the part of herself that came from her father. I think she always felt incomplete because she
grew up in a completely non-Hispanic way and yet she

was Iris Chavez. But"—and Gina's voice was abruptly grim—"if I've learned one thing in life, it's to let the past go, let it go."

"Do you think her disappearance could be connected in any way with her search for her father?" Detective Hess's hands were poised above her keyboard.

"I think it's unlikely," Gina said slowly. "She told me quite soon after she arrived in San Antonio that she'd found a cousin of her father's who said Arturo died in a car wreck a few years after he came home. So I don't think her father can have any bearing on her absence. She sounded sad but, after all, she'd never known him. But she said she felt very close to him, being in San Antonio, so I stopped trying to persuade her to go back to California."

Detective Hess typed for a moment.

Her final question surprised me. But, of course, given the realities of our time, it shouldn't have. The detective leaned back in her swivel chair, folded her arms. "Mrs. Wilson, you said your granddaughter has no history of drug use. But you can't be sure."

"Yes. Yes, I can." I knew that if Gina were here, she would be leaning forward, green eyes flashing, narrow face intent.

The detective looked sadly at the speakerphone. "A fortune in drugs can be carried in an attaché case."

A fortune in drugs can be carried in an attaché case . . .

I unlocked the door to Iris's apartment. At my nod, Detective Hess stepped inside.

I looked at the disarray with new eyes. It could be drugs. If it was, the police would find out. In those circles, they had connections. Someone sold to someone else who sold to someone else. The police would find out if Iris was involved in a trade that routinely dealt death in one form or another.

"Not random." The detective's crisp statement confirmed my earlier judgment. "And not an ordinary robbery." She pointed first at the painting in the chair. "That looks like something special. And there's the regular stuff"—her hand gestured toward the television and the computer—"so something unusual is going on. " Her mouth twisted in a wry smile. "Or the girl's split but dumped everything out to make it look like somebody searched the place. That could be why nothing's messed up." She saw my surprise. "Yeah. People do funny things, especially when they're walking out on somebody. And this is a funny one. No sign of a break-in. Either the girl threw things around herself or she let in the person who made the mess or the searcher had a key." She turned, studied the door. "But this kind of lock can be opened pretty easily if you have the right tools."

Detective Hess closed the door, moved to the middle of the room and surveyed the small area. She didn't touch anything. No fingerprints would be marred if their taking should ever be necessary. Using the tip of her pocketknife, she delicately explored every pile of debris that appeared to contain papers. She spent at least ten minutes crouched on the floor beside the telephone table, patiently edging through that mess.

I stared at the telephone table. Had the drawer been pulled out, the contents emptied? I tried to remember, couldn't be certain. But that drawer was too small to hold anything larger than a notepad. Or an address book.

When Hess rose, stiffly, one hand on her left knee, I said, "No address book?"

"I didn't find one. Not in this stuff." She pointed at

the floor. "Not in any of it. I'll check with her grandmother tomorrow, see if she knows whether the girl
had one."

We walked to the door.

Detective Hess took one last look. "If she didn't set
this up, I'm pretty sure she wasn't here when the apartment was searched."

I looked at her with interest.

She pointed at the kitchen table, at the chairs in
place, at the lamps at either end of the sofa, at the
untouched painter's easel, at the painting propped in a
chair.

"People fight when they're attacked. You'd be surprised at the damage." Her eyes, for an instant, were
dark with memory. She continued matter-of-factly,
"There's too much stuff here that's untouched. Whatever happened to her, it didn't happen here. If something happened to her."

I led the way down the concrete steps. At the base
of the stairs, Detective Hess stopped. "Are you going
to return the key? Or hold on to it?"

My answer was quick. "Hold on to it."

"Where can I find you?" Detective Hess flipped
open her small notebook.

I'd had time to think about that. I wanted to stay on
the River Walk. There was plenty of choice, from the
massive Hilton to the elegant La Mansion del Rio. But
I had a definite destination in mind. "There's a bed-
and-breakfast upstairs from Tesoros. La Mariposa.
B&Bs usually empty out on Sunday afternoons. I
probably wouldn't stand a chance late in the week, but
tonight I expect they'll have a vacancy."

"Let me know if that doesn't work out. Upstairs
from the store." Her voice was thoughtful, her blue
eyes interested. "Why so near? The guy?"

Yes, Rick Reyes worked downstairs in Tesoros and Rick was Iris's latest love, except not according to him. But that wasn't my prime reason. "Yes, I want to know more about Rick. But most of all, I want to know why Iris left her job without a word to anyone. Was she ill? Frightened? What happened at the store?"

Detective Hess shrugged. "Maybe nothing. Maybe she just decided to split. If you find out, call me." She slipped her pad into her pocket. "I'll be in touch." She turned and walked with a swift, confident stride toward the manager's office.

A crow burst from the magnolia. In the light beaming down from the corners of the apartment house, the crow's shadow was a sudden dark streak across the courtyard, a quick, quickly gone picture, quite similar to the shadow against the wall created by the swift hands of the silent window washer at the elegant River Walk art gallery.

The oversize wooden doors must have been carved a hundred years ago. Even in a city that often surprises with glimpses of a long ago world, the doors to La Mariposa were spectacular. I grasped a heavy bronze ring and pulled. I stepped into another century.

Large lacquerware trays, some painted, some inlaid, decorated the ocher walls. The reddish brown walls glowed like sunrise on adobe, providing a perfect backdrop. Each tray was distinctive: one with red and yellow flowers, a second with gold and cream, a third with orange and pink. The trays echoed the vivid glory of flower markets and fields of wildflowers. Bright blue tiles framed a huge fireplace. Muted paintings of saints hung above the fireplace. Antique wooden chairs surrounded a massive table that quite likely had once graced a mission refectory.

My shoes clicked on the red tile floor. At the sound, a huge black cat with glistening green eyes lifted his head to watch me. He stretched half the length of the rustic wooden cart that served as a desk. Barely decipherable against the cart's yellowed canvas awning were faded red letters proclaiming "Chili."

I touched the bell. The cat yawned. His ears pricked as the door behind the cart opened.

"Hello." The tall young man in a sports shirt and slacks beamed a welcome. "Bienvenida a La Mariposa. I'm Tom Garza."

He looked quite a bit like Rick Reyes. I wondered if they were cousins. I liked his welcoming smile. I wasn't sure how long the welcome would last.

I smiled in return. "I don't have a reservation. Do you have a single available?"

"Yes, ma'am. We're fully booked beginning Friday evening. Will that work out for you?"

I certainly hoped so.

I gave him my charge card, explained I'd left my luggage in the car, parked in a nearby lot, and inquired about restaurants. I smiled when he handed me a key that was at least five inches long.

He grinned in return. "Old doors. Seriously old. But actually, the locks work very well. And we have good security at night. Because of the store."

"Tesoros. It's very lovely."

"So you've already visited it."

"Oh, yes. A young friend of mine, Iris Chavez, works there. She's told me a lot about it."

"Is she back?" He looked surprised.

"No. Actually, I'm looking for her. Do you know Iris?"

"Sure." He held out a brochure with a floor plan. "She's dating my cousin."

So my guess was right. This place teemed with sons and daughters, aunts and uncles, sisters and brothers.

"Or she was. Rick said—" His eyes dropped and he said quickly, "Your room is the last one down the hall on this floor. Number six. Through that door." He pointed to his right, just past the end of the cart.

"What did Rick say?" My tone was unemphatic.

"Oh, I don't know exactly. Something about Iris going to Padre with"—a careful pause—"with some friends. Anyway, it must have come up suddenly. But that's life, isn't it?" His grin was ebullient. "One day everything's great, the next it all blows up in your face. That's what I told Rick."

"So she and Rick had quarreled?"

"Hey, I don't know that. But Rick and Iris didn't come to our cousin Rosa Herrera's quinceañera Friday night. I figured then that something was up. That's a big party to miss." He glanced at me.

I nodded. Many Hispanic families continue the old tradition of la quinceañera to celebrate a daughter's fifteenth birthday. This is a major family occasion, when a young girl is presented first to God in thanksgiving and then to society as her life as a young woman begins.

"That was—well, Rick should've come. And then he told me later that Iris didn't show up for work Friday and Aunt Susana was furious. So, I guess Iris has moved on." He shrugged. His bright smile dismissed Iris. "If I can get anything for you, please let me know." He stepped from behind the cart, held open the door to a wide corridor.

Light glowed from golden-globed wall sconces next to each door. Bright red numbers glistened above the lintels. A painted butterfly, wings outspread in glory, decorated each door.

Butterflies have to be one of God's loveliest creatures. I never see a butterfly without thinking of my husband and my son. The year before Bobby died, he and his father created a scrapbook with pictures they'd taken in Chapultepec Park. Bobby had carefully printed the names beneath each photograph. "Hey, Mom, look at this one—he's as big as a bat! Isn't he terrific?"

The artist at La Mariposa obviously agreed. The butterfly on each door flew with joy, every iridescent color sparkling as if viewed in a sun that never set. I recognized the butterflies as I walked up the hall— yellow sulphur, black swallowtail, pearl crescent, painted lady, spring azure.

At the end of the hall I stood a long moment, clutching the key, looking at the magnificent monarch on my own door. The fall before Bobby was killed in a car wreck, Richard and I and Bobby and our daughter Emily had hiked up the torturous trail on a remote mountain in Mexico to see the nesting place of the monarchs. Our legs aching, gasping for breath in the thin dry air, we'd come to the top of a rugged hillock and looked out into a wonderland—millions of monarchs clinging to the trees, obscuring the trees, their brownish-orange wings a surfeit of beauty. Just for an instant, I was there, my own special circle of love unbroken, Richard and Bobby and Emily and I. Then the image dissolved, and I looked at a butterfly painted on a door.

The big key turned the lock smoothly. I closed the door behind me, leaned against it, suddenly too weary to appreciate the spare beauty of the room, buffeted by my own sense of never quite accepted loss and by the uneasy sense of danger that had moved with me ever since I first saw Iris's littered apartment.

I pushed away from the door. I had much to do before tomorrow.

I nibbled on pumpkin candy, dulce de calabaza. The grainy sweetness reminded me it takes as much sugar as pumpkin to make the crystallized candy. After a wonderful dinner of tostadas de pollo topped by a creamy avocado dressing and corn fritters, I was fortified for work with the aid of the candy and steaming coffee made in the small pot on a marble-topped table in my room.

Not too surprisingly, my room at La Mariposa had no telephone. But I could use my cell phone. I called my daughter. Emily and her husband own and run a small-town newspaper in east Texas. They are both seasoned reporters and I knew Emily could find out anything about anyone.

"Mother! Any luck with Iris?"

The fatigue vanished and in its place spread the warm glow of delight that her voice always brings me. She has a lovely, lilting tone full of gaiety and vigor. It was as if she stood beside me, glossy ebony hair, vivid aquamarine eyes, a vibrant, eager face.

"No, and I need help." Emily, too, is a good listener. When I finished, she said confidently, "I'll have it all to you first thing in the morning. I'll find a copy shop where you can pick up a fax. Check with me in the morning."

"Thanks, Emily. As always."

"Mother," she spoke swiftly, "you know I'd come and help if I could."

I knew that. But Emily and Warren were truly a mom-and-pop operation and it took every moment they had to run their small newspaper. Moreover, they were doubling up on duties. Their wire editor, no spring chicken, had broken her hip in a fall in mid-August and was now in rehabilitation. I'd come at Emily's call and enjoyed being on the desk, once again a part of the pulse of news. But it was not only fun, it was protecting my investment. I'd used an unexpected (and unwelcome) bequest to help them buy the newspaper. Emily hadn't wished to take the money. I'd insisted. It was, more than she would ever know, money to which she had every right. I occasionally thought of the testator, Chase Prescott. I could not remember Chase with pleasure, but I knew this use of his money would please him.

"Mother"—now her tone was firm—"will it do any good to ask you to be careful?"

"I'm always careful." It sounded a little disingenuous even to me.

"Oh, Mother. Okay. If not careful, then cautious. Okay?"

"Sure."

I smiled as I clicked off the call. Emily's buoyant voice gone, fatigue struck. As I plunged into sleep, I thought of the questions Emily couldn't answer for me, the questions I would try to answer tomorrow. Why was Iris hired at Tesoros? Where did Iris get the small painting that she was copying? What was Rick Reyes trying to hide?

One of the joys of stopping at a bed and breakfast is, reasonably enough, breakfast. La Mariposa didn't disappoint. I was served eggs scrambled with green chilies and fresh corn tortillas that had a spongy texture and were faintly sweet, like a fine white cake. The orange juice was just squeezed and the coffee a rich, dark Colombian. But I wasn't on a holiday. I ate swiftly. Back in my room, I talked to Emily and got the address of the copy shop. I called the copy shop for directions. Fifteen minutes later I was on my way, the map on the passenger seat, heading northeast. I knew I was going in the right direction when I passed the public library. The copy shop clerk had said, "You can't miss it. We call it the Big Red Enchilada." He was right. A huge multihued building, predominantly golden red, catches the eye, as the architect no doubt intended. But libraries should stand up and shout; they are America's greatest bargain.

Three more blocks and I pulled into a strip shopping center. The material was waiting for me, faxed by Emily. Twenty minutes later, I was back on the River Walk at the sidewalk café opposite Tesoros. I glanced across the river.

It was so early that few people wandered along the River Walk. An occasional jogger loped past. It was so quiet I could hear the swish of the window washer's squeegee. He worked slowly, methodically. The window glistened in the sun like a new-minted penny.

I ordered coffee and picked up Emily's report. There was a brief heading:

Compiled from Newspaper Archives

Maria Elena Herrera Garza created Tesoros, now one of the River Walk's premier art galleries, in 1960. It was a dream that grew out of her father's heartbreak. Her father, Manuel, was a streetcar conductor who saved every penny, hoping to open a small store downtown that would offer lovely artworks from Mexico. Her mother, Rose, was a wonderful cook who worked for a family that lived in the King William district. The Herreras saved for years and finally opened a tiny store on Crockett Street ten years before their youngest child, Maria Elena, was born. The 1921 flood destroyed that store. Growing up, Maria Elena heard so much about the wonderful store, the store that could have made their fortune, the store that her father was never able to open again. "It was not only stories about the store that captured my imagination. There was The Family Trip. That's how we always remembered it because it was the only trip we ever made and, as I look back, I am surprised my mother and father used money needed for so many other purposes for that one glorious, unforgettable journey. It was in 1933. We all—my parents, my brothers Julio and Pablo and Ramon and I—crammed into our old rattletrap car and went to Mexico. We traveled through the central highlands and into the states of Puebla and Morelos. We visited old churches, saw pre-Columbian sculptures, but, most of all, we went from marketplace to marketplace and at each there was color and excitement and, always, wonderful art. We didn't buy, but we looked and admired and my father would tell us, 'Oh, that is a wonderful piece. We would have put that at the front of the store.' I was only eight years old but I've never forgotten some of the things we saw: a glazed pottery pitcher for pulque that was shaped like a woman's boot, a brilliant orange-red-lacquered wood chest for some young woman's dowry, wooden carvings of plumed dancers bright with scraps of shiny rayon and brocade, miniatures of a bullfight, another pulque jar with a leaping lizard for the handle, a wooden stool shaped like an armadillo, a walking stick formed like a tangle of snakes. For years I dreamed of those things. I could see them so clearly and always I pictured them in a store window." In 1935, her father died from influenza. Maria Elena married Juan Garza in 1946 and became a homemaker. But even in the most modest of circumstances, she always taught her children about art and music and told stories of their grandfather's wonderful store. Her husband taught school. He died in 1958. Left a widow with five children, Maria Elena took her savings, almost three thousand dollars, and bought a dilapidated old building on the River Walk. The River Walk had opened in 1941 with grand expectations of becoming America's Venice. But the River Walk in 1960 was a decaying, after-dark dangerous, pale reflection of Robert Hugman's glorious dream. It was not a choice place when Maria Elena bought, but she could afford that particular building and she was determined to have a store. Call it luck, call it prescience, call it fate, she purchased property that would be in the heart of the River Walk when its glory days finally arrived after the refurbishing for the 1968 HemisFair. Even when the River Walk was still shabby and spurned by most shops, Tesoros was attracting collectors. Maria Elena's unerring choice of superior artwork attracted a clientele that stretched from Corpus Christi to Dallas. Word spread about the quality of her offerings and, eventually, the breadth of arts she displayed. Maria Elena lived above the shop with her five children, Francisco, Antonio, Manuel, Magda, and Celestina.

Maria Elena, now in her seventies, is still at

the helm of her own commercial destiny, although she has relinquished the everyday running of the shop to her second son Antonio. A daughter, Magda Reyes, buys the merchandise. Another daughter, Celestina, creates the catalogs and directs the advertising. Her oldest son, Francisco, oversees the operation of La Mariposa, considered one of the premier bed-and-breakfasts in the southwest. La Mariposa had accidental beginnings. Occasionally, collectors from far away would schedule visits to San Antonio during Fiesta Week. Hotel rooms sell out months in advance of the ten-day April extravaganza with its famous Parade of the Flowers and Nights in Old San Antonio. When this happened, Maria Elena, of course, invited the visitors to stay in her home. Her hospitality was already legendary, a true reflection of the Spanish welcome, "Mi casa es su casa." Gradually, a portion of the old building was set aside for a two-story, twelve-room inn. Maria Elena also introduced the concept of a private auction to San Antonio art circles. Once a year, the store's most prized customers are invited to a one-day auction offering the artworks Maria Elena herself has chosen as masterpieces of the year.

The business is now estimated to exceed two million dollars a year in gross receipts. It can only be an estimate because Maria Elena refuses to discuss publicly the success of her family-owned store and she still continues to live modestly above the store with her son Manuel. Her other grown children also live quietly. Frank and his wife, Isabel, own an older home in the King William district. Tony and his wife, Susana, have their own apartment on the third floor of La Mariposa. Celestina Garza has a downtown apartment, as does Maria Elena's widowed daughter, Magda Reyes. Magda is often out of town, as she is the principal buyer for the store, a role Maria Elena reluctantly relinquished a decade ago.

In the margin, Emily had scrawled, "Check out who wants money and why. Maybe the third generation doesn't like Maria Elena's 'modest' lifestyle. Maybe Iris tumbled to something crooked. Although from what I remember of Iris, I'd think she and a spreadsheet would have about as much in common as a nun and a luxury hotel. And, to be accurate, every source emphasizes that Tesoros has an absolutely unassailable reputation for honest dealing. No stolen goods. No fakes. No artworks with suspect provenances. Promises made are promises kept. Mrs. Garza was once quoted as saying the store would always be in family hands because then she would always be certain that only the best and the finest went through her showroom."

Emily had scanned several news photos. Maria Elena Herrera Garza beamed out from the center of a family photograph taken two years earlier. My initial impression? A lady loaded with charm.

Maria Elena's dark eyes glowed with good humor. Her oblong face was alight with eagerness. Her mouth curved in a merry, infectious smile. A youthful zest almost erased the lines of age.

I realized I'd responded and was smiling at the photograph.

She was so interesting, so alive, so vivid that those around her receded into the background. But this was a good photographer. Every face told a story. I looked at each of her children and their spouses in turn.

Frank Garza. A narrow face with the distinctive Garza chin. Deep-set eyes looked out at the world diffidently, almost defensively. He didn't smile and his mouth in repose had a forlorn droop.

Isabel Garza. Honey-bright hair curved around a delicate face. Her brown eyes had a distant gaze. Rings with stones of many colors shone from the hands lying in total relaxation in her lap. She had the air of a confident house cat, beautiful, self-absorbed, capable of unthinking cruelty.

Tony Garza. Even in a group photo he exuded magnetism, the macho swagger of a matador. His eyes glittered with energy, a hungry, questing, demanding look. His full lips spread in a boisterous smile. He'd be the loudest man at the poker table. A fun companion if his jokes and chatter didn't distract you from your cards.

Susana Garza. She was as alive and arresting as her husband, her dark head flung back, her vivid eyes arrogantly defiant, her scarlet lips both inviting and contemptuous.

Celestina Garza. Sleek black hair drawn back in a tight bun. Gold-wire glasses. Reserved, inquiring, suspicious eyes. A surprisingly prim mouth for a woman near fifty.

Magda Reyes. The Garza face, long and lean, but artfully applied makeup highlighted her eyes, softened the blunt chin. Bright, cheerful, confident eyes. A bubbly smile. She had an air of good humor, but her firm mouth and bold chin argued decisiveness and determination, qualities quite useful for a buyer of artworks.

Manuel Garza. He alone had not looked at the photographer. His wide eyes, luminous and loving, were fastened on his mother. The odd mixture of innocence and age made his face the most affecting of them all.

The other photographs weren't as interesting, business publicity pictures that had appeared with various news stories. There was only one that mattered to me, a formal shot of a rather stiff Rick Reyes when he joined the staff at his grandmother's store upon graduation from Texas A&M. I separated that print and the family portrait from the sheaf of papers, carefully folded them and put them in my purse.

I waved away the waiter with an offer of more coffee, put down a bill on my check. Across the river, Manuel Garza was nearing completion of the first window. The door to Tesoros swung open.

But I had one more stop to make before I crossed the river to meet Maria Elena Garza, a stop that might make my visit simpler. Or more difficult.

four

THE air was sharply cool. I'd left the window unit running in Iris's apartment. I shivered as I crossed to turn it off. The room seemed even shabbier, dustier, its disarray more ominous. I turned on the lights, opened the blinds. Even so, the room was dingy. Yet, when I stood and looked at the small oil painting still propped on the wooden chair, its colors glistened as if brushed moments ago.

It was such a small painting to have so great an impact, perhaps twelve inches by eighteen. A weathered wooden cross leaned against a mission wall, next to a stone doorway and massive wooden doors. That was all, wood and stone and sunlight, shades of brown and gray and a faintly apricot peach, evoking a cry to God, humble and hopeful.

What was a painting of this stature and depth doing in Iris's apartment?

Oh, the quick answer was obvious. She was trying to copy the work. Actually, her half-finished effort was well done. But the greater question had no ready answer. At least, I knew I wouldn't find the answer here.

I lifted my hand to knock, waited until the tinny blast of trumpets subsided.

The door opened grudgingly. A blue smock this morning. No makeup. The apartment manager scowled. "You have her key. Why bother me?"

The mariachis on the television program swung into a rollicking polka. The danceable music made the unkempt room seem even more forlorn. Or perhaps it was the bright sunlight spearing in through opened window blinds, teeming with dust motes, highlighting the scuffed floor, bleaching color from a sofa arm. The blinds looking out into the courtyard were open, as were the blinds on the window facing the alley and another overlooking the parking lot.

"I came to see you. I know you take great care of this property."

She brushed crumbs from her smock, stared at me woodenly.

I opened my purse, found a fifty dollar bill, clasped it between my fingers and my purse. "I know you have much to do. Your time is valuable. I would only ask a few minutes, Mrs.—" I waited.

"Hernandez." Her dark eyes dropped to the bill. She stepped back, held the door for me.

I sat on the sofa, placed the bill on the side table. Neither of us looked at it.

She eased into her rocking chair. Her eyes were both sullen and curious, her face cautious.

I waved my hand around the room, at the windows. "Obviously, you are careful to keep an eye out for anyone who does not belong."

She folded her big arms across her chest and, after a moment, slowly nodded. But she didn't speak. She was waiting.

I had to be careful. Iris's searched apartment revealed many things. Perhaps the most important were Detective Hess's conclusion that either Iris admitted the person who searched the apartment or that the searcher had a key or the expertise to deal with an inexpensive lock. I could be sure Detective Hess had asked this woman about keys and, quite likely, about strangers.

I doubted the manager had been particularly forthcoming. This was not a forthcoming woman. She might know something, but why would she bother to tell anyone? The detective's questions didn't matter to her. Iris didn't matter to her. I was going to find out if money mattered. It does to a great many people.

"Now, I don't know whether Detective Hess—"

The manager's face was abruptly stone still.

"—explained that Iris has officially been listed as missing."

"She was fine when she left here." Mrs. Hernandez spoke loudly. "That last time I saw her. I think it was Thursday. Yes, I'm sure it was Thursday. So there is nothing wrong here."

"I'm sure of that. But it occurred to me"—I nodded at the windows—"that you may have seen something that might help. Perhaps Iris sent someone to pick something up for her."

Her face didn't change. That suggested to me that Detective Hess had said nothing about the apartment's having been searched. It's been my experience with police that they never reveal anything except for a reason. There would be no reason to tell the apartment manager. I would guess the detective inquired about the presence of any strangers.

"Mrs. Hernandez, did you see anyone you didn't know going up the stairs after Iris left on Thursday? Or even on Friday or Saturday?"

Her eyes flickered toward the table and the bill.

"I have some pictures here. If you wouldn't mind looking at them . . ."

That interested her. Her heavy face was suddenly attentive, less combative. She took the papers, then picked up the television remote, punched off the program. She was quick, scanning the family gathering, then the publicity photos. She pointed to a picture.

I saw Rick's young, serious, ambitious face. And was surprised at the sadness that touched me.

Her voice was brusque. "That's her boyfriend. Pretty nice kid. Always says hello and smiles. Here all the time. But I haven't seen him lately."

"Not on Thursday?"

"No. Iris was by herself. But she was in a hurry."

Rick could have been waiting in his car for Iris.

"You haven't seen him since she left?"

"No. Of course, I don't sit here all day. I have things to do. I have to keep a check on the laundry room, see to repairs." She glanced at the bill, smoothed a large worn hand across her chin. "I did see a man I didn't know Thursday afternoon. But that was after Iris left."

Just as Detective Hess suggested, Iris may not have been in the apartment when it was searched.

Mrs. Hernandez relaxed in her chair, began to rock. She spoke with interest. "I noticed this guy. It must have been close to five Thursday. I noticed because most of my people aren't home from work yet. I didn't know who he could be going up to see. Unless it was Mrs. Wentz. In twenty-four. She's old and she doesn't get out much. But I'd never seen him before. Anyway, he went up the stairs about five and he came down at five-thirty. I know because the news comes on then. So maybe he went to see Mrs. Wentz."

I looked at her attentively. Would she hold out the family photo? Who could it have been?

"He looked all right." Her voice was steely. "Believe me, I don't let anybody hang around here that doesn't look right. Yes, I keep an eye out. I don't want any trouble here. This man looked fine."

Yes, I supposed he would. In the family portrait, the Garza men had the air of successful, substantial businessmen.

But she didn't even glance at the sheets she held loosely in one hand. "Nice-looking guy about forty-five or fifty. Big head. Curly blond hair. Blue eyes. A big mouth. Blue shirt. Gray slacks." She pushed up from the rocker. "That's all I remember. Nothing special about him. Maybe five-ten, two hundred pounds. Not fat. Strong-looking."

Slowly, I stood. She handed me the photographs I'd brought with such expectations.

"A big blond man." I suppose the blankness of my voice made my surprise evident.

She lifted her big shoulders in an expressive shrug. "All I can say is what I saw."

I looked at her searchingly.

She pointed at the papers in my hand. "I could have pointed to someone there. I suppose that would have pleased you. But"—she drew herself up—"I am an honest woman."

"I'm sure you are. And I appreciate your helping me. It's wonderful of you to keep such a careful lookout for your tenants."

"Not much gets past me." She looked toward the courtyard.

"If that man comes around again, please leave a message for me at my bed-and-breakfast, La Mariposa. I'm in Room Six." I glanced toward the fifty dollar bill. "You needn't leave your name, simply say, 'The man came back.' "

As the door closed behind me, the television blared to life.

I hurried back to the stairs and up to the second floor. I knocked on the door to 24 and noticed that the blinds to the front window were open, though slanted, so it was hard to see inside.

It took a moment before the door opened slowly.

Mrs. Wentz must once have been tall. Now she was bent, her spine curved by age. Gnarled hands gripped a walker. A cold intelligence glistened in sharp blue eyes. Iron gray hair curled in tight ringlets. She observed me unsmilingly from a worn, remote face.

"What do you want?" Her diction was perfect, her tone commanding.

"Were you a teacher?" I offered a smile.

Her eyes tried to pluck secrets from my face. I suspect she'd had great success through the years.

"Think you're clever, I suppose. And if I was?" But her voice, though still crisp, was amused.

"Then you know how to think—and I'm looking for a good mind."

"I don't know you." She made no move to get out of the doorway.

I pointed at the door to Iris's apartment. "The girl who lives there—"

"Yes. A nice girl. A sweet girl." She very deliberately didn't speak Iris's name. Yes, indeed, I'd found a good mind. "She brings me cookies. She actually makes them. I told her that wasn't politically correct these days."

"And Iris laughed."

Her eyes warmed. "Yes, she did. What do you want with Iris?"

I told her. ". . . and no one has seen Iris since Thursday."

She maneuvered her walker, gestured for me to enter.

Bookcases served as a room divider, creating a small living room, a sleeping area and a breakfast room. The filled shelves provided color. The walls were bare, as were the floors. The room could have had an air of proud poverty. Instead, it was bright and airy, and the books piled on end tables, many of them open, promised information and adventure and beauty.

Mrs. Wentz didn't waste time, neither hers nor mine. An open book lay on the end table beside her. "I saw Iris Thursday afternoon." She gestured toward her front window. "I keep my blinds open during the day. I like sunshine. And I like to look out, though there isn't much to see: the railing, the corridor that fronts the apartments, a portion of the tree in the courtyard. Anyone going to Iris's apartment."

I understood her point at once. "Iris had to pass your apartment, arriving or departing. Unless she chose to walk the long way around." And there would be no point to that.

A slight smile. The pupil was to be commended. "Correct. There are two stairways to the second floor, but the shortest route to Iris's apartment is past my window. I saw her every day. But I haven't seen her since Thursday afternoon."

"Was she arriving or leaving?"

"She arrived at shortly after four. I was a little surprised. That isn't a usual time for her. And she was walking very fast. Then, it couldn't have been more than five minutes later, she left. I heard her steps. And again, I suppose I looked more closely than I might because even her steps sounded hurried. I glimpsed her face."

She paused and stared thoughtfully out the window.

I didn't try to hurry her. I knew that when she spoke, she would speak with precision.

"She appeared excited. Not so much worried or fearful as intensely absorbed. She walked quickly." Mrs. Wentz placed her fingertips together. "She had a backpack hanging from one arm." She gave a short, firm nod. "I've not seen her since."

"Have any strangers passed your window since you last saw Iris?"

"Just one. At five o'clock . . ." Her precise voice described the blond man.

So the blond man—the unexpected, unexplained blond man—wasn't a creation of the manager. She had earned her fifty dollars.

". . . Reminded me of a boy I had in class many years ago. If things didn't go his way, he glowered. He bullied the younger, smaller children. I once told him, 'Harry, someday you're going to meet a bully bigger than you are'."

I couldn't resist. "What happened to Harry?"

A slight shake of her head. "Barroom brawl. Harry picked on the wrong man."

I had a little picture of Harry. And of the blond man who searched Iris's apartment.

I thanked Mrs. Wentz for her help and she promised to get in touch if the blond man returned.

In the parking lot, I called Tesoros from my car.

Tony Garza answered. There was no mistaking his full, deep, lively voice.

"Maria Elena Garza, please."

"Mrs. Collins?"

I was startled. I was surprised he recognized my voice. I'd had good reason to listen to his. I wondered if that was true of him? "Yes. How are you, Mr. Garza?"

"Fine, fine. Have you heard from Iris? We're hoping nothing's really wrong." His smooth voice dropped in concern.

"I've not found her yet. I wanted a chance to visit with your mother."

"Oh, sure. Mother's worried, too. Hold on and I'll put you through." A click. Another.

"Hello." A melodious voice. Unpretentious, yet firm. This was a woman who had started with little and succeeded beyond all expectation. That told me she was smart, capable, far-sighted, tough. And, of course, lucky. I do believe in luck, but it's interesting how people who work the hardest are usually the luck-iest.

"Mrs. Garza, my name is Henrietta Collins—"

"Of course. I'm so glad you called. Have you had any success looking for Iris?" There had been polite concern in Tony Garza's voice, but Maria Elena sounded truly troubled.

"Not yet. I've reported her as missing to the police. But there is something I'd especially like to discuss with you. There is a painting in Iris's apartment." I described that haunting, memorable canvas, how the shadow of a tree dappled part of the door and the wall, the way the sunlight brought out the amber color of some of the chunks of stone, the uneven shadow of the small wooden cross. "Do you know that painting?"

"Yes." The answer was quick. "Oh, yes."

"May I come and talk to you?"

"Yes. Please do." She gave me directions, how to come into La Mariposa and ask for her. "We have much to discuss. The police were here this morning to ask about Iris."

* * *

I don't know what I expected of the owner of a shop like Tesoros. A plethora of beautiful possessions, so many that the room would shout of her success? But the room where I awaited her was small, almost monastic, painted a stark white, a crucifix on one wall, a straw mosaic on another. The furniture was simple: two woven chairs, a plain wooden sofa. The sharpest splash of color in the room was the red-and-orange-figured material of the cushions. A low blue tile table sat between the sofa and the chairs. A Talavera jar with blue Aztec figures sat in the center of the table. Nothing else. I found the simplicity of the room enchanting.

Maria Elena Garza surprised me, from the first moment that we met. She was taller than I'd thought from the photograph and she moved with a quick, confident, youthful step. The face that glowed with good humor in the picture was grave this morning but not hostile. In fact, her handclasp was warm.

She went directly to the point. "How do you know Iris?" Her vivid brown eyes plumbed mine.

"I am her grandmother's best friend. Gina and I have been friends for years. Iris is a good granddaughter. She keeps in touch with Gina. But Gina's heard nothing for several days and she hasn't been able to get in touch with Iris. Gina is frightened."

"So you've come to find Iris." She gestured toward a comfortable chair and sat across from me on the sofa.

"Yes, I have." I spoke firmly.

We regarded each other. Her hair was as dark as mine, though mine does not have a raven gloss. My face is the more lined, hers smooth with a creamy complexion. I'm afraid that through years of asking questions and so often hearing lies or distortions, perhaps my gaze is more skeptical than accepting. But in the warmth of her regard, I felt my own defenses crumbling. She looked at me with eyes that have surely seen as much as mine and yet there was an eagerness and a vivacity I have lost.

"You are frightened for Iris." Her voice was high and clear and sweet with that liquid grace of those who also speak Spanish. "So am I." Her fine black brows drew into a frown. "My daughter-in-law Susana tells me that Iris left Thursday without saying a word to anyone. I find that surprising. You see, Iris has been very much involved in the preparations for our annual auction and excited at being able to help. I saw her that morning and she was simply glowing. She'd been helping Rick prepare the auction area and she was planning to work that afternoon in the receiving room. So, yes, I am surprised. Please tell me what has happened."

I began with Gina and the E-mail that never came, the apartment in disarray, and concluded with the painting that I'd studied so carefully that morning.

Maria Elena smoothed a tendril of ebony hair at her temple. A single gold band on her left hand, no other rings. "Even though the apartment was in disorder, you don't believe there had been a struggle?"

I looked at her with respect. That was surely the most important fact of all. "That's right."

Her dark eyes narrowed. "Yet, Iris's apartment was searched. That has to mean someone was looking for something, presumably something of value. But the painting"—this time her eyes accorded me respect—"wasn't taken. The painting bothers you."

"Yes." My voice was crisp. "Yes, the painting bothers me."

"Little Iris is not a thief." She answered my unspoken question. Because how did Iris, penniless, budget-conscious Iris, have what I felt sure was a very valuable canvas?

I relaxed back into the comfortable cushion.

Maria Elena smiled gently. "I gave the painting to Iris."

I looked at her sharply.

"I know. That puzzles you. Because it is indeed a painting that is worth quite a bit of money. But blood and bones count for more than cash. You will find that everything here has to do with family." She was matter-of-fact. But there was an undercurrent in her voice now, uneasiness, concern.

I didn't understand. "Family?"

"Iris came to the store last April, asked to see me. She'd come to San Antonio hoping to find her father, Arturo. She'd found a cousin who told her Arturo died in a car crash. Yes, a young man driving too fast on a rainy night. He was so young and so gifted. The cousin knew I'd bought several paintings from Arturo. The painting you saw this morning is one of his finest. I gave it to Iris to remember her father. You see, Arturo's mother was my cousin, a cousin I adored. I remember Arturo when he was a little boy. Even then he loved to draw and paint. He would have been a great success."

"So the painting doesn't mean anything." I sighed. I was glad I didn't have to tell Gina her granddaughter was a thief, and yes, that's what had occurred to me because the painting had no place in that shabby apartment. And the second anomaly was also answered. Now I knew why Iris had been hired to work in a store that was exclusively family. Iris was, in a distant fashion and certainly in this generous woman's heart, a part of the extended family.

I was left with nothing to explore. Except—

"The manager and another resident noticed a man who doesn't live there. He's stocky, blond, probably in his late forties, with a big head and tight curly hair and bright blue eyes. Do you know this person?"

She considered it, then slowly shook her head. "No. But I very much want him to exist."

Maria Elena was continuing to surprise me. "I don't understand."

"Because there must be a reason why Iris disappeared. This morning the police lady came and talked to my grandson Rick." She lifted a hand, touched the white ruffle at her throat. She looked away from me. The planes of her face sharpened. Suddenly she looked old.

Now fear sat between us, fear and uncertainty, and bourgeoning anguish.

"I love Rick," she said softly. "He is—oh, I will admit it—so much like me when I was young. He loves beautiful things and he is so proud of who he is and what the store is and that everyone respects us. Collectors come from all over the world to see what we have. And I was so pleased that he and Iris—well, what is an old woman but a matchmaker at heart—it seemed such a good choice. Iris has laughter that can set a room alight. And a sweet, silly happiness that she wants so much to share." Maria Elena clapped her hands together. "So I must know what has happened. Because, in my heart, I know something has happened. Iris loved Tesoros. She would never run away, leave us behind." Maria Elena rose, still as swift and graceful as a young woman, but the steps she took across the room were measured. She stopped, clasped her hands, and looked up at the crucifix. "I believe the good God sends us not only angels—often, when we are unaware, he sends us messengers when there is a path we must take, no matter how hard and difficult." She turned, suddenly a majestic figure, and gazed at me with somber, sorrowful eyes. "You have come to discover the truth. That is God's wish. The truth. I have tried to live my life, teach my family, practice in the world that which God wishes us to do."

I don't think I have ever felt so humble. Or in the presence of such goodness. I wanted to please this woman as I've rarely wanted to please anyone. And yet I felt overwhelmed. In her heart, she was hoping that whatever had happened to Iris, her family, her beloved grandson, were not involved.

And she was looking to me, I realized with a sinking heart, to finish what I'd begun, to solve the mystery of Iris's disappearance.

A sudden smile curved her lips. "I know. It is much to ask. But you have come. It was intended. And so"— the smile fled, the haunted look returned—"let us begin."

She walked to the door, opened it. "Tommy, tell Rick to come." She closed the door and returned to the sofa. "Another of my grandsons"—she gestured toward the closed door—"Tommy is still in school. He works here between classes, in the evenings."

Family. All family.

Then she fell silent, once again her face composed, her hands in her lap. But every so often her eyes strayed to the crucifix.

Quick steps sounded in the hallway leading to this front room.

"He's coming through the house."

I'd already figured in my mind the arrangement of the store, the bed-and-breakfast, and Maria Elena's living quarters. Tesoros was the ground floor, with the display area, the storeroom and the offices. Portions of the ground, second, and third floors made up La Mariposa. Tony and Susana Garza had an apartment on the top floor above La Mariposa. Maria Elena's rooms were directly above Tesoros.

Rick strode into the room, his dark eyes seeking his grandmother's face, his wide mouth curved in a smile. "What is it, Abuelita? I—" Then he saw me. He stopped, his body rigid. Whatever he was, this young man was not schooled in subterfuge. His long face was a study in dismay, his eyes flicking from my face to hers, his mouth open but with no words, scarcely any breath.

"Rick." She stood, her fine-boned face stern. "What do you know about Iris's disappearance?"

He swallowed. "Abuelita, I swear to you the last time I saw Iris she was fine. She was wonderful." His voice was low and husky. "Abuelita, I swear it."

Abuelita, the term of endearment, little grandmother.

"Rick, you haven't answered my question." There was a steely ring of authority, but her eyes were anguished and her tightly clasped hands trembled.

Rick stared at his grandmother, his eyes strained, his face pleading. "Iris"—he swallowed jerkily—"she and I talked Thursday. I was upset about the idea of her going to Padre with a guy. She ran out of the store. But she said"—he picked his words carefully—"that she could be back sometime Tuesday. That's tomorrow. So, like I told the police, I'm sure she'll be back tomorrow. She'll turn up. I'm sure of it." His voice throbbed with sincerity. He shoved back a tangle of dark hair. "Look," and now he spoke to me, "I'd tell you where she is if I could." Again there was a sound of truth.

I believed him. And so did his grandmother. The tension that had gripped Maria Elena eased. She smiled, a smile of relief.

And yet . . . I leaned forward. "Do you know anything about the search of Iris's apartment?"

Rick's dark eyes flared. His full lips parted.

I would swear he was stunned, that he had no knowledge of that littered, disturbing room. I didn't think Rick was acting. If he were an accomplished liar, he would have managed to appear at ease when I first arrived at Tesoros to inquire about Iris. Instead, he'd alternated between uneasiness and outright fear.

"The searcher was looking for something about this size." I spread my hands in the shape of an attaché case. "Not too big, not too small. What do you think he was looking for?"

"He?" His voice was sharp. I certainly had his attention.

"A blond man." Maria Elena watched her grandson. "In his late forties. Muscular."

"With a big head," I added. "Bright blue eyes. Curly hair. Do you know this man?"

He shook his head, but his eyes were remote, as if he were thinking and thinking hard. Finally, he realized we both were staring at him. He looked at his grandmother. "I don't know him. I've never seen anybody like that."

I asked quickly, "Do you know what Iris might have that someone would want?"

"Iris?" He looked incredulous. "She doesn't have anything anybody would want to steal. I'm sure of that. Maybe somebody saw her leaving with that guy and decided to break into her place. Maybe it's a good thing she's gone. Anyway, I'm sure she'll be back." He crossed the room, gave his grandmother a hug, held her tight for a moment, pressed his chin against her head. "Don't worry, Abuelita. Everything will be all right." His voice was deep and reassuring. Then his eyes sought mine. "Please tell Iris's grandmother not to worry. I'm sure she'll be back." He gave his grandmother a gentle squeeze and stepped away, but his handsome face was still strained.

Maria Elena patted his arm. "Rick, I know how Iris's grandmother feels. She will not be content until she knows Iris is safe. Mrs. Collins"—a nod toward me—"is going to stay in San Antonio until she finds Iris. I want you to help her."

He kept his face smooth, but dismay, if not hostility, flickered in his eyes. His voice was genial. "Of course. If there's anything I can do, I will." Once again he shrugged. "But I don't know anything else. I told the police officer everything I know."

I smiled cheerfully. "That's wonderful."

Rick's face looked frozen.

I wasn't surprised. He didn't want to be helpful. But he had no choice. I was going to spend some time with this young man whether he liked it or not. As far as I could gauge, his responses to our questions had been an intriguing mixture of truth and diversion.

Once I knew why Iris left the store, why she went to her apartment, where she went from there, then maybe I would be on the trail to finding her.

five

OUR shoes clanged on the spiral staircase. I'd noticed the staircase yesterday when Susana Garza took me into the back area of the store, but I'd only glanced at the end of the corridor and had no real sense of how steep and difficult the stairs were.

"Does your grandmother still use these stairs?" I don't mind heights, but these steep steel steps were daunting.

Rick had bounded ahead of me. He stopped and looked back at me. "Oh, yes. It's the most direct way. Is this hard for you?" His courtesy was automatic, even though he obviously didn't want to deal with me.

"Not at all." I knew my reply came too quickly. It is an odd truth about aging that we never want to admit we can't do something that was once easy. I hoped that pride didn't, in this case, literally precede a fall. I concentrated on placing each foot firmly in the center of the metal grid. My hand slid along the railing. I was blithe in my speech, but my body was exhibiting intelligent caution. And I didn't trust the young man below me.

Rick waited until I reached the step above him. "This is the quickest way down to the store. Of course, it's possible to take the outside steps from La Mari-

73

posa, but it's definitely the long way around. Everyone in the family comes this way." He clattered down the remaining steps.

As I followed sedately, he chattered, "The interior back stairs in La Mariposa end in the ground-floor hall. Tony and Susana live on the third floor. They walk down to the ground floor and use these stairs." He pointed up at a door next to the one we'd opened to leave Maria Elena's quarters. I knew that door was close to my room.

Rick was apparently delighted to share nonessential information. The better, I suspected, to avoid any more questions about his relationship with Iris.

"Now, down here—"

I reached the base of the staircase.

"—we have the offices." He gestured across the hall.

A large floor fan at the far end of the long hall stirred the cool air. There was no need of air-conditioning here. Old, thick walls kept the temperature cool. The air, though moving, had a dry mustiness that reminded me of a visit on a fall day many years ago to the catacombs in Rome.

"And there is the receiving area." Rick gestured toward closed double doors as he led the way to the doorway into the store.

I said quickly, "I'd like to see the receiving area." Susana had said that Iris left the shipping area unattended. "That's where Iris was working Thursday, isn't it?"

He waited an instant too long to reply. Where was Iris working Thursday? A simple question requiring a simple answer. Instead, he said blandly, "Really? I didn't know that. I didn't see her after she told me about going to Padre. And that was upstairs in La Mariposa. We hold the auction in one of the large rooms

on the main floor of La Mariposa. I was working on
the display tables, setting up the electronic bidders.
But you said you wanted to talk to everyone. When
Abuelita called for me, I was at Tesoros. We're final-
izing plans for the auction. If we hurry, we may find
everyone still there."

"Everyone? The whole family?"

He grinned. "Well, it's never everyone in the Garza
family unless you've made room for a hundred or so.
All the aunts and uncles and cousins. Whenever anybody gets sick or wants to take a vacation, somebody
in the family fills in. And trouble? They come through
the door in droves." He spoke easily with the security
of a man who knows where he belongs and is comfortable there and with the fluency of a man determined to control the course of the conversation. "But
day to day, Tony and Susana oversee the store. Along
with me and Celestina. I don't think you've met my
Aunt Celestina. Or my Uncle Frank and Aunt Isabel.
They run La Mariposa. So, of course, they're right in
the middle of the planning for the auction. Anyway,
everybody's in Tesoros."

Was Rick simply trying to divert me from asking
questions of him? Or did hc want to steer clear of the
receiving area? Whatever, I knew his volubility had a
definite purpose.

I smiled. "I'm certainly eager to meet everyone.
Whatever they can tell me about Iris will be a help.
But it will only take a minute to look at the receiving
area." I walked determinedly to the closed doors.

Rick reluctantly followed. He punched a keypad
mounted on the wall. I tried to recreate in my mind
the movement of his hand. Oh-nine-two-one. It was
certainly not a combination which would occur to an
intruder in a hurry.

Rick pulled open the nearer door. We stepped into a cavernous room that was perhaps twenty feet wide, thirty feet deep. A single globed light hung from the ceiling. Shelving ran around the four walls, broken only by the wide metal door of a freight elevator in the far wall. The throaty hum of a dehumidifier explained the dust-free, dry air.

Rick flipped a switch and bright fluorescent light glowed, running in panels above four long worktables. The sharp white glow transformed a dusky cavern into a storeroom with colorful treasures everywhere. On the shelves, I glimpsed a variety of artworks of every color and kind imaginable: pottery, marionettes, sarapes, clay figures, straw mosaics, wax figures, bas-relief wood panels, lacquerware, wooden carvings, baskets, earthenware vessels, stone sculptures, toys, dolls, masks, retablos, Day of the Dead offerings.

"Everything comes down in the elevator." Rick pointed toward the back of the room. "We unpack at the first table. Every item is recorded in the Tesoros great log. Over there"—Rick pointed to a huge leather-bound book on a stand—"that's Maria Elena's original journal. Then we put everything into the computer"—now he swung to his left and gestured toward a computer station against the near wall—"and index it so we can find an entry by type, point of origin, price, age, provenance." Pride lifted his voice. "We have one of the most modern systems available."

My shoes clipped on the cement floor as I walked briskly to the old journal. "What does Iris do when she works in here?" I glanced at the facing pages. The date was handwritten in the center of the page above a listing of items received. Nothing for today's date. Nothing for Sunday.

On Saturday, a shipment of six late-classic sarapes

from San Miguel de Allende, circa 1920, fine, tight weave with diamond medallions in the center against alternating red and black horizontal designs, purchase price $4,500 each, sale price $5,750.

I backtracked, scanning the entries made on the previous Friday, turned the page and found the entries for Thursday:

Sixteen wax figures, Jalisco, matadors, circa 1950, purchase price $110 each, sale price $250.

Lacquerware, Uruapan, seven trays, purchase price $350 each, sale price $450.

There were more entries—for pottery from Guadalajara, Tonalá, and Santa Cruz de las Huertas, some old, some new, ranging in price from a few hundred dollars to several thousand. All of this was in a schoolgirlish handwriting. I pointed to these lines.

"Is this Iris's handwriting?"

Rick barely glanced at the page. "Yes. She did a lot of unpacking. It's really a lot of fun. We check the invoice, unpack, then get out the right collector's book for the current pricing. Of course, Maria Elena goes over a printout from the computer every day. Sometimes she changes the prices. But if she approves the shipping-room price, the next step is to tag the work and place it according to price within its storage area. We rotate pieces in the front of the shop. Our turnover rate is excellent. We usually don't keep any particular piece more than a month. That keeps our inventory manageable. And we don't buy in a particular area unless our inventory is low." He reached out, turned the pages gently forward. There was pride and delight, almost reverence, in that touch.

I smiled at him. "You enjoy being a part of the store?"

"Tesoros." He savored the name, his hand smoothed

his sleek black goatee. "That's what we have, treasures. And to be surrounded by all of this"—he looked around the room from one lovely piece to another—"how could life be any better?"

His grandmother's instinct was sound. This young man indeed appreciated Maria Elena's lifework.

"Does Iris feel the same way about the store?"

"Oh, yes." Rick was too swept up in his eagerness to realize for a moment to whom he spoke. And why. His eyes glowed. His mouth spread in a huge smile. "It's amazing how quickly she's learned. She cares more than—" He broke off. The happiness fled from his face, leaving it wooden.

"If Iris loves Tesoros so much, why did she leave?" I stared up at him.

He turned away. "I already told you." His voice was harsh. "She found somebody else. She's gone to Padre." He strode toward the door to the hall.

I followed, hurrying to catch up.

He yanked open the door. Despite his anger, he held the panel, waited for me to precede him.

I stopped in the doorway, facing him. "What time did you last see Iris?"

He scowled. "About four, I guess."

"She came from the shipping area"—I pointed back into the huge room—"upstairs into La Mariposa to find you?"

"I don't know. I don't know where she was." The muscles ridged in his face.

"Why did she come at that particular moment?"

Anger flashed in his dark eyes. "How should I know? You can ask her. When she gets back from Padre."

I wished I could calibrate Rick's emotion. He towered over me, his face sullen. Yet, his anger seemed hollow, forced. I didn't understand this young man. I had a conflicting sense of him in every way: he loved his grandmother, he loved this store, he eagerly told of Iris's interest in the store, but every inquiry ended with his claim that Iris had run away because of another man.

"Rick, please." I spoke gently. "Please help me."

"I tell you, Iris"—he broke off, looked past me, his eyes suddenly guarded—"Iris told me she was going to Padre. Hi, Celestina."

A small woman glided toward us from the door to the main showroom. She had a mouselike face, the features small and tight. Wire-rimmed glasses and raven dark hair drawn back in a bun gave her an air of severity. "Tony's looking for you, Rick." Her voice had a dry, gritty sound, like gravel crunching underfoot on a country road. "The computer hookup in the auction room isn't working." She held out a hand. "Hello, I'm Celestina Garza." Her hand was limp and cool and faintly moist.

"This is Mrs. Collins." Rick put a firm hand on my elbow and I was out in the hall and the doors to the delivery area closed behind us. "She's a friend of Iris's grandmother and she wants to know all about Iris's job here. If you'll show her around, I'll run up and see what's going on with the hookup. See you later, Mrs. Collins." He strode to the steel stairway and hurried up, his shoes clanging on the metal. I doubted he was nearly as eager to deal with computer problems as he was delighted to be done with me.

Celestina Garza's eyes glittered with dislike. But not of me. Her disdainful glance followed Rick's noisy ascent, then she turned toward me with a smile. At least I supposed it was intended as a smile. The tiny movement of thin lips in tightly drawn skin evoked all the warmth of a face chiseled in mortuary stone.

I beamed at her. "I'm so glad to meet you, Celestina. I'm so impressed at how the family all works together here in the store. I'd like to learn all about it. For Iris's grandmother. When Iris comes back—"

"Is she coming back?" Celestina looked at me curiously. "I heard she ran out on Rick. But maybe Maria Elena doesn't care. She's been terribly interested in Iris. And for what reason, I'd like to know?" Her tone was sharp. "That girl came out of nowhere and Maria Elena treats her like family." Her eyes glinted with resentment. "So she's coming back, even though Rick has his nose out of joint. What do you know about that! Maybe for once Abuelita's darling won't get his way." Now she smiled fully, her lips curving in malicious delight.

"Iris told me you'd been very kind. And that you are very important in running the store." I learned long ago in interviews that it never hurts to toss in a bit of butter.

She blinked in surprise. Then she preened. "Well, I'm glad Iris recognizes how things really work. Why, to hear Tony or Rick talk, you wouldn't even think I existed. But who works behind the scenes, making sure that everything happens when it should? I do. And never a word of thanks from anyone. As for Mother, she's never let me do as much as I wanted. At least she has the sense to get Magda out on the road. That's my sister, Rick's mother. She's in Jalisco now on a buying trip. Magda and Tony never could be in the same room without fighting. Tony bulls his way around and everyone runs to do what he says. But not Magda. And not Susana, for that matter. And if a man can't control his own wife, that tells you something, doesn't it?" A short laugh. "Susana thinks she's better than everyone else but she'd better be careful. The walls can have ears. And eyes. Although I don't know if I blame her. How many little friends is a man supposed to have? But Susana takes too much on herself. And then she's never satisfied, always jealous when Frank buys Isabel new jewelry." A thin hand straightened the plain collar of her beige silk blouse. "Jewelry!" She tossed her head and not a hair in that taut bun quivered. "That's all Isabel thinks about, jewelry and trips and fine furniture and silver. Well, it's a good thing I'm here. And I'm glad to know Iris appreciates me. When is she going to be back? I didn't understand why she left, with the auction coming up." Celestina peered at me and the thick lens magnified her brooding brown eyes.

I watched her carefully as I spoke. "I understand from Rick that he expects Iris to return sometime tomorrow."

But Celestina merely nodded, as if the fact were of only marginal interest. "Well, we'll have to make you welcome until she gets here. So you want to find out about the store for Iris's grandmother? Is her grandmother an old friend of Maria Elena's?"

It was like being at the end of a long line when a message is whispered to one, then another in turn, and the final account is entirely garbled. Fun, when it's a game. Interesting to me now, and very helpful, in dealing with Celestina Garza. I was being accorded a legitimacy I hadn't expected. Instead of posing questions, perhaps unwelcome questions, about Iris's last day at the store—and why she'd left in secrecy if not in haste—I was now merely an honored guest to be shown every respect.

"Maria Elena?" I spoke easily, as if I knew her well. "Actually, she and I have known each other longer than she's known Iris's grandmother." It's always such a pleasure to speak the truth. And it sounds so well. "But, Celestina, tell me more about Tesoros. I feel like I have so much to learn. And I don't know anyone who could be a better guide. Now"—I pointed at the closed doors to the delivery area—"what's the procedure for working there? I suppose with so much valuable artwork, you are very careful about security?"

"Oh, yes, of course," she said importantly. "You see the electronic keypad. The code changes every day. But it's so simple. And so clever. I thought of it. The code depends upon the date. The first number is the month, the second the day of the month. Say it's May seventh. You punch oh-five-oh-seven. But"—she paused importantly—"if it's the twenty-first, like today, you punch in oh-nine-two-one."

"Oh." My tone was admiring. "And if it's the twenty sixth, it's oh-nine-two-six."

"Yes." Her tight smile awarded me a gold star.

I nodded in admiration. "And if it's the thirtieth, you punch oh-nine-three-oh. That's very clever, Celestina."

Starved for applause, she bloomed, like a parched plant splashed by water.

Her small, neat fingers, the nails glistening with colorless polish, danced on the keypad. She opened the double door, stepped inside, and flipped the switch. Once again the bright fluorescent lights illuminated the long room.

"And Iris works . . ."

Celestina was already leading the way to the first table. She bustled importantly to the grand ledger, explained it to me. I listened, but this time I was looking carefully around the room.

Iris was here on Thursday, involved in an ordinary

workday. What led her to hurry from the room, leaving that guarded door open?

"It's important to proceed in the proper order. First, the shipment is opened, its contents examined. It's necessary not only to confirm the invoice but to be certain the materials have arrived undamaged. All of this . . ."

No telephone. I scanned the area again. I didn't see a telephone anywhere. Of course, Iris could have brought down a mobile phone or a cell phone. I couldn't be certain she hadn't received a telephone message. But there was no standard, connected-to-a-jack office telephone.

Celestina was beaming at me.

"That's very impressive. A well-designed process. And I see there's no telephone."

If anything, she looked even jollier. "I felt it was unnecessary. Tony was furious, but for once Mother stood up for me. Tony never likes to be away from a telephone."

So Iris's departure probably wasn't triggered by a telephone call. Then it had to be something here, something in this room. Thursday's shipment? I walked over to the grand ledger, turned the pages.

Celestina stood at my elbow. "Yes, Iris was working here Thursday." A tight frown pulled her brows down. "I came in the next day and found a shipment—some candlesticks—still in the box. She shouldn't have opened a box if she didn't intend to finish with it."

So Iris left in the middle of a task. Once again, I had a sense of urgency, of something happening, something shocking. But what? I closed the ledger. "Did you see Iris Thursday?"

"Oh, yes. You couldn't help knowing she was around. Always laughing so much. And that Thursday at noon, I found her and Rick having a picnic in the showroom. They'd taken over for Susana—she'd gone to a meeting—and I told them the showroom was no place for food. They were laughing and giggling like a couple of kids. Even after a customer came in! That's no way to run a business. I sent them outside, gave them fifteen minutes. It's a good thing I keep an eye on things. Of course, no one cares about my lunch hour."

Certainly if Iris intended to announce an imminent departure to Rick, she could have done so then. I doubted she'd met a new love and accepted an invitation to Padre between lunch and four o'clock. Which brought me back to this brightly lit room with its carefully cataloged artworks.

I said admiringly, "You certainly have the best interests of the store at heart."

Celestina looked at me gratefully, her tight little features almost lively.

"Did you see Iris later in the afternoon?"

"No." Her voice was sharp. "I'd come back to the storeroom, a customer wanted to know if we had any more of Teodoro Blanco's ceramic dolls. Susana was here in the hall, furious. She'd just discovered the door open and Iris nowhere to be found. She and I looked everywhere." She pointed at the doors behind us. "I thought she'd just run upstairs for something. These young people, they can't follow a routine. And, of course, she was always going off on tangents."

"Tangents?" I faced her.

Celestina brushed a speck of lint from the ledger. She straightened the huge book. Perhaps it was a quarter inch askew on its stand. "Really"—she eyed me carefully—"Iris could be supremely silly. It was hard for her to stay focused. Why, she was as likely as not to decide it was time to sweep out the floor by the recycling bins. Or she'd hear a noise and squeal and say a mouse must be in one of the shelves. I'm sorry to say it, but I imagine her grandmother knows full well that Iris can't be depended on to remember what she's supposed to be doing. Why, once I thought she was busy unpacking and I came down to check and she was arranging the tin paintings of the saints in alphabetical order, said it would be easier for us to find them. She was covered with dust and had completely lost track of the time."

Supremely silly Iris. I wish I felt amused instead of scared. Iris with her short attention span and overweening curiosity. What had she found? I was sure of only two things. The object or objects were smaller than a bread box, bigger than an orange. And she'd gone with her discovery to Rick.

I couldn't prove this. I couldn't even make a particularly good case for my theory. But it made better sense than an imaginary trip to Padre Island. And maybe, just maybe, it gave me some ammunition for a confrontation with Rick. It definitely increased my interest in each and every person with access to this storage area.

Celestina's thin hand turned the ledger page to today. "But we won't get any more unpacking done until Iris gets back. Everyone is too busy setting up for the auction." She glanced at her watch. "I need to pick up the catalog from the printer's this morning."

"Do Iris and Rick do most of the unpacking?"

"We all do our share. Mother insists. She says we need to remember what we are all about. Even Isabel helps from time to time. That always upsets Susana." Celestina's thin mouth curved in a satisfied smile. "Susana likes to think she's in charge of everything."

So I couldn't knock anyone off my list, but it was a small-enough list: the Garza family.

"But Tony's actually in charge of the store." Outgoing, handsome, charming Tony. I could well understand why Maria Elena had chosen Tony to run Tesoros.

Celestina's tiny nose wrinkled as if she smelled something disagreeable. "At least he thinks he is. But Mother keeps track of everything. Tony has such big ideas. Even Susana's more sensible than Tony. And of course it bothered Frank when Mother put Tony in charge of Tesoros, but Mother acted as if running La Mariposa was terribly important. Mother knew Frank would make a complete botch of the store. Of course, he's awfully retiring to try and run a hotel. Now Isabel certainly knows how to behave. She can charm the devil if she puts her mind to it. Frank pretends it was all his idea for him to do La Mariposa, but sometimes when he looks at Tony . . ." She shivered and her little face was suddenly uneasy. "I know Mother keeps an eye on the books, both at Tesoros and La Mariposa. She'd better. Tony's a gambler, but he knows he'd better keep the accounts straight for Mother. And Frank always needs money. Isabel spends money like it's water. If it weren't for me, Mother wouldn't even know how many problems there are." She sighed, a prophet scorned.

And, I thought, a whiny tattletale who'd never outgrown that pleasure.

"But the auction's always a great success, isn't it?"

"Yes." Her tone was grudging. "I suppose it is. But really that was all Mother's idea. Frank and Tony just keep things going."

"Can we go up to the auction room? I'd love to see how it's organized."

She glanced at her watch. "I have to see about the printing—"

"I can find my way." I smiled and headed for the door.

In the hallway, she pointed to the circular staircase. "Straight up to the landing and through that door."

Malicious Celestina. Tentative Frank. Spendthrift Isabel. Charming Tony. Prickly Susana. Proud Rick. And I shouldn't forget Manuel. Sweet Manuel. Sweet and worried Manuel. I must be sure to see him. He couldn't speak, yet I felt he knew something of Iris's unexpected departure. I remembered his hands and their swift movement. Yes, I, too, felt Iris left in a hurry.

I reached the landing, stepped into the back hallway of La Mariposa. As the door closed behind me, I saw the electronic keypad and realized access to the stairs was controlled in the same way as entry to the delivery area. I punched oh-nine-two-one. The handle turned, the door opened. I closed it, then glanced at the interior stairway, which offered access to the upper floors of La Mariposa.

Iris must have come this way on Thursday. I reached the lobby and walked to the desk, the weathered old chili cart. The resident black cat looked up with a measuring gaze. I held out my hand for him to sniff, then stroked his cashmere soft fur. He rewarded me with a gurgle in his throat.

Rick's cousin Tom greeted me with a smile from a face I was beginning to know, the oblong Garza face with thick dark brows, high cheekbones and blunt dimpled chin. "Good morning, Mrs. Collins. There's a message for you." He turned to the pigeonhole desk and retrieved a white envelope.

I took it with a smile. "Thank you." I glanced at the

envelope. My name was printed in block letters. Otherwise the envelope was plain, giving no hint of its origin. "When did this come?" I was still smiling, but I looked at him intently.

"Sometime this morning," he said casually. "I found it on the counter a few minutes ago."

"I see." That could be true. It could be a lie. I needed to remember that I knew nothing about this young man. He spoke easily about Iris. But I wasn't ready to trust anyone in the Garza family and I felt certain that this note, whatever message it held, had to be in response to my search for Iris. I was burning to know the contents, but I didn't want Tom Garza or anyone in his family to know my eagerness. So I held the envelope as if it were of no importance and asked, "Tom, where is the room where the auction will be held?"

"The auction?" he temporized.

I realized that no matter Tom's charming courtesy to guests, the Thursday auction was a closed affair, by invitation only, and my name was not on that select list.

"When I was visiting with Maria Elena this morning, she insisted I see how everything is coming along. She said the electronic bidders are very impressive."

As soon as Tom heard Maria Elena's name, his manner changed. "That's all Rick's doing. He put the bidders in last year and everyone loves it. You know how the auction works?"

I was familiar with all kinds of auctions, from the raucous to the silent. I fished. "As I understand it, everyone attending the auction has a number—"

He interrupted eagerly. "Not a number, a letter. It's really cool. The items are placed on tables around the room. Each table has a keypad with a small screen, kind of like a notebook. The most recent bid shows on the screen plus a letter. Say it's $2,000P, that means the bidder with the code name P bid $2,000. If the new person wants to raise the bid, they can type in $2,500C or whatever their letter is. The bids are recorded in a central computer, and at the end of the morning the bidders receive an envelope containing the list of the objects they've bought. This way no one else attending knows the identity of any bidder."

Which mattered to a great many quite well-to-do art collectors who prefer always to remain unknown not only to the general public but to their fellow collectors and who do not broadcast their acquisitions. Neat, yes.

"This was Rick's idea?"

"Oh, sure. He's really on top of it with everything that can help the store. He's in the auction room now, making sure there aren't any glitches." Tom pointed toward a wide doorway framed with red velvet hangings. "There's a reception area and our meeting rooms." A big grin curved his mouth. "All two of them."

I crossed the tiled lobby, skirting the huge refectory table, but stopped next to a collection of wooden panels. A card noted they were created by R. D. de la Selva in the 1930s, probably in Mexico City, and were painted white mahogany, the bas-relief scenes depicting Mexicans at work. With my back to the desk, I opened the envelope. On a single sheet of paper, block capital letters informed:

THE RIVER WALK BEHIND THE KING WILLIAM
DISTRICT PROVIDES ONE OF THE LOVELIEST
VIEWS OF THE SAN ANTONIO RIVER.
2 P.M.

That was all. No instructions. No hint of what might await me on this stretch of the River Walk. Or who. Was the message purposefully vague to entice me? The printing was uneven, the letters odd sizes. Definitely the writer did not want to be identified. That thought was unsettling. Who wanted to be utterly certain that the author of this message remained unknown? Who could have written it? The list was small indeed: Tony Garza, Susana Garza, Rick Reyes, Tom Garza. But I couldn't limit the possibilities quite so closely. Although I'd just met Celestina and had yet to meet Frank and his wife, I was willing to guess the entire family knew of me since Officer Hess had preceded me this morning. So, add Celestina Garza, Frank Garza, Isabel Garza. Perhaps one of them knew something about Iris's disappearance and wanted to talk to me away from Tesoros. I stared at the note and felt the stirring of caution like a storm flag rippling in a rising wind.

Two o'clock. I glanced at my watch. Almost noon. There was time enough to pursue my interest in the Garza family. As for the summons? I'd do some scouting in advance. I'm always open to new experiences. But I try not to be stupid.

I tucked the note in my purse and moved toward the red velvet hangings. I stepped through the opening into a reception area. Light spilled in a golden cascade from the shimmering swirl of copper chandeliers, illuminating a floor-to-ceiling mural of a Mexican village square: a woman rolled tortillas, a man led his firewood-laden donkey, children played with ragtag dogs, a family walked toward the church.

I was startled for an instant that the door to the church in the mural stood open, then realized the doors to La Mariposa's two meeting rooms had been painted to appear part of the mural. A second door was in a wall around a hacienda. I crossed to the open door.

As I neared the doorway, the low rumble of men's voices was overborne by a woman's disdainful pronouncement. "Rick, it's the aesthetics you don't understand. Those wires are hideous!"

I stood to one side of the door and, unnoticed, looked into the big room. Small tiled tables on wrought-iron legs were placed around the perimeter of the room. In addition, two rows projected into the center of the room from the far-right wall. It was cleverly done. A visitor would travel either right or left along the walls and around the center rows. At the present moment, a low wooden pedestal sat on each table along with a keypad and small screen.

Bright murals adorned these walls, too. Each wall depicted artisans at work: weavers with bright yarns; potters shaping clay, working at wheels, firing ovens; artists dying straw and sketching scenes to be covered by beeswax to hold the straw; sculptors carving figures from blocks of beeswax and creating bright costumes from silk and cotton scraps.

I hadn't met the speaker, but I recognized Frank's wife, Isabel, from the family photograph: honey-blond hair as shiny as burnished gold, sloe eyes emphasized with strokes of ocher shading, full lips brighter than poppies in the summer sun. A fawn-colored silk jumpsuit clung to her voluptuous figure. Red and blue stones glistened in her rings as she pointed to the silver-sheathed wires snaking across each table, dangling from the back, ending in a tangle of connecting plates.

"I'll cover the wires with dark crepe paper on the tabletops." Rick's voice was edgy and determined. "The way it's set up"—he strode to the nearest table, traced the wire—"the lines go over the back of each table and run along the floor to come together."

"I'm surprised Maria Elena agreed to this." Isabel's full lips pouted. "When Frank and I organized the auction, each piece was the focus of its own place. Now that ugly keypad completely detracts."

Frank Garza scratched his salt and pepper hair and affected a surprised look. "You know, Rick, I have to agree with Isabel. The kind of people who come to this—the Harrisons and Joshua Campbell and Mr. King—they're accustomed to the finest. We don't want to tarnish a grand tradition. Perhaps it's time to rethink—"

Tony Garza leaned negligently against a wall, hands in his pockets. "Don't let a woman do your thinking for you, Frank. Rick can cover the wires, that's not a problem, and the concept's excellent." Tony pushed away from the wall and reached down to punch the keypad. "Anonymity. Speed. Accuracy. Way to go, Rick." He gave his brother a contemptuous glance. "Thing about it is, Frank, you've never had a real head for business, have you?"

Isabel tensed, like a cat poised to leap. Frank reached out, caught her arm. He blinked, like someone startled by a too-bright light. "Business is more than a row of figures, Tony. You've never learned how to treat people. I heard that Jack Ramirez told a bunch of his friends he'd never deal with Tesoros again because you refused to make good on a broken plate."

Tony Garza's full mouth split in a huge grin. "That plate wasn't broken when his wife left with it. He wanted the money for his little friend. I'd be dammed if he was going to make Tesoros pay for her."

Just as he finished, Susana Garza stopped beside me. Frank looked toward the door. His indeterminate

mouth curved in a sly smile. "Hi, Susana." Then he
shot a satisfied look at his brother. "I'd think you'd
know better than anyone what a man will do for his
mistress, Tony."

Isabel Garza gave a tinkling laugh. Her richly red
lips spread in a delighted smile. She had looked catlike
in the family photograph. Now she watched Tony with
the pleasure of a feline with a mouse between its paws.

Beside me Susana stood rigid, her haggard face
flushed. Tony carefully did not look toward his wife
as he reached out to the nearest table. "Come on, let's
see how this is working."

Rick busily adjusted the electronic keypad and
smoothed out a cord. "I'll get busy with the crepe paper. It will work. And Uncle Frank, your idea of placing a floor on some of the items makes a lot of sense.
Aunt Celestina's used your figures for the catalog. I'll
bring you a copy this afternoon."

Susana, her eyes glittering, strode to her husband.
"Celestina wants you to come down and see about the
catalog."

"Hello," I said cheerfully, stepping inside. "Rick,
I'm so glad I found you. Your Aunt Celestina told me
a lot about the store. She said this is the area for the
auction. I'm eager to hear all about it." I looked at the
older Garzas. "I'm Henrietta Collins, a friend of Iris
Chavez's grandmother. Maria Elena has made me feel
very welcome. And I feel there is so much to learn
about Tesoros."

Frank nodded, switching from sly to polite. Isabel
flicked me a measuring glance. I suspected she'd totted
up the cost of my cotton blouse and skirt and inexpensive sandals, noted the single gold wedding band,
been briefly intrigued by a necklace made of old jade-
ite beads. Then her eyes moved on, dismissing me,

returning to Tony Garza, fastening there with pleased malice.

Tony Garza, although very aware of his wife's presence, concentrated on smiling at me.

Did anyone care that I was a connection to Iris Chavez? Not on the surface. But if my guess about Iris and a discovery in the receiving area had any validity, one of them should be very interested indeed. I debated whether to stir the pot. Yes, sometimes I can be reckless. In the course of an interview, an unexpected, perhaps confrontational question can evoke anger, fear, despair—and a lot of words. Some of my best stories were gleaned from heated responses. But as my husband Richard once observed, if you toss a piece of meat into a lion's den, be sure you're on the other side of the fence.

"In fact, I was fascinated by my tour of the shipping area." I looked at each in turn. "There are so many nooks and crannies. Who knows what you might find there?"

Rick's oblong, darkly handsome face was carefully blank.

Isabel, her head to one side, surveyed her nails, then lifted slim fingers to pat away a tiny yawn.

Frank waved a hand in dismissal. "There's nothing of interest down there. It's the buyers who are interesting. I'll have to tell you about the people who are coming for the auction."

Tony beamed at me, probably glad to have a diversion. "It's a heck of a place, all right. I remember when I was a little kid, I was always scared of the devil masks."

Susana said briskly, "Everything in the shipping area is in its proper place, Mrs. Collins. But," and she abruptly moved toward the door, "that will have to wait until after the auction. We're all very busy at the moment." She paused in the doorway. "Especially," and her voice was cold, "since we're shorthanded." She stalked away.

As we moved toward the hallway, Isabel said sweetly, "Oh, I'm sure Susana will have time for you. She's always eager to please Maria Elena. I'd hurry right after her."

"If you think that's all right," I murmured. We stepped into the lobby of La Mariposa.

"Don't pay any attention to Susana." Frank's voice was soft. "She was born crossways. And she isn't really up to things. The auction always worries her. Isabel and I like it better than anything but Fiesta. But there is plenty to do. If you'll excuse us, we need to huddle about our party Wednesday night. You're coming, of course."

"I'd love to. I never miss a party."

Isabel smiled brightly. "You certainly won't want to miss ours. The best food, the best music, everything the best." Her bright lips curved in satisfaction. "We live in the King William area. Our house is on the National Register."

"The King William area?" I looked at her intently.

"San Antonio's oldest, loveliest homes," she announced proudly. "German businessmen settled the area in the 1870s. Our house is one of the oldest."

"I'll look forward to it." As they moved away, I looked for Rick and realized he'd left while I talked with his uncle and aunt. So, Rick didn't want to engage in a tête-à-tête about the interesting nooks and crannies of the receiving area. But the day wasn't over.

I checked my watch. A quarter to one. I walked across the tiled floor to the chili-cart desk. No one was in attendance, so it had obviously been easy for someone to leave that anonymous note without being seen. I picked up a silver bell and jangled it.

Tom came out of the office. "Yes, ma'am."

"I'm interested in the King William area."

"Oh, yes, there are some wonderful houses there." He found a map and opened it. "Here it is. It's only a few minutes by car."

"I understand some of it is on the River Walk." I scanned the map and realized there was a three-block area of the walk between Durango and Johnson.

"Oh, sure. But you might want to drive over there. It will give you a chance to look at the houses, too. You can take the River Walk, but it's at least a couple of miles." He traced the way. "If you plan to walk, go down the steps to the River Walk and turn left."

I thanked him and tucked the map in my purse, along with the summons. I took the outside steps down to the River Walk and went to the front of Tesoros. Manuel was wiping a shining window with a soft cloth. I stopped behind him. Now that I had met all of the Garza men, I had a clear sense of the family appearance. Strong faces. Manuel sensed my presence and turned toward me, his luminous eyes shyly welcoming, his broad mouth spread in a sweet smile, the Garza face with no pretense.

I felt suddenly sad. How many places do any of us feel safe to be open and unaffected? I hoped Manuel would always feel safe enough to offer his sweet, undemanding, lovely smile.

"Hello, Manuel," I said gently. "You make the windows very beautiful."

His eyes glowed. He looked at me for a moment, then held out his cloth.

After only an instant's hesitation, I took the soft cotton swath in my hand. I wasn't sure what he meant, what he expected. I wanted to please him, to do the right thing. I stepped close to the window, reached up and polished a patch of glass. When I finished, I nodded at my own reflection. I held the cloth out to Manuel. "Thank you, Manuel, for letting me help. It's fun to make the glass shine."

Tucking the cloth in his pocket, he lifted his hands, tanned, lean hands, and moved them swiftly, quickly. Shadows flickered against the shining glass. I thought I discerned a smiling mouth, a slim figure moving quickly, a hand industriously polishing.

"Iris?" I guessed. "She likes to help clean the glass, too."

Manuel beamed, his hands came together in a gentle clapping, and I knew I was right.

"Was she in too much of a hurry to help, the last time you saw her?"

His face drooped. Once again those swift movements, a taut mouth, a hunched figure running.

"Manuel, was she carrying anything—"

Manuel's shoulders drew in, his eyes skittered away. He picked up his bucket, and, head bent, scurried away. Slowly, I turned and looked into another Garza face. For once handsome Tony Garza wasn't smiling. "My brother is quite simple, Mrs. Collins. He can't answer questions. It would be kinder to leave him alone. As for Iris, none of us know where she is."

"I am going to find her." But I spoke to a closing door.

As I turned away, I carried with me the impact of two faces—long, oval, strong-boned, so similar, yet so different; one so open, the other vivid, commanding, somehow hawklike. And dangerous? Tony Garza had kept me from speaking with Manuel. Was his aim to protect his brother? Or was he protecting himself? Or someone else?

I could be certain of only one fact. Apparently, it would not be Tony Garza waiting for me on the River Walk near the King William district.

six

ON a holiday, I would have strolled all the way on the River Walk. But I wasn't on a holiday. Besides, I wanted a chance to look over the terrain before the scheduled time. I pulled out of the parking garage and drove south on Alamo, took Turner to the King William Park, where I left the car. I walked past another marvelous bed-and-breakfast, then took the first access down to the River Walk. The steps wound down past lush greenery. The river curved, so I could only see a little way ahead and behind. I strolled with the bright look of a tourist.

Palm trees, red oaks, magnolias, and sycamores flourished, affording only glimpses of the lovely homes. The placid water sparkled in the bright sun. Two young mothers pushed strollers. I passed an elderly woman tossing seed to eager ducks. I followed the curving walk all the way to the Johnson Street footbridge. In the center of the footbridge, I shaded my eyes and looked over the smooth green water and the shady walk.

Two sunburned women power-walked past me. The little one, scrawny legs a blur, chirped, "Margie, I just have to take home an armadillo. Aren't they the cutest things you've ever seen!" Margie was tall, with bushy red hair and dangling silver earrings that jangled as she moved. She said mournfully, "Armadillos carry leprosy." Her red-nosed companion squealed. "Oh, that's awful. But I don't want a real one. They're always squashed in the middle of the road. But there's the cutest shop in La Villita . . ."

Their voices faded. I returned to the River Walk at a leisurely pace and began to wonder at the summons I had received. It was a few minutes past two. Everywhere I looked, I saw ordinary people on a beautiful September afternoon—a young couple holding hands, occasional joggers, a family picnicking. I didn't feel uneasy. At no time was I more than thirty feet from others. But what was the point—

A whoosh and a lithe figure in a pink tank top and white shorts swooped around a curve and raced up to me on Rollerblades, dark hair flying, big eyes nervously scanning the walkway. The exertion had added a rosy flush to her creamy skin. As she toed to a stop, she looked at me imploringly, her limpid green eyes the exact color of her grandmother's.

I felt a sudden breathlessness, a welling of relief that left me almost light-headed. And a spurt of exasperation laced with indignation.

"Aunt Henrie!" Her light, high voice was rushed, breathless. "Tell Grandmother I'm fine. I just can't be home for a while. Tell her I'm okay and please let the police know I'm all right. That's why I came today. I can't explain—"

"Oh yes, you can," I replied sharply. I grasped her arm, surprised at the intensity of my anger. The anger showed me how worried I'd been, how uncertain of her safety. I was relieved, yes, but furious. What did this young woman think she was up to? She'd put her grandmother through sleepless nights filled with hideous imaginings; caused disruption at her work place; worried Maria Elena, who had befriended her; taken the time of police, who are always pressed, always behind; and, of course, interrupted my visit at Emily's. "Iris, the police are looking for you. What's going on? Why did you disappear? And what did you find—"

"Please let me go." Her huge eyes begged. "I'd tell you if I could. But I can't, Aunt Henrie, I really can't. This is terribly important, something I have to do—"

"Iris, Maria Elena welcomed you to her store." My voice was icy. "To her life. She opened her heart to you, and you repay her by frightening her. She knows Rick is involved in your disappearance. Iris, you have to explain. Come with me—"

She shook her head and her shining black hair rippled. Tears glistened in her eyes. "Oh, Aunt Henrie, I wish I could. Maybe we did the wrong thing. But we thought it was best. I'll tell you when I can. But I have to help Rick. Oh, you just don't understand . . ." Her voice rose in a wail.

"I'll understand if you tell me what's going on." My grip on her arm tightened as I felt her try to pull away. "Help Rick with what? Did he follow you home from the store Thursday and take you away?"

"How did you know?" Her face was an image of astonishment.

I could have shaken her. "Iris, listen to me. You're in big trouble. The police are looking for you. Someone searched your apartment—"

She shivered. "That's so scary. Rick told me. But that's proof that we have to—"

The bushes behind us rustled. Without that warning, I don't know what might have happened. We swung toward the sound. The moment stretched in time, the sense of danger and menace making the seconds seem endless. A stocky blond man lunged toward us, his face malevolent, big blunt hands outstretched, muscular arms tensed. On the back of his right forearm was the tattoo of an eagle with wings outspread.

Iris gave a frightened yelp.

The blond man was almost upon us, his face twisted with anger and urgency. He was big, strong, and determined. I knew he must not reach Iris. "Go, go," I screamed. I pushed her away.

He was close, so close. His right hand swiped through the air, but Iris was moving. She escaped his grasp by inches. In an instant, head down, arms pumping, she sped on the cement walk back toward town, twenty feet away, thirty, then gone around a bend.

He ran heavily after her for a little way, then lurched to a stop. He raised a fist in frustration. "Bitch." His voice was low and thick in his throat. He took one step, another, then gave it up and swung to face me.

I stood in the center of the walk. I flipped open my purse, grabbed my cell phone, held it up.

He moved toward me, his big face red with anger, his blue eyes glittering.

I spoke calmly but emphatically. "One more step and I'll punch nine-one-one. And scream. There are plenty of people around." As I held his gaze, I cataloged his appearance: tight blond curls; square face with a broad nose; red-veined blue eyes with puffy pouches; heavy jowls; a thin, angry gash of a mouth; a bristle of blondish beard; fiftyish; stocky but muscular, especially his arms; short-sleeved light blue T-shirt; navy slacks; tasseled loafers.

He glared. Anger undulated from him, a wild, pulsing fury. He was close to losing all control. I could see it in the tight line of his mouth, in the clenching of his big hands, in the tautness of his body, poised and ready to spring. He wanted to batter me into a bloodied heap.

I turned on the cell phone.

"I could kill you and be gone before anybody got here." The hoarse whisper trembled with rage.

I backed away, looked desperately past him as a mother and little girl came nearer.

"Listen to me, lady. Listen close." He was close enough now that I could see a tic jerking one eyelid. "Tell the little bitch she'd better bring it back." Each word was as clear and distinct and menacing as ice crackling underfoot on a frozen lake. "Tell her I won't be double-crossed. Tell her she's got twenty-four hours."

"Twenty-four hours?" I knew my voice was high and thin.

He was across the space between us in a swift step. He grabbed my arm, twisted, the cell phone dropped to the pavement. He bent so close to me I could see beads of sweat on his bristly cheeks, smell the rank scent of whiskey, feel the warmth of his fetid breath. "Tell her to put it back. Or she won't like the way her boyfriend looks. I've got a knife. I'll use it. Tell her. Tell him."

His grip tightened until I winced in pain. He came close—oh, so close—to flinging me down on the pavement. But, as quickly as he'd grabbed me, he dropped my arm, whirled and ran.

I didn't try to follow. I would never catch him. Instead, my hands shaking, my heart thudding, I picked up the cell phone, but I made no move to call. There was no point in calling for help now. He was gone. I could describe him but what could the police do? If I lodged a complaint, accused him of assault, they could swear out a warrant for his arrest. But certainly the facts wouldn't support an all-out search. Moreover, a charge of assaulting me didn't get at the real problem: What had Iris found in the Tesoros receiving room? Who put it there? Why? Who was this man? What connection did he have with Tesoros?

Reporters learn early to focus on the who, what, when, where, why, and how. It was time for me to remember my early training. But first, there was a call I could make.

The cell phone squawked and buzzed. Gina's voice was faint.

"Gina, good news. I just saw Iris. She's fine, absolutely fine . . ." But once I reassured her, I didn't mince words. Gina had every right to know that Iris was mixed up in something that was probably illegal and certainly dangerous. I described the man who had burst from the bushes. "He tried to get Iris. When she got away, he wanted to hurt me, Gina. And he said Rick and Iris have twenty-four hours to return whatever it is they've taken."

The connection worsened. I could barely hear Gina. ". . . she's such a fool. Henrie O, please, try to protect her."

I promised. I stuffed the phone in my purse, noting the splotchy red marks on my arm and headed back toward my car. I remembered the blond man's heavy, angry face. Where was he now and what did he plan to do?

As I pushed through the main door of the downtown police station, a young woman, one arm in a sling, moved wearily past. I looked the other way, but I carried the picture of her swollen, purplish face with me as I walked down the hall to the Youth Bureau. Probably domestic abuse. Just another day at your local police station. I'd seen a bumper sticker on a car in the lot across from the station: "So You Don't Like Cops. Ever Thought About Living in a World Without Them?"

I waited about ten minutes on a hard bench in the small waiting area, then Detective Hess came to the doorway and gestured for me to come into the main office. I took the chair facing her gray desk and talked. Fast.

When I'd finished, Hess said quietly, "So, she isn't missing. But she's mixed up in something ugly." She turned to her computer. In a few minutes, she handed me some color printouts. I studied a half dozen faces, middle aged blond men all, and shook my head.

The detective leaned back in her swivel chair, folded her arms. "I can't help you. We don't know who he is, we don't know what he's after. If anything. He may be a nut. Maybe he's a guy who got fresh, maybe Iris is trying to get away from him. As for his threats, no judge is going to swear out a John Doe warrant on the basis of a threat made to a third party. Now, if he surfaces, directly threatens"—she glanced down at her notepad—"Rick Reyes, we might be able to get a restraining order. But I'll tell you what it sounds like to me. It sounds like a drug deal gone wrong. I'm going to alert the drug unit. I'm sorry if the girl's in that kind of trouble." Her face hardened. "But people who deal drugs pretty much deserve what they get."

A harsh assessment, but she knew the devastation that flows from drugs.

"Detective Hess, I don't think this has to do with drugs. Iris may be foolish, but I can't imagine her getting involved in that kind of evil."

"I hope not," the detective said quietly.

I nodded, stood. "Thanks for your help. I'm sorry about the missing-person report."

She shrugged. "That's all right. That's the way most missing persons investigations turn out. Or up." A tired smile.

As I turned to go, she called out, "Good luck. If it isn't drugs."

Rick was waiting on a customer. I wandered over to a collection of small painted boxes. Two were dated circa 1780. The smaller was painted in now faded red and green flowers and ferns. I touched the brass lock plate and wondered what the box had contained through the years. Had it kept safe the precious Psalter of a priest who traveled by donkey for many months to reach the far-flung missions? Or protected a land-owner's deeds and records of transactions? Or served as a repository for necklaces of pearl or coral or gold belonging to a grand lady impressed by the French court?

"You have good taste, Mrs. Collins." Rick spoke loudly, his voice easy and genial. He stood with his back to the main floor. Only I could see his face and it was far from genial. His eyes were anxious and wary. He stepped closer. "That box is a fine example of old lacquerware from Zacatecas." He whispered so low only I could hear, "You've seen Iris. Now leave us alone."

As in, butt out. Frankly, I would have liked nothing better. But Gina had asked me to do my best for her granddaughter, however ill advised Iris's actions were. Moreover, I had to tell this handsome, worried young man that a bigger, heavier, stronger man, a man who'd obviously been drinking and was close to an explosion, had a knife and intended to use it.

And now I was once again being manipulated by him. Obviously, Rick was afraid unfriendly eyes might be watching us and he was afraid to speak openly and publicly with me. There could not have been a stronger pointer that the blond man had to be allied with someone at Tesoros.

I stepped closed to the table, picked up a long, slender box. The card on the table identified it as a sewing box circa 1840. "This one's very lovely," I said and then I murmured softly, "Did Iris tell you about the blond man?"

He took the box from me, opened the lid. "Isn't the interior lid spectacular?" Then the whisper, "Yes. Don't worry—"

My voice was soft, but it sheathed steel. "Don't be a fool. He didn't get Iris, but he's going to get you. I have to tell you—"

His lips barely moved. "Tonight. I'll come to your room tonight. Please, don't do anything until I talk to you." His eyes, such young, intense, desperate eyes, beseeched me. Then he put the box down and turned to greet Susana. "Oh, Susana, you've met Mrs. Collins. I know you'll enjoy telling her more about the store. I need to run upstairs and tell Maria Elena that Iris called. She's coming back from Padre tomorrow."

Susana frowned and the deep lines by her mouth pulled her bright red lips down. Her dark eyes glittered with irritation. She lifted a hand to the smooth obsidian necklace that fit her throat like a collar and grasped it with magenta-nailed fingers. It was an effort for control, then the words burst like a torrent. "Back tomorrow! And is she going to waltz in here like she owns Tesoros? Who does she think she is, running off to the beach when we're trying to get ready for the auction? Surely Maria Elena will send her away."

Rick held up his hands, as if to stop the angry flow of words. "I had it all wrong. She didn't go with a guy. It was a friend who was sick. It wasn't anything like we thought. Maria Elena will understand." And he turned away to stride toward the back of the store.

Susana's angry glance followed him. "He's just a fool for a pretty face. How can Iris be going off with a man one minute and the next thing we hear it's a girlfriend. I don't believe a word of it." She threw up her hands, bracelets jangled. Abruptly, she lifted her shoulders in a shrug. "I can't take care of everything around here. And I can't waste any more time worrying about that silly girl. You can tell her grandmother that she's more trouble than she's worth. Now," she tossed her head and the high black pouf wavered like a bird's crest, "you're welcome to come along with me, but I have to work. What would you like to do?"

What I wanted to do was chase after Rick and insist he tell his grandmother—and me—the truth. But I knew that would not happen. He'd made it abundantly clear that Maria Elena wasn't to know the circumstances around Iris's disappearance. I could gain access to Maria Elena, tell her what I knew, which seemed at this point to be very little, and what would that accomplish? Rick could deny all of it and I had no proof. I'd planned to see Maria Elena next to tell her Iris was safe. Rick had beat me to it. And he'd left without my making it clear to him that he was in danger. I'd find him as soon as he finished talking to Maria Elena.

For now, I smiled encouragingly at Susana. "Oh, I'd love to follow you about and learn more about the family and the store. I know Iris is exasperating, but since"—I bent nearer, dropped my voice conspiratorially—"she may soon truly be a part of the family, and I know you'll keep that confidential"—let Rick work himself out of this one if his intentions weren't honorable—"I promised Iris's grandmother I'd find out everything about all of you." I cocked my head to one side and peered at Susana inquisitively. She could chalk me up as one of those old women who love to ask personal questions, the more intrusive, the better. "Maria Elena told me she's sure I'll enjoy getting to know all of you. Now you and Tony are the real backbone of the store, aren't you?"

Susana's sour look softened. "Maria Elena knows who does the work. She depends on me. Oh, there's lip service to the men, of course. But she knows that Celestina and I keep things going. Tony always has grand plans that come to nothing and Frank's too busy pleasing Isabel. When it comes down to work, you'll find Celestina and me taking care of everything." Her brows drew into a tight frown. "As for Rick," she spoke grudgingly, "I'll admit he tries hard. But he thinks he knows all about everything. Half the time he doesn't even check with me. I have to be sure everything runs right. No one really understands how hard I work. And now I'm so behind since Iris has run off. There are three shipments to be unpacked—"

"Could I help?" I wouldn't mind another chance to nose around the shipping room.

Susana shook her head quickly. "That's nice of you, but we can't have anyone except employees working in receiving. Liability, you know. But if you'd like to watch while I unpack—" She bustled to the front desk and I followed. She pushed the buzzer beneath the counter. "Tony, can you take over out here for a while? I need to get to those shipments from Guadalajara."

In a moment, Tony joined us. He seemed to have forgotten his irritation with me earlier, when I was talking to Manuel. He greeted me with an ebullient smile. "Enjoying yourself, Mrs. Collins?" He focused his charm on me without even a glance at his wife, who watched him sourly. I had a city editor once who had a motto framed on his desk: "Attitude Is Everything." As Susana and I walked away, I glanced at her, at her cold eyes, tightly pressed lips. Okay, maybe Tony deserved to be ignored, but she had all the charm of a porcupine despite her haggard beauty.

In the workroom, I perched on a high stool near the first table. Away from Tony, Susana relaxed and worked quickly and efficiently, occasionally holding up pieces for me to admire. "These plates have Aztec motifs." I recognized the magnificent green plumes of the quetzal, the crested bird famous for its glorious feathers. "They were made in the nineteen thirties. Aren't they lovely?"

"Everything you have here"—I spread my hand around the room—"is lovely. Have you always been interested in pottery? Or did that interest come after your marriage?"

She traced a finger around the patterned rim of the plate. "I knew when I married Tony that I would be a part of Tesoros. But it's odd when I think about it. The store means more to me than it does to him. He only stays because of Maria Elena." She stepped to the stand and wrote swiftly in the ledger. When she turned back to the table, the pen clattered to the floor.

"What would he like to do?" I slipped off the stool, picked up the pen and placed it by the ledger. I stood close enough to see the fine blue veins in her hands, the rich purplish red of her fingernail polish, the deep lines on her face.

She lifted out another plate, the blue background richer than a Cozumel sky. "Tony? Who knows?"

I looked at her curiously. Surely a wife should know better than anyone the desires of her husband's heart.

She added the new plate to the list, placed it in the stack to be shelved. "His place is here." She spoke with finality.

"How did you meet?" My tone was chatty. Is there a woman in the world who doesn't enjoy remembering how she and her husband met?

Susana was so long in answering, I thought she was going to ignore the question. But, as she poured popcorn packing material into a barrel, she said indifferently, "At Central Catholic. He was a senior and I was a sophomore at Providence. I thought he was the handsomest boy in the world." Her tone was curiously remote, as if she looked back across a chasm of time. "His cousin Lucia introduced us at a rally before a football game. He was the only boy I ever dated."

"Love at first sight," I said lightly.

She crushed a cardboard packing box flat, tossed it on a pile near the door. "Kids," she said disdainfully. "They don't know a thing."

"I suppose it was exciting to marry into the Garza family. Maria Elena seems to be a marvelous person."

Susana carried another box to the table, opened it, carefully unwrapped protective plastic from a wax figure of a bent Indian woman with a load of pottery on her back. She worked fast now, unwrapping, cataloging, checking current prices, tagging and shelving the figures. As she worked, she talked. "Everyone thinks Maria Elena is so perfect. Of course, she was a wonderful businesswoman, but she expected her sons to be able to take over. And the truth of the matter is that they can't. Even she knew better than to let Frank run the store. Frank has no confidence. Maybe that's why he married someone like Isabel. She may look like an empty-headed figurine, but to her the finest sport is figuring out the chink in someone's armor and shoving in a stiletto. She likes to know everything and she's willing to use everything she knows. And expensive? Frank could have a dozen mistresses for what Isabel costs him . . ."

There was no hint of that moment in the auction room when Isabel taunted Tony about his little friends.

". . . and Frank's always in debt. She spends the money faster than he makes it. He's always trying to figure out some scheme to make more. That's one thing about Tony, he is very careful about money. We never buy a new car unless we have money in the bank. But Frank has plenty of places to spend money. He dotes on their kids. Their daughter, Gabriela, is in France for her junior year in college, and every time Isabel talks about her, Gabby's been to London or Spain or somewhere extra. And they have two girls in school in California. Frank has to be careful that Isabel doesn't get jealous of the kids, so whenever he does something special for one of them, he buys more jewelry for Isabel. All she thinks about are things—more jewels, more antiques for her house, more clothes. She doesn't ever look past things she can hold and wear and see. And now Maria Elena is so crazy about Rick and Iris, but she'd better remember who makes things work." She lined up a row of wax figures in blue uniforms, each playing a different musical instrument. She tapped the head of the trumpet player and the golden tassel on his cap fluttered. "The heads are spring-mounted," she murmured and for an instant a smile lighted her face and she looked years younger. And happy. "See how perfect the detail is—the buttons on the jacket, the red stripe down the pant legs, even the little brown boots."

I gently touched a head and watched it wobble. "When were these made?"

She studied the figures. "Around eighteen ninety, nineteen hundred. This is very special because it's the complete set. It's quite hard to find a complete set."

I looked around the huge room, brightly revealed by the overhead lights. "There's certainly a great deal of value here. I see now why Celestina was upset when Iris left the door unlocked last Thursday."

Susana finished her entry into the ledger, then looked up with flashing eyes. "Celestina ran around looking for Iris. When we found the door open, I was scared to death something had been taken. I don't mind telling you I came back and looked the place over very carefully." She frowned and her dark brows drew down. "It was very odd. Iris had finished unloading and cataloging a box of wax figures"—she pointed across the room—"do you see the matadors? She'd started on a shipment of lacquerware. She was only half done when she went off and left it! But I looked around the entire room. Nothing seemed to be disturbed except that wardrobe over there. We just received it a few weeks ago. One of the doors was ajar."

I crossed to the lovely piece, more than six feet tall, the rich red wood panels hand carved.

Susana was at my elbow. "Carved pine and mesquite. It's very old, perhaps late seventeenth century. Isn't that huge iron bolt magnificent?" The bolt was perhaps eight to ten inches long. At the moment, it was secure in its loop.

I reached out. "May I?" As she nodded, I touched the cold metal, drew it back. The door creaked as I opened it and there was a musty smell of old wood, dark recesses, and age. I poked my head inside. There was light enough to see that the wardrobe was empty. I would have liked to shine a bright light into the interior, see if there was any scrap of material, any suggestion of what the space might have held.

Susana peered past my shoulder. ". . . nothing in there, of course. But I know I would have noticed if it had been open that morning." She put both hands on her narrow hips. "Iris must have opened the door. But I can't imagine why she would . . ."

"Curiosity," I murmured, stepped back. And more than that, perhaps a variation on the old axiom of whenever you count on surreptitiousness, someone is sure to be looking. I'm not especially given to positing cosmic connections. But if nothing had been hidden in that ancient wardrobe, Iris would never have looked. Or, put another way, Iris looked because something was hidden. I was reminded of an old friend's story. When he was a young lieutenant in Vietnam, he was on leave in Tokyo. One night a fellow lieutenant said they could pick up girls, have a great night. The young officer thought of his wife in Sacramento, told his friend that no, he wasn't going to do that. The other officer kept insisting, saying that his wife would never know. As they came around a corner, the young man heard a call. Coming toward him, smiling and waving, was the priest who had performed their marriage.

Susana reached out, closed the old, old door. ". . . she should have been attending to business. And then to go away and leave the main door open. Maria Elena needs to know about that." She slid a sideways look at me.

"I suppose it's important to keep Maria Elena informed of anything out of the ordinary." I was still looking at the wardrobe. "This is such a fine piece. Do you know where it came from?"

"We bought it at an estate sale here in town last week. It cost two thousand. But we can probably get almost four for it."

"I suppose it was packed with old things."

Her head shake was swift. "Oh, no. It was empty. At that kind of sale, everything of value is offered separately."

"So it arrived empty?"

"Yes. I cleaned it out myself. I think it must have been empty for years." Her nose wrinkled. "Cobwebs and what looked like a dried up mouse. I wore gloves to clean it out and then I used a hand vacuum."

"Why isn't it out on the main floor?"

She slid home the bolt. "We have several large pieces there already. We'll wait until one of those sells."

So the wardrobe arrived, was logged in, cleaned, and should have sat undisturbed until a place was available in the showroom. No one should have had occasion to look into it, so it must have seemed a fine place to stash—what? Drugs? Money? Something of value.

"You'll probably have plenty of room after the auction Thursday." The auction, something of value, people arriving, a nebulous thought began to grow. "Do you have a great deal more to do to get ready?"

"Much of it has to be done at the last minute. Frank and Isabel want me to move everything upstairs now, but I refuse. We simply can't have that many valuable objects in that room for more than one night. It's too great a security risk. We have to put the pieces in place Wednesday because we have a preview in the afternoon for the auction guests. It's really very exciting.

They all try to act as if they're just strolling about, but there's a huge undercurrent of excitement. They love it. I love it." Her eyes glittered and her face was wreathed in a vivid smile, making it even clearer how beautiful she could be if she so often didn't look unhappy and irritable. "We'll all be working madly Wednesday morning. I'll need everyone to help."

We walked toward the double doors. I stepped out into the hall. "I can see that I've had the good fortune to visit at a very special time. People are already starting to arrive at La Mariposa. Who is that heavyset blond man, about forty-five? He has the most piercing blue eyes. And his arms, they're so muscular. There's an eagle tattooed on one arm."

Susana pulled the heavy door shut. She shook her head absently. "That doesn't sound like any of the guests. There's Jolene and Wiley Harrison from Abilene. She's as skinny as a wraith and he's tall and almost as thin and he walks with his head jutting out like a giraffe. Cara Kendall is so blond she reminds you of Jean Harlow in the old movies. She always wears designer clothes and she flaunts even more jewels than Isabel. Bud Morgan from Chicago is bald and fat, but he's reputed to be worth more than thirty-five million dollars. Joshua Chandler wears thick glasses and looks like a college professor but he's a professional golfer from Scottsdale, Arizona. Kenny King has red hair in a ponytail. He's in the movie business. Let me see," she counted them off on her fingers, "the Harrisons, Cara Kendall, Bud Morgan, Joshua Chandler, and Kenny King. That's it. You'll find them so interesting. They are all extremely rich." Her tone was touched by awe.

"That's nice," I said dryly. I glanced at my watch. It was almost four. "Susana, thanks for being such good company. I'll tell Maria Elena how much I enjoyed visiting with you." I gestured toward the circular staircase. "I believe I'll go up that way. I'm still in time for tea." I'd noticed an announcement on a card in my room, announcing tea every weekday afternoon from three to five in the main lobby. And I could try and find Rick.

Susana's lips curved into an odd smile, part smirk, part grimace. "Oh yes, tea with Isabel. I'm sure you'll enjoy it. She'll tell you all about herself. It will be such a treat." She looked past me. "Hello, Frank. I was just telling Mrs. Collins how much she'll enjoy tea with Isabel."

Frank Garza bustled across the hall. "Hello, Susana, Mrs. Collins." He gave me a diffident smile. "Looking us over from top to bottom? I'm a little prejudiced but I don't think you'll find a finer store in Texas." He reached the double doors to the shipping area, punched the code. "Susana, I've looked everywhere for those chrome easels for the auction. I thought we kept them in the supply closet."

Susana frowned. "Not in the closet, Frank. I'll show you—" She nodded toward me. "Enjoy your tea, Mrs. Collins."

I took the circular staircase, holding carefully to the handrail. But once inside La Mariposa, I went straight to the door leading to Maria Elena's quarters.

A tiny elderly woman in a starched high-necked white blouse and long ruffled skirt opened the door.

"Hello, I'm Henrie Collins. I visited with Maria Elena earlier today," I said cheerfully. "I understand her grandson, Rick, is with her and I've come to join them." I'd learned long ago that a positive approach can get you a long way.

She smiled in return. "Mr. Rick has already left and

Maria Elena isn't home. I will tell her she missed you."

The door closed and I turned away. I felt a stab of worry. Damn Rick. I was sure he'd left quickly to avoid seeing me. But I wasn't going to give up this easily. I hurried to the main lobby.

The young man behind the desk turned. I almost called out for Rick, then, seeing the broad smile and stockier build, knew it was Tom Garza. The cousins' resemblance was almost startling. But I'd never seen Rick smile. Certainly not at me.

"Hi, Mrs. Collins. Did you have a good time on the River Walk?"

"It was interesting." I managed not to sound as grim as I felt. I no longer suspected him of writing the note that had taken me to that ugly encounter. Was Tom aware of the odd game being played by Rick and Iris? But it didn't matter at this point. In fact, if he was, I wouldn't mind worrying him a little, and I had to get in touch with Rick. "Tom, can you help me find Rick?"

"Sure." His manner didn't change. He was cheerful and obliging, but a half dozen phone calls later, he shrugged. "Not at the store. Not home. Not at our cousin Serena's. Not at his favorite Starbucks. Do you want to leave a message on his home phone?"

He dialed and I held out my hand for the phone. "Rick, this is Henrietta Collins. I have some information that I know"—I emphasized the verb—"will be of extreme interest to you. Please contact me immediately." I put the phone down.

Tom's eyes were curious. "Anything I can help you with, Mrs. Collins?"

"No. No, but thanks, Tom."

When I turned away, I looked across the lobby. Isabel sat at a tea table. She smiled and gestured for me to join her. Two other women sipped from fine china cups.

After an instant's hesitation, I crossed the lobby to join them. It seemed highly inappropriate to stop for tea when I needed to find a stubborn young man who might be in deadly danger. But I'd done all I could do for the moment to warn Rick Reyes. And maybe if I kept rooting around the Garza family, I'd figure out the connection between Tesoros and the blond man with a knife.

Isabel had changed from the fawn-colored jumpsuit. She wore a fuchsia jacket over a white silk dress with miniature maritime flags in bright gold, navy, and green. Rubies glittered in a gold pin on the lapel, matching ruby and gold earrings. The hands poised over the tea table glistened with gold and bright stones.

"Mrs. Collins. Come and meet two delightful guests." She was as satisfied as a cat sunning on a cushion.

I slipped onto a brocaded chair, accepted a cup of steaming tea.

A dark, witchlike woman with intense black eyes, a hooked nose, and a tiny mouth flashed a cheery smile. "Jolene Harrison." Her voice was incongruously deep and reminded me of sea lions barking for fish.

"Henrie Collins." And I looked to my right at a Dresden-china blonde with cold sea-green eyes and smooth red lips in a face devoid of lines. Except, of course, for tiny telltale marks at the base of the jaw.

"Cara Kendall." Her voice was languid, her glance indifferent.

"Sandwiches, Mrs. Collins? Or scones?" Isabel moved the three-tiered dish nearer to me.

Jolene Harrison barked, "Best scones I've had in

years. Can't say too many nice things about this place. Now, Isabel, tell me more about the gold necklaces." She smiled at me and confided in that foghorn voice, "I really love gold. Don't you, Cara?"

I took a scone, added a dollop of raspberry jam.

"Sometimes." Cara Kendall stared dreamily into her tea. "But it has to be very, very special."

I stirred some sugar in my tea. "What do you collect, Mrs. Kendall?"

"This and that." She spoke lazily, just this side of overtly rude. She looked past me as if there might possibly be something of interest in the room if she simply persevered.

I like a challenge. "Oh, Mrs. Kendall. I believe I've heard of you. You're quite renowned as a collector."

For an instant, a tiny spike of interest glinted in those eyes shiny as polished jade. "And who told you that?"

I wanted to break through that shell of indifference. "A man I spoke with in the store. This afternoon. I suppose he's here for the auction." I smiled agreeably. "I don't know his name, but he's very blond and stocky, and he has especially noticeable blue eyes."

I kept on smiling and looked at each in turn: self-absorbed Isabel, gold-loving Jolene, indifferent Cara. Apparently, not one of them gave a damn about a stocky blond man.

I finished my tea amid Jolene's rhapsodic descriptions of the polished gold disks called espejitos, or little mirrors, and Cara's absorption in the delicate cakes and excused myself. Cara's green eyes passed over me without interest. Jolene, assuming I was a co-attendee of the auction, said huskily, "Well, we all just have to be patient until Wednesday afternoon. You know why they let us have a preview, don't you?" She looked at me with an urchin's street-wise grin.

I don't mind being the straight man. "No, Mrs. Harrison. Why do they have a preview?"

She had a huge laugh. If I hadn't been looking at her, I'd have searched the room for a hungry sea lion. Her eyes glittered with delight. "So we can lust for a day before we get to bid! More fun than chemin de fer at Monte Carlo."

"It should be exciting. I'm certainly looking forward to the auction." I put down my cup, the tea half-drunk. "Thanks so much for the tea, Isabel." As I stood, I felt totally thwarted. I'd not found Rick. I'd learned nothing helpful from tea. And I realized as I pushed through the door into the hallway and walked by the doors with their magnificent butterflies that I'd managed to become a co-conspirator with Rick and Iris—and I didn't even know what the conspiracy involved. I considered that unsettling conclusion all the way down the hall. But I felt certain Rick cared about his grandmother and I thought he cared about Iris. I was willing to give him a chance to explain. Besides, I didn't see any other options. I'd gone to the police after the encounter with the angry blond man. I'd tried to talk with Rick when I returned to Tesoros. Later I'd tried to catch Rick with Maria Elena and failed. As for Maria Elena, talking to her wouldn't make Iris any safer. Only Rick could do that. So I had to play his game.

I had my key in my hand. I was reaching out to unlock the door when I stopped and stared. The door was ajar.

seven

THE door to my room slowly swung in.

I moved back, fumbling with my purse. I clutched the cell phone, not that it had availed me much on the River Walk. I'd throw it . . .

A muscular arm held the door open.

I lifted my hand, ready to throw the instant a face came into view.

Dark hair, neat goatee. Rick Reyes stepped to the threshold, peered up and down the hall, and gestured urgently for me to come in. "Hurry, please, before anyone comes."

When I stepped inside and closed the door, I leaned against it, waiting for my heart to stop thudding.

"I didn't mean to scare you," he said contritely. He wasn't as large as his uncle Tony, but he definitely took up most of the extra space between the bed and the wardrobe.

I didn't bother to answer. I was looking around the room. I'd not brought much with me, a small suitcase with clothes and toiletries for a few days, so there wasn't much to strew about. But my few belongings had been tossed onto the floor, the bed, the white wicker chair by the small table. The pillows were flung into a corner, the comforter and sheets piled by the bathroom door, the mattress hung askew from the box springs, the dust ruffle was hiked up. The doors to the wardrobe stood open.

"I didn't do it, Mrs. Collins." Rick's large dark eyes watched me anxiously, like a spaniel near a chewed-up shoe.

"I didn't think you did." I folded my arms. "Rick, did you leave the note asking me to go to the River Walk near King William?"

He rubbed at his goatee, looked at me uncertainly. I think he'd told so many lies since last Thursday that he was still wary of telling the truth.

"It had to be you." I answered for him. "Because you're the only one who knows where Iris is." I paused and added softly, "I hope to God."

He plowed a hand through his curly hair. "Yeah. Well, we figured if you saw Iris, you'd tell her grandmother she was okay. But we knew you'd have to see her and be sure she wasn't in any danger—"

"No danger!" I exploded. "How about the man who damn near grabbed her? I tell you, Rick, if he'd gotten his hands on Iris, he would have hurt her."

"I didn't figure on that." His voice was husky. "God, I would never have told her to go if I'd had any idea that would happen. See, the guy had to be following you. That's where we went wrong."

"Who is he, Rick? Who told him I was here to look for Iris?"

"If I knew that," he said somberly, "I'd know—" He broke off, looked away from me.

"Rick, you've got to tell me what's going on. You are in danger. Iris is in danger." And I didn't feel especially safe myself. "The man wants his stuff. Whatever it is."

Just for an instant, a lopsided grin gave me a

glimpse of a likable Rick. "Hasn't found it, has he?" he said cheerfully.

"Rick, I want you to listen, and listen hard." I spoke quickly and my voice was harsh. "After Iris skated away, the blond man grabbed me"—I held out my arm and now the splotches were purplish—"he said you and Iris have twenty-four hours to get 'it' back." Rick started to speak, but I kept on, "No, let me finish." I held his gaze and enunciated clearly, "He said he has a knife and he's going to use it—on you."

Rick's eyes widened. Just for an instant, he looked young and scared, then his chin jutted. "He has to find me first. And believe me, I'm looking around wherever I go. I'm not going to walk down any dark streets by myself."

"What about Iris?" I wished I could take him by the shoulders and shake him. "Where is she? What if he finds her, like he did earlier today?"

"He doesn't have a clue." Rick sounded confident now. "He found her because he was following you. But she got away—"

"She's not far from Tesoros." I watched him closely.

He stared at me. "How do you—"

I was impatient. "Look, Rick, don't count on that guy being a fool. Anybody can figure it. She doesn't have a car. Her car's in the parking lot of her apartment. She came on skates. She headed toward town when she got away."

"Yeah, well," he blustered, "that doesn't mean anything. She could have got a bus or a cab when she got to town."

"She could have. She didn't. He may be closing in on her right now. Think about it," I demanded.

"No." His assurance came back. He swept his arm

around my room. "No, you're the one he was following. He doesn't know where she is or he wouldn't have torn everything apart here. Iris is okay. And tomorrow—" He broke off.

"What happens tomorrow?" I eased past him, gestured toward the tilted mattress. "Shove it back and sit down. You've got a lot to tell me."

He flipped down the dust ruffle, and, in one smooth movement, slid the mattress back in place. He bent over, grabbed the bottom sheet. I stepped to the opposite side and smoothed the fitted sheet in place. In a moment, the bed was made.

"We make a pretty good team, Rick. Maybe this can set a precedent." I sat in the wicker chair. "What did Iris find?"

He grabbed the poster of the headboard and looked at me unhappily. "I can't tell you. Look, Mrs. Collins, I know you think this is crazy—but you've met Maria Elena"—his dark eyes were full of anguish—"don't you see how wonderful she is?"

"Yes," I said gently, "Maria Elena is remarkable."

He flung away from the bed and loomed over me. "More than that. Better than that. She's good and kind and honorable. She lives with honor. Do you know what it would do to her if Tesoros were involved in"—he paused, picked his words—"something dishonest? It would break her heart." He took a ragged breath. "It could kill her."

I almost told him that old women are more durable than he realized. But I understood what he was saying. To people who value honesty, nothing could be worse than to be accused of dishonesty. It might not kill Maria Elena, but it would shrivel her soul.

I spent my life as a reporter. I did my best. Perhaps nothing could matter as much to me as an accusation of writing lies or distortions. Yes, I have made mistakes in fact, errors in judgment, sometimes failed to understand. But never, never, never did I write a deliberate untruth.

"So Iris found something in the wardrobe that shouldn't have been there." It was what I had guessed. "She brought it to you. You took Iris and the package—about the size of an attaché case?"

Alarm flickered in his eyes.

"The search of her apartment was for something of that size," I explained absently. "Anyway, you have Iris and the package hidden somewhere. What happens tomorrow?"

"Tomorrow, we'll give the stuff to someone who can see that it goes to the right place."

"I foresee a small problem," I said quietly. "No matter what you do with the package, the blond man is going to keep after you. He seems to feel strongly that he has a right—"

"To hell with him. He can't do a damn thing when the stuff is gone." His voice was bullish, but his eyes were uncertain.

"Except slice you and Iris up with his knife." Ugly words, uglier possibility. "And how will he know that you and Iris no longer have what he wants?"

"I'll get the word out." He spoke with grim deliberation, almost as if to himself, not to me. He still leaned toward me and his oblong, interesting face was hard and unyielding.

But I heard and I understood far more than he intended. "To everyone at Tesoros who has access to the receiving room?"

His dark eyes snapped toward me.

I ticked them off on one hand. "Tony. Susana. Celestina. Frank. Isabel."

"Yeah." It was a sudden angry spurt. "It has to be one of them. I can't figure it any other way."

"A partnership with our blond friend." I made it a statement. "Someone in the family making some kind of dishonest deal that would tarnish the store, is that what you figure? Is it tied up with the auction?"

His handsome face creased with worry and uncertainty and a tired anger. "Look, Mrs. Collins, let it go. Okay? I promise, Iris is safe. Tomorrow it will be over with. All I want to do is protect Maria Elena." He crouched in front of me, big and earnest and hopeful, still so young, full of pride and love. "I won't let anything happen to Iris. I"—he took a deep breath "—I love Iris."

He was foolish and rash, naive and courageous, well-meaning and impetuous, and I knew nothing I would say could sway him.

He reached out, clasped my hands, squeezed them hard. "It will be okay. I promise." And he was on his feet and at the door.

I stood, reached out a hand, let it fall. The door closed behind him. I wished it hadn't sounded eerily like the click of a closing coffin.

I slept restlessly. In one particularly unpleasant dream, I was running, running, running, but no matter how I twisted and turned, spotlights found me and I was pinpointed, exposed for any follower to see in a hard white glare. It didn't take a guru of the subconscious to interpret the feeling of insecurity engendered by the search of my room. I woke up the second time and struggled to my feet to check the straight chair wedged beneath the knob. It was in place.

I'd just settled back in bed, eyes firmly closed, determinedly recalling the lighter-than-air sensation of dancing a Strauss waltz with a wonderful partner when the first siren pealed.

There are some lonely sounds in the world—the faraway whistle of a train as the wheels rumble good-bye, good-bye, good-bye; a dog's forlorn howl when clouds cover the moon; the crackle of ice-laden branches in a winter wind. Those sounds pierce all our defenses if they come in the depths of night when the soul is tired and eyes see dimly. The loneliest sound of all is a siren. Sirens always herald disaster.

One siren. Two. Another. A dissonant chorus rising and falling, warning, wailing.

I flung away the light cover. I didn't turn on the light, but groped my way to the balcony door. I unlocked it and stepped out. The gentle breeze was mild, rustling the glossy magnolia leaves of branches that spread not too far from me. Moonlight spangled the dark water.

More sirens. Shouts. Calls. I strained to see. Although lamps illuminated patches below, most of the River Walk was in darkness. The cafés were closed. I knew it must be very late. The sounds came from around the bend, then I saw spotlights playing on the sides of an apartment building.

A stentorian voice, amplified by a megaphone, intoned: "Stay calm. If your door is hot, go to your balcony and await instruction. If your door is cool, proceed to your nearest fire stairs and exit the building. Firemen are presently extinguishing a blaze which appears to be confined to the basement. Stay calm. If . . ."

I covered my first fire for the *Houston Post*. I was a young reporter, not long out of J School, no seniority, so I was working the Christmas shift and that's when a five-alarm fire broke out. I got my first Page One byline. I remembered jumping over snarled hoses and watching glass explode from the force of flames within and scribbling frantic notes and ignoring the burn of tears and rush of nausea as a wall collapsed on a crew. The memories ran like a subterranean river as I looked toward the lights flickering on shiny glass. But tonight there were no billows of gray smoke against the starry sky, no acrid smell biting into my throat and lungs and the breeze was coming my way, ruffling my hair, stirring the begonias in the pot—

I gripped the iron railing, leaned forward. This balcony afforded a good view of the stone stairs that led down to the River Walk from La Mariposa. A lamppost shed a golden pool of radiance just past the steps. Movement caught my eye even though I was watching the lights around the bend. I jerked my eyes back to the scene just below me and recognized Rick's tall, familiar figure, running hard. Then he was gone, pounding around the curve of the River Walk, heading for the site of the fire. Where had he come from? Tesoros or La Mariposa? And what was he doing at either at this time of night?

I was pulling off my T-shirt and shorts, discarding it as I whirled into my room. I found a blouse and slacks, slipped into tennis shoes, and was on my way downstairs, my key in my pocket, my travel flash in my hand.

I took the exit to the River Walk stairs and hurried down. I walked fast past Tesoros and a café and an empty stretch beneath a bridge. When I came around the bend, I saw across the river a milling crowd of tousled people scantily dressed in whatever they'd found to pull on hurriedly. A cordon of police kept the crowd back from the building. Firemen lugged hoses, mounted ladders, moved in orderly haste. The calm voice over the megaphone continued its exhortations. People streamed from a stairway, pouring out onto the sidewalk. I hurried up the wide stone steps to a footbridge. I stopped midway across the river and looked down, scanning the surging, nervous crowd.

From my overlook, I saw them at the same time, Rick pushing his way toward the apartment house, struggling against the crowd, and Iris stumbling out from beneath the bridge, trying to shrug free of a tangled mass of cloth.

"Help, help, please, help me." Iris's frantic voice cut above the melee of sounds. Or perhaps I heard because I was listening and Rick heard because it was the voice which mattered above all others to him.

By the time I clattered down the stone steps to the River Walk, she was in his arms, clinging to him and sobbing. Her words were choked, her tone stricken. "They're gone. Oh, God, Rick, I'm so sorry, they're gone. I tried my best, but he got—"

Rick saw me and clapped his hand firmly over her mouth. "Hush, Iris, hush. Mrs. Collins is here." His tone was sharp. Then his fingers slipped up to smooth a tangle of hair away from her flushed face. "Are you all right? What happened?"

She pulled away from him, stared at me. Tears streaked her face, her soft young lips trembled, then tears flooded her eyes and she turned again to cling to him. "I'm so sorry, Rick."

He bent his head, his lips against her ear. I couldn't hear his whisper, but I didn't need to. Whatever it was that had been taken, Iris wasn't to reveal it to me.

I did hear him say quietly, "Let's walk this way," and he led her away from the continuing bustle on the River Walk. He didn't say anything to me, but I followed. When Rick and Iris reached the bridge, they climbed the stone steps. I was right behind them. Once on the other side of the river and around the bend, it was quiet, no sirens now, just an occasional rumble of sound and murmur of faraway voices. The River Walk was deserted here. In front of a closed café, Rick pulled out a chair from a wire table.

Iris sat down gingerly.

Rick and I saw her scraped and bloodied knees at the same time.

"Oh, God." He knelt beside her. "Are you hurt?"

I found a handkerchief in my pocket, held it out to Iris.

She waved it away. "It doesn't matter. My knees sting, but I'm all right."

I glanced back toward the building, no longer spotted with light from the searchlights. Lights in apartments flickered on, off. "Looks like the residents are going back inside. What happened, Iris? Did the fire alarm go off?"

She pressed fingertips against her temples. "God, it was so scary. The alarm jangled and buzzed and it was like waking up in a hornet's nest. Then I heard the sirens. I grabbed"—she glanced toward me—"my backpack. I ran down the stairs and came out on the River Walk. People were yelling and shouting. I smelled something burning." She looked at Rick, her face forlorn. "I thought the best thing to do was to come to you."

I, too, looked at Rick, but my gaze was puzzled. "Were you at Tesoros?"

"No. I bunked in an extra room at La Mariposa." He looked uncomfortable. "I thought I'd better stay close to Iris."

I wondered if my concern for Iris after our River Walk adventure accounted for his presence.

Iris confirmed my guess. "Rick called this evening

and told me he'd be at the inn. He said he'd keep his cell phone on. But I didn't bring mine downstairs with me."

No, she'd concentrated on saving the backpack.

Iris shivered. "When I got downstairs, I thought I'd hurry to La Mariposa and find him. When I went under the bridge, I heard someone coming up behind me, running. I thought someone else wanted to get away from the fire and the noise. It was dark under the bridge and all of a sudden I was covered up, a blanket or something like that. I struggled, but somebody pinned my arms against my sides and yanked at the backpack and then it came loose. I tried to scream but the blanket was in my face, against my mouth. By the time I pulled it off, no one was there." Her hands dropped to the table. She clasped them tightly together to try and stop their trembling.

"You never saw anyone?" I asked, but I knew the answer before she shook her head.

Rick reached out, took her shaking hands in his. "I'm sorry, Iris. I thought you were safe."

And she hadn't been. I had an idea why. "Whose apartment were you in, Iris?"

Iris spoke in a small voice, "Rick's mom."

"Is that where you were when you called Rick at Tesoros to tell him what happened when we met?" She'd skated away to safety and the first thing she did was call Rick. She'd already talked to him before I got back to the store.

Rick looked at me sharply.

But Iris answered like a lamb. "Yes. I mean, I know he told me not to call him, but I thought I could just hang up if anyone else answered. In fact," she said proudly, "Celestina answered once. I waited awhile and tried again. That time Tony answered. I hung up. But the third time Rick answered."

"So she was safe as could be. Right, Rick?" I tapped on the wire tabletop and remembered the untidy desk in the main office of Tesoros—the computer, the printer, the speaker phone and the caller ID, all the appurtenances of a successful business. "And your mom's number came up three times on the caller ID in the back office."

He looked stunned.

"Don't you see?" I sounded tired. I was tired. "The Caller ID was a dead giveaway. You told everyone at Tesoros that Iris left town with somebody new and that you and she were all washed up."

A soft gasp from Iris indicated she'd not known of this. She looked at Rick in dismay.

But I didn't have time to worry about her feelings. "Somebody never did believe that story, Rick. Then you get three calls from your mother's apartment and everyone knows your mother is out of town. You gave a pretty good performance, but you were way too nervous. I didn't believe you and neither did someone else at Tesoros. And today, when your mother's telephone number surfaced, the answer was pretty clear. So who's calling the store from that number? Somebody who wanted desperately to find Iris saw those numbers and figured it out. Then the objective was to get the package."

"A fire in the basement," Rick said hoarsely. "But that's awful. All those people in the apartment house! What if the firemen couldn't put out the fire, what if it spread too quickly and people were trapped?"

I had some respect for our adversary. "The point was to get the package. I'm willing to bet the fire was contained in a barrel, oily rags giving off smoke, then the alarm pulled. Lots of smoke, little danger. Wait and watch for Iris. When she came out, she headed for help. That's what the watcher expected. As soon as she was away from the congestion, he ran up behind her, flung a blanket over her head, grabbed the backpack, and by the time she picked herself up and pulled off the cover, he was gone."

"Gone." Rick said it crisply. "Gone. By God, it's gone." His head lifted. Tension eased out of his face. "So, it's not our problem any longer."

I looked at him in surprise.

He looked back defiantly. "None of it happened. I mean, what do we care? All I wanted was to protect Maria Elena. If that guy—"

I frowned. "What guy?"

Now it was his turn to look surprised. "The blond guy. The guy who tried to grab Iris, who threatened me. The guy who searched your room."

I was shaking my head.

But Rick ignored me, talked faster. "Sure it was him. He—"

"What about the calls Iris made from your mother's apartment?" I wasn't going to budge on this one.

Rick waved his hand in dismissal. "That's all your idea. Maybe it's a lot simpler. Like you said, anybody could figure out Iris was hiding downtown. And this guy has to know a lot about all of us—"

"And why is that?" I demanded.

Rick shrugged. "So we don't know why he's picked us. Maybe the whole thing doesn't have anything to do with the store. Maybe he's some guy who delivered stuff. Maybe he delivered that wardrobe and he'd hidden something in it—"

"Susana cleaned out the wardrobe," I objected. "Vacuumed it. After she found a mummified mouse."

"Yeah, but it doesn't matter any longer," he said happily. "I can take Iris home. She's okay because she doesn't have it any longer. Nobody's after her." He pushed back his chair, reached out a hand to pull Iris to her feet.

I was on my feet, too, and standing in front of him, feeling a little like an irritable old cat facing a bumptious mastiff puppy. "Rick, listen to me, please."

Iris clutched his arm. "We don't know who got the"—a quick look at me—"got my backpack."

"Think about this, Rick." I looked straight into reluctant eyes, held his gaze. "You want to believe it was the blond guy. That puts some distance between you and Iris and the backpack snatcher. So let's agree maybe it was, though I don't know how he could be privy to the caller ID in the office, but we'll let that go for now. Let's assume it's the blond man. What if he's hotfooting it right back to Tesoros? And if it wasn't the blond man, if it was someone from Tesoros, your problems aren't over. You want to protect Maria Elena, don't you? Shouldn't we make damn sure the backpack and whatever it contains aren't right back where they started from, hidden somewhere in Tesoros?"

He rested back on his heels, his forward motion stayed for the moment.

I took advantage of his silence to ask Iris, "What did you smell when the man grabbed you?"

She looked at me blankly. "Smell?"

"Close your eyes. Try to remember." At noon, when the blond man gripped my arm, he came so near that I could see his sweat and smell his breath, and there was the distinct, unmistakable sour odor of alcohol, present and past. He'd been drinking for more than a day, I was sure of it.

Iris obediently closed her eyes.

I smiled a little. She looked so young, almost like a child in her shorty pajamas with a pink ribbon bow at the neck.

"The blanket was dusty," she said uncertainly. "It made my nose itch. And I was hot. It hurt the way he held me, one arm circled around me." She shuddered. "I hated the feel of his arm, rigid and hard, crushing me. I didn't smell anything except dust."

The blond man smelled like hell at noon. That smell—and I'd bet he'd had a few more drinks in the interim—wouldn't be gone by night. If he'd flung the blanket over Iris, he was close enough for that rank odor to reach her. It didn't prove my idea that her attacker was someone else, but it convinced me. I glanced at Rick, but he hadn't paid any attention to my questions of Iris.

He glared down at the flagstones, unhappy at my suggestions, but well aware that I could be right.

"Okay." His voice was resigned. "We'll go to Tesoros. And we won't stop looking until we've checked out every inch. If there's anything there that shouldn't be, we'll find it."

He and Iris moved ahead of me. I was close behind, but I didn't try to talk. I was still working out probabilities in my mind. I didn't think the engineer of the fire and theft—if retrieving contraband can be termed theft—was the blond man who'd scared me on the River Walk and later searched my room. If he'd known where Iris was, there would have been no need to search my room. No, I felt we were looking for someone else and that someone could be picked from a short list—Tony, Susana, Celestina, Frank, or Isabel—all of whom had access to the Tesoros receiving room. And that list should include Tom Garza. Although he and Frank and Isabel worked at La Mariposa, they were part of the family. To me, that was the key determinant. That list, of course, included Rick Reyes, but I had seen him sprinting on the River Walk in answer to the cry of the sirens and witnessed his search for Iris. Although I'm fond of young lovers, that status does not guarantee innocence. I was glad I knew from my own observation that he could not have taken Iris's backpack.

But he could be in league with someone else.

The bleak thought chilled me. I added him back to my list of suspects in the crime at large. If he was involved in hiding contraband at Tesoros, he certainly wouldn't admit it to Iris if she came clutching that material, appalled at her discovery. He could, in fact, have mounted a complicated charade, culminating tonight in the apparent disappearance of the stolen goods, whatever they were, enabling him to announce with great relief that, after all, the problem was solved, the goods were gone, and all was well in the world.

I sighed and walked faster, noting how protectively Rick held Iris's arm, how solicitous he was. Iris leaned against him. Obviously, she adored him.

I wasn't happy at the possibility of his involvement. I wasn't sure I thought it feasible. I liked him. But I couldn't be positive of his innocence. That uncertainty was one more reason I was unwilling to pretend the receiving-room mystery could be dismissed. I wanted to be sure not only that I could like Rick, I wanted to be able to tell Gina she could trust him with her granddaughter's heart.

We were passing another café front, perhaps twenty-five feet from Tesoros, when Rick stopped. Iris stumbled to a halt, looked up at him nervously.

I came up beside them. In the moonlight, Rick's

face was blank with shock. He leaned forward. "My God. Stay here. Both of you." He plunged forward, running toward Tesoros. A bright sheath of light spilled out from the open door and a dark shape huddled on the River Walk.

We didn't wait, of course. Iris's rubber-soled house slippers slapped on the flagstones as she ran. I broke into a slow lope. I was about ten feet behind them when they careened to a stop just past one of the pair of park benches that flanked that open door. I hurried to join them.

The golden wedge of light spilling out of Tesoros illuminated the flagstones and the trickle of blood from the battered head of a man lying face down, absolutely inert, halfway between the open door of Tesoros and the dark, silent water of the river. Blood matted the man's hair, but there was no mistaking the soaring eagle on his limp arm. The blond man had not changed clothes since our noon encounter. He still wore the light blue T-shirt and the navy slacks. He looked smaller in death. He'd given Rick and Iris twenty-four hours, not knowing he had less than twelve left for himself.

"Oh my God." Rick shuddered, then took a deep breath. "Wait here. I'd better see." He edged reluctantly toward that still form.

I could have told him we were too late, but Rick forced himself closer, sank to one knee, and lifted a flaccid hand. When he stood and came back to us, his face was greenish. "He's dead."

Iris gave a small moan. She reached out, clung to my arm. Her tear-streaked face was pale and frightened. "Aunt Henrie, it's that man. It's that man!"

Rick stiffened. "Oh, Christ. Iris, are you sure?"

She nodded wordlessly.

"Yes, Rick," I said grimly.

Rick's head swung back toward the murdered man. "But—" Then he broke off, shook his head, said briskly, "Iris, go up to Mrs. Collins's room. I'll call the police and—"

The sudden, startling sound was incongruously ordinary, the clank of a galvanized metal pail against the cement. The three of us turned in unison to stare at the open door of Tesoros. In the vivid stream of light, Manuel Garza slowly straightened. One hand clutched a mop. Sudsy liquid sloshed around the rim of the pail placed neatly to one side of the door. Oblivious alike to the sprawled body and to us, Manuel stepped back to the entrance and moved the mop back and forth, back and forth. He was neatly dressed, a short-sleeved blue work shirt, faded jeans, high-topped black sports shoes.

"Manuel." Rick's tone was muted, but stricken.

Manuel poked the mop into the foamy liquid, released his hold. The mop began to tilt. He reached out, grabbed the handle, carefully balanced the mop. This time it remained in place. He stared at it for a moment, then turned and looked at his nephew. Manuel's long face was creased with worry. He pointed at the body, waved his hand toward the open doorway, then he turned away, reaching for the mop.

"Wait, Manuel, wait." Rick took two long strides. He reached out and gently held his uncle's arm. "Come over here and sit down on the bench." He turned the older man toward us.

Manuel stiffened, leaned back on his heels. I've seen recalcitrant children do the same thing, pit their bodies in opposition when they cannot combat an adult's verbal command. He leaned far back, almost overbalancing, and tried to squirm free. All the while, his hands groped for the mop.

Iris's eyes glazed with horror. She backed away, sank down on a bench. She wrapped her arms tight across her front.

I skirted the body and the tendrils of blood. "Manuel, come sit with me." I pointed at the companion bench. "Rick needs to make a telephone call. He'll take care of the man. And you know, it isn't the right time to clean. We'll wait and clean in the morning."

Manuel's arm trembled under my touch. He stared at me with bewildered, frightened eyes. Then the tension in his arm fled, and he was limp and docile. I slipped my arm around his back and felt those muscles softening. "Everything's going to be all right. I know you are upset. Come and sit down. I'll stay close to you."

As I settled him on the bench, I gestured behind my back to Rick, out of Manuel's sight.

Rick nodded. He started to go inside Tesoros.

"La Mariposa," I said quickly. I kept my voice low and conversational.

Manuel sat on the bench, his natural pose unaffected and childlike, straight back, feet planted apart, hands loose in his lap. His eyes huge and worried, he stared at the dead man. Suddenly he lifted his hands, pressed them to his head, made a mournful cry in his throat.

Iris drew her breath in sharply.

I sat down beside him. "I'm sorry, too. His head hurt. But he is not in pain now, Manuel."

Manuel placed his hands together. I looked down and saw the shadow on the flagstones, hands cupped in prayer.

"Yes," I said softly.

There was an instant of peace, then once again his

hands flew to his head, he made that little cry, and he struggled to his feet. His chest rose and fell as his breathing quickened. Suddenly his hands moved rapidly and shadows flickered on the flagstones by our feet, swift and evanescent as cloud forms.

I was tired. My eyes burned from fatigue. It was long past midnight in that deep watch of the night when the body functions on adrenaline and will. I blinked and tried to understand and realized that he was making the same sequence of motions, over and over. I might be dreaming, but I thought I knew what he was telling me, what he had seen—a body, a wound, rivulets of blood, and a round object. This last he cupped in one hand and plunged, lifted, plunged. His fluid hands made the shape of the body again and long straggling shadows that were streaks of blood. The mop was easy to discern, then slow, steady sweeps with the mop.

"You found the body on the River Walk? And there was blood in the store and you wanted to clean it up?"

Manuel clapped his hands, then pointed at the mop and bucket and tried to step around me.

"Not now," I said firmly. "We have to wait until it is time to work. Now isn't the time, Manuel. It's the middle of the night. That's not when you clean."

His face creased in perplexity. He pointed at the body.

"I know. You want to make everything clean. But we are going to have some help and when it is daytime again, you will be able to clean." I took his hand. "Manuel, please come and sit by Iris. She would like for you to keep her company."

The pupils of her eyes were huge. She sat as still as a bird watching a snake approach.

I bent down, whispered, "Please, Iris. He won't hurt you."

She swallowed, edged over on the bench, patted the space beside her. "Here, Manuel, you can sit here." Her voice was as thin as a soprano on an old phonograph record.

It was as if Manuel hadn't seen Iris earlier, and perhaps he hadn't. His world had been encompassed by the body and by his terrible urgency to rid Tesoros of despoilment. Now he stood shyly in front of the bench, his face illumined by a great smile, a smile that began in his eyes and softened and smoothed his face of all distress, leaving only gentle adoration. He reached out, touched her dark head softly.

Iris sat stiff and still, staring up. Slowly, she began to smile.

He pointed questioningly at the space beside her.

"Yes." Her voice was soft. "Yes, sit here, Manuel."

He sat down very precisely. His eyes never left her face. His hands began to move. As Iris watched those flickering shadows, I slipped quietly through the front door of Tesoros, watching where I stepped, avoiding the still glistening darker path where Manuel had mopped.

Sirens squalled. When the police arrived, this area would be closed to all of us. Us. Funny. Was I aligning myself with the Garza clan? Not exactly, though I was charmed by Maria Elena, and I liked—or wanted to like—her grandson Rick. But I wasn't kidding myself that the death of the blond man wouldn't cause trouble for Iris. Whatever she'd found in the wardrobe, it had to be connected to this murder. And I wanted a look inside Tesoros before Rick had a chance to grab Iris's backpack should it be there. That was why I'd told Rick to make the call to the police from La Mariposa.

The central light was on. That was the golden pool that spread through the open door. The small recessed spots above the limestone display islands were dark, so the rest of the store was dim and shadowy.

I followed alongside the path revealed by Manuel's mop. It was beginning to dry at the farther reach, but there was still enough moisture to tell the story I was sure the police would understand. The body had been moved along this path, leaving a trail of bloodstains. That's what Manuel had mopped up.

The sirens were louder, nearer.

The trail ended in the middle of the store near an island with a charming display of pottery banks— a lion, a bull, a big-cheeked balding man, a donkey, a rounded head with bright red cheeks. Arranged in a semicircle, each was equidistant from its neighbor. One was missing.

I used my pocket flashlight, snaked the beam high and low. I didn't find the missing bank. Or Iris's backpack.

The sirens choked in mid-wail.

I hurried, moving back and forth across the store, swinging the beam of my flashlight. No pottery bank, no backpack. Nothing else appeared out of order or disturbed in any way. The only oddity was the rapidly drying area of freshly mopped floor, a three-foot swath leading from the paperweight-display island to the front door.

I reached the front entrance and stepped outside. In trying to stay clear of the mopped area, I almost stumbled into the pail and mop. I leaned down, wrinkled my nose against the sour smell of ammonia, and pointed the flashlight beam into the faintly discolored water, no longer foamy with suds. The water's brownish tinge didn't obscure the round pink snout of a pottery pig bank.

Swift, heavy footsteps sounded on the steps leading down from La Mariposa. I moved quickly to stand by the bench. Iris looked with wide and frightened eyes at the policemen following Rick and his Uncle Frank into the brightness spilling out from Tesoros. I supposed Rick had wakened his uncle to tell him of the murder.

Iris reached out, grabbed my hand. Rick stopped a few feet from the body, pointed at it, then at the open door. Frank Garza peered around the shoulder of a short policeman with sandy hair and thick glasses. Rick was pale and strained. He spoke in short, jerky sentences to a burly policeman with ink-black hair, an expressionless face, and one capable hand resting on the butt of his pistol. Frank patted his hair, disarranged from sleep, stuffed his misbuttoned shirt into his trousers.

When Rick stopped, the policeman turned and looked toward the bench. Iris's fingers tightened on mine, but I knew the policeman wasn't looking at us. He was looking at Manuel, sitting quietly with his usual excellent posture, back straight, feet apart, hands loose in his lap.

Manuel slowly realized that everyone was looking at him. He blinked, looked at us eagerly, slowly lifted his hands, and began to clap.

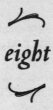

eight

THE burly, dark-haired policeman hunched forward, his eyes wide as he stared at Manuel. His right hand curved tightly over the leather-strapped butt of his holstered gun.

Manuel's palms hit softly together, but as silence surrounded him, dropped over all of us like a sooty pall of ash, Manuel's hands moved more and more slowly and finally dropped to his knees, upturned and open, defenseless.

Frank moved quickly across the pavement. He slid his arm around Manuel. "Officer"—Frank's voice shook—"my brother is handicapped. He doesn't understand. Please, he's perfectly harmless."

The policeman looked from Manuel to the body. "Yeah. Sure." Finally, he looked at Frank. "I'm Officer Flores. Homicide's on the way. You people can sit on those benches. No talking. Officer Wagner will stay with you."

Frank avoided glancing at the body and the pooling blood. "Would it be possible for us to wait in the lobby of our hotel, officer? After all, we have two ladies here. It's upstairs." He pointed toward the stone steps leading up to La Mariposa.

Officer Flores glanced at Iris and me. He stepped

away, conferred with his partner, then said woodenly, "Officer Wagner will escort you."

Frank led the way, obviously relieved to leave the River Walk and that still body behind.

Iris kept close to me and I realized she was self-conscious at the scantiness of her shorty pajamas. I gave her a reassuring hug. "I'll get a jacket—"

"Please, ma'am." Wagner's voice was polite but insistent. "No talking until Detective Borroel comes."

In the background, Officer Flores spoke into a hand radio, his voice too low for us to hear.

Rick came up beside us. Wagner waited for us to precede him. We'd gone a half dozen steps when Wagner said, "Wait, please." He gestured for Manuel to come. "You, too, sir."

Manuel hunched on the bench, stared at the ground.

Rick turned back. "Officer, he doesn't understand. Please let me—"

"Doesn't he speak English?" Wagner didn't wait for an answer, said quickly, "Por favor, señor, venga."

Frank Garza said hurriedly, "He doesn't speak at all, officer. I'll try to persuade him." Frank stepped close to the bench. He spoke gently. "Manuel, it's time to go inside. We're going upstairs to La Mariposa. We have to wait there for a while."

Manuel drew his legs up on the bench, pressed his face against his knees.

"It's all right, Joey. Gus is almost here." Officer Flores held up the radio. "Take the rest of them up there. I'll keep an eye on this guy." Once again his hand rested on the butt of his gun.

"Officer Flores." It's no effort to sound imperious at my age. "Manuel is handicapped. He is a son of Maria Elena Garza, who owns this store." I pointed at Tesoros. "I'm sure she can communicate with him. We should inform his mother, have her join us. And I think it would be better if he remained with us. He might become confused if we leave him behind." I didn't look at Officer Flores's hand resting on his gun. "Moreover, the detective who is coming will be better able to learn what Manuel knows if his mother is here."

Frank Garza shot me a look of gratitude. "That's a good idea, Officer. I can go upstairs—"

"Sorry, sir." Flores was brisk. "I can't permit you to speak with anyone until Detective Borroel has interviewed you. As for your brother, he'll have to go along with you right now or stay here. No one can communicate with anyone until Detective Borroel has seen all of you."

"Officer, let me try." I definitely didn't want to leave Manuel there by himself.

Flores looked from me to Frank, shrugged. "All right."

I walked slowly to the bench and put my hand on Manuel's shoulder. It was as taut as a piano wire. "Manuel, you remember how we talked about the shiny windows? You keep them so clean. They're beautiful. But the tiles in the fireplace of La Mariposa are smudged. Will you come with me? We can find a cloth and you can polish the tiles, make them beautiful, too."

Slowly Manuel's head lifted. He looked at me with huge questioning eyes. Then his body uncurled. He swung his feet to the ground and stood. He looked at the windows, then at the pail and mop. He began to walk toward the pail, his hand outstretched.

Officer Wagner took a quick step, but I caught Manuel's hand, held it loosely in mine. "We don't need water. Frank will find us a nice clean cloth, and you can make the tiles shine like the windows."

Manuel balled one hand and made a steady, circular motion. The shadow on the ground reminded me eerily of a buffer.

"That's right." I slipped my arm through his. "You can polish and polish. Let's go upstairs together."

The others followed us. Manuel's arm relaxed, his skin was smooth and warm against mine. As we started up the wide stairs to La Mariposa, I felt I'd won Manuel a reprieve, but I knew that there would soon be ugly questions. And Manuel could not answer.

Surely the detective in charge of the investigation would permit us to rouse Maria Elena. I would insist. I knew Frank would help me.

Once inside the lobby, Frank found a soft puffy cloth in a drawer behind the desk. He gave it to Manuel and pointed toward the fireplace.

Obediently, Manuel moved across the tiled floor, his sneakered feet making no sound. He started at the top left of the fireplace and carefully began to smooth the tiles with his cloth.

I sank wearily into a wicker chair, bunched a cushion behind my tired back. Iris and Rick sat close together on a sofa, his arm protectively around her shoulders. Frank hurried to the french windows that overlooked the river. He opened one, stepped out onto the balcony with its view of the River Walk and Tesoros.

Officer Wagner took a step or two after Frank, then gave a small shrug. It didn't matter if Frank watched the homicide unit at work.

I closed my eyes. I didn't need to stand beside Frank to know what was happening: photographs—videocams these days—measurements, sketches, arrival of the medical examiner, removal of the body, taking the mop and pail into evidence, fingerprinting. I know the

basics of crime scene procedures. The major changes
since I was a young reporter are in technology. I covered the crime beat once for a small Kansas daily. I
tried to learn how to think like a detective. Now I
emptied my mind of foreknowledge and looked at the
facts as they would appear to the police:

1. *The murder apparently occurred inside Tesoros.*
2. *The weapon is probably the pottery bank in
   the pail of water.*
3. *The cause of death—I recalled the battered
   back of the dead man's head—was blunt force.*
4. *The location of the injuries indicated the victim was caught unaware or was attempting to
   escape an assailant. There could be no claim
   of self-defense.*
5. *After death, the body was dragged from the
   middle of the store, through the front door of
   Tesoros, to the point where it was discovered.*
6. *The site of the crime and the path along which
   the body was dragged had been mopped clean
   with a solution of ammonia and water.*
7. *A pail containing water and ammonia and a
   mop were found outside the door of Tesoros.
   A pottery bank, similar to those displayed inside the store, was found in the pail.*
8. *Witnesses who discovered the body (Rick
   Reyes, Iris Chavez, Henrietta Collins) observed Manuel Garza with the mop and pail,
   saw him mopping.*

That was all apparent at first glance. In their investigation the police would learn:

1. *Manuel Garza lived above the store.*
2. *Manuel was incapable of speech, communicating through shadows on a wall or floor created by hand gestures in front of a light source.*

The police would have these questions:

1. *Who was the victim?*
2. *Why was he inside Tesoros?*
3. *Did Manuel know the dead man?*
4. *Did Manuel move the body?*
5. *Why did Manuel mop away traces of that removal?*

Following hard on these questions would come this conclusion: Manuel committed the murder and was trying to get rid of the body and erase all traces of the crime.

It all made perfect sense—if you'd never had any contact with Manuel. Certainly I could not pretend I knew him, but his gentleness appeared to be so genuine and so pervasive that it seemed absurd to suspect him of violence.

But as the police well know, many murders occur with no prior history of violence. Moreover, the police deal with facts, and the facts were damning. The police could suggest various scenarios: Manuel surprised an intruder in the store, struggled with him and chased him, perhaps in self-defense in his own mind, battering the man from behind long past any necessity for submission but perhaps not possessing the judgment to recognize when the threat was over. That was the most innocent explanation. There could be other, uglier suggestions. If the police linked Manuel and the victim, they could posit a personal grudge, a late-night meeting, a quarrel, murder.

I opened my eyes.

Officer Wagner stood in an easy stance with his hands behind his back, feet apart, but his blue eyes moved constantly, keeping his charges in view.

Manuel was on his knees in front of the fireplace, assiduously polishing the bottom line of tiles. Despite the gray in his hair, he looked young and supple and he continued the steady work without apparent effort. His jeans were old and soft, faded lighter than robin's egg blue. That made the bloody smear on the left pant leg highly visible. His athletic shoes had white honeycomb soles. These, too, had traces of dark stains.

Frank still stood on the balcony. From the back, with his heavy shoulders curved, he looked like a bear, still and intent, hunched forward for a better view. Muted sounds of activity drifted through the open windows—low voices and the scrape of shoes on the flagstones. Occasionally a bright light flickered. Still photographs, too?

Iris and Rick sat close together on a sofa opposite me. Rick held Iris tight in the crook of his arm. His cheek was pressed against the top of her head.

The only sounds were the faint scuff as Manuel's cloth made its endless circles on the tiles and the noises drifting up from the River Walk.

Officer Wagner was near the chili-cart desk. His gaze constantly circled the room as he tracked Manuel at the fireplace, Frank on the balcony, me in my wicker chair, and Rick and Iris huddled on the sofa. He had a side view of Rick and Iris. They sat opposite me.

I looked casually at them, snuggled so close together. Rick's face was bent against Iris's hair, his mouth hidden from Officer Flores's view. Rick's lips were moving.

Officer Flores would not be happy to know two of the witnesses were communicating. I wasn't unhappy, but I was thoughtful. I glanced at Rick and Iris occasionally, casually. Rick kept his face carefully blank, as if he rested his face against Iris's dark hair, sunk in a tired stupor. But his lips kept moving.

Soon, the homicide detective would leave the final work at the crime scene to the technicians, and he would climb the steps to La Mariposa.

What was I going to tell him? More important, I imagined, what was Rick going to tell him?

"I'm Gus Borroel, detective investigator." The clear tenor voice was both melodic and commanding.

I jerked awake. My eyes were grainy with fatigue, my vision indistinct. I blinked and focused on a middle-aged man standing beside Officer Wagner.

"Who found the body?" He looked at us in turn. No one would ever have trouble hearing this man and no one would ever doubt that he was in charge. Short-cut jet black hair without a trace of gray topped a seamed face with deep-set dark eyes, a hawk's curving nose, and a wide mouth. He was just under six feet, slender but not thin. His white dress shirt was clearly fresh, his red tie with a silver diamond design neatly tied, his gray slacks unwrinkled. He would have looked at home in an office or a bank. Or, because he had the unmistakable air of a tough dude, in a bar. At this time and in this place, he seemed larger than life.

Uncertainly, Rick raised his hand, a student in an unfamiliar class.

Borroel studied him, a long look by eyes that had

seen every aspect of humanity, from the celestial to the dregs.

Rick scrambled to his feet. "Rick Reyes, sir. I saw him first."

The detective's eyes moved to Iris.

Rick spoke. "Iris Chavez. She was with me. But she doesn't know—"

Borroel lifted his hand, his eyes moved to me.

"Henrietta Collins. I was with Rick and Iris." My head ached, my eyes burned, and my mouth felt like sandpaper. Surely I could get a glass of water soon.

Frank Garza hurried across the room, his eyes blinking nervously. "Frank Garza. I can speak for the family. I placed the call to the police. We hope this is cleared up quickly." He pumped the detective's hand.

Borroel's wide mouth curved fleetingly in a cool, dry smile that was gone so quickly I wasn't certain it ever existed. His tone was polite. "We always hope to clear up murders quickly, Mr. Garza. I know everyone here will give us as much help as possible." The detective turned away, walked to the fireplace. Manuel had completed the left panel of tiles and the top frieze. He was midway down the right panel, his arm moving rhythmically.

Borroel stood behind Manuel. "Hello." The detective spoke quietly.

Manuel kept on polishing.

"Officer—" Frank rubbed his head as if it ached. "My brother cannot speak. If you wish to communicate with him, it would be better if we called for my mother."

Borroel looked down and I knew he was seeing the stains. He didn't answer Frank directly. Instead, he glanced around the lobby. "Is there a room where I can speak to witnesses privately?"

Frank gestured toward the chili cart. "We have a small office behind the desk. Or if you need more room—"

"The office will be fine. I'll talk to you first, Mr. Garza." Borroel was polite but brisk.

Frank led the way behind the cart, opening a door next to the pigeonholes for guests' messages. When the door closed behind them, it was once again very quiet in the lobby.

Rick lifted his arm from Iris's shoulders, smoothed his hair. Manuel polished. Officer Wagner watched.

It was only a moment or so and the door opened. Frank turned toward the door leading to the hallway of the first floor. Borroel looked at Rick. "Mr. Reyes, please."

Rick gave Iris's hands a hard squeeze. She looked after him with wide, strained eyes.

I wished desperately for a glass of water. My tongue was as dry as desert sand, my mouth felt like flannel. I would have given a kingdom for a tall frosted glass of clear sparkling cold water. But I forgot about my discomfort when the hall doorway opened and Maria Elena hurried through, followed by Frank. Manuel was no longer alone. I felt tension draining away, leaving me wearier but bolstered.

Maria Elena's white seersucker robe was crisp and unwrinkled. Her dark hair hung straight, shiny as ebony. She moved with grace, her head held high.

God, it's hard to be a mother. I understood the look on her face, the anxiety for a child at risk, the almost sickening wash of relief when she saw Manuel, the utter determination to do whatever had to be done. She came up to him and touched his shoulder.

He paused in his polishing, looked up, and a sweet smile lighted his face. He pointed at the tiles.

"That's very good, Manuel." She managed to speak softly, evenly. I knew the effort it had taken.

Officer Wagner walked across the lobby. He said quietly, "Ma'am."

"I know," she said quickly. "We won't talk." She looked at Manuel, her eyes filled with fear. Frank reached out, held her arm. She smiled at him. They sat in the large leather chairs on opposite sides of the fireplace. Maria Elena cupped her chin in her hand, her eyes following Manuel's movements. Frank slumped in his chair.

We all looked wearily across the lobby when Rick stepped out of the office.

Detective Borroel's dark glance found me.

I stumbled getting to my feet. I was so dreadfully tired. He held the door of the office, waited until I settled in the straight chair. His questions came fast, but he was pleasant and he gave me time to answer. I felt as though I were speaking beneath tons of water . . .

"Henrietta Collins." I repeated the story I'd related so many times: Iris, her grandmother, my arrival, the apartment, Detective Hess, Tesoros . . ." When I finished, I gave a great sigh.

"We'll be quick, Mrs. Collins. First, can you identify this picture?" He stood and held out a Polaroid picture of the dead man, lying on his back, eyes open. The wound didn't show in the print.

"This is the man who tried to grab Iris this afternoon." I felt a wash of sadness. I didn't know him. He had frightened me, but he had been alive, and life is so fragile and so precious. Every life. "He smelled of alcohol. He was furious. I think he was dangerous."

"Do you know his name?" Borroel tapped his pen on his pad.

I'd already answered that, but I did again. "No. I have no idea who he is. Or was."

"He wanted Miss Chavez and Mr. Reyes to return some object to him. What was it, Mrs. Collins?" His dark eyes watched me intently.

"I don't know." I had an idea. I'd worked the wire desk in Emily's newsroom for several weeks. A big story had crossed the desk. It seemed a wild possibility, too wild to suggest until I did some checking.

Borroel tapped the desk. "So apparently this object was at one time hidden in a wardrobe presently in the store receiving area. Do you know how that could have occurred?"

I pressed my fingers against my face, then said with a hint of impatience, "Detective Borroel, I don't *know* anything. Everything I've told you is supposition. All I *know* is that Iris ran away from the store, taking something with her; Rick hid Iris and whatever she possessed in his mother's apartment; the dead man wanted Iris and Rick to return 'it'; someone took Iris's backpack; someone killed the blond man."

He was looking at me with a dry smile. "But no one has ever revealed to you what the dead man wanted?"

"No. But he wanted it badly." He died for it.

Borroel pushed back from the desk. "Thank you for your assistance. I understand you are staying here?"

I nodded, struggled to my feet.

Borroel walked to the door. "We will be in touch if necessary." He was already dismissing me from his mind, his hand pulling the door open.

I was midway through the doorway when I stopped. He was following so closely, he almost stepped on my heel.

I looked up at his seamed, amazingly fresh face. "Do you know what the man was looking for?"

"That," he said carefully, "has not yet been determined."

But he had an idea. Or someone had told him something. Despite my fatigue and a brain that felt like bread pudding, I hadn't stopping thinking altogether. Detective Borroel could never be accused of revealing information to a witness. Or, possibly, a suspect.

I didn't give up. "Who was he?"

"We do not have formal identification yet. Thank you, Mrs. Collins." He still held the door.

So go peddle your papers, lady, that was his attitude, though a good deal more politely expressed.

I moved on into the lobby. The detective stepped past me and nodded to Iris. I stood by the chili cart as the door closed behind Borroel and Iris. It was still very quiet in the lobby except for the scuff of Manuel's cloth. Dear God, didn't he ever tire? I looked at him, happily, busily engaged. Then Maria Elena's face turned toward me and my heart ached.

I walked across the lobby.

Officer Wagner lifted his hand.

I spoke before he could stop me. "Call a lawyer for Manuel."

Her eyes were dark with misery and fear. "I have done so."

I leaned forward and we embraced for a moment, drawn together by fear for defenseless Manuel.

The pounding in my head separated from a steadier, heavier thud. I pulled free of the twisted sheets, rumpled from a deep but restless sleep, and propped on my elbow.

The knock on the door sounded again.

I sleep in a T-shirt and running shorts, each to his

own taste. I reached the door, opened the peephole, then held the door wide.

Maria Elena carried a small tray with a coffee thermos, two cups, and a cloth-lined basket filled with golden-brown fruit empanadas. "I'm so sorry—" she began.

I waved away the apology. "I overslept. Come in. If you'll excuse me for a moment—"

She sat at the small table. I hurried in the bath, washing my face, brushing my hair, slipping into a blouse and slacks. I didn't take much time over my face, but it was certainly a road map of the night— bluish pouches beneath tired eyes, frown lines that were verging on permanent.

When I joined Maria Elena, she poured our coffee. I welcomed the harsh brew. She stirred sugar, but never lifted the cup to her lips. When we'd met, I'd been entranced by her creamy complexion and bright eyes and lustrous hair. They'd given her a youthfulness that was gone this morning. She, too, had dark circles beneath her eyes, and her face sagged as if weight pressed against the skin.

"Will you help me?" She spoke without pretense, simply, directly, and those dark eyes burned into mine. She didn't remind me that I had accepted her help in my search for Iris. She made her request and waited.

"Yes. Although"—the coffee was beginning to reduce the throbbing in my head to a dull ache—"I don't know what I can do."

The sun spilled brightly through the window, shining on her raven-dark hair, her vivid eyes. She smiled at me suddenly and I was sharply reminded of Manuel's face and the way it glowed with love and life. "You will find out the truth."

I stared at her in surprise.

She nodded firmly. "You see"—and now the smile was gone, supplanted by an icy calm—"Manuel is very good. You know that, don't you?"

"Yes. Yes, I know that." Despite the blood on his jeans, despite the blood on his shoes.

"He polished the tiles for you. Because you asked him. He always wants everything to be clean. That's what I tried to explain to that detective. But I'm afraid, I'm terribly afraid, that he is going to arrest Manuel. We called a lawyer before I came down to the lobby last night. That's what Frank told me to do when he came for me. And the lawyer—one of my nephews— was with us when we talked to the detective."

"What did Manuel say?" It didn't seem an odd comment. Manuel spoke with his hands.

"We aren't sure what happened. All he can show us is that he went downstairs, he found the door open and the body on the River Walk. We don't know if something woke him up or perhaps he was wandering about. He does that. Perhaps a noise woke him last night. His room is over the main part of Tesoros. If only he'd come for me . . ." She shook her head. "Instead he went downstairs and found the front door standing open. He walked out and saw the body on the River Walk, but he was upset by the trail of blood, the smears. He hurried for his mop and pail. The detective . . ." She squeezed her eyes shut for a moment.

I finished it. "Thinks Manuel killed him. Because he was breaking in, something like that?"

"They don't care. It's enough that Manuel tried to clean up the blood. They think it was he who moved the body. And this morning, one of my cousins who works in the police department found out that the dead man was drunk. He said now they think perhaps he threatened Manuel." She threw up her hands. "Manuel would not." Her voice was low and harsh. "He would not."

I reached over for the thermos, refilled my cup. "Have they told you who the dead man was?"

"No. But my cousin gave me that information." Now her face was bleak. She closed her eyes. "I thought I recognized the picture."

I waited. This was hard for Maria Elena.

"He was in Frank's class in high school. Ed Schmidt. Sometimes he came here after school. After they graduated, I don't think any of my children kept in touch with him. Years later, Ed made buying trips to Mexico, though I rarely dealt with him. He would buy anything, anything, and ask so much money for it." She spoke with disdain.

"He wasn't a regular supplier to Tesoros?" The flaky pastry was sweet and good and I could feel a spark of energy.

"No." She was definite. Then, a pause. "At least, I don't think so. I've left that to Tony and Celestina in recent years. I will find out." She picked up the lacy napkin from her lap, twisted it tightly between her fingers. "But there are some things I cannot find out. There are questions I cannot ask, questions that would stain the future with my family." She studied me. "I don't think you ever find it hard to ask questions."

I wished that were true. Then the thought came sharp and quick. No, I didn't want it ever to be true that I could poke and prod another human being without effort and sometimes with pain. It can be as hard to ask a question as to be asked. That didn't mean I hadn't asked sharp questions over the years. If I didn't think truth mattered, I would have given up reporting long ago. I wasn't a reporter now, but I still knew how to ask the questions that had to be asked.

I said simply, "I will do what has to be done." For Manuel. For Iris. For Rick, I hoped.

She took a deep breath. "I love my children. I love all my children. They treat me gently, with kindness. Dear Mamacita. To me they are dear children. In a family, there are many fictions. We pretend that we do not see what we should not wish to admit to each other. I love my uncertain, worried Frank, who would so much like to be in charge but who cannot bear the pressure of responsibility. I would never speak to him about his wife who spends more money than he can afford, or his children whom he spoils with gifts beyond his means. I love my adventurous Tony who climbs high mountains, dives deep into the sea. I will never ask Tony why he and Susana have no children, why Susana's eyes are filled with anger. I can't ask Celestina why she is jealous of her brothers. I can't ask Isabel if she has a lover. I can't ask Susana why she pours the passion of her life into Tesoros. I can't ask Magda why she so dislikes her brother Tony. I want safety for them and goodness for them all, but I will not buy it with Manuel's life. So we have to find out what happened, why this man was killed in Tesoros. I talked to Rick this morning. He told me Iris found a package of cocaine in the wardrobe. He thinks it doesn't have anything to do with us, that the drugs were hidden there, perhaps by Ed Schmidt, perhaps by someone else, and the wardrobe was shipped to us and Schmidt was trying to get the drugs back."

"Nonsense. Susana said the wardrobe was empty when it arrived." I spoke crisply. Moreover, a package of cocaine could be worth several hundred thousand dollars, depending upon its purity. Drug dealers don't accidentally misplace shipments. "Sure, Schmidt was trying to get the package. He followed me to try and find Iris. But how did he know I was hunting for Iris? Who told him about me? How did he know Iris took the package out of the wardrobe? Who told him? It had to be someone at Tesoros. And it couldn't be Manuel."

"No," she said quietly, "it couldn't be Manuel. So, we have to find out what actually happened. Otherwise, the police will arrest Manuel."

Arrest him. Charge him. Convict him.

As for Rick, I wondered if he was willing to sacrifice Manuel to save Tesoros. Apparently he was. "Did Rick tell Borroel that Iris found cocaine?"

"Yes." Her eyes ached with questions.

Cocaine. All right, it was possible. But I didn't believe it. I had an idea, but I needed some confirmation before I told Borroel. Or Maria Elena.

Maria Elena looked toward the balcony. "Mrs. Collins, Manuel found the door to Tesoros open. Who opened it? Did Ed Schmidt have a key? If so, who gave it to him? Or did Schmidt meet someone at Tesoros last night? Who opened that front door? I know it wasn't Manuel. He has no key."

"Who has keys?" I asked.

"Frank, Isabel, Celestina, Tony, Susana, Rick. And Magda, but she is still out of town. And Tom could come through La Mariposa. No one else. No one else," she repeated wearily. She drew a deep breath. "I want you to find out who opened the door."

Which hand unlocked the door and later picked up a pottery bank and battered life away?

"I will do my best," I said quietly.

She stood. "Because we both must know the truth, I for Manuel and you for Iris." Her eyes were grim. She knew what she was asking. If I succeeded, I might save her one child but lose another.

nine

I sat at the café across the river, watching Tesoros. The scene was uncannily similar to my first observation on Sunday: the slight figure hard at work on the shiny, shiny windows; the occasional passersby— joggers, honeymoon couples, and, at this early hour, people on their way to work. The homicide unit obviously had completed its investigation. There was not even a crime-scene tape to recall last night's violence. The only indication of anything unusual was the increased traffic into the store, a half dozen middle-aged women, two young men in business suits, an elderly man. And, standing not too far from the front door, a uniformed policeman, watching Manuel.

I drank coffee and punched Emily's number into my cell phone. She answered on the first ring. When we finished talking, I had set in motion a search for information about Ed Schmidt and requested coverage of a story I'd handled on the wire desk two weeks ago, a big story about the robbery of the National Museum of Anthropology in Mexico City. Since I knew the museum well, I'd followed that story with great interest. Yes, it was a hunch, and maybe a crazy one. But in my own mind, the tantalizing possibilities were clear: the amazing theft; a gathering of exceedingly

wealthy, fanatical collectors; a family steeped in
knowledge about Mexican art of all kinds; the frantic,
desperate search for something obviously of great
value; and murder.

Emily said, "Okay, Mom. I'll fax the stuff within
an hour."

"Thanks, honcy."

"Mother—" Her voice was stern. "Be careful."

"Aren't I always?" I was smiling as I clicked off
the phone. It's nice to be loved. Love and family,
that's what life is all about. I looked across the river.

I was somewhat prepared for the crowd inside Tesoros, since I'd been watching the visitors streaming
inside. I spotted many faces that reminded me of the
Garza family. The gathering was a cross between a
wedding reception and a wake. Susana Garza, her eyes
bright and her cheeks glowing, suddenly surfaced beside me. "Moral support," she said loudly, gesturing
at the throng. "Let me take you around." She introduced me to almost a dozen relatives—Cousin Fernando, Cousin Louisa, Cousin Rita . . . "Mrs. Collins,
an old friend of Maria Elena's."

My hand was pumped. I received a couple of hugs.
Everyone spoke earnestly and loudly about the dreadful amount of crime today. A plump woman with dark
hair piled high on her head and jangling earrings announced firmly, "Maria Elena simply has to hire a
night watchman." A courtly older man with great side
whiskers and bright black eyes said softly, "I don't
understand why Manuel moved the body. That seems
odd, doesn't it?" He straightened the string tie at his
neck.

If it seemed odd to someone in the family, how

much more sinister it must appear to Detective Borroel.

Susana steered me to the back of the showroom and
a tall, slender woman whose face looked familiar. "My
sister-in-law, Magda."

I smiled. "Of course, you're Rick's mother. He fa-
vors you."

"Thank you." Magda Reyes managed a tight smile,
then looked at me intently. "Yes, Rick told me you
were close to Iris's family."

I met her questioning gaze steadily. "Her grandmother and I have been friends for many years."

Magda brushed back a tangle of dark curls. "Can
you tell me what's going on?" Her tone was impatient.
"My brother Tony claims Iris disappeared without a
word on Thursday. Then you arrived and went to the
police." There wasn't quite a note of anger, but close.
"And now it turns out Iris says she found drugs in that
big wardrobe and Rick took her to my apartment. Rick
told me he and Iris were keeping the stuff until I got
back. As if I could do anything about it! Why didn't
they go to the police?"

"I suppose," I said slowly, "that Rick didn't want to
get Tesoros involved in a scandal." But Magda's return, perhaps irrationally, made me feel more confident
about Rick. Yes, I believed he was lying about drugs,
but I suddenly understood his insistence upon when
Iris would come back to the store. That return was
connected to his mother's arrival. Rick had a problem;
he was going to hand it over to his mother to solve.

Magda Reyes gazed around the crowded room. "I'd
say we're involved in worse than a scandal now. I
can't believe any of this. And Manuel—" She lifted
her shoulders.

Celestina Garza sidled up to us. She looked spitefully at her sister. "Magda, I can't imagine what Rick thought he was doing."

Magda's gaze was steely. "The best he could, Celestina, the best he could." And she turned and walked away.

"Well!" Celestina sniffed. "If I were Magda, I don't think I'd get on my high horse now." Celestina almost managed to keep the pleasure out of her voice when she continued, "Isn't this dreadful? Did you know the dead man was an old friend of Frank's? Frank says he hasn't seen him in a long time. That's what he says. I hope it's true." Her eyes glittered with malice.

We were pushed up against the back wall, close enough to smell the musky, dry scent of a diablo mask hanging at head level. It was like having a third party to the conversation, one with goat, cow, and bull horns protruding from its head and stripes of red, gold, and green paint on its cheeks.

Celestina stood on tiptoe, hissed, "I always know when Frank's lying. He looks even more like a failure than usual and his eyes blink and get all watery. He can't fool me."

"Maybe he wants to avoid having to talk to the police." I rubbed my nose, stifling a sneeze triggered by the thick, curly fringe of sheep hair on the mask.

"Well"—Celestina placed her small hands on her hips—"why should he do that? But then," she answered herself, "Frank's always been afraid of his shadow. I'm surprised he ever asked Isabel to marry him." She gave a little spurt of ugly laughter. "Isabel probably asked him. She's no fool where money's concerned and Tesoros was a great success even then."

"Frank and Ed Schmidt went to school together, didn't they?" I eased away from the wall, ignoring the almond-shaped painted eyes on the horned goat mask near my shoulder.

Celestina peered past me, then moved so close I could smell the distinctive scent of White Linen. She whispered, "They almost got into big trouble. Sister Agnes talked to Mother. I think Frank and Ed were selling pot at school. But they weren't expelled, so I guess it wasn't ever proved. But I knew it was true"—once again her tone was utterly smug—"Frank had his hangdog look. And he and Ed stopped running around together."

It's a big leap from schoolboys' selling pot to a stash of cocaine, but baby steps sometimes lead to giant strides.

"Are you going to tell your mother?" I turned my head so I couldn't see the empty eyes of the mask.

Celestina jiggled on her feet, a little dance step of desire. "It would serve him right." Her voice was low and satisfied, then the eagerness drained away. "Oh, Mama wouldn't believe a word of it. Not about Frank." Her lips twisted in bitterness. "Anyway, it probably doesn't matter." Her tone was almost regretful. "Rick says Ed got inside last night and he must have had someone with him. Rick says it doesn't have anything to do with us. And poor Manuel found a mess and didn't know any better than to try and clean it up."

"How did Schmidt get inside?" My tone was sharp.

But Celestina was looking past me, waving to an old woman with bright eyes who lifted an imperious hand. "Oh, there's Aunt Josefina." She darted away.

Some of the visitors were moving toward the door. No one was paying any attention to me. I turned and moved to the back door. I pushed it open and slipped into the broad concrete hall. After the door closed, I waited for a moment. The doors to the offices were open. The offices were dark. The double doors to the receiving area were shut. I had the back area to myself. I hurried down the hall to the circular staircase. It was easier going up the steep treads than coming down. I stopped a moment to catch my breath on the landing, then stepped into the hallway of La Mariposa. The cleaning cart was next to my room. I glanced inside. A small, wiry woman with a bright kerchief on her head was bent over the bed.

I followed the hallway to the lobby. It, too, was alive with visitors. I was getting used to the extended Garza clan now and thought perhaps a half dozen faces belonged to more cousins. There were also workmen carrying sound equipment toward the auction rooms and La Mariposa guests standing by piles of luggage. Frank was hard at work behind the chili-cart desk, along with young Tom.

Frank, obviously, was not going to take time to talk to me. I glanced around the lobby. Isabel, looking svelte and elegant in an obviously expensive orange-and-gold jacket and beige linen slacks, smiled at one of the auction guests I'd met yesterday. What was her name? Kendall, Cara Kendall. Today she wore a jade green silk blouse and flared trousers. Her sleek blond hair shimmered like moonlight, but this morning her smooth face was puckered in irritation.

I resisted the temptation to march across the room and caution her that frowns made the incisions quite apparent. But that was an uncharitable thought. After all, wasn't I simply lucky that I'd escaped the great American obsession to appear young? It's very hard to separate ourselves from our culture, and American women are taught from childhood on that thin is good, thinner is better, and now estrogen will keep them ageless. But my flash of empathy with Cara Kendall died stillborn when she waved her hand pettishly at Isabel and swung away, her face a pinched white mask.

Isabel lifted a hand after the retreating sharp-spined back, which looked like a walking skeleton despite the expensive blouse.

When I reached Isabel, I murmured softly, "Maybe it's possible not to be too rich. But it is possible to be too thin. She is about as attractive as a pile of dinosaur bones pinned together by steel rods."

For an instant, malicious delight danced in Isabel's eyes. But quickly she smoothed out her face, looked at me gravely. "Mrs. Kendall is upset by the unpleasantness."

Unpleasantness. Yes, that was one way to describe murder. "What bothers her, Isabel? The body? Or the police nosing around?"

"Mrs. Kendall isn't accustomed to having contact with anything"—Isabel's lips thinned—"anything so sordid as murder. She acted as though we had something to do with it because it happened in the store."

"Really." I kept my voice uninflected. "Actually, the family is involved, isn't it?"

Isabel's sloe eyes blinked. One hand touched her creamy throat. "Why, no, of course not. None of us knew the man. Rick—"

I interrupted impatiently. "Your husband knew Ed Schmidt. They went to school together. I understand they were involved in illegal drug sales a long time ago. You've heard about the hidden cocaine? So, of course, that's sure to make the police wonder. Especially since Frank always needs money." I glanced down at the ornate rings on her soft, beautifully manicured hands. "For you." I paused. "And for the children."

Her smooth face hardened. She'd always appeared catlike, with her air of sleek satisfaction and arrogant contentment. Now her eyes glowed with a dangerous anger. She leaned forward like a feline arching her back, and words spewed through bright red lips.

"Who told you that? Susana? She's jealous of Frank. God, she's jealous. She hates us because she has no children and she's spent her life a barren woman with nothing to care for except the store." Isabel kept her voice low but the softness did nothing to disguise the rage, bubbling like witches' brew in a cauldron. "She's trapped in marriage with a man who has eyes for every woman but her. I'd feel sorry for her except that she's like a poisonous toad, fouling everything she touches. If you want to know who knew Ed Schmidt—knew him better than he ever should—you talk to Tony."

I ordered a chicken fajita salad and iced tea at Mi Tierra for an early lunch and spread out the faxed sheets from Emily.

I read her cover sheet:

Dear Mother,

The robbery at the National Museum of Anthropology in Mexico City is one of the biggest art thefts in history. There was a huge exhibition of ancient gold from all of the pre-Hispanic cultures and the thief took pieces that are absolutely irreplaceable and considered among the finest pieces of gold workmanship ever created. I'm including a bunch of clips and also an inventory of the stolen gold. It's reputed to be worth millions. That's easy to believe when you look at the pix.

In re Ed Schmidt, this information is for your

*eyes only. Warren talked to Cal Jenkins, a police
reporter in San Antonio who knows a secretary
in Homicide. Cal obtained a dossier on the victim
and the latest info on the investigation. He says
Manuel Garza is the prime suspect. Cal also got
a bunch of stuff about Manuel Garza. Warren
promised Cal that you wouldn't reveal this information and that you'll keep the source confidential.*

*How does the jewel theft figure in? From what
you've told me, I don't see how Manuel Garza
would be interested in money. Is it a mix-up of a
pointless homicide and a grand heist? Please be
careful.*

Love, Emily

I thumbed through my sheaf of papers. One of the
news stories was from a Mexico City daily. The head-
line said it all:

AUDAZ LADRÓN ROBA ORO ANTIGUO

I scanned the story from the L. A. *Times* that ran
the day after the robbery:

BOLD THIEF SNATCHES ANCIENT GOLD

A bold thief last night entered the Exhibition Hall
at the National Museum of Anthropology in Mexico City and in a daring robbery escaped with
priceless ancient gold treasures, including an
eleven-strand necklace from Monte Alban and
four breastplates. The largest piece taken was a
sheet of gold measuring 16.5 times 2.6 centime-
ters.

The gold had been collected from museums around the country for an extraordinary exhibition running from June 1 to September 1. Police said the thief sabotaged an electric transformer serving the Chapultepec area, thereby disabling the alarm system. Authorities are at a loss to explain how the thief gained entrance to the Exhibition Hall because there was no sign of forcible entry.

I smiled dryly. Bribes are part of everyday life in Mexico. I could well imagine how the thief obtained a key to the particular hall. Of course, bribery in one form or another is certainly alive and well in Mexico's northern neighbor. But here we call it campaign contributions.

Once inside the Exhibition Hall, the thief used glass cutters to gain access to the exhibited gold. Although museum guards were quick to rush to that hall, they found the door locked and were not aware of the theft until much later in the evening, when a general search was undertaken.

I quickly checked a few more news articles and the inventory of the stolen gold and made some notes:

The robbery occurred on the night of Saturday, August 22.

No trace of the thief was found.

The stolen jewelry included four gold pectorals, a gold sheet with serpent head, two gold brooches, five gold necklaces, two gold masks, one of them representing a jaguar and encrusted with pearls and garnets, eight gold lip rings, four gold bells, six gold projectile points.

*   *   *

I remembered one of the pieces from a long ago-visit to the museum, the brooch with its unique centerpiece of a turquoise mosaic on gold and the distinctive filigree edge so reminiscent of the border of feathers that decorated the shields of Moctezuma's warriors. When red-bearded Hernán Cortés, imposing in his armor, rode into Tenochtitlan, or Mexico City, he was greeted by the royal leader adorned with gold, even his gold-covered sandals glistening in the sunlight. Cortés must have gaped in awe at the buttery-colored pectoral and necklaces and beads, gold that fueled insatiable desire in the wealth-lusting Spaniards.

Intellectually, I began to grasp the enormity of this theft. But it wasn't until I turned to the next few sheets that I had a sense of the glory that had been taken. Thanks to the miracle of color transmission via computer, I held a sheaf of spectacular pictures. Though these were only photographs, they captured much of the almost unimaginable richness and artistry of the stolen gold.

The most spectacular piece, of course, was the eleven-strand necklace, the gold as bright and beautiful as captured sunlight or a field of buttercups. I counted the eleven strands—the first three with fairly uniform beads, though, since each was crafted by hand, there were obvious variations; then six strands of small beads in series of ten separated by larger oblongs; a tenth strand with twenty-three dangling globes at the center; and a final magnificent strand with large dangling globes decorated with double drops.

The list of stolen gold was dry and scholarly, the actual images startling. I stared at the breastplate from Veracruz, at the god's heavy-lidded face, at the fangs protruding from round thick lips. Huge rosettes and horizontal bands of gold decorated with delicate swirls hung from either side of the ornate crown.

I turned over page after page, and when I was done I shivered. Man has always been tempted by gold, seduced by gold. This was a blood-drenched treasure.

If I was right, if these were the objects that had been found by Iris in the wardrobe, there was danger indeed at Tesoros. But I had no proof. I needed to know more, much more. The place to start was with the dead man.

Yes, this was the dossier I desperately wanted and now I had it, thanks to Emily and Warren's friend Cal. I read swiftly:

Edward Friedrich Schmidt, b. July 18, 1950, San Antonio, father clerk in a hardware store, mother homemaker. Only child. Father alcoholic, died when Ed was twelve. Mother worked as a clerk at local grocery store. Graduate Catholic High School. Two years at San Antonio University. Drafted 1970, one year tour Vietnam, honorable discharge 1972. Grew up in a modest neighborhood near the King William district. Area now undergoing gentrification, arts and craft shops and upscale restaurants near by on Alamo. Inherited the house from his widowed mother, lives there alone. Erratic work history. Heavy drinker. Spent several years in Houston working at a petrochemical plant after his discharge from the Army. Ten years in El Paso, clerking in an art store. Returned to San Antonio in 1990, when his mother became ill. A neighbor, Julian Worth, often traveled to Mexico on buying trips for local galleries and Ed sometimes accompanied him. In recent years, Ed made solo buying trips. Another neighbor, Rollo Barrett, complained to the police

*about Schmidt's cat, claimed he trespassed on his
property and destroyed flowerbeds.*

In re investigation, Cal Jenkins's report continued,
*police source says Detective Borroel conferring with
DA. Charges expected against Manuel Garza, perhaps
as soon as tomorrow. Pottery bank in cleaning pail
determined to be murder weapon. Polished clean, no
fingerprints or bloodstains, but shape consistent with
contusions on victim's head. Motive thought to be attack on intruder in Tesoros, possibly second degree
murder or even manslaughter because of suspect's im-
paired capability.*

The next sheet contained the data on Manuel:

*Manuel Alphonso Garza, b. March 11, 1955. At-
tended private classes for handicapped children.
Although he has never spoken, Manuel compre-
hends a great deal about his surroundings. He
communicates by creating shadows with hand
movements. Manuel focuses on cleanliness,
spending most of his days washing the front windows of Tesoros. Despite his handicap, Manuel
has a sunny temperament, smiling often. He is
affectionate with family members. He has never
been known to exhibit anger or hostility. However, he withdraws and will cry when confused
or frightened and becomes uneasy if taken away
from familiar surroundings.*

I put down the fax sheets and felt a wash of anguish.
What would it do to Manuel to be jailed? Even though
no one would abuse him, he would be cut off from his
family, placed in a cell, made to wear strange clothing.

He would be utterly terrified. And to be arraigned in a courtroom . . .

Anguish was succeeded by an icy anger—anger at Rick, who was still lying, and anger at the unknown member of that clever family who had unlocked the front door of Tesoros for a drunken Ed Schmidt.

I glanced at my watch. Almost noon. The tables and booths were filling. Light, cheerful voices surrounded me. I pushed away my half-eaten lunch. I paid my bill and hurried out into another steamy forenoon. I found a pay phone with a tattered phone book still attached to a twisted chain. I looked up three addresses.

Odd how appearances deceive. The front of Tesoros had presented its customary elegance to the world this morning, untouched by violent death. The modest frame house on the quiet street off Alamo appeared equally unaffected by the bloody end of its owner.

Ed Schmidt's house, his childhood residence, his last home, was a one-story bungalow, probably built in the early thirties. I loved that old-fashioned style of house that always reminded me of the Uncle Wiggily stories I long ago read to the children. There was a front porch, of course, another vestige of a different America. A forest-green wooden swing was tucked close to a lattice covered with honeysuckle.

Someone—Ed?—was a dedicated gardener. Pansies, impatiens, and petunias flourished in the front beds. A Whitmani fern grew lushly in a striking blue-and-white pottery pot near the door.

A folded newspaper lay near the steps. That was the only hint of disorder.

As I started up the steps, a gate creaked. "I didn't know whether to pick up the newspaper." The voice was thin and wheezy. "I always kept them for Ed when he was out of town." An old woman, a very old woman, shuffled the few feet from her dandelion-spangled lawn to the weedless, recently mowed grass in Ed's yard. Gauzy black hair, almost purplish from cheap dye, fluffed over her head, revealing patches of shiny scalp. Her face was as wrinkled as an ancient elephant's hide, but her rheumy eyes scanned me carefully. "You with the police?" She sounded doubtful.

"No, ma'am. I was hoping to talk to someone here." I pointed at Ed's house. "You know he went on buying trips to Mexico—"

Her head bobbed like a marionette.

"—and he was going to look for a silver-and-tortoiseshell necklace for me. He told me he'd have it for me today, but when I called this morning, a policeman answered."

Again that fluffy head nodded.

"Of course, I'm dreadfully sorry about what happened." There was no delicate way to say one regretted a man's murder.

She wore a pink housecoat with a frenzy of lace at the neck and scuffed, once-pink terry-cloth slippers. "I saw the police car." No doubt little escaped her notice. "I came out on my porch. The policeman came over to see me. He wanted to know if I'd seen Ed last night and if he was with anybody. He said Ed was found dead on the River Walk outside that fancy store, Tesoros."

Obviously, Detective Borroel was running true to form. He said little and what he said was true but unrevealing.

"The detective said someone hit him on the head." She put her hands on her hips and peered at me. "I always thought Ed would come to a bad end, but I figured it would be in a bar somewhere or a car wreck. Ed drank too much."

It was my turn to nod. I gestured toward the house. "Is there anyone I can talk to? I don't want to intrude, but I'm leaving town soon and I'd like to know if he was able to make that purchase for me. Do you know who's in charge of the estate?"

She rubbed her nose with a thin finger. "Probably Ed's cousin, Greta. Lives in Pampas, I think. But if you know what the necklace looks like—"

"Oh yes, black tortoiseshell interspersed with oblong silver beads and a clasp shaped like a beetle." I put on my most earnest expression. "I wouldn't take it with me," I said virtuously. "I haven't paid for it yet. But if it's there, I'll get in touch with his cousin. If it isn't in his house, I won't take up her time."

"Well"—she dropped a hand into the pocket of her housecoat and metal jangled—"I have keys to his house 'cause I kept things right for him when he was gone. He always said, 'Mrs. Jackson, I never worry about the place when I'm gone.' And he was good to me, always brought me a present and sometimes he gave me cash. I don't have much money, you know," she confided, "just my late husband's social security and it doesn't stretch too far. I was glad to help out and when I saw the police car this morning, I went out to look. The detective was very nice to me. After he told me about Ed, I went over and brought Sammie home. That's Ed's cat."

As we stepped onto the porch, she reached down to stroke a huge orange tom. "Papa's not coming home, Sammie. But you'll be all right. I'll take care of you."

She poked a key into the front door. I asked casually, "Now, Ed's last trip, let's see, that was in August, wasn't it?"

She stepped inside, flipped on the living room light. "Yes. He was gone the last two weeks in August."

I kept my expression pleasant, but I felt like shouting. It was like poking the right piece into a complicated puzzle. The robbery at the National Museum occurred August 22. The odds on cocaine in the wardrobe continued to dwindle in my mind.

We stood in the little entryway, the small living room to the right, the dining room to the left. The living room surprised me, cheerful with bright cushions on white wicker furniture, a crimson-and-black sārape on one wall, small oil paintings, mostly of San Miguel de Allende, on another, and brilliantly glazed pottery scattered everywhere. A spectacular big black-glazed pot stood near the fireplace, obviously the finest piece in the room.

The room smelled fuggily of bourbon and stale cigarette smoke. A bottle, a shot glass, and a half-filled tumbler sat by a stub-filled brass ashtray on a low coffee table. An oversize coffee table book lay open to a glittering green scene of rolling pastoral country. Even from here, I could read the script: *The Glory of the Emerald Isle*. The open bottle, the murky half-filled tumbler, and the ashtray were the only signs of disorder, clashing with the serenity of the room.

"Ed kept a nice house. I do give him credit there. And when he was himself, he was the best neighbor in the world." She glanced at the profusion of greenery in glazed pots. "I suppose I'd better water his ferns, keep them nice for his cousin." She pattered away toward the kitchen.

I moved swiftly around the room. Ed Schmidt had been an orderly man. I stepped close to the bookcase and photos of Ed when young—in the Army, on a small boat, walking along a beach, on a tennis court.

Sometimes alone, sometimes with friends. Always men.

I heard steps behind me. I turned, shaking my head. "I don't see anything here that could be mine." I pointed at an unframed snapshot lying in the bookcase. "That's a very nice picture, the one with Ed standing by that huge sculpture." The sun splashed on Ed's face. He looked powerful, determined, and smug. I thought this photograph—had he asked another tourist to take it? I felt certain he'd been alone—was the equivalent of thumbing his nose at the world. Unless I was mightily mistaken, this picture was taken in front of the monument to the god Tlaloc at the entrance to the National Museum of Anthropology. I smiled at Mrs. Jackson. "I've been there. The National Museum of Anthropology in Mexico City."

For all the reaction in his elderly neighbor's face, I might equally have named an orbiting space station.

She squinted at the photo. "Sad to see him having so much fun and not knowing he had so little time left. I think this was made on his last trip. It wasn't here until this week." She looked around the room. "If you didn't see your necklace, let's take a look in his office. It's a little cubbyhole by his bedroom."

I followed her down the short hall. There is something incredibly intimate about seeing a man's bedroom. The green cotton spread stretched tight and smooth on the old fashioned maple spool bed. A monogrammed silver-backed hairbrush and matching comb sat atop a lace doily on the dresser. I'd bet doilies had been scattered about the house when he was young. Had he kept this one out of deference to his mother? It appeared freshly washed. A paperback of Barbara Tuchman's *The Zimmerman Telegram* and a half-empty pack of Camels lay on the bedside table. The closet door was closed. No clothing was discarded on the bed or straight chair near the dresser.

"Here's his little office." She stood aside for me to look into a pine-paneled room that had obviously been added to the back of the house.

I would have loved to go through the green filing cabinets, though I doubted there was a folder tabbed "Stolen Gold." Another fern graced the top of the cabinet. The desk was bare except for the hand tooled leather pad and a fishbowl. Two goldfish darted excitedly.

"Oh, yes, I'd better feed Spenser and Hawk." She pulled out the shallow desk drawer and picked out a shaker of fish food.

Maybe that's when my distasteful recollection of a whisky-breathed man trembling with anger and a shrunken bloodied corpse was overlaid by another picture, that of a cultivated lonely man who drank too much but loved his cat, sought structure and order and beauty in his surroundings and harbored a hunger for gallantry and romance.

She slid the cover shut on the fish food, replaced the container in the drawer. "I don't see anything like that necklace you wanted."

I shook my head regretfully and walked toward the hallway. "I guess he didn't have a chance to get it. Or who knows," I said brightly, "perhaps he'd already mailed it to me and I'll find it when I get home." On the front porch, I waited as she shut the door, locked it.

When we reached the sidewalk, I opened my purse. "Mrs. Jackson, Ed told me he had a friend who also dealt in jewelry. Now I can't remember who he said. Do you know any of these faces?"

She squinted at the newspaper clip of the Garza

family. "Can't say that I do. But I didn't know Ed's friends." Her eyes dropped to the ground. "He went out a lot but when he came home with company it was usually late at night."

I put the sheet back in my purse, pulled a twenty-dollar bill from a side pocket. I smiled at her. "I like cats a lot, Mrs. Jackson. Please use this to help take care of Sammie."

For an instant, she hesitated. But I wasn't offering her money. It was for Sammie. Her wrinkled face shone. "Thank you, ma'am."

As I walked away, she called out. "I'm sorry about your necklace."

I wasn't. It had turned out to be a damn fine piece of work.

I checked my second address. Across the street. The distance was short but the contrast dramatic. I climbed the steps to an almost identical bungalow, but there were no ferns here. Instead, broken pieces of shingles littered the porch, the raffia mat in front of the door was scuffed with mud, and a dog barked ferociously when I pushed the doorbell.

Old venetian blinds, some of the slats missing, masked the windows. A thud against the inside of the door suggested Rover was big, irritable, and would be pleased to imprint his canines on my throat.

I rang several more times, but apparently Rollo Barrett was not at home. If he held a nine-to-five job, that figured. I glanced at my watch. Shortly after noon. So I couldn't ask Mr. Barrett about the neighbor he obviously didn't like and why he didn't like him. I doubted it had to do with big bad Sammie. These flower-erbeds hadn't been cultivated in years.

I skirted a broken-down pickup leaning on a bare

axle, and stepped into a beautifully kept yard with a magnificent magnolia as its centerpiece. As I neared the steps of a freshly painted white frame house with bright green shutters, the front door opened.

Perhaps nothing tells you more about a man or woman than how they dress. Dress reveals class, attitude, status, mood, and temperament.

At a glance, I knew the man on the porch loved fine clothing, resisted change, and took pride in himself. The embroidered soft cotton shirt had been washed many times, but each ruffle was painstaking ironed. His gray worsted-wool trousers, unpleated, were worn but the crease was perfect. The heavy belt buckle, a ram's head, glistened like a tea-shop pitcher. His moccasin-style loafers had the supple softness of old leather, lovingly polished. Gnarled hands gripped the silver knob of a thick black cane. He wore his silvery hair long, held back with a turquoise-beaded thong. But it was his eyes that held fascination and power, coal-dark eyes in a face made interesting because it was slightly off center, the left eyebrow lifted into the domed forehead, the jutting high-bridged nose with a lumpy middle, the thin mouth so long tilted in a quizzical moue that it never changed.

I reached the porch steps. "Mr. Worth?" Ed Schmidt had often traveled with his neighbor Julian Worth on art-seeking trips in Mexico.

"Yes. I'm Julian Worth." He was frowning. "You went into Ed's house." His voice was somber. Abruptly his dark eyes filmed with tears.

"I'm sorry." And I was.

"We were old friends. Very old friends." He stared at the now deserted house, struggling with the awful finality of death, knowing that Ed Schmidt would never again kneel beside a flowerbed and feel moist dirt on his hands and the hot San Antonio sun on his back. Then he looked at me. "I don't know you." Worth's voice was cold.

I didn't dare claim a friendship with Ed Schmidt. This man, this neighbor across the street, this fellow seeker of art treasures, knew that I was a stranger. But Worth's eyes had filled with tears . . . I took a chance.

"I'm trying to find out what happened to Ed Schmidt. I'm Henrie Collins, a friend of Maria Elena Garza's. You may know that Ed was found in front of Tesoros . . ." I broke off at his nod. No, I didn't need to explain Tesoros to a man who knew Mexican art. "There is a terrible possibility that the police may try and blame her handicapped son Manuel for Ed's murder. I'm trying to help Maria Elena discover what happened last night."

I climbed the steps, stood beside him on the porch, smelled the after-aroma of a cigar and a faint touch of spicy cologne. "Will you tell me about Ed?"

He lifted his shoulders. "Why should I?"

"It is something you can do in his memory," I said softly.

Finally, he nodded. "I haven't seen much of Ed for a long time now." His mouth curled down. "He hasn't had any time for me the last few years." He turned away, the cane jabbing against the wooden floor. He sat on a white wicker chair and glared across the street.

I took the chair on the other side of a garden table. "Why not?"

"Too busy. He just took what he wanted from me, learned enough about buying to do it on his own. As soon as he could manage by himself, he didn't go to Mexico with me anymore. But until then we had so many grand trips. Ed was always ready to try anything, go anywhere. Once—" he looked at me, eyes shining with memory—"in Acapulco, he dived from the cliffs. Ed did. Oh, it was late at night and no one saw, no one except me." Remembered awe lifted his voice. "I never knew anyone like Ed. He would do anything, try anything. But he was insatiable, always looking for more excitement, a greater thrill . . ." His hands gripped the cane, his face ridged. "But finally he was always too busy to see me and then"—he turned his head and his eyes bored into mine—"he lied to me. He deceived me. For money." His mouth twisted in that wry, weary half-smile, half-grimace.

"So Ed liked money." That did not surprise me. What was he willing to do for money? "And Ed liked to take chances. Did you know Ed was in Mexico a month ago? That's when someone broke into the National Anthropology Museum and—"

His heavy silver brows arched in surprise. "The gold!"

I wasn't surprised that he knew of the theft. Anyone who cared about Mexico's treasures would certainly know.

Suddenly the off-kilter face erupted into laughter, booming deep laughter. Finally, he clapped a stubby hand over his mouth, subsided finally into sporadic chuckles. "Damn him. By God, he would do it. Only Ed. God, I wish I'd been there." He looked at me and broke into another peal of laughter. Finally, gasping for breath, he waggled a bony finger at me. "You should see your face. You despise Ed because he was a thief. But, by God, that's stealing on a grand scale, woman. And why not? That bloody gold has left dead in its wake since the first piece was created. Do you know why? Human beings are no goddamn good. There will always be the lust for riches. It doesn't purify gold to put it in a museum. Isn't it almost worse to think of all the thousands of sheep mewing and stirring in front of the cases, awed by gold? Don't glorify art that's been touched by the devil. Why shouldn't Ed take advantage of lust?" He nodded, his sleek ponytail swinging. "Let some greedy fool have the stuff. Add another lost soul tied to that gold, like scalps to a tomahawk." His right thumb rubbed the silver top of his cane as his excitement subsided, replaced by cold calculation. "If Ed took the gold, where is it now?" He didn't wait for me to answer. Obviously, I didn't know. "Gold. So that's why he died." His dark eyes glowed with an unholy light. He stared at me, his eyes trying to pluck information. "Why have you come to me?"

"I want to know more about Ed."

That long mouth twisted. "Ed?" His dark eyes were skeptical. "Or are you trying to find the gold?"

"When I find the gold," I said it baldly, "we'll know who killed Ed."

His silvery eyebrows bunched. "So Ed died in front of Tesoros."

"Yes." I decided not to be as reticent as Detective Borroel. Maybe if I told Julian Worth what I knew, he would help me. "That's where his body was found. But apparently he died inside Tesoros and someone pulled the body out of the store."

"Inside Tesoros." His eyes glinted. "Tesoros. Stolen gold. I see." His voice pulsed with satisfaction. "The most respectable gallery of all, owned by the famous Maria Elena Garza. The great Garza family. Ed was no fool." Worth used the cane to push himself to his feet. "That's the perfect way to dispose of the gold and make enough money to live like a king."

I rose, ready to keep step with him. I didn't like his combative tone, the sudden aura of fervid excitement.

This man clearly knew Maria Elena and her children well. "Do you know which one of the Garzas might be Ed's partner?"

Julian Worth's lips drew back in a cold smile. "You're a smart woman. But then you'd have to be if you're on the track of the gold. That's definitely the question, isn't it? If Ed took the gold to Tesoros, it had to be to arrange a secret sale. Oh yes, very secret. And this is the week of Maria Elena's famous auction, with only the richest of the rich invited to attend." He smiled.

It was as ugly a smile as I've ever seen, contemptuous and confident.

"One of them now has a treasure beyond price." Worth's eyes glowed. "A treasure far beyond the works to be sold at the auction. Oh yes, Ed was clever, Ed and his partner. But only a member of the family could make this happen. Which one, which one?" It was almost a soft chant. His eyes looked through me, seeing other faces in my place. "I know them all. I should be able to guess." He tapped his cane as he spoke each name. "Frank's a fool. Isabel loves riches. Tony's a gambler. Susana puts the store above everything. Magda's quick and smart. Celestina hates them all. Rick Reyes, he's an arrogant young ass. And that earnest young man who works at the hotel, Frank's son Tom. One of them. Which one?"

He turned away, the cane thumping on the porch.

"Mr. Worth . . ."

But he had no more time for me. The front door slammed.

I felt eerily unsettled. Sometimes as a reporter I'd ask a question that totally changed the course and complexion of an interview. Often the question was an afterthought. The sometimes astonishing results always awed me. That was a simple example of the Law of Unintended Consequences. On a more complex level, sometimes a decision made carelessly and without thought has a profound impact on my life.

The Law of Unintended Consequences. I wondered if I'd just set that law in motion.

ten

IF I'd found Tesoros crowded in the morning, this afternoon it rivaled market day in a Mexican village. I wormed my way into the main showroom, noting the elongated faces that I attributed to the Garza family, likely more cousins, aunts, and uncles. Others I tabbed as friends and well-wishers, both Hispanic and Anglo. Celestina Garza hovered attentively near a covey of nuns. Voices rose in vigorous conversation, the sound magnified by the tile floor and plaster ceiling.

I paused near an elderly priest gazing in delight at a display of Oaxacan wood carvings. He picked up a winged horse with red and white splotches of polka dots, a black ruffled mane, and a streaming red-and-white tail. The lower half of the horse's upswept wings were decorated with blue and white lines of boxes, the upper in pink accented with thin white stripes. The decorations were so fluid, the wings seemed to undulate. A gray-and-black-striped cow peered earnestly at her calf, whose eager mouth was open to suckle. Black spots decorated an arched green cat with a pink-spotted muzzle and wide golden eyes circled in black. More wings lifted skyward from the backs of blue or pink angels. The nearest angel wore a pink robe, the carving so skilled the skirt appeared to ripple. Tiny gold crescents streaked her wings; gold stars spattered her gown; gold glistened in her crown.

Of all Mexican folk art, I most enjoy Oaxacan wood carvings. Just to glimpse one of the carved figures makes me feel privileged to be human and thereby akin to an artist who sees such a vivid world with unlimited possibilities: flying green sheep, rabbits playing the drums, a frog reading a book, a gorilla family on an outing.

I gave another admiring look at the display as I eased past the priest. I sought a quiet refuge near the back wall and found myself once again near the mask collection, standing next to a Indian mask from Guerrero State. This mask was created for the dance of the seven vices and was eerily affecting—the skin a dusky orange, the eye sockets empty, the red mouth turned down, a hissing salamander running down one cheek and a black snake coiled on the other. Vices. I was looking for someone who had succumbed to vice.

I stood on tiptoe scanning the crowd. I wasn't surprised when I spotted Julian Worth, measurably taller than most in the room, distinctive with his silvery hair in its sleek ponytail. He, too, was gazing purposefully around the room.

Our eyes met. For an instant, his off-center face was stony, then he gave his derisive smile and made a courtly bow in my direction. I was under no illusion that he was pleased to see me. I felt the gesture was more on the order of a contemptuous challenge. We both knew he was here to contact the man—or woman—he suspected of having conspired with Ed Schmidt. Worth's goal? He wasn't a Knight Templar seeking justice. I suspected his aim was much simpler and seedier. Worth wanted a piece of the action.

He headed straight for Celestina Garza, still talking to a tall, thin nun with bright blue eyes.

Celestina Garza! I felt a surge of astonishment. She looked smaller than ever facing the tall nun. Could that petite woman have battered a man to death? I pictured Ed Schmidt and Celestina Garza. I might have difficulty perceiving tight-featured Celestina as a conspirator in a daring and imaginative robbery, but I could easily imagine Ed Schmidt and Celestina Garza quarreling. She was born to argue and certainly he had downed enough whiskey to make him quarrelsome and quite possibly abusive. Celestina was small, but if Schmidt had been walking away from her, had not seen her grab up the heavy pottery bank, if she had attacked with sufficient force and utter determination, if he fell and she moved swiftly to strike and strike and strike . . . yes, Celestina Garza could have killed Schmidt. Would she? Jealousy had corroded her spirit, made her spiteful and envious. She wanted desperately to win her mother's approval, gain appreciation for her efforts at Tesoros. Had years of perceived neglect twisted her love for Tesoros into disdain? But what would Celestina do with an illicit hoard of money? Surely she didn't hope to escape from San Antonio and create a new life on some exotic South Sea isle. Perhaps there was no particular plan. There are some to whom the mere possession of wealth, even if hidden, provides a sinister pleasure.

A tall man stopped beside me, cocked his head to look at a winking diablo mask with rubber ears and horns and a gaping watermelon red mouth decorated with goat teeth and a split tongue.

I slipped around him, in time to see Celestina's tiny features suffused with an ugly saffron flush.

Julian Worth bowed to her and stepped away, his eyes circling the room.

I realized as I skirted visiting groups, waited patiently for congestion to ease in the clogged aisles, that almost all of the family members were in the showroom. I passed by a clump of chattering old ladies with Maria Elena in their center. She was nodding, speaking quietly, reaching out to clasp seeking hands. Everyone was here in a surge of family support.

By the time I reached Celestina, I'd lost sight of Julian Worth.

"Hello, Celestina. This is quite a turnout, isn't it?" I looked around approvingly.

Her eyes still glittered with anger, but she smoothed out her face and managed a meaningless smile.

"It's lovely the way everyone's come to show their support for Maria Elena." I spread my hand at the jammed room.

"The family." There was no warmth in her colorless voice. "Of course they've all come. It's an even bigger draw than a funeral. Everybody wants to know what happened. And there are already whispers about Frank and Ed. People remember things. They show a sweet face to Mother, but a lot of them are pleased to see us in trouble."

I looked with interest at her hostile little face. And you don't like anybody very much, do you, lady? "Is that why Julian Worth came?"

Obsidian-cold eyes stared up at me. "How do you know Julian Worth?"

Good question. "I met him this morning." Let her wonder about that. "What did he say that made you so angry?"

"Angry?" Those icy eyes bored into mine.

"Yes. I saw him talking to you." I was glad I spoke

with her in the midst of a crowd. I was startled to find myself made uneasy by such a small creature, but antagonism emanated from her in almost palpable waves.

"It would make anyone angry." Her scratchy voice exuded distaste. "He said he'd been sorry to hear that a known thief had been killed inside Tesoros. He said it had to make everyone wonder why Ed had come to Tesoros. He said it certainly was a shame for an old establishment such as ours to be tainted by scandal. I told him in no uncertain terms that Ed Schmidt had nothing to do with any of us." Her bleak face hardened.

"What did he say to that?" Across the room, I caught a glimpse of Julian Worth walking away from Susana Garza. Today her shining black hair was piled high atop her head, emphasizing the filigree earrings that hung straight and still from her stone-still head. One hand held tight to her necklace. Even from a distance, I could see the coral and turquoise insets in her heavy silver necklace. The spectacular jewelry only emphasized the somberness of her discontented face. I wished I had observed Worth's tête-à-tête with Susana.

Celestina and I stood beside the display island with the pink and blue and orange pottery banks. I noticed they'd been rearranged so there was no longer an empty spot. She pointed a shaking finger at the floor. "He said we couldn't pretend the murder had nothing to do with Tesoros when the man died in this very room." She stared toward the front door, her face pinched.

Some of the visitors walked where blood must have run, where Manuel's mop had swiped away traces of death.

"Celestina, oh, Celestina!" Frank Garza stood near

the front door. His thin voice could barely be heard. His worried face glistened with perspiration. He gripped the elbow of a portly-white haired man in a black suit and clerical collar. "Father Hernandez wants to say hello." Frank beckoned to his sister.

Celestina's sallow face cheered. Murmuring, "Excuse me, please," she headed toward Frank and the priest, sidestepping a child's stroller pushed by a grandmother and darting around a group of plump animated women.

Once again I looked for Julian Worth. He stood in the nook filled with Day of the Dead decorations. A line of toy skeletons hung near his shoulder. Behind him on a shelf ranged an array of grinning papier-mâché skulls, each with a distinctive head covering: the matador, the nun, the nurse, the soldier, the scuba diver, the motorcyclist, the mantilla-graced grande dame. Worth bent toward Tony Garza, speaking rapidly, his hands moving, one ending in a thrust toward the front door.

A shaft of light from overhead spotlighted Tony, as always extraordinarily handsome, his midnight black hair in tight curls, his lantern-jawed face bold and commanding, his sensuous mouth curved in an enigmatic smile. When Worth concluded, Tony lifted his broad shoulders in a dismissive shrug. Obviously, if Worth had spun him the same tale, the effect was much less dramatic than it had been on Celestina. Tony grinned, gestured at the throngs of people, then, with a final comment, moved away from Worth.

This time it was Worth, his face sour, who watched Tony stride away.

Once again, our glances met.

I glared at Worth. I'd hoped to keep the murderer from realizing that anyone else knew about the gold.

Julian's circuit of the family dashed that plan. Now, if I told Detective Borroel about the gold, there would be no element of surprise when he began to investigate.

Worth's sloping smile exuded satisfaction and a complete lack of regret. He walked directly toward Frank, giving me a sardonic nod as he passed, his cane thumping on the tiles. He was moving slowly and I thought he was laboring. Was it fatigue? Or had he put himself under a great strain?

I said sharply, "You realize you're warning the murderer."

Worth ignored me and walked on, leaning heavily on his cane. I watched as he drew even with Frank, thrust out his hand and began to talk. Clearly, he intended to speak with each member of the family, except, I supposed, Maria Elena.

I looked at the pottery banks and reached out, touching the nearest, a prosperous looking, big-cheeked, balding man in a green coat and blue slacks, entitled "The Landlord." The pottery was cold to my touch, but not as cold as my thoughts. Worth had severely complicated my hope of discovering who had conspired with Schmidt. I could no more hope to determine the identity of Ed Schmidt's co-conspirator from the reactions of those to whom Worth spoke than I could divine by my proximity to the banks the hand that had grabbed one up as a lethal weapon. More than that, Worth's charade here on the showroom floor definitely alerted the murderer that the gold was no longer a secret. And, damn Worth, I didn't know whether he suspected a particular member of the Garza family or whether he was gambling that his description of Ed as a thief would trigger a response from the murderer. Worth could then demand money.

No, keeping track of Julian Worth wasn't going to help me find Ed Schmidt's co-conspirator and murderer. I still had no proof Ed had stolen the ancient gold, but I now knew he could have done so; he was in Mexico when the theft occurred, and Julian Worth's revelations about Ed proved he definitely had the right mental and physical equipment for such a venture. Ed Schmidt loved excitement and danger and he was strong and fit.

Julian Worth wasn't losing any time. Now he leaned on his cane, talking with Isabel. She smoothed back a drooping ringlet of her lustrous golden-toned hair. Her hand was delicate, exquisitely groomed, soft and smooth, and the fire of rubies and the glow of emeralds flashed from a half dozen rings. She stared up at Worth, her delicate face elegant and alert, her eyes unwinking, like a cat silently appraising a witless bird.

My gaze moved on. Worth, as far as I was concerned, could talk to everyone in the store. He no longer interested me. Instead, I was seeking yet another handsome Garza face. But I didn't find Rick Reyes. Odd. Everyone else was here. Well, not quite everyone. I didn't see Iris either.

Dammit, I wanted to see Rick now. I had to know for a certainty that my guess was correct—that the treasure found and taken by Iris was indeed the ancient gold. Only Rick or Iris could tell me if I was right. I worked my way around the crowded room, ending up by the front door. I took my time. I knew when I finished the circuit that Rick definitely was not in the showroom.

I stepped out onto the River Walk. I welcomed the soft, moist heat and the stir of a fitful breeze. I'd not realized how oppressive it had been inside Tesoros.

The air-conditioning in the showroom wasn't geared for a capacity crowd.

I heard the faint swipe of cloth against glass. Manuel was polishing at the far end of the second window. When I stopped behind him, he froze for an instant. His narrow shoulders hunched. He darted a swift, fearful glance at the glass and my reflection.

I, too, could see his face, watch as recognition lighted his eyes, brought a sweet smile, eased the tightness of his body.

I gently touched his shoulder. "Good job, Manuel."

He twisted toward me. His hand rose. Hesitantly, he offered me the pad of thick white toweling.

I reached out, took the cloth, stepped near enough to buff the glass. I polished a broad horizontal stripe above and below our reflections, then swiped vertically as if creating a frame.

Manuel clapped his hands. We smiled at each other. I handed back the cloth, gave him another pat on his shoulder, turned away and looked straight into the cool, measuring gaze of a uniformed patrolman. He was young, with reddish hair in a quarter-inch crew, a freckle-spangled face and an athletic build. He was only a few feet away.

As I walked toward the stairs leading to La Mariposa, the policeman's gaze followed me for a moment, then returned to Manuel, once again busy with his cloth, his face reflected in the window, calm, intent, happy.

At the top of the stairs, I looked down and found it a disquieting tableau, Manuel and the so-attentive policeman. It was time for me to do what I could to expand the investigation, but I wanted to present Borroel with credible evidence, not simply my hypothesis. To do this, I needed Rick Reyes to tell the truth.

The lobby of La Mariposa seemed an oasis of tranquillity after the bustle of Tesoros, the only sound Cara Kendall's piercing voice as she stood by the chili-cart desk and berated Tom Garza, who nodded and continued to look pleasant, though I imagined it took some effort.

Her frown stretched the too-tight skin of her glazed face. ". . . simply can't tolerate such inferior quality. My poor face was rubbed raw, raw!" Emaciated fingers touched an inelastic cheek. "If you can't arrange for a finer quality of pillowcases, I will simply have to move to La Mansion. You must understand that I am accustomed to the very best." She swung around, almost cannoning into me, gave me a haughty stare and flounced away.

Tom's smile vanished faster than a quarter in a slot machine.

"Feel free," I offered.

He grinned, looking extremely young and likable. "Thanks. But for all the"—he paused, probably to choose another word—"difficult guests, there are dozens like you."

Ah, this young man had a future as a hotelier.

We exchanged mutually approving smiles. "Tom, I'm looking for Rick. Have you seen him?"

Tom pointed toward the exit to the outside steps. "Rick's downstairs. Everybody but me's at Tesoros, busy greeting the extended family. You know, in a Hispanic family whenever there's trouble, everyone rallies around."

"I just came from Tesoros. Rick isn't there." I glanced toward the red velvet curtains at the archway leading to the foyer and meeting rooms. "Could he be working in the auction room?"

"I don't think so," he said doubtfully. "I haven't

noticed anyone going through the arch this afternoon. Of course," and he shrugged, "maybe I was busy and missed him. Why don't you take a look?"

"Thanks, I will. And if you see him, please tell him I would very much like to speak to him." I paused, wondering just how to ask this attractive young man where he had been last night when Ed Schmidt was battered to death. I liked Tom, but he, too, was certainly part of this family. He, too, would know very well how to take advantage of the auction to transfer a fortune in gold to a wealthy collector. "Tom, did you know the man who was killed?"

He shook his head. "No. But he went to school with my dad. Dad says he hadn't seen the guy in a long time." Tom's face was earnest, but unworried. "Rick told me it was pretty awful last night."

"Yes." I didn't want to remember that still body looking so much smaller than in life. "You weren't here last night?"

"No, ma'am. After we close down for the night, the front bell rings in Uncle Tony's room. Nope, the most exciting thing in the history of Tesoros and I'm home in bed."

Maybe. Maybe not. I smiled a thank-you and walked across the lobby. Inside the foyer, I saw the entrances to the two meeting rooms were shut. I tried both doors. They were locked. I knocked sharply. It was very quiet in this lobby. The store downstairs might have been a thousand miles away. And obviously, if Rick, or anyone else, was in either meeting room, he didn't care to answer my summons.

After I unlocked the door to my room, I reached up and stroked the painting of the monarch. But it was just a painted butterfly, and it could not bring me close to Bobby.

I'd left word with Tom for Rick to get in touch with me as soon as possible. If I didn't hear from Rick soon, I'd find Maria Elena. I had no doubt that if she put out the word for Rick to come to her, he would come.

I found ice in the little bucket in the bath and an assortment of sodas in a small refrigerator. I chose a club soda, poured it, and carried the glass with me onto the tiny balcony. I sipped the cool drink, leaned against the warm wall and looked down at the entrance to Tesoros. Manuel was now working on the first window. The late-afternoon shadows reached all the way to the river. I got a notepad from my purse and settled at the small table on the balcony and swiftly made notes. As soon as I had bullied the truth from Rick, I would present Detective Borroel with these facts:

Ed Schmidt was in Mexico City when the antique gold pieces were stolen.

Ed Schmidt was a daredevil, and he was greedy. See Julian Worth for confirmation.

Ed Schmidt had a long history with the Garza family, especially Frank.

Iris Chavez found the gold in a wardrobe in the Tesoros receiving room on Thursday. She took it to Rick Reyes.

From Thursday until Monday evening, Iris stayed in the apartment of Rick's mother, Magda Reyes, with the gold.

Ed Schmidt must have been informed by someone at Tesoros that Iris had left without explanation and that the gold was gone from the wardrobe. Ed searched Iris's apartment, probably shortly after she left the store on Thursday.

I arrived on Sunday, seeking Iris. I went to her apartment, to Tesoros, and to the police.

Monday afternoon, I responded to instructions to be on the River Walk near the King William district. Iris met me. Ed Schmidt attempted to grab Iris. She escaped on Rollerblades. Schmidt threatened to knife Rick if the "package" taken by Iris wasn't returned.

If Schmidt was following me, as seemed apparent, someone at Tesoros must have informed him that I was looking for Iris.

After that encounter, Iris called Tesoros several times, seeking Rick. The Tesoros office was equipped with Caller ID.

My room at La Mariposa was searched on Monday.

Monday night a fake fire erupted in the apartment house where Iris was hiding.

When Iris fled the building, carrying the gold in her backpack, she was attacked, a blanket thrown over her so she could not see her assailant, and the backpack was taken.

Moments later Rick, Iris, and I found Ed Schmidt's body in front of Tesoros.

I tapped the pen on the pad. Several conclusions seemed obvious. Ed Schmidt was in league with someone at Tesoros. It was the only way he could have learned that the gold was not in its hiding place, that Iris was missing and likely had taken it, that I was connected to Iris and that following me might lead him to her and the gold. It seemed equally apparent that Ed Schmidt was not the person who figured out Iris's hiding place from the Caller ID and who set the fake fire and retrieved the gold from Iris.

I sipped the bubbly soda and felt curiously disturbed. The timing was out of kilter. I'd assumed that

Ed's co-conspirator killed him. It seemed the obvious conclusion—that they'd quarreled and the conspirator struck Ed down. But why? The gold was going to be retrieved. What caused the murder? Okay, figure a quarrel. That wasn't hard to imagine. Ed drank too much. Alcohol not only distorts judgment, it engenders violence. Ed had been drinking heavily Monday night, nursing his grievance, his anger growing that his fellow conspirator, call him X, claimed the gold was gone. Did Ed think that was a lie, simply a method of cheating him out of the money that would be realized in a sale of the gold? I could easily imagine Ed arriving at Tesoros in a state of drunken fury. But now it got complicated. Who met him there? Who opened the front door? What happened? And how did he end up dead in the main showroom at almost the same time frightened people, including Iris, were streaming out of the apartment house?

I finished the soda, my face in a tight frown. Even if Detective Borroel accepted my theories about the stolen gold and Ed Schmidt's involvement with a member of the family, he'd point to my conclusion that X couldn't have committed the murder because he or she was busy retrieving the gold. Moreover, the suggestion of a conspiracy made it not improbable that Ed had a key to Tesoros. What if Ed unlocked the door? But who could have attacked him? If not X, then who?

The quick answer, of course, was Manuel. Manuel was at Tesoros, Manuel tried to remove all traces of the crime; therefore Manuel committed the murder.

Damn. The last thing I wanted to do was make Manuel an even more attractive suspect to Borroel. I pushed up from the little table, moved to the railing and stared down at Tesoros. Surely I had made a miscalculation.

But there seemed to be no way X, in only the few minutes between Rick and me finding Iris and reaching Tesoros, could have run with the gold, returned to Tesoros, quarreled with Ed, killed him, moved the body out onto the sidewalk, and disappeared when Manuel arrived. But X could have killed Schmidt, left the body in the store—after all, no one would be on the floor until morning—and gone to flush out Iris. Why leave the body? Wasn't that terribly reckless? But perhaps the effort to get the gold from Iris provided time to think what to do. I did believe the murder was unpremeditated.

In any event, the murder occurred early enough for Manuel to have time to mop the bloody path from the piggy-bank display through the front door.

Borroel would have worked out the time very carefully.

So X could have killed Ed before setting the fire. But it was hard to imagine why he would leave the body on the showroom floor and leave the front door open. Manuel said he found the body on the River Walk and the front door open.

Borroel would insist it was Manuel who moved the body, not a shadowy X.

Damn, I was afraid—

The front door of Tesoros opened, and Frank Garza bolted outside, his face pasty, his eyes staring. He gestured frantically to the red-haired policeman. The young officer took two quick strides. Frank's hands rose and fell and he spoke rapidly. He turned and led the way back into the store, the officer close behind.

Manuel was on his knees by the second window. His gentle face looked perplexed. He neatly folded his cloth, tucked it in a back pocket. Slowly, he stood, picked up his pail, and walked inside.

I took the quickest route. I stepped out into an empty hall and walked swiftly to the door that opened to the circular staircase. I recalled the date, punched the digits into the keypad. I pulled the door open and stepped onto the metal grille of the landing. I looked over the railing and felt the blood drain from my face.

I looked down at death.

There was no doubt Julian Worth was dead. The blood wreathing his silvery hair foretold massive injury, but the unnatural crook of his neck as he lay, splayed at the bottom of the steps, signaled that life was gone.

". . . he must have fallen." Frank's voice shook.

I edged back from the railing, out of sight of those below. Turning, I looked at the door into La Mariposa. From this side, the door opened with a push on a bar. The keypad lock was in operation only from the hotel side. My mind was working on two levels, wondering who had pushed Worth and whether my fingerprints on the keypads put me at risk. I was in no mood to try and explain my presence at the top of these stairs. I wondered if I could push the bar without disturbing fingerprints on this side.

There were three exits from the broad hallway downstairs. The killer could have come up these steps to the hotel or to the family apartments. Or the killer could have opened the back door to the showroom and slipped into that milling throng. Or, and I thought this unlikely, the killer could have opened the keypad door to the receiving area and taken the freight elevator upstairs. If the killer escaped into the showroom or the receiving area, it meant climbing down the steps and edging past or stepping over Julian Worth's body.

A murderer, I've been told, is high on adrenaline so skirting the body would be easy. But there must have been a dreadful long moment going down the steel steps when someone else could have appeared, pushing through the doorway from the showroom. Alternatively, someone in the family could have chosen that moment to enter the stairway from La Mariposa. But actually, everyone in the family was in the showroom with the crowd of well-wishers except for Tom, at the desk in La Mariposa, and Rick, who was curiously absent. So maybe, once the murderer and his quarry were alone on the staircase, maybe there could not have been a better moment.

Shoes gritted on the cement below. I hesitated, then used my hip against the bar to push the door just wide enough to slip into the hallway. The hallway still stretched empty before me.

When the door closed, I gazed at it thoughtfully. I imagined the murderer's path. The murderer would have led the way up the circular stairs. Worth would have had no sense of danger. No doubt the murderer emphasized the need for discretion, saying they needed a quiet place to talk, perhaps they could find a spot in La Mariposa, and discuss business because it was certainly an intriguing suggestion that stolen gold had been hidden at Tesoros. Worth's deadly companion, of course, insisted that he—or she—had no personal knowledge of such a thing but it was surely a subject that needed to be explored. After all, Mr. Worth obviously was an excellent businessman and two people with a common goal could easily reach an understanding. The murderer no doubt spoke calmly, reasonably, and Worth followed, pleased with his success. Quite likely, he was laboring for breath. He'd seemed physically drained as he made the rounds of the family in the showroom. At the top of the staircase, the murderer probably maneuvered Worth into turning to descend the stairs. Perhaps the murderer opened the door into La Mariposa, shut it quickly, saying, "Sorry, we'll have to hurry down. Here comes my husband/wife/that detective." Once Worth turned, he was vulnerable. One powerful shove was all that was needed. Then the murderer either stepped into La Mariposa and exited through the lobby or moved swiftly down the circular stairs, heading for the receiving area and the freight elevator or darting across the hallway and slipping into the showroom to meld into the throng of visitors.

As long as no one heard Worth's scream and found him immediately, the murderer was clear and free of any connection to the point of death. At this moment, the area around the staircase was certainly alive with sound as the police investigated. I heard nothing. As for the showroom, no one there would hear a cry over the hum of voices. Moreover, Worth may scarcely have made any sound. The blow to his back could have emptied his lungs.

The choices were clear: into La Mariposa or down the steps to the receiving area or into the showroom. If I were the murderer, I'd take my chances slipping into the crowd. The likelihood of being noticed was minimal, and once again entry from the back area didn't matter if it couldn't be tied to the time when Worth fell.

I needed to talk to Borroel, but I took a moment longer. Hurrying to the lobby, I saw Tom leaning out of the balcony, craning to see below. I came up behind him. "Tom?"

He spun around, his good-natured face creased with worry. "Do you know what's going on down there? There were sirens and then a bunch of police arrived and somebody just pushed a gurney through the door. And people have been coming out, one at a time, then standing around in groups, staring at Tesoros."

It sounded as though everything was in good order. "I suppose the police are taking the names of everyone in the store so they can interview them later. Tom—"

"Interview them for what? What's happened?" His eyes widened in apprehension.

"A man fell down the circular steps. He's dead. He was a friend of Ed Schmidt's." Even as I spoke, I wondered why I didn't say he was pushed. But it is a habit to cushion our words when breaking hurtful news to others. There was time enough to talk of murder. Besides, I didn't want Tom to be thinking of murder, not until I asked my questions. "Look, Tom, you've been here all afternoon, haven't you?"

"Yes." He pointed at the chili cart. "Dad told me to stay on the desk all day today, there are so many people in and out. And Mom and Dad needed to be downstairs to help my grandmother welcome everybody. Mrs. Collins, how did this guy get on the circular staircase? Was he coming up here?"

"I don't know." That was accurate. I had a darn good idea, but I didn't know. "Listen, you've been here. So who came through the door from the hall"—I figured quickly, I'd last seen Julian Worth taking to Isabel Garza about a quarter to three; it was now half past—"from about ten to three until twenty after?"

"Oh gee, I don't know. Mrs. Kendall. You remember, you saw her. But she didn't go back to her room. She went out the River Walk exit. Then"—his face wrinkled—"I don't think anybody else came from the hall door. But I could have missed somebody just now. I've been watching from here"—he waved his hand at the balcony—"ever since the sirens."

My quarry would have moved through the lobby long before the police were called.

"What did this guy look like?" Tom's gaze was worried.

Tom didn't understand the point of my questions and that was fine. "Tall, white-haired, wore his hair in a ponytail, white ruffled shirt, gray slacks."

His head shake was definite. "Nope. Nobody like that came through the lobby."

I smiled at Tom. "It probably doesn't matter," I said carelessly.

I knew he was looking after me as I headed for the River Walk stairs. He might figure it out. I hesitated, swung around. "Tom, should you recall someone—anyone—coming through the door, don't tell anyone but me. Not even if it's someone you know very, very well."

Stricken dark eyes clung to mine. I wished I could recall the words, but that I couldn't do. I had to warn Tom. He had moved to the bottom of my suspect list. I could almost be certain he'd not been downstairs to the Tesoros showroom while Julian Worth made his fatally foolish circuit. No, Tom was not involved in the murders at Tesoros—unless he'd seen a killer come through the door into the lobby.

A small placard in the first window of Tesoros read "Closed." Manuel was not polishing the glass. The crowd in front of the store had thinned. The red-haired policeman, arms folded, stood in front of the door. He squinted against the bright sunlight, sweat glistening on his pink face.

I walked up to him. "Officer, it is important that I speak with Detective Borroel about Mr. Worth, the man who was killed."

"Are you a relative, ma'am?" He pulled a small notebook from his back pocket.

"No, but I have information relevant to his murder." I didn't have to pick and choose my words here. The time to unburden myself of anything I knew or guessed was definitely now and was, in fact, past due. If I had spoken to Borroel when I simply had a good guess about the gold, Julian Worth could now be alive. To be fair to myself, Worth was a gambler, a man attracted to danger. If I had suggested to Borroel that he talk to Worth, the result of that interview might have been exactly the result my visit produced. I wasn't, as a matter of fact, going to harbor a sense of guilt. It was Worth who chose to use what he learned from me to his own advantage. He could have made other choices.

But the young policeman gave me a kindly, patient look. "Ma'am, there was a murder here last night. But the man today died in an accident." His youthful voice was a little loud, probably to be certain I could hear him. "It's all been seen to. Seems he was an old gentleman and he got dizzy on these real steep metal stairs and he fell down and broke his neck. Kind of a shock to the folks who have the store after what happened last night. Now, if you want to give me your name—if you know something about the murder last night—I'll be sure Detective Borroel gets the message."

eleven

I was getting to know the San Antonio police station. I hurried across the lobby and through the door on the right. I gave my name at the counter. "I have information for Detective Borroel about the Schmidt murder."

"Yes, ma'am." She checked me out with tired, wary blue eyes. She'd been a pretty girl with a long gentle horsey face. Now she was on the shady side of forty and the drooping lines by her eyes and mouth exaggerated the jut of her cheekbones. "If you'll take a seat over there, ma'am."

The golden oak bench was hard and had an oddly curved back. This anteroom served both the homicide and sex crimes units. Most people waiting here had much worse worries than an uncomfortable bench. I carefully did not study the faces of the three other people waiting, but glimpsed enough—a lanky young man who held his shaking hands tightly together, a couple with reddened eyes—to remind me that it takes a special courage to be a good policeman, the kind of courage that makes it possible to deal with heartbreak and evil without losing all belief in humanity.

I had plenty of time to think while I waited to see Borroel. I'd tried my best to find Rick and Iris—no answer at his apartment or hers—but I realized I could not put off talking to Borroel. I didn't have confirmation from Rick or Iris that the wardrobe had held stolen gold, but it seemed to me that Worth's death was more proof than I needed. It was well after six when the clerk called out my name. My early lunch seemed eons ago. I felt a tiny wave of light-headedness when I stood.

"Are you all right, ma'am?" The clerk held open the gray door. Her words were solicitous; her exasperated sigh was not.

"Fine." I followed her down a hall into a wide room filled with desks, only a few occupied. One detective sloped in his chair, spoke quietly into the telephone crooked by his neck. Another typed on his computer keypad. The clerk led me to a desk next to a planter with a limp fern.

Detective Borroel stood. "Mrs. Collins." He was polite, but that was all. He didn't offer his hand.

I took the straight chair at the side of the gray metal desk.

He sat down and waited, his dark eyes cool, his seamed face impassive. As always, he looked crisp, energetic, and capable. But this evening there was also an edginess, a barely leashed impatience, as if he had much to do and was intent upon doing it and would plunge back into work as soon as he had dealt with me.

During the course of my career, I interviewed lots of smart, tough, combative people. You can't charm them, fool them, or maneuver them. I didn't try. I had to get this man's attention and get it quickly. "Detective Borroel, Julian Worth was murdered this afternoon. Ed Schmidt's killer shoved Worth down those steel stairs." I opened my purse, pulled out my neatly written sketch of events. I leaned forward. "It started with Ed Schmidt's theft of ancient gold from the National Museum of Anthropology in Mexico City. If you'll glance over this—" I handed the sheet to Borroel.

The mention of ancient gold evoked absolutely no reaction. None. But, in a way, that was an illuminating response and a discouraging one. Borroel scanned the sheet, placed it at the precise center of his desk, next to a manila folder. There was nothing else on the desktop except a group of picture frames, one a studio portrait of a woman with masses of dark curly hair frosted with silver, wide eyes, and a joyful smile. The other frames held snapshots of boys—boys playing baseball, climbing trees, paddling canoes, camping, rock climbing; several with their mother's wide eyes, two with Borroel's hawklike nose.

Borroel leaned back, but the fingers of one hand drummed on the arm of his chair. "How did you know Julian Worth?"

Of all the questions he could have asked, this one was least to my liking. I wanted to start with Iris and her discovery in the wardrobe, her disappearance, Ed Schmidt's searches for her and the obvious conclusion that someone at Tesoros told Schmidt that the gold went missing at the same time Iris departed.

Instead, I had to start with my visit to Ed Schmidt's house. I was barely underway when Borroel interrupted. "Why did you go there?"

I could be as direct as he. "To find out if Schmidt was in Mexico when the gold was stolen."

"Gold." His impatience and irritation bubbled to the surface, imbuing the single word with a tone of utter disgust. "Mrs. Collins, there's no hint anywhere of stolen gold." He flipped open the folder, riffled through a stack of papers. "Detective Hess's report indicated a good likelihood of drugs and that turned out to be the case. The package hidden in the wardrobe was cocaine. Certainly Schmidt tried to get the stuff back when Iris Chavez ran away with it. A lot of trouble would have been saved if she and Reyes had come to us when she first found it."

"There is no proof the package held drugs." My voice was icy.

He tapped the papers. "Reyes admits it, so does the girl."

I almost demanded if he always believed witnesses in murder cases, but making Borroel angry wouldn't help my cause. I spoke reasonably. "Detective Borroel, Rick Reyes wants to protect his grandmother's store from association with a scandalous theft. He lied to you."

For an instant, a glint of humor moved in his eyes. "Drugs are not scandalous, Mrs. Collins?"

I tried a different tack. "Do you agree that Schmidt was in league with someone in Tesoros?"

Borroel shrugged. "Possibly. But equally well, Mrs. Collins, possibly not. In any—"

I interrupted angrily. "He had to be in contact with someone at Tesoros. There's no other way he could have known that Iris took the package and certainly no way he could have known I was in town looking for Iris."

Borroel planted his elbows on the desk. He spoke deliberately. "Mrs. Collins, give us a little credit. Obviously, Schmidt was involved in something dishonest and it doesn't really matter whether it was drugs or gold." He glanced at my sheet. "I'll agree that Schmidt probably was working with someone in the Garza family. And it makes sense that the person who got Iris's backpack is a member of the family. But as you clearly point out, that person could not possibly have killed Ed Schmidt. What seems very likely is that Schmidt had a key to the store, that he arrived drunk Monday night, let himself inside, and made enough noise to awaken Manuel Garza. Garza came downstairs, there was a confrontation, Garza grabbed up one of the ceramic banks—"

"No." I was surprised at the emotion in my voice. But I could see Manuel so clearly—the shining light in his eyes, the soft, smooth, unlined skin of his face, his shy smile. "Detective Borroel, I know you see all kinds of murderers—old women, children, teenagers. Anyone and everyone. But can't you look at Manuel Garza and see that he would never hurt anyone?" I wanted to grip this man's shoulders and tell him that Maria Elena said it best: Manuel was good; dammit, he was good!

Surprisingly, Borroel's face softened. "I understand your feelings. But even the most gentle creature may attack if frightened. We'll never know—Manuel Garza can't tell us—what happened in the store. Schmidt's blood level indicates he was drunk. He was abusive earlier in the day to you and to the girl. He may have threatened to storm up the stairs and rouse Mrs. Garza. What if Schmidt shouted, bulled his way past Manuel? If Manuel thought his mother was in danger, what would he do? And"—now his voice was steely—"the facts are irrefutable: Schmidt was killed by blows to the back of his head from the pottery pig found in the cleaning bucket; Manuel's fingerprints are on the pig; Manuel's fingerprints are on the bucket which contained water, ammonia, and blood; Manuel's fingerprints are on the mop used to clean up the blood on the floor of the store; Manuel's jeans were streaked with blood; Manuel's shoes carried traces of blood. So," he flipped shut the folder, stood, "the DA's office will decide tomorrow what charges to file."

I stood, too, but I didn't intend to leave. Not yet. "You won't listen about the gold. But Julian Worth believed me, and Worth knew Ed Schmidt as well as anyone ever did. Julian Worth died for that gold."

"Mrs. Collins"—he leaned forward, his voice dangerously quiet—"every mention of gold has come from you. It's your invention. I don't give a damn what Worth did or said. I don't care why he went to the store. I talked to dozens of people this afternoon and everyone who spoke with Worth said the same: his color was bad, he was short of breath. We checked, he had a bad heart. Who knows why he went up those steps? Maybe he got to feeling real sick and ducked through the door to the office area. Maybe he wasn't thinking too straight and figured if he got upstairs somebody could help him. All we know is he went up those stairs, got dizzy, and fell. He was an old man and he fell. And if there was cocaine hidden somewhere, it's gone now. With Mrs. Garza's permission, we searched every foot of that store. No drugs. And"—his voice was sardonic—"no gold. What we have is a murder case and it's solved. Case closed, Mrs. Collins."

I drove to Mi Tierra, had a chicken-and-rice chalupa with sour cream and guacamole, drank several glasses of iced tea. Maybe it was the food, maybe the caffeine, maybe sheer desperation, but I headed back to La Mariposa and I had a plan of attack. I tried not to think how little time remained and how clever—and lucky—I would have to be.

When I reached the lobby, I went directly to the

door leading to Maria Elena's quarters. I rang the bell.

"Excuse me." The call came from behind me. The voice was high and querulous. "Can I help you?"

I looked toward the chili-cart desk. A woman I'd not seen before nodded formally. She was close to my age—white hair piled atop a regal head, the familiar long-jawed face, myopic eyes behind thick glasses, a prim mouth.

"I must see Maria Elena." And I hoped a meeting with her would be more successful than my encounter with Borroel.

The woman behind the cart shook her head, her white hair glistening in the golden glow of an amber-shaded wall sconce. "I'll be happy to take a message, but Maria Elena is engaged this evening."

"She will see me," I said crisply. "I am Henrietta Collins, and I've come from the police station. I have news about Manuel."

She surveyed me from head to foot, calibrating my dress, age, and social status, picked up a phone and punched. She spoke softly, hung up. She looked toward me, pushed the glasses higher on her nose. "The door is unlocked. You may go through and go past the entry room into a corridor. It leads to the family room. Maria Elena is there."

I followed directions, passing through the simple yet elegant room where I'd spoken with Maria Elena yesterday. I pushed through the interior door and stepped into a corridor. Light glowed ahead through a curved archway.

I have occasionally been the focus of group attention—at seminars, when teaching, the odd speech. But when I stepped through that archway, I realized I was facing the most rapt attention I would likely ever have. At any other time, I would have immersed myself in the beauty of that long, wide room—the soft apricot walls, the red-tiled floor, the enormous Guerrero lacquerware trays and brilliant sārapes on two walls, a wall of bookcases filled with pottery of every age and style, from Guadalajara to Oaxaca, sturdy nineteenth-century Spanish green wooden straight chairs with woven cane bottoms, a cluster of jaunty wooden pigs near the Talavera tiled fireplace, curved sabino wood chairs covered with age-mellowed leather. But not now, not with a frozen tableau of familiar faces turned toward the doorway.

I rapidly cataloged those intent figures:

Frank's hands were planted firmly on his thighs and he leaned forward, his face creased in a querulous frown, like a man too tired to think and uncertain he understood the conversation.

Isabel was curled on a white wicker couch with bright flowered cushions, her beautiful face smooth and enigmatic, elbow propped on the couch arm, legs tucked to one side, apparently as relaxed as a sleepy cat, except for too-bright eyes that probed my face.

Tom stood behind his mother's couch, his broad face puckered in a worried frown that was amazingly similar to his father's.

Tony gripped the bronze pole of a majestic white-maned carousel horse with a pink bridle, gaudy reins bright with glass jewels, and pink stirrups. Tony's eyes glittered with a fervid eagerness. If murder distressed Frank, it excited Tony.

Celestina looked even more petite than usual, perched on the edge of a long bench that must once have graced a mission church. Her expression was sour, her eyes cold. She still did not like anybody very much, and that included both her siblings and the intruder in the doorway.

Maria Elena stood in front of the fireplace, her long, slender hands clasped before her. Her shoulders drooped beneath her delicate cotton blouse. She did not look as tall and regal as when we'd met, fear tightening her muscles, anxiety etching itself in sharp lines on her once merry face.

Rick and Iris shared a sofa, sitting stiff and straight with a cushion between them. Rick's glance slid away from me and Iris's gaze dropped, too, her face turning a bright pink. I wondered if that space between them meant disagreement on their course. They had followed a definite course of action with, to my mind, disastrous results. Or whether it simply revealed reserve in front of the gathered family.

Rick's mother Magda sat in an oversize wicker chair. One hand nervously worked the fringe on a cushion. She looked at me, then at her son, her gaze guarded.

Susana was at my far right, obviously as distant from Tony as possible in that long room. She stood quite straight and tall, head up, eyes burning with intensity, perhaps with even more than their usual fire. One hand restlessly rubbed the rim of a waist-high burnished jar with a glorious peacock against a bright red background.

In all the room, only one face was not turned toward the archway. Manuel sat on the floor, knees to his chin, arms loosely circling his legs, his placid gaze on his mother's face, his lips curved in a gentle smile.

I'd not expected this assembly, but, if I could, I would use it to advantage. Obviously, Maria Elena had called the family into council. I didn't know how long they'd been gathered, what had been said. I had to tread carefully. All I had to help me was my conviction that Ed Schmidt had stolen the antique gold and that

Julian Worth was pushed to his death. I felt certain that my claims about the gold and about Worth would never be repeated by Borroel. He didn't believe me, and he never volunteered information. Rick and Iris had lied and lied about the gold. I didn't need to worry about them telling anyone. I would hoard my knowledge until I could use it with force. But for now—

"I've just come from the police station." I may not often have an audience, but I knew how to capture this one. I spoke distinctly, forcefully, and with measured cadence. "Detective Borroel will consult with the district attorney's office tomorrow about bringing charges against Manuel."

Manuel's smile never wavered.

Maria Elena's face aged as I watched, her cheeks sagging, her lips drooping. But it wasn't Maria Elena who mattered, not at this moment. Frank stared at the floor. Isabel toyed with a lock of her honey bright hair, her face remote. Tom looked anxiously at his grandmother. Celestina's eyes narrowed behind her wire-rimmed glasses. Tony glanced at Manuel, looked quickly away, his face in a troubled frown. Rick clenched his hands into tight fists, his eyes dark with horror. Iris shuddered. Magda clasped her hands tightly together, looked toward Manuel in dismay. Susana rubbed the rim of the vase, around and around, but she watched her husband, not Manuel.

I pointed at Manuel, resting contentedly near his mother. "If anyone here can tell us anything about Ed Schmidt, now is the time. If not, the police are going to arrest Manuel, take him to jail, take his clothes away, put him in coveralls—"

Maria Elena, bred to courtesy, always thoughtful of others, was too distraught to wait for me to finish. She broke in, "Please, please, my children, speak. One of

you knows why that man was in Tesoros. Tell me."
Maria Elena's voice was high, quavering. She looked
deep into the eyes of each of her children and their
spouses.

The silence was taut, pulsing with alarm and with
fear. When no one spoke, Maria Elena spread out her
arms in appeal.

"Mother." Frank was across the room, reaching out
to his mother.

She held up both hands and he stopped a foot away,
his head jerking back as if he'd been slapped.

I threw gasoline on the open flame. "Frank knew Ed
Schmidt. Frank, why did you meet with Schmidt?" He
was as good a place to start as any.

Frank's uncertain face turned ashy white. He looked
stunned, a fighter popped by an uppercut he never saw.

Isabel was on her feet and across the room with the
lithe ferocity of a jungle cat. Her delicate face sharpened by rage, her sultry eyes glistening with icy deliberation, she came to her husband, gripped his arm, then
faced the others. "All of you dealt with Ed. I know it
and I won't stand here and let Frank be treated like a
common criminal. All of you had dealings with Ed.
Oh, no one spoke about it. Of course not. You"—an
accusing finger pointed at Maria Elena—"expected
Tesoros to make money, but you forbade Tony to buy
from Ed. We've missed out on a lot of money that
could have been made. But we all knew who to call
when we wanted a little something special and we
wanted it cheap, cheap, cheap. Nobody was better than
Ed at bringing home a shipment of goods with a few
extras well hidden." She tossed her thick mane of burnished honey hair. "Ask Tony about the silver bracelets for all his little friends. Ask Susana about the
marijuana that she keeps in a coconut bank carved like

a dancing dog. Ask Celestina about that garnet necklace, the heavy beaten-silver one—"

Celestina jumped to her feet, shouting, "That's a lie, a lie, a lie," but she didn't look toward her mother.

Tony jammed a hand through his thick black curls. He, too, avoided his mother's gaze. And his wife's cold measuring glance. He blustered, "If a man can't deal occasionally with an old friend, I don't know what the world's coming to. Ed had some good deals sometimes. What's wrong with that?" His voice trailed away and he pulled at the collar of his knit sport shirt.

"Cocaine?" Maria Elena's face was terrible in its anger.

"Mother, no. Never." Frank faced her, his trembling hand outstretched.

"Absurd," Celestina sniffed, but her eyes slid hungrily from one face to another.

"Bracelets, not drugs." Tony almost managed his usual insouciant smile. "Come on, Mama, you know us better than that. And the police looked, they looked everywhere. Nothing."

Frank said urgently, "Tony's right, Mother. The police checked every vase, every corner, every shelf in the storeroom. There are no drugs in Tesoros. Someone got them from Iris, and who knows where they are. But it doesn't have anything to do with us."

I knew better. It had everything to do with Tesoros because it was gold and not cocaine. The timing of the theft, the arrival of the gold last week, all proved, at least to me, that Tesoros was the very heart of the scheme, Tesoros and its annual auction that drew a handful of very, very rich collectors, gave those collectors a bona fide reason to be in La Mariposa. Someone in this room was at ease because the mission had been accomplished. There was no gold found in the police search because one of the Garzas had already made delivery.

Susana said sharply, "Ed Schmidt was a terrible man. He may have put drugs in that wardrobe simply to involve Tesoros. He was jealous of us. He hated us. And what if he somehow got a key to Tesoros? What if he came in that night and Manuel found him and—" She broke off when Maria Elena's head swiveled toward her. "Or," she said hurriedly, "maybe someone was with him and they quarreled about the drugs and that person killed him."

Isabel looked around the room, at the stricken faces of her husband's siblings, and smiled, a slow, satisfied smile full of malice.

"Someone, someone," Maria Elena said bitterly. "We have to find this person. Don't you see? If we don't—" Her voice broke.

"Mother, Tony and I will see to it," Frank said importantly. "We'll hire a private detective, see what we can find out about Ed. Don't you worry. We know Manuel could never hurt anyone. It will all come right." His voice had the same tone a parent uses to dismiss fears of the bogeyman.

"Tomorrow." Maria Elena pressed her hand against her trembling lips. She looked down at Manuel.

Manuel smiled and it was as if a shaft of sunlight pierced a purple cloud. He was a center of light, surrounded by darkness.

That smile caused an instant of stricken silence, then voices sounded together. Susana insisted, "There had to be someone with Ed." Celestina snapped, "Why borrow trouble? They can't prove anything about Manuel!" "We all know it wasn't Manuel," Magda said sharply. Tony shrugged. "Who knows what will turn up?" Isabel favored Tony with a smile, her venom spent. Frank's shoulders slumped. He looked at his mother hopefully. "Don't worry, Mother, Tony and I'll see to everything tomorrow. And now, we'd better go. You're tired. We'll see to everything tomorrow." And he turned away. Celestina was already scooting through the archway, Susana close behind. Tony clapped his hands. "Remember, tomorrow afternoon everybody needs to be on hand to help with the auction preview." Isabel added cheerily, "And, of course, we're having the party tomorrow night." Only Rick and Iris and Tom were silent, Rick staring at the floor, his mouth a tight line, Iris clutching his arm and looking up at him anxiously, Tom hurrying after his parents.

I stepped to one side of the archway as they fled the room. Rick was moving fast, pushing Iris ahead of him.

I stepped in front of him. "Oh, Rick, Iris. I've missed seeing you all day." I gave them a bright smile, clearly visible to Maria Elena.

Rick was trying to sidestep.

I turned, slipped my arm through his and said low enough that only he could hear, "Come to my room. Make sure no one sees you. If you do not come within fifteen minutes, I will return here and tell Maria Elena about the gold."

A bolt of electricity couldn't have shocked him more. His face looked like putty in a hot sun, gray and soft.

I gave his arm a squeeze, flashed another smile for any watching eyes, though the others seemed to have left without paying any attention to us, then turned back toward Maria Elena.

She was at the fireplace, looking up at a portrait of all the family.

In the sudden quiet after the departure of the others, my shoes clicked loudly on the tile floor.

She faced me, and I was shocked at how old and frail she appeared.

I wished I could promise success. I couldn't do that. "Maria Elena, I know you might be tempted to cancel the auction preview tomorrow afternoon if Manuel is arrested. Please don't do that. Keep everything on schedule."

Her eyes blazed with sudden hope. "What are you going to do?"

I was not as old as she, but my bones ached with fatigue. I was guessing and groping. I didn't dare tell her what I hoped to do. I answered indirectly. "My husband was a correspondent in England during World War Two. He covered the Battle of Britain. Whenever things got really tough later in life, he said he remembered the RAF pilots. When the sirens pealed, they ran to their Spitfires and went up against enormous odds, time after time. They called it scrambling." I took a deep breath. "I'm going to scramble."

I opened my door at the whisper of a rap.

Rick and Iris slid inside.

I waved Iris toward the bed, Rick to the easy chair. I remained standing.

Rick rubbed hard at his goatee. "Look, Mrs. Collins, we've got to get it straight. There was cocaine in the wardrobe." He looked at me earnestly, eyes wide, long face solemn.

I almost told him he'd better study politicians at press conferences if he intended to make a career of lying. But there was no time to waste. "Give it up, Rick. I know. I was on the wire desk at my daughter's newspaper when the stories came over about the robbery at the National Museum of Anthropology. The thief took his pick from the greatest collection of ancient gold ever placed on exhibit. That thief was Ed Schmidt. He brought the gold to Tesoros and someone hid it in the wardrobe. Rick, that someone comes from a short list—Frank, Isabel, Celestina, Tony, Susana." I looked at his young, frantic face and wondered if I should add his name to that list. But first there was something I had to know, a fact that would determine everything I was going to say to Rick. "Rick, where were you and Iris this afternoon?"

"This afternoon—" He looked bewildered at my sudden shift.

"Between two-thirty and three-thirty?" That was when Julian Worth died. I watched his face and Iris's.

Iris's face flushed, a becoming rose stained her cheeks. She jerked her eyes away from me, stared fixedly at her hands clasped in her lap.

Rick avoided my gaze, too. "Well," he mumbled, "we were at Iris's place. Uh, we cleaned up the mess. Yeah, we put everything back where it belonged."

I grinned. No wonder the phone went unanswered when I called Iris's apartment. Thank God for sex. I liked these kids. I wanted them to be happy. How sweet that they were old-fashioned enough to be uncomfortable at the prospect of discussing afternoon delight with Iris's grandmother's best friend. No doubt they would have been shocked had I told them I hoped they always found such pleasure together.

I made it easy. "Oh yes," I said briskly, "the apartment needed a lot of work. But you're certain of the time?"

Iris leaned forward eagerly, the becoming flush beginning to fade. "Oh, yes, I'm sure. On our way home, we passed the high school not far from where I live and the kids were coming out and that means it had to be two-thirty." She looked at Rick. "Don't you remember?"

Rick scratched his goatee. "I wasn't paying any attention, but it was the middle of the afternoon." I understood. He was not at that point a young man with time on his mind.

Iris's transparent relief in focusing on a subject far, far from their activity at the apartment sealed my conviction they were indeed at her apartment during the critical period. And that's all I needed to know to be sure it was not Rick who conspired with Ed Schmidt, not Rick who pushed an old man down steep metal steps.

"I'm glad you were not here." I looked at them gravely. "The murderer killed again this afternoon."

Rick jerked forward in his chair. Iris gasped.

"This morning I talked to an old friend of Ed's. I told him about the gold—"

Rick winced.

"—he won't give you away, Rick. He won't give anyone away. He came to Tesoros this afternoon. He went from one person to another—Frank, Isabel, Celestina, Tony, Susana—and minutes later, he was dead at the foot of the circular staircase."

Rick came to his feet, pulling air into his lungs. "God, you scared me for a minute. Look, I heard all about it. Some old man got dizzy—"

"He got pushed." I walked close to him, looked up into dark, worried eyes. "How much help are you going to give a killer, Rick?"

He pressed his fingers hard against his face, let his hands fall. "No, no."

"The same person hid the gold in the wardrobe, Rick."

He reached out, grabbed one of the bedposts, held tight. "It's too late," he said dully. "The police searched. They looked everywhere, Celestina told me about it. If the"—he paused, still unwilling to admit to the gold—"the stuff's gone, what difference will it make now what it was?"

"It makes a difference. It makes a hell of a difference to you and Iris." My voice was cold. My eyes bored into his. "You do realize, Rick, that you and Iris committed a felony by taking possession of goods you knew to be stolen; goods, in fact, that not only were stolen but were priceless objects being hunted by police around the world."

"You can't prove it." He was a dog at bay, ready to jump for my throat.

Iris wriggled uncomfortably

"Yes, I can. And I will." It was hard to say it, hard to put this kind of pressure on Iris. I ached for her.

Iris began to cry, little sobs that made her shoulders shake.

I wanted so much to move forward, comfort her. I wanted to put my arms around her and tell her everything was all right.

But it wasn't all right.

Rick reached out, pulled Iris to her feet, held her tight. He glared at me over the dark head pressed against his chest. "The stuff's gone. It doesn't matter what you say. It's your word against ours."

"Not if I find the gold." I took a deep breath. From here on out, I was pitting myself against this frightened young man, against a wily murderer, against a rabid collector who didn't care how much blood had been shed in pursuit of golden artifacts. "You see, I know the gold is in La Mariposa." If it wasn't, Maria Elena's heart would be broken and Manuel would go to jail.

Dammit, I was sure of it. Almost sure of it.

If Rick had looked like old putty in Maria Elena's living room, now his face was the color of custard. "Uncle Frank?" he whispered.

"One of them; maybe Frank, maybe not. But you're going to help me find the gold, Rick, or I am going to call Detective Borroel." I reached for my purse, pulled out my cell phone. I fished out my small notebook, flipped it open, read the number. My hand was poised above the phone. Yes, it was a colossal bluff. But Rick could have no way of knowing Borroel had dismissed the gold as absurd, an old woman's flight of fancy. "The police didn't find anything when they searched Tesoros. But what will happen if they search La Mariposa? Do you want the police to search La Mariposa, find the gold? Can't you see the headlines now?" My voice capitalized the words, "STOLEN TREASURE FOUND IN RIVER WALK HOTEL or TESOROS MURDER LINKED TO ANCIENT TREASURE." I punched the cell phone on. "How will Maria Elena like those headlines? And how do you think you and Iris will find the city jail?" I punched in the first digit of the number.

Rick flung up a hand. "Wait, wait a minute. Please, Mrs. Collins." He pressed his chin against the top of Iris's head.

I depressed the end button.

Iris pulled back from his chest, looked up at him, her face tear-streaked. "Rick, it's okay. It doesn't matter. I'll go to jail."

At that moment, I wasn't nearly as enchanted with youthful love. This was no time for Iris to offer herself as a sacrifice to the Garza family's reputation. But I didn't speak to her. "Rick, do you want Iris in a holding cell? Ever visit one on a sociology-class tour? Do you know what might happen—"

"Oh, God," he said violently, "I wish we'd never found the damn stuff. I wish—"

Iris flung herself toward the bed. "It's my fault. Everything's my fault. That man and Manuel—" She huddled on the bed, sobbing.

Now I did move, reached out, grasped a trembling hand. "Iris, listen to me." She was too fragile to bear this. Even to save Manuel, I couldn't permit her to suffer like this. "You didn't steal the gold." I felt like shouting it, but no one must hear these words. I kept my voice down, but she must have heard the steel in my words. She lifted a blotchy face to stare at me. "Iris, you didn't hide the gold. You didn't club down Ed Schmidt. Yes, you found it, but you did the right thing. You took it to Rick."

I looked at him, slumped against the old-fashioned wardrobe, misery in every line of his body. I ached for him, too, and that made my voice gentle. "Rick, stop beating up on yourself. You did your best. But now it's time to do your best again. There's a murderer in Tesoros and it isn't Manuel. You can save Manuel. It's up to you."

"Manuel could have heard Schmidt." The words were tortured. "That's what the police think. God, maybe they're right. Schmidt was there because he thought the gold might be hidden somewhere. Maybe Manuel heard him and came downstairs." Tears glistened in Rick's eyes. He was thinking that if he and Iris hadn't hidden the gold, Schmidt would never have forced his way into the showroom and Manuel would not have killed him.

I said gently, "Rick, tell me about Manuel."

His lips trembled. He was trying not to cry. "He's so helpless." Rick tried to control his breathing, but the words were still choked. "He gets really nervous anywhere but home. If they put him in jail—"

"We aren't going to let that happen." I held his gaze. "Rick, can you understand when Manuel uses his hands to make shadows?"

He nodded, his lips pressed hard together.

"He tells simple stories, isn't that right?" I remembered the quick flicker of his hands, the stick figure running away. "Someone's at the door, a dog ran by, he's drinking a cup of cocoa?"

"Yes." Rick used the back of his hand to swipe at his reddened eyes. "Just what he sees."

"Then how could Manuel lie, Rick?" It was this truth that Borroel didn't understand or wouldn't accept. Manuel Garza was incapable of deception. "Don't you see? Manuel couldn't have committed the murder because he found the body on the River Walk. But Schmidt was killed by the pottery-bank display. If he wasn't clubbed down there, his body would not have been there and wouldn't have to be moved, leaving a bloody trail that Manuel tried to clean."

Rick's face lightened. It was like watching the sun spill into a dungeon, dispersing the phantasms of the night. "No," his voice lifted, "no, Manuel can't lie. He could never lie. Look," he was eager, his eyes bright, "we'll explain to the police. Then they'll leave Manuel alone."

"Detective Borroel's nobody's fool." Even if he'd ignored my theories, the man was good and smart and clever. But he was a cop with a cop's mind for evidence. I ticked off the facts for Rick: "Manuel was there. Manuel got his pail and water and cleaned up the blood trail. Manuel's fingerprints are on the pottery pig that killed Schmidt—"

Rick's eyes widened. He didn't know about the fingerprints.

"—Manuel's clothes and shoes were bloodstained. That's what Borroel sees. What we tell him about Manuel is irrelevant. Borroel's got the evidence. So, yes, you're right about one thing, Rick. If you and Iris hadn't taken the gold, Schmidt wouldn't have died. But Schmidt's the one who showed up drunk at Tesoros, ready to brawl. And you and Iris didn't steal the gold and you didn't batter Schmidt. But if you continue to lie about the gold, Manuel will go to jail."

"I don't want Manuel to go to jail." Iris's soft voice shook.

"I don't either." Rick sat down beside her on the bed, gripped her hand. He looked up at me. "What can we do?"

"Find the gold." Now was time to offer a carrot or the closest equivalent I had. "I think there's a way I can find the gold and no one will ever know." I didn't owe Detective Borroel a damn thing. Saving Manuel came first. I'd worry about the gold later. And there might possibly be a way to achieve it all, though I didn't intend to spell it out for Rick. The scramble had begun.

twelve

WEDNESDAY morning I drove south on Alamo to St. Mary's, turned left and found a Pig Stand restaurant, so old-fashioned I could have been on a road journey across America in the 1950s. I wanted breakfast and privacy. The restaurant was almost full, but I could be certain no one from La Mariposa or Tesoros was there. Most of the customers were working people en route to jobs. The conversation level was loud, a jukebox played Mexicali Rose, the coffee was hot and fresh, the pig in a blanket tasty. I had a booth near the jukebox, but that was fine. I didn't want to talk. I wanted to study the slim folder that had been pushed beneath the door of my room at shortly after six that morning.

The pale blue folder had no identifying tabs. I knew the source. I riffled through the pages. Rick may not have wanted to cooperate, but my quick scan told me he'd done everything I asked. And even more. Way to go, son. Maybe, just maybe we could pull off a scam right on the level of the original theft.

I unfolded a double sheet and spread it out, taking care to stay free of the sticky maple syrup container. I supposed the drawing had been made by Rick, a precise floor-by-floor rendering of both Tesoros and La

Mariposa. The showroom and back offices of Tesoros were on the River Walk level. Also on the River Walk level was a closed portion of the building that ran beneath La Mariposa. This area served as a basement, containing heating and cooling units, a laundry, and supply closets. The lobby of La Mariposa, the meeting rooms, and the wing with rooms one through six were on the ground floor that opened to the street. Maria Elena's apartment was also on the ground floor. Her apartment was above Tesoros. The second floor was devoted entirely to La Mariposa. Tony and Susana's apartment was on the third floor.

I looked especially closely at the access to the circular staircase. There were three doors on that landing: one led to the stairs up to the second floor of La Mariposa and to Tony and Susana's third-floor apartment, the second opened into the serene room where I first spoke with Maria Elena, the third provided access to the ground-floor hallway of La Mariposa. Maria Elena could also leave her apartment from that first room by stepping into the main lobby.

As I had asked, Rick had marked the location of the bedrooms—Maria Elena's on the street side of that apartment, Manuel's on the River Walk side. I tried to picture Manuel's descent on Monday night. His room was indeed over part of the main showroom of Tesoros. Yet the building which housed Tesoros and La Mariposa was very old, with foot-thick walls to keep out heat and cool. I suspected it would take a great deal of noise to rouse Manuel. Yet, the quarrel between Schmidt and his murderer, no matter how intense and violent, surely was not loud enough to permeate those walls. But there could be a heating register, some alteration in the original structure where sound might pass through. If only Manuel could speak.

I sipped coffee, studied the drawings. Manuel found Schmidt's body on the River Walk ... I sipped my coffee. What if Manuel had been awake late Monday night? Maria Elena said he often wandered about the apartment at night. Certainly it was possible that he might sometimes stand on his balcony, looking out into the magic of the night, watching the play of moonlight on the still water, taking pleasure in the passage of the occasional solitary pedestrian, smiling as the nocturnal creatures—cats, raccoons, possums— took possession of the River Walk. If he was on his balcony on Monday night, then at the very least he saw Schmidt enter Tesoros. Manuel lived in a restricted world, a world of definite order. He would know the pulse of the night. He would know the door opening into Tesoros at night was wrong. Yes, that's how it must have happened. He either saw Schmidt enter or he saw the murderer dragging out the body.

If he saw Schmidt enter, he might dress and go downstairs. But if that was so, the timing would likely be that Manuel would have arrived soon after the murder and while the murderer was moving the body. It was equally possible that Manuel looked down from his balcony and saw the body. In fact, Manuel "said" that he saw the body on the River Walk. But he had not been asked if he had seen anyone. Would his swift-moving hands then picture an opening door, a moving figure?

I tried to recreate the night. Schmidt entered Tesoros, there was a quarrel, the attack. The murderer turned off the lights and pulled the body out onto the River Walk, intending to push Schmidt into the river, then clean up the store.

And here came Manuel.

Yes, that was my guess. Manuel saw someone pulling a body from the store. This would have been a scene played out in darkness, the figures dimly seen, unrecognizable. But Manuel was disturbed enough to go downstairs. Moving slowly as he always did, Manuel dressed and went down the circular staircase. But, and this was the critical point, it was Manuel who turned on the lights, the golden swath that spilled out of the open front door, revealing blood and death.

Where was the murderer then? Likely, on the River Walk. The sudden harsh brightness must have been an ugly, heart-stopping shock. The murderer darted away from that merciless revealing stream, probably hiding in the shadows beneath the stairway to La Mariposa. When Manuel turned back into Tesoros, going for the mop and pail, the murderer escaped, either slipping back through the store, carefully avoiding Manuel, then up the circular stairway if the murderer was Tony or Susana, or, in the case of Frank or Isabel or Celestina, melting into the night and returning home.

But when did the murderer go to the apartment house and set the fire? The murder must have occurred before the fire. There simply wasn't time enough for the quarrel, the murder, and the removal of the body to have occurred after the fire. It didn't take Rick and Iris and me that long to reach Tesoros, and when we found Manuel he'd already mopped his way out to the River Walk.

That had to mean that Schmidt's body had remained inside Tesoros when the murderer hurried across the river to set the fake fire. Once the gold was retrieved from Iris, the murderer returned to Tesoros to move the body out onto the River Walk. It was then that Manuel looked down from his balcony.

I shook my head, uncertain. Manuel worked at a slow pace. He had mopped from the pottery-bank display island to the front door by the time Rick and Iris and I arrived at Tesoros.

I wished I could better estimate how long we took after we first found Iris. First, we consoled Iris, then we talked. It was I who finally urged the return to Tesoros.

Manuel would be no help in determining how long he had mopped. I was sure of that.

But if Manuel was attracted downstairs by what he had seen from his balcony, could he tell us who the murderer was? No. The body was moved in darkness. All Manuel would have seen was a figure.

I finished my coffee, refilled the cup from the plastic carafe. It was helpful to have a clearer view of what happened Monday night. I wondered if Borroel would listen to me, then pushed the thought aside. I wasn't counting on Borroel. I had my own agenda, one he would never approve.

I hunched over the floor plan of La Mariposa. I knew the layout, of course: the stairs from the River Walk to the lobby, the door into the lobby from street level, the big archway leading from the lobby to the meeting rooms now set up for Thursday morning's auction, the hallway behind the chili-cart desk leading to the rooms on my floor, the stairs just past the chili cart leading up to the second floor.

I smiled at the neat precision of the drawing. On the street level floor, there were rooms on either side of my corridor. There were twice as many rooms on the second floor because the space included the area devoted to the lobby and the meeting rooms on the street floor.

I counted the rooms, six on my floor, twelve on the second floor, making La Mariposa more of a small hotel than an actual bed and breakfast. Three rooms were occupied on my floor, four on the second. An asterisk marked one room. I glanced at the legend below. The asterisk was followed in neat printing by: "Not Attending Auction."

Rick had listened well. I had no interest in the Wallaces from Canton, Ohio, in room 9. But I had a great deal of interest in the other guests, the Harrisons in room 2, Cara Kendall in room 4, Bud Morgan in room 8, Joshua Chandler in room 12, and Kenny King in room 14, all invited guests to the annual Tesoros auction.

If Borroel had given me a chance, I would have laid it out for him. The grand exhibition of ancient gold at the Museum of Anthropology in Mexico City was a stellar event in the world of antiquities, running throughout the summer. The robbery could have occurred at any time during that period. I was sure Ed Schmidt had been in the district several times since summer began. So why did the theft occur when it did? Because the quicker the thief disposed of the gold, the shorter the period he would have it in his possession and the less danger of exposure he faced. Therefore, the sale of the gold had already been arranged. That was the only smart way to set it up. Who has the money or the lust for possession to buy that kind of treasure? Very, very rich collectors. Where did a handful of such collectors turn up every year? At the annual auction at Tesoros. Yes, I felt certain that the entire transaction had been planned long in advance, the date selected for the theft, the gold brought to Tesoros and hidden in the wardrobe to await the arrival of its purchaser.

All would have gone according to plan if it weren't for a young woman's curiosity. For want of a nail . . .

But I was confident that once the murderer had retrieved the gold from Iris, the rest of the plan went into effect. I knew that because Maria Elena had permitted a police search of Tesoros and the searchers found nothing. To me, that meant the transfer had been made, gold for money. I tapped the rooms of the auction guests. Yes, I was certain the antique gold was still close at hand, hidden in the room of one of the guests, guests who would be at La Mariposa until noon tomorrow, when the auction ended.

I had to figure out which one had the gold. I had to do that today. I had to narrow down my search this morning because the only chance I would ever have to find the gold was this afternoon. The guests would be engaged from one to three at a preview of the auction items. By tonight, if the pieces all clicked into place, I would be equipped to trap a killer. No, I had no idea how that could be accomplished. That was definitely the next challenge on a slippery slope that could end in disaster at any moment. But first, I had to find the gold.

I slipped the drawings to the bottom of the folder, lifted up six sheets of paper.

The guests, rich, powerful, sophisticated, imbued with the status that wealth creates, they were now my quarries.

The first sheet was handwritten in obvious haste, the writing deeply impressed on the page:

Mrs. Collins—The material contained in the following pages is highly confidential. Should it be revealed that this information was made available to you, the damage to Tesoros would be incalculable, irreparable. I have to depend upon your sense of honor never to tell anyone about this betrayal of client confidentiality. As you will see, we go to great lengths to obtain personal information about our highly valued customers. Maria Elena has always made the point that the more you know about a client, the more you can sell to that client. There is no intent to take advantage of a client. The hope is always to be prepared to respond to that client's needs and interests. Maria Elena began the program of obtaining personal information about prized customers after an incident early in her career which always saddened her. The client was an elderly woman who collected straw mosaics. Maria Elena had obtained a mosaic picturing the Boy Heroes jumping from the cliff rather than surrender to the Americans. The woman looked at the mosaic, broke into tears. Her only son had died in a firefight in the South Pacific, his valor credited with saving the lives of most of his platoon. Maria Elena realized that sparing clients pain or embarrassment for whatever reason was essential. The most positive result of understanding the circumstances of a client's life is the ability to provide that client with artworks that will have a genuinely personal importance. There are many instances in the history of Tesoros when this kind of information has been invaluable. The invitations to the annual auction are a result of this gathering of information. These are not only customers who buy heavily through the year, these are customers who approach collecting with passion, lifting it to a level of artistry. It is my hope that however you intend to use this information, it will remain confidential.

The scrawled letter was unsigned. Its stiff tenor revealed, as perhaps nothing else could, the despair I'd engendered in Rick. But he'd seen himself with no option. If he didn't produce what I demanded, I would destroy the efforts he had made to protect Tesoros and Maria Elena from a scandal that would explode in the world of art.

I put his note aside, picked up the typewritten sheets:

WILEY AND JOLENE HARRISON, ABILENE, TEXAS

Fifth-generation Texas cattle ranchers. Wiley Harrison's great-grandfather, Jasper, rode into Texas in the 1850s with a sackful of nuggets from the Gold Rush. He bought a head of cattle and from that sprang the great Harrison empire. Wiley's grandfather, Claud, went east to Harvard and met a young heiress from Philadelphia. When she came to Texas, she brought with her a love for fine art and the Harrison family has spearheaded the promotion of arts in central Texas ever since. Wiley's great enthusiasms are rodeoing and ranching. His taste in art is eclectic and the Harrison personal collection includes native artworks from around the world. Jolene searches only for gold, loves to say she and Jasper are soul mates. She prefers unusual pieces, especially crosses and brooches. Last year paid fifty thousand dollars for a brooch with gold in three different hues shaped in a filigree of roses and leaves, with three drops of wreathed leaves centered with rose petals. Wiley is tenacious as a collector, willing to overpay if he wants an object, ready to ignore import/export laws. Wiley has left the running of the ranch to his son-in-

law. He and Jolene spend most of their time traveling in search of art objects. Wiley is in his sixties, has high blood pressure, is easily angered. Jolene pampers him and he never refuses to buy her anything, no matter the cost. Jolene is vivacious and outgoing, an excellent golfer, and as a young woman excelled in barrel racing. Their daughter, Amanda, is a gracious and lovely woman very active in supporting local charities, not a major collector. However, Amanda adores antique dolls and the Harrisons are always eager to add to her collection.

I'd met Jolene Harrison, bony face, bony body, eyes like tar, a resounding raspy voice. Susana had described Wiley as whip-thin and moving like a giraffe with his head poked forward.

JOSHUA CHANDLER, SCOTTSDALE, ARIZONA

Grew up in Charleston, South Carolina. Graduate Wake Forest. Professional golfer, has finished fourth at the Masters, seventh at the U.S. Open. As a golfer, respected but not liked. Never speaks during a round. No personal friends on the tour. Twice divorced. Rumored to have paid huge settlements to avoid messy court battles. Has no apparent interests other than golf and art. Collects widely from American Southwest and Mexico. Interested in Tlaquepaque-style pottery, especially glazed, petatillo works attributed to the artist known as the Yellow Brick Road because of the yellow roads on many pieces. Chandler is in his mid-thirties, remains expressionless at most times, especially when negotiating over price. Refuses to pay more than he deems a piece worth on the market. Stubborn, determined, utterly ruthless when attempting to get a good price. If he can take advantage of a seller, he will.

Susana described Chandler as a man who looked more like a college professor than a professional golfer.

CARA KENDALL, FORT WORTH, TEXAS

Fourth wife of a very old man who owns enough banks and oil wells to start his own third world country. He runs his businesses very much like a third world despot and is reputed to have all the charm of a granite mausoleum. Cara was his secretary. Cara is probably forty-five, admits to thirty-two. Fort Worth society treats her politely but distantly. Cara, however, has achieved stature as a collector. Her collection of wooden puppets created by Alejandro Aguierre was recently featured at a local Fort Worth museum and was widely acclaimed as extraordinary. Cara's infatuation with puppets is extreme. She will talk to a puppet when deciding whether to buy it, ignoring the seller. She is only interested in very rare pieces. She has also amassed a remarkable collection of clay figures created by the renowned Pantaleon Panduro and possesses almost all of his famous bullfighters, a collection without peer and beyond price. She is bad-tempered, irritable, and probably emotionally unstable. Needs constant reassurance of her perspicacity as a collec-

*tor. Succumbs to flattery. Rarity is the trump card
with Kendall.*

I recalled the stretched-face, cherry-lipped blonde
without pleasure. She'd been obviously bored by the
company at the tea Monday and in the lobby Tuesday
she was petulant and demanding. Not, I would think,
a fun customer. But clearly a valued one.

WALTER (BUD) MORGAN,
CHICAGO, ILLINOIS

*Morgan runs his own investment company. His
financial newsletter is considered one of the best
in the country and has a hefty subscription price
of five thousand dollars a year. A bachelor, Morgan spends every free moment collecting. One of
his proudest accomplishments is a room in his
Winnetka home which contains almost fifty table-
ros, scenes made up of Talavera tiles from
Pueblo with their magnificent cobalt blue back-
grounds and rich green and yellow colors. An
entire wall is decorated with pictorial tiles that
picture Mexicans in everyday life in the early
nineteen hundreds. In his forties, Morgan is genial, a raconteur, smokes Cuban cigars bought in
Mexico, fond of unusual beers including a straw-
berry beer from England, and a gourmet. Tesoros sends him gift packages occasionally. He
especially enjoys unusual salsas. When vacation-
ing in Hawaii, Frank and Isabel found a mango
salsa which they sent to him.*

Susana described Morgan as bald and fat. He
shouldn't be hard to identify in this thin crowd.

KENNY KING,
LOS ANGELES, CALIFORNIA

King is a movie producer who specializes in raunchy, quick-take R-rated films that appeal to teenage boys. His movies are cheap to shoot. He casts actors who are just about to hit or actors just past their peak, avoiding star-level salaries. Single, he's in the gossip columns a lot with his love interests, usually wannabe starlets. He's a local boy, went to Beverly Hills High School, his dad a psychiatrist, his mother an English professor, specialty Chaucer. Edging up on thirty, he has a seaside house in Malibu, a quick smile, hard eyes, and a world class collection of massive Aztec sculpture, much of it displayed in an interior garden.

Susana described him as having a red ponytail. I had yet to meet King, but his hair had to be the least interesting aspect of a young man who favored huge and, I was sure, often illegally obtained sculptures of a society that nourished the sun and glorified life by ripping the heart from sacrificial victims.

Five valued guests. One of them had a great deal in common with the Spaniards who rampaged across Mexico in their lust for gold. Missionary Father Bernardino de Sahagún carefully transcribed the feelings of the beleaguered natives who said of Cortés and his men upon their receipt of gifts of gold from Moctezuma:

"It is a certainty that they desire it with a great thirst. Their bodies swell for it. They have a furious hunger for it."

That was four hundred and seventy years ago, but the continuum of human greed apparently never ends. Someone at La Mariposa had a furious hunger, too.

Cell phones aren't secure from electronic eavesdroppers. I found a pay phone on the River Walk and called Maria Elena.

The maid said politely, "I am sorry. Mrs. Garza is not available."

"She will talk to me," I insisted. "Tell her that Henrietta Collins must speak with her."

"She is not at home." There was a sudden quaver in her voice.

"Please," I said quickly, "it's important that I know. Where is she?"

She spoke reluctantly, unwilling to admit the truth. "She and Manuel have gone to the police station."

I hung on to the phone for a moment after I hung up. I'd known it was coming, but I'd hoped we might have today, I'd hoped Manuel would not have to be frightened and bewildered.

Susana's haggard face had the brooding quality of a stone sculpture deep in the Yucatán jungle as she watched me walk through the main showroom of Tesoros. She stood at the cash desk with the prim-faced older woman who had served at the chili-cart desk last night. Susana paused in her obvious role of instructing to stare at me. She wanted to boot me out, but didn't dare. I ignored her and scanned the room. There were a few off-the-River Walk customers, none of the special guests who interested me. I didn't expect to find them here. Their location was unimportant to me until the preview opened in the auction room in half an hour. I knew where to find them and find them I would. But now I needed Rick and I wanted to talk to him without anyone observing our contact.

As I pushed through the rear door into the back hallway, I could feel Susana's consuming stare. The door closed behind me, and it was abruptly as quiet as a monk's cell. I looked up at the circular staircase. The quiet in the big hallway was as oppressive as a heavy, wet snowfall. No wonder Julian Worth's fall wasn't heard by anyone. I hurried, checking the offices and the big showroom. The sound of my footsteps seemed overloud and ominous. No Rick. No Iris.

I clattered up the circular staircase and had to stop at the top to catch my breath. When I opened the door into the hallway of La Mariposa, I saw the maid's cart outside the third doorway. I squeezed past and entered the lobby.

I looked across the sparkling room toward the red velvet hangings. I glimpsed Tony and Celestina. Rick must be in the auction room. I turned toward the chili-cart desk.

The smile on Tom Garza's face slid away faster than a margarita chasing jalapeño-laced chili. I felt like a cat in a dog pound. Obviously, he resented my attack on his father last night. When I placed my hands on the rim of the cart, he stood as stiff as a wooden soldier. "Tom, do you love your grandmother?"

His young face creased in misery. "You tried to get my dad in trouble."

I avoided that bog. And I had to trust Tom. I didn't think he'd had any opportunity to talk with Julian Worth. I'd better have guessed right. "I'm trying to save Manuel. Your grandmother wants me to do this. Will you please take a note to Rick and not tell anyone it came from me?"

I looked up at the massive old clock on the wall

behind him. Twenty-two minutes from now the auction preview would begin. Even as I watched, the hall door opened and Susana scooted across the lobby. Everyone was gathering.

"A note." He rubbed the edge of the old-fashioned ledger where guests were invited to sign their names and share their impressions of La Mariposa. "You are a guest." He spoke slowly. "Every effort is made to satisfy any request made by a guest. Information about guests is never revealed." He took a deep breath, stared at me with puzzled, worried eyes. "If you wish to have a note delivered by the staff, that will be done."

Yes, I was taking a chance, but the clock now stood at twenty to the hour. I yanked out a pad, ripped off a sheet, scrawled, "Urgent. Room 6," folded the paper, handed it to Tom.

I paced in the small room, forcing myself to stop looking at the clock and trying to decide what I could do if Rick didn't respond. At ten minutes to the hour, the sharp knock sounded on my door.

I checked through the peephole. I had no difficulty remembering that I was hunting not only for a thief, but for a killer. The curved glass skewed Rick's oblong face, made even longer by his sleek goatee. I yanked open the door, motioned him inside. Before he could say anything, I outlined what I wanted, precisely and specifically.

He hunched his shoulders, glared at me. "Why—"

"It's better if we don't get into that. And Rick, you've got to hurry. I want everything in here by no later than one-fifteen." That gave him twenty minutes, which should be more than enough. "Finally—"

He was reaching for the door.

"—I want keys to these rooms." I rattled them off.

He froze, looking like a law-abiding burgher face-to-face with a rampaging mob. "You can't—"

"I must."

Lights blazed in the copper chandeliers of the reception area outside the auction room. Crystal champagne glasses glistened on a table near the room. Nodding in satisfaction, Isabel shepherded a waiter with a service cart toward the serving table. She watched as he carefully unloaded the hors d'oeuvre trays. Everything looked fresh and appealing—guacamole, bite-size tostadas topped with chicken, cheese, lettuce and tomato, and picadillo, a spicy meat hash with corn chips.

Susana held open the double doors to the auction room for Tony, who was rolling a dolly with a worn stone statue of a jaguar. One eye still contained gleaming jade. Celestina trotted alongside. "Hurry, Tony. What took you so long? You've been hours."

"Relax, Tina. Once I get this dude on his platform, we're done. Ferocious looking beast, isn't he?" His voice bubbled with good humor.

Celestina shot him a poisonous glance. "Tony, why are you so juvenile? Don't let our guests hear you talk like that."

Tony ignored her, maneuvering the dolly through the doorway with a flourish.

Susana tossed her dark hair and her silver earrings jangled. She, too, watched Tony with disdain. Magda looked irritated. Tony wasn't charming anyone.

I was no more than a couple of feet inside the foyer when Frank barred my way. For once his diffident face looked bullish and determined. Obviously, he'd neither forgiven nor forgotten my demand of last night to know about his association with Ed Schmidt. Just as he stepped in front of me, I saw Isabel's head jerk toward us, her eyes flare. She lifted a hand as if to restrain him, but he was looking at me.

"Excuse me, Mrs. Collins." There was no regret in his deep voice. "I'll have to ask you to leave. This is a private affair and—"

"Maria Elena asked me very particularly to come," I said firmly. "I have a commission from her since she's unable to be here."

That caught him by surprise. Some of the bluster seeped from his voice. "Not here? But she always opens the doors, invites everyone to come in and see what Tesoros has gathered for its most favored customers."

"Not this year. She's at the police station, Frank. With Manuel." I tried to hold his gaze.

But I no longer mattered to him. As clearly as though he spoke, I read in his face the stunning realization that his mother had not called upon him—he looked around the room—or upon any one of her children to accompany her and Manuel to the police station. Clearly she did not trust them and she intended to protect Manuel whatever the cost.

His face perplexed and stricken, Frank turned, seeking his wife. As he moved away, he looked diminished, a man whose world had suddenly been transformed from a familiar and comfortable landscape to uncertain terrain with all paths obscured and no boundaries in place.

Magda stood with her hands on her hips. She gave me a hard look, then turned to follow Frank.

The double doorway to the auction room, painted to appear as the doors of a village church, were now firmly closed. I scanned the foyer. All of the auction guests were there. Jolene Harrison gripped the arm of a tall, too-thin man whose head poked forward on a long neck. She and Wiley were poised like greyhounds waiting for the starter pistol. Cara Kendall gulped down a glass of champagne and leaned forward, her cherry red lips widened in expectation. Joshua Chandler leaned against a wall, a distant look on his sun-burned face, an unlit pipe in his hand. Chandler looked vaguely professorial except for his sunburn. Bald, pudgy Bud Morgan watched the closed doors with avid eyes. Kenny King was unmistakable with his red ponytail and cold gray eyes. His moon face had a doughy, unhealthy look and he looked much older than thirty.

The Garza family had drawn apart in a half-circle, Frank, Isabel, Celestina, Tony, Susana, Magda, Rick. Iris stood a few feet away, her eyes on Rick. Frank waved his hands, pointed toward me. Like marionettes seeking the enemy, their heads swiveled toward me.

I looked up at the oversize clock and moved to the closed double doors. As the clock struck one, I faced the foyer. Ignoring the Garza family, I smiled at the assemblage. "Hello, I'm Henrietta Collins and I want to welcome all of you to the annual Tesoros auction, one of the premier art auctions of the world. I am speaking on behalf of Maria Elena, who regrets that a family emergency has taken her away this afternoon. However, she will be here in the morning when the auction begins at nine. For now, she has asked me to bid you bienvenidos." I stepped to one side and flung open the doors.

On a chutzpah scale, it had to be off the meter and my heart thudded uncomfortably. I hoped my face wasn't as red as Frank's. I hadn't catapulted myself into the limelight to offend the Garzas irremediably, although I was sure that had been the effect. It was a push-the-chips-into-the-pot attempt to convince the auction guests I was Maria Elena's emissary. I would put that position to the test as soon as I could because the time was inexorably dwindling when I could count on these five people being engaged in this room.

The Harrisons beat Cara Kendall through the doorway by a nose. King slouched into the room, his cold eyes scanning the displays. Morgan's thick-fingered hands were outstretched, like a seeking insect's feelers. Chandler drifted to the right, going counterclockwise to the other guests.

Susana stalked toward me, her high heels clicking on the tiled floor. Her eyes glittered with fury. She stood so close I could see the fine drawn lines of her mascara and smell the penetrating scent of Obsession. Vermilion-tipped fingers clutched at her heavy silver necklace. The huge pendant was decorated with symbols from the Aztec Calendar Stone. She kept her voice low, as cognizant of the auction guests as I. "What do you think you're doing?"

"Maria Elena sent me. Now, if you'll excuse me, I have work to do." I brushed past her. As I stepped into the room, the utter quiet assaulted me, a thick, suffocating quality like the airless confines of a huge bank vault, the same sense of unimaginable riches contained within reach.

I've seen vultures circling, huge, powerful birds with predatory eyes, skimming silently on air currents, seeking prey. There was the same aura in this room as the auction guests roved past the tables. There were riches indeed: an entire collection of mid-eighteenth-century paintings, oil on canvas, of the Stations of the Cross, the distinctive use of red, white, and green emphasizing the adaptation of the religious theme to Mexico; a concha from Guanajuato, the twelve-stringed instrument decorated with mother-of-pearl and armadillo shell; a magnificent Danza de los Negritos mask decorated with beads and foil and long silk ribbons; a brilliantly blue-and-white Talavera jar made by the Uriarte family in the late eighteen hundreds; and more and more and more—earthenware statues, animal pottery banks, lacquered dishes and plaques, jungle watercoolers, saddles with silver filigree; and more and more and more.

I looked at the collectors, moving as if in a stately dance, a step here, a glance there, but always their expressions determinedly empty so that their competitors could have no inkling of which pieces they coveted most.

Tony was striding purposefully toward me, no hint of good humor in his handsome face now.

On a high diving board, you can't teeter on the end too long or you'll never dive. Which one first, which one?

Joshua Chandler was nearest, stopping for an instant at a display of almost a dozen alebriges, the fantastic and inventively ominous papier-mâché flying monsters created by Pedro Linares. Chandler picked up a horned green dragon with glistening white teeth and curved red wings. A tiny smile flickered on his smooth sunburnished face.

"Mr. Chandler." I looked into pale green eyes with all the warmth of jammed glacier ice. Up close, I had a clear sense of his muscular grace and power. "Maria Elena wishes, of course, for all the guests to be able to enjoy their visit from beginning to end. She wants to offer transport to the airport after the auction."

"Don't need it. Thanks. Driving." He turned away from me, gently replaced the green dragon, picked up a more serpentine creature with rippling orange-and-bronze-and-gold-striped wings. His back was to me, the message clear.

Tony hung a foot or so back. He obviously didn't want to accost me within hearing of the guests.

I stepped past Tony and smiled at Wiley Harrison. Wiley's face glistened red, too, but from rising blood pressure, not sun. I doubted collecting was going to do too much for his longevity. He poked his narrow head forward, lanky arms folded behind his back, as he studied a jaguar mask from Guerrero dating from the eighteen nineties. "The lord of the animals," Wiley announced, his eyes dreamy, his voice a caress.

I had a sudden uncomfortable feeling he envisioned himself as a jaguar, striding through the night, sinuous and powerful, a force without peer. And yet he was just a man of late middle age with thin strands of graying hair, watery-blue eyes, and a too-tall, too-thin frame. But he was, of course, a very rich man of late middle age with thinning hair, a vacuous gaze, and weedy build.

I stepped close and spoke perhaps a little loudly. "We want to make sure your visit is quite comfortable. Can we give you a ride to the airport?"

Harrison blinked. "Oh, we haven't decided when we're leaving." He spoke absently, his eyes still studying the mask. "May take a little spin down to Oaxaca. But Jolene heard about a new shop in Santa Fe. May spin up there."

Anyone flying went off my list of suspects because no one would be fool enough to check a fortune in stolen gold, and even the most incurious of airport X-ray attendants might wonder about a valise filled with jewelry. So I almost turned away. But because I had spent a lifetime as a reporter—"The sky is blue.

Check it out"—I asked, "So you haven't even bought your airline tickets yet?"

"Don't need tickets when you own the plane, honey." And he hunkered down for an up-front and personal look at the mask. The jaguar's whiskers were made of boar bristle. I wondered if they had an odor.

The tick of an old grandfather clock was loud in the absorbed silence. Fifteen after one. I had to hurry. Out of the corner of my eyes, I saw Tony and Susana in a whispered disagreement.

I skirted the central line of tables. Jolene lifted an elegant necklace of black pearls and gold filigree, touched it to her neck, her smile as dreamy as her husband's. But I didn't need to speak to her. The Harrisons could easily have the stolen gold. A private plane made lots of sense.

Cara Kendall gave me a petulant glare when I stopped beside her. "Don't know why I drove all this way. I simply don't see a thing I want." But her mouth had a secretive little curl.

"I'm so sorry." No need to ask my question. "But I'll certainly tell Maria Elena we've fallen short this year."

She flounced away, but her eyes slid sideways for a swift look at the table with the very rare oil paintings of the Stations of the Cross. I forbore to pursue any philosophical thoughts about her choice.

Bud Morgan watched her go. "Ah, the stage lost quite an actress. Might buy the damn things just to thwart her." He gave me a roguish grin. "And I'm lapsed. What the hell, may lead me back to piety. Heard your offer. Sure. I'd like a lift to the airport. Flying Southwest Friday morning." Then he moved away, his pudgy face intent.

I wasn't surprised to find Kenny King's cold gray

eyes studying the stone jaguar. He ignored me when I
stopped beside him. If I'd sensed athletic power with
Chandler, I had a darker sweep of unease near this
man. "Mr. King, we'll be glad to provide you with
transportation to the airport."

His eyes moved from the jaguar to me. He might
have looked unimpressive, with his round freckled
face, the swaying red ponytail. Instead, I had to force
myself to stand my ground. He was young, but the
eyes that looked at me knew evil I'd never envisioned.
His lips quirked in a grotesque parody of a smile.
"You're so kind to ask. But I won't need any help."
The words were deliberately arch, the tone offensive.

I was the one who turned away.

My heart was thudding as I headed for the doorway,
trying to walk as if in no hurry, glancing about as if
looking for a way to be helpful.

I moved through the open doorway, paused at the
champagne table, said clearly enough for anyone
nearby to hear, "Magda, Isabel, perhaps you should
take trays around. I'm going to check on Maria Elena,
see if she's returned. I'll be back in a few minutes."

I walked slowly, carefully, casually, and then I was
past the red velvet hangings into the lobby. I glanced
at my watch, my thoughts whirling. God, it was already one-thirty. I had so little time.

thirteen

AS I hurried up the hall toward my room, I knew
that everything depended upon Rick. Had he followed my instructions? I was stymied without his help.
I flung open the door, intent on what I should find. I
scarcely glanced at Rick, standing by the end of the
bed. Yes, black-and-rose lacquered trays were there,
on my bed, each with a crystal bud vase with a single
creamy rose, two wineglasses, and a bottle of the finest
California sauvignon blanc. There was also a stack of
downy towels with the La Mariposa crest, a gorgeous
embroidered black-and-yellow monarch. But where
were the keys? They were most important of all. The
keys were essential. Then I saw them, oversize, with
wooden tags bearing their numbers, clutched in Rick's
fist. He held the keys, his long face closed and remote.

I spoke as I moved, grabbing a tray, tucking the
towels beneath one arm, holding out a hand for the
keys. "I don't have time to quarrel, Rick. If I don't
find the gold, Manuel will be arrested, charged, con-
victed. Do you think Maria Elena would rather keep
Tesoros free of scandal or save Manuel?"

I reached for the keys, trying desperately to think. I
had at the most a little more than an hour, and in that
time I might have to search as many as four rooms. I

decided to discard Bud Morgan as a possible buyer of the gold. He'd been casual and open about his airline reservations. There was no possibility the possessor of that ancient and distinctive gold would check it in a bag on an airline, and even the most incurious checkpoint attendant would wonder at a case containing these pieces. Of course, Morgan could have received the treasure and handed it off to a lackey of some sort, or to a lover, servant, confidante. But I didn't believe the person who conspired to buy the most famous missing gold treasure in the world would trust it to anyone else. This was a collector satisfied to enjoy the gold in total secrecy. A collector who would keep that treasure very close at hand and very private.

But which one now possessed the gold? The Harrisons, who could have whatever they wished whenever they wished? Cara Kendall, who accreted things of value to build her own worth? Joshua Chandler, who might be playing the most competitive game of his life? Kenny King, who exuded an aura of sheer evil?

"What are you going to do if you find the gold?" Rick's voice was urgent and scared.

"Use it," I said briefly. "Rick, I want you to go back to the auction room. Wait there for me. If I find the gold, I'll come for you."

"But what will we do with it?" He still held tight to the keys.

I was back on the high dive. Damn if I didn't wish I knew, but there would be a way once I found the gold. I gripped his wrist. "Give me the keys, Rick."

Cara Kendall's room had an overpowering scent, several perfume bottles carelessly unstoppered, potpourri in assorted cut glass bowls. I placed the tray on the writing desk, moving aside a clump of silk blouses. The bed was made, the bathroom clean, but Cara's untidiness gave the room the air of a very expensive jumble sale—dresses draped on the chairs, a wardrobe crammed with more clothes. Did the woman change outfits every half hour?

I worked quickly. She wasn't the likeliest suspect on my list, but she was definitely the likeliest to be the first to saunter out of the auction room, ostensibly bored and unimpressed, making it, in her view, impossible for anyone to detect which objects she wanted. Tomorrow I suspected Bud Morgan would enjoy upping and upping the bids on the paintings of the Stations of the Cross. I felt behind the clothes, checked beneath the extra pillows on the shelf in the wardrobe, peered under the bed, opened the drawers in the chest. Her luggage was locked. Damn and damn and damn. I picked up each piece. No, the cases had to be empty. The weight of the gold would surely be evident.

I was pulling out the draperies when I heard the scrape of a key and the door began to open.

Swiftly, I picked up the stack of towels.

As she stepped into the room and stopped, her eyes flaring, I moved toward her with a smile. "Just checking to make sure you have plenty of towels. And we hope you will enjoy the very special wine." I gestured at the tray on the writing desk. I stepped past her. "Let us know if there's anything at all we can do to make your stay more comfortable."

She pressed a hand against her temple. "I have the worst headache. Such a disappointing preview. And to think I came all this way for a roomful of junk. Get me some alka seltzer."

"Certainly. I'll have some sent right to you."

The door closed on her petulant face.

* * *

Now it was ten minutes to two. My knock was sharp. At the same moment, I turned the key, pushed in the door with my shoulder, the tray carefully upright. The Harrisons' room had an air of casual disarray. I carried the tray to the writing table, pushed aside the rumpled sections of a *USA Today* and an open box of Godiva chocolates. An ornately tooled leather jewel box sat atop the dresser. I lifted the lid and was shocked at the profusion of jewelry—rings, necklaces, bracelets—all in gold. But this wasn't the gold I sought.

Jolene's clothes filled the wardrobe, red and chartreuse and orange blouses, long multicolored cotton skirts. The peculiar bulge in a clothes bag was a shoe shine kit. I scooted aside shoes on the floor, reached up to check out the upper shelf.

The floral suitcases stacked next to the wardrobe were unlocked and empty. A big leather suitcase rested on a luggage rack. I lifted the lid, felt quickly through the shirts. I knelt and looked under the bed.

I gave the room one final sharp survey, then pulled the heavy door shut. I hurried to my room, grabbed a tray, then I ran to the end of the hall and the stairway to the next floor.

It took every bit of courage I had to step into room 14. I'd deliberately chosen to explore the other rooms first. I closed the door behind me, placed the tray on the table. I wanted to be out of here as fast as I could. All right, yes, I was scared of the young man with the moon face and red ponytail and eyes that had seen visions I never wanted to see. But searching this room should only take a moment. The room was almost bare of personal possessions. In the bathroom, a closed shaving kit sat on the towel rack. In the bedroom, there was nothing on the writing table, nothing on the chairs, nothing—

I stared at the fake alligator attaché case on the top the dresser. Yes, I could tell it was fake. The real thing has an unmistakable sheen and texture, attractive to some, repellent to me. But however King felt about alligator leather, it seemed sharply out of character for him to have a cheap case. Even though he dressed at odds with convention, his clothing was expensive and his loafers, as I recalled, the richest of cordovan.

The oddity drew me toward the case, but at the same time my flare of excitement ebbed. Even though La Mariposa was a first class hotel and no guest would ever be concerned about a maid poking into a case, surely no one would be this casual about a fortune in stolen jewelry. But I went ahead and lifted down the case, though when I realized it was unlocked, my momentary interest faded. If King hadn't even bothered to lock the attaché case, its contents must be unremarkable. As the lid rose, I expected to find papers, a script, or perhaps a cell phone or a laptop.

Velvet. My eyes widened. Purple velvet cloth bags. I knew even before I picked up the top bag. So heavy. Lumpy. As I loosened the drawstrings, I was struck by the incredible arrogance of Kenny King, an unlocked case containing stolen gold worth a fortune casually left atop the chest. Arrogance compounded by recklessness?

I lifted the flap, partially pulled out a strand of gold, part of the huge, magnificent necklace from Monte Alban, and looked at richness beyond belief. The gold drops felt oddly greasy. My heart beat fast. Quickly, I pushed the necklace into its covering, put the velvet container back in the attaché case. Now I must get to Rick and—

"I see we have a common interest." The voice was silky, with a touch of amusement, but beneath the light tone anger throbbed, dark and dangerous.

I'd been so absorbed in my discovery, so amazed at the presence of unimaginably beautiful gold, that I'd not heard the door. I jerked around and stared into cold gray eyes with pinpoint black pupils.

King closed the door, leaned back against it, his muscular arms folded. I had a sudden memory of the masks on the wall of Tesoros, one in particular, stark black-and-white, human features with overtones of a reptile. Looking at King's face was like seeing a living representation of that mask, his features utterly motionless, his deep-socketed eyes rounded like an iguana's, his mouth stretched thin like a crawling snake. He looked as immovable and menacing as one of the monolithic sculptures he admired.

Somehow I managed to look at him coolly. And I tucked the case under my arm.

Those round hostile eyes narrowed. "Put the case down, Mrs. Collins."

It surprised me a little that he had remembered my name. He'd left the auction preview much sooner than I would have imagined. But, of course, the auction was not his true reason for coming to La Mariposa.

"No, Mr. King." I'd hoped to find the gold, then enlist Rick's aid. I'd told Rick to return to the auction room, that I'd come for him if I found the gold. But Kenny King had no knowledge at all of what I intended, what I knew, who I was or why I stood in his room clutching a case worth millions of dollars.

He pushed away from the door, stepping as softly and determinedly as any jungle cat. His hands hung loose by his side. His eyes skittered around the room.

I knew I had seconds before those hands closed on my throat. Then, abruptly, he stopped, still a foot away. Was he judging the danger? How to dispose of a body from here?

My arm crooked tightly around the case. "Yes, you'd better think, and think hard. You can't kill me here. Not now, Mr. King. You don't think I'd be fool enough to come in here without a backup? And you can't take this away from me"—I tapped the case—"because the police will be after you immediately. You might as well face the truth. You gambled. You lost. Now, there is a way that you can save yourself from a great deal of interest by the San Antonio police."

The snakelike mouth rippled. I recognized malignant fury. But he waited, his hands dangling by his sides. He was rich, spoiled, vicious, but, for the moment, stymied.

I spoke fast. "I assume you would prefer that the police not know about your involvement in the theft of this gold from the National Museum of Anthropology?" I looked at him steadily. I had to keep him talking, convince him that it would be smart to cooperate with me. "It would be hard to make movies from a Texas prison."

He might be willful and arrogant, but he wasn't stupid. His muscles relaxed. He was no longer poised to jump. For a moment that seemed endless, there was no sound but his light breathing. Then he shrugged. "I have no idea what you're talking about. I've never seen that case you're holding. Now, if you'll excuse me, I'm on my way—" He moved toward the door.

"Just one point before you go." Here it was, the moment I'd worked for, the information I had to have. "Who sold the gold to you?"

His mouth curved in an ugly smile. "What gold, Mrs. Collins?" he asked softly. His hand gripped the door handle.

I walked around the bed, my arm curved around the case, pressing it to my body. There wasn't much room between the bed and the wardrobe. We stood face-to-face. He was so close I could see a fleck of saliva on his thin lips, smell a mixture of cologne and skin. "You can walk out of here without a worry in the world, Mr. King, as soon as you give me that name. If you don't give it to me, I'll tell the police precisely where I found this case"—I held up my hand to forestall him—"and they'll believe me because your fingerprints are all over the gold."

His muscles flexed.

"Don't try it." It was almost a shout.

He stopped, his hands inches from me, large, powerful hands.

"You don't think I'd be stupid enough to come into this room without someone nearby ready to help me?" This was the ultimate bluff. "If I cry out, you're through. And you can save yourself so easily. I'll tell the police I found the gold hidden in Tesoros. How would they ever know it was a lie? The police searched Tesoros yesterday, found nothing. But the gold could have been put there last night. All I need is the name of the person who sold it to you."

Slowly King's hands dropped. Despite the fury glittering in his eyes, there was thought, too.

I played the trump card. "Because it isn't just a matter of stolen gold. It's a matter of murder."

He was as still as a basking lizard.

"You never met the thief, the man who scaled the walls of the National Museum, cut into the cases, grabbed up the gold." I edged toward the door, put my hand on the handle. At the least I could now yank it open and scream. "You never will. Somebody battered him to death Monday night and dragged the body out of Tesoros onto the River Walk. There's a link that stretches all the way from Mexico City to this room. But I can cut that link. All you have to do is give me the name."

I pulled down the handle, edged the door open.

King ignored that. He'd made the decision to let me go. But his doughy face curdled with resentment. That didn't surprise me. The rich not only don't like to lose, they especially don't like to be ripped off.

As long as I was promising immunity—and wouldn't Borroel find this exercise interesting?—I might as well create a little goodwill. "If you want your money back, there may be a way. The family doesn't want a scandal. If the money can be found, it will be returned."

"I want the money back." His hands clenched.

"Give me the name." I held his corrosive gaze. "And keep your mouth shut for twenty-four hours."

"Why?" The demand bristled with reluctance.

"You don't get it even yet, do you?" My tone was scathing. "You know, you're going to be lucky if you don't end up dead or in a Tijuana jail. Think about it. Your contact, the person you paid, is more than just a conduit for the gold. That person's a killer. Now, the cops don't care about the gold. They care about catching a murderer. Give me the name; I'll keep you out of it, and when the case is over, the family will try to find your money for you."

So the logic was shaky, the premise crazy. But this was a man who dealt in stolen treasure. Why should anything sound weird to him as long as he got his? Or got his back?

"Yeah." A dark pleasure shone in his eyes. He'd lost the gold. He couldn't, at this point, touch me. But he could cause trouble for the bastard who had his money. "Yeah. Have a little talk with Tony Garza."

I've never been happier to close a door. I hoped I never again saw that young, decadent, dangerous face, never. The hallway seemed graced by light and life, the butterfly-adorned doors harbingers of freedom. I hurried down the hallway, still scared, but holding tight to the case and to the name. But knowing wasn't proving. Certainly Tony Garza fit the profile of an art thief. Tony was an adventurer, a risk-taker, a gambler, a man who would think it was fun to mastermind the heist of the century. No Brinks robbery could compare to a cat burglar scaling the walls of the National Museum. No wonder he'd been alive with excitement today. Somewhere nearby he had hidden a suitcase full of cash, enough money for him to indulge any taste at all. I quashed a sharp sense of sadness. If it came to a choice between Manuel and Tony, that choice was easy. At least, it was for me. But it was sad that Tony's ebullience and charm and undeniable magnetism masked the heart of a killer. I pushed away any thought of Maria Elena. I was indeed going to bring her one heartbreak in place of another. Tony was the son she'd chosen to run Tesoros, and that told everything about her feelings for him.

But right now, the fake alligator case seemed leaden in my arms, and I had to find a safe place for the gold. Certainly I couldn't trust Kenny King. I thought I'd precluded any move by him because certainly his fingerprints were on the gold. But he might simply have decided it would be smart to remove any contest between us from the hotel. There were two possibilities.

He might intend to get the gold back, if at all possible. Or he might now be hurrying down to the River Walk, seeking a public phone. All it would take was one anonymous call. Borroel might not have believed in my tales of treasure, but he couldn't ignore a phone call with descriptions of the specific pieces, descriptions that could easily be confirmed.

It might please Borroel a great deal if that stolen gold was found in the possession of one Henrietta O'Dwyer Collins.

I was in the middle of the lobby and felt as out of place as a Democrat at a Newt Gingrich rally. By the time I reached my car, I was trembling and well aware I carried with me a fabulous treasure. I could march to the police station, plump it down on Borroel's desk, but that would not only sabotage Tesoros, it would betray Rick. The only reason I ever found the gold was through Rick's cooperation. So far today, I'd spun so many lies, skirted so much truth, that wily coyote would seem the archetype of honor in comparison. No, whatever I did, within the bounds of protecting Manuel and trapping Tony, I intended to keep my word to Rick.

But what could I do with the gold?

I unlocked the car, slipped inside, and gasped at the pocket of heat trapped within. But I didn't roll down the windows. I started the car, put the air-conditioning on high, and eased down the parking-garage ramp.

Where to go? What to do?

After I had paid and zipped the window shut again, I paused and glanced at the rental car map on the seat. Okay. It was a straight shot to the airport on 281 North. I'd find the lockers, indigenous to all major airports, and stash the case. I'd mail the key to Emily.

It was damned hot in the car, but that didn't account for the sweat beading my face.

The Bible urges us to be kind to strangers because we thereby often entertain angels unaware. I was totally absorbed, fighting panic, frantic to be free of the gold. A troupe of angelic strangers could have perched on the car hood and I would scarcely have glanced. So an angel's wing brushed my shoulder. How else can I explain the impulse that made me check the rearview mirror as I drove up Commerce? But look I did. I looked and saw a gray Jaguar in the next lane and the gleam of copper-red hair. So I jockeyed lanes and instead of heading for the expressway, I drove straight to Santa Rosa and turned left. I pulled into the parking lot at Nueva and Santa Rosa and looked across the street at the blue-and-white-tiled facade of the San Antonio Police Department.

The gray Jaguar kept right on going.

I waited until the Jaguar was past and hurried across the street and up the low steps. It was an odd sensation to walk past the smudged glass doors carrying a trophy sought by police on every continent. If I'd been bluffing before, I was now gambling high, wide and handsome. I stopped at the pay phone, dialed La Mariposa.

Tom Garza answered.

"Tom, this is Mrs. Collins. Please take this number"—I read off the pay phone number—"to Rick in the auction room. Tell him to call immediately and to do so where he cannot be overheard. Tom, this is urgent." I hung up. I didn't want to answer questions, I didn't want to talk any longer. I wanted Rick. I stood close to the wall on the interior side of the phone. If Kenny King dared to follow me inside, I'd have to make some tough decisions the minute I saw him.

By my watch, it took four minutes for the phone to

ring. By my nerves, it was a millennium, and all the while I watched through the smudged glass for that moon face and powerful body. At the first buzz, I grabbed the receiver. "Rick? I have the materials we discussed earlier, obtained from Mr. King. But he's not giving up. He's following me. I'm in the lobby of the police department on Nueva. Send somebody absolutely unconnected with Tesoros and La Mariposa with a big purse or gym bag. Not you. Not Iris. And fast."

I hung up, wiped my face and pushed through the second set of doors into the main lobby. Fortunately, the traffic in and out is fairly heavy and constant. I took up a post by the entrance to Sex Crimes/Homicide and tried to look inquiring and impatient, occasionally checking my watch.

I didn't imagine Rick was thrilled at the prospect of taking charge of the gold again, but nine minutes later a tall, slender girl in a T-shirt, shorts, and athletic shoes strode purposefully into the lobby, glanced around. When her eyes slid over me, she gave an infinitesimal nod.

I waggled a hand and walked into the waiting room where I'd spent so much time yesterday. She followed. Once out of sight of the main lobby, I greeted her, my back to the counter and the long-faced receptionist, my eyes on the doorway into the main lobby. She came close, opened her gym bag. I pushed in the fake alligator case. It took a half minute, neither of us spoke, no one saw.

I stayed in the reception area, sat on the uncomfortable bench. The receptionist looked at me incuriously. I had to decide what to do. I knew what I wished I could do. I wished I could walk up to the receptionist, demand to see Detective Borroel. I wanted to tell him this was his job, not mine. But I'd

already made one decision when I handed off the gold.
I was going to try and keep faith with Rick. I wouldn't
have the tag on Tony Garza except for Rick. But how
could Tony be revealed as Schmidt's murderer without
any reference to the stolen gold? I held fast to the fact
that it didn't matter what had been hidden in the wardrobe; all that mattered was the confrontation between
Tony and Ed that ended in Ed's death. But every piece
of physical evidence pointed to Manuel. Somehow I
had to lead the police to Tony instead. If only Manuel
had not looked down from his balcony that night . . .

I was no longer aware of the hard wood of the bench
or the fatigue after my horrific encounter with Kenny
King. I sat still and tense, the beginnings of an idea in
my mind.

Manuel looking down from his balcony . . .

What Manuel saw didn't really matter. He obviously
saw enough to bring him downstairs. If Tony could be
persuaded that Manuel saw him and that somehow
Manuel was going to be able to describe that moment
Tony would be forced to act. I glanced at my watch.
Almost four. The party at Frank and Isabel's home in
the King William district, the party to which I'd been
so gaily invited, would not begin until eight. With luck
and hard effort, there should be time enough.

I grabbed my notebook from my purse, flipped it
open, began to write:

*Maria Elena—Do whatever you must to ensure
that you and Manuel are present at the party tonight. Promise Borroel you will take personal responsibility for Manuel, stress that he is in no
way a danger to anyone. Come to my room immediately upon your return home. Make sure that
no one—I underlined the last two words—sees*

*you. There is a chance we can resolve everything
tonight. Henrietta Collins.*

I folded the note, addressed it to Maria Elena Garza.
But still I sat on the hard bench, knowing that once
Maria Elena received it, there would be set in motion
a chain of events that had to end in sadness, that could
end in horror. I wasn't certain that I would take this
gamble if I were Maria Elena. It was a choice only
she could make. Was it a choice I should offer her?

Was there an alternative? What if I told Borroel
about the gold? But that wouldn't make any difference.
The result was still the same: Tony Garza identified as
the conspirator with Ed Schmidt was no proof at all
that it was Tony who battered Schmidt to death. Borroel could still argue that the evidence proved Manuel
committed the murder, that the gold didn't matter. He
would, of course, be pleased to be the police officer
responsible for returning the gold to Mexico. That
would be a plume in his hat. But I was afraid it would
make no difference at all in his judgment about the
murder. So, if it wouldn't help to link the gold to Tesoros, there was no reason not to try and protect the
store. As for the gold, with luck and planning, we
should be able to return it to the museum without a
hint it had ever been in the United States, much less
at Tesoros in San Antonio. The gold mattered, but it
didn't matter as much as Manuel. And the gold didn't
exonerate Manuel. The only possible way to prove
Manuel's innocence was to prove Tony's guilt.

What if I proposed my plan to both Borroel and
Maria Elena? Whatever happened, Maria Elena had to
make the final decision. Would Borroel cooperate, help
us create a short span of time in which the murderer
would reveal himself?

I recalled the detective's dismissive gaze, his barely repressed irritation. He was smart, tough, and convinced he had his murderer. I suspected he would warn us against any such endeavor. In fact, instead of providing undercover men to watch over and protect Manuel, he might even arrest Manuel immediately, effectively making a trap impossible, or he might send a police officer to the party to be in public attendance upon Manuel, equally effective at scotching any effort to draw a move from the murderer.

But wasn't it too dangerous to expose Manuel's life to a man who could grab an unseen moment and kill so cleverly that Julian Worth's death was officially accepted as an accident?

I looked down at the folded note. That's what the murderer would have to do with Manuel. Manuel's death would of necessity have to appear to be either an accident or a suicide. If the latter could be arranged, so much the better. The murder of Ed Schmidt would be closed and the murderer safe forever.

Accident, suicide. I suppressed a shudder. Tony Garza was quick and ruthless. Would Maria Elena and I be any match for him? Our only chance was to create an atmosphere of utter urgency and contain the possibility of murder to a short span of time.

Could we do it? Dare we do it?

Manuel, so defenseless, so unable to help us in protecting himself. To put him in danger was terrifying. How could I even suggest to Maria Elena that she place the life of this cherished child in peril?

I opened the note, reread the words. I don't know if I have ever felt such a grave sense of responsibility. I wished I'd never envisioned this possibility. Then I wouldn't have to decide whether to seek out Maria Elena. But once I foresaw a way to save Manuel, how could I refuse to offer it to his mother? It might be the only way in the world to save him from prison.

I opened my purse, reached for my cell phone. I held it, not wanting to call, feeling I must call.

The door near the counter opened. A young man in a dark suit held it open for Maria Elena and Manuel. Dear Lord, they'd been here all these hours, all day. I guessed the young man was Manuel's lawyer and likely one of the extended family. His face was carefully composed, lawyers always keep their cards hidden, but a muscle ridged in his jaw. Maria Elena looked a decade older than when we'd first met, her dark eyes haunted and stricken, her mouth drooping, her creamy complexion tinged with gray. She held tight to Manuel's arm. He shambled alongside her, staring down at the floor, his shoulders drawn tight. Oh, God, he was so frightened, so bewildered, even with his mother at his side. And what would happen if they took him away from Maria Elena?

Fate. Karma. The brush of an angel's wings. None of these or all, I didn't know, could never know. But I was here at this moment as this despairing woman walked near.

I gave one last quick glance toward the greater lobby, then stood and moved in front of Maria Elena. I stood with my back to the lobby, though surely Kenny King was now far away from here. I reached out, embraced Maria Elena and tucked the note into her hand.

Her eyes shot toward my face, her fingers squeezed around the paper, and then she was past.

I gazed after the three of them and knew exactly how Caesar must have felt when he stood at the Rubicon.

*   *   *

I brewed coffee in the small coffeemaker and sat in the comfortable chair near the open french door. Shadows slipped across the river as the sun sank behind the buildings. I sipped the coffee and waited in an odd state of relaxation. I'd done all I could do.

Yes, I was ostensibly relaxed, but my thoughts darted from one challenge to the next, should Maria Elena say yes. I needed a clear description of Frank and Isabel's house and grounds. Where could an accident occur? Not even gambling Tony would choose the circular staircase for another accident. No, an accident would have to be natural, an outgrowth of the surroundings. I picked up a map of San Antonio, located Isabel and Frank's house on King William Street. Its backyard sloped to the river. How deep was the river there? Could Manuel swim?

An accident. That was my bet. My hope. A suicide? An overdose of some kind, but surely Manuel had no access to drugs of any kind and would not be likely to have enough knowledge to use them. A hanging? I felt a curl of horror. Yes, that was possible, and the police might believe it within Manuel's capabilities. I doubted it. I didn't think Manuel would understand suicide. I didn't believe that he would imagine ending his life no matter how frightened and despairing he might be. But if a hanging occurred, wouldn't Borroel be quick to see it as the simple solution for a difficult case? No matter how much Maria Elena might object, the truth was, of course, that such a death could be suicide. No one could ever prove differently.

I finished the coffee, pressed my fingers against my temples. Water. Rope. What else?

The door to my room opened and Maria Elena slipped inside. There was a faint flush on her cheeks and hope in her eyes.

I rose and once again we embraced, two old women who knew how precious and fragile life was. When we drew apart, her hands still gripped my arms.

"What can we do?" Her voice was strong, lifted by the promise of action.

"I'm going to offer you a terrible choice." I drew her toward the chair, I sat on the edge of the bed. Her eyes never left my face. I knew she saw there the fear and uncertainty in my heart. "You understand that whoever killed Ed Schmidt and pushed Julian Worth down the circular stairs—"

Maria Elena's hand rose to her throat.

"—is one of the family." I did not need to list the names for her. She knew those names only too well. "Julian Worth came to Tesoros yesterday to try and discover who took the stolen goods from Ed Schmidt. He went from person to person, making it clear his silence was for sale. But Ed Schmidt's murderer wasn't buying and he wasn't going to take any chances that Worth might talk to the police. He moved quickly. Worth came to the store and he was dead within the hour. So we are dealing with someone who is frightened, who thinks fast, and who is very dangerous." No, I did not want to tell her that her beloved second son was the murderer. Call it cowardice, call it foolishness, but in my own mind, I called it caution. In a moment, Maria Elena must deal with a heart-stopping decision. I refused to subject her to more stress than I must at this moment. She would have to deal with a hideous truth soon enough. But not at this moment. "Now let me tell you how I think Manuel got involved Monday night . . ."

When I finished, she slowly nodded. "It could be so. He often does wander about the apartment during the night. I've never known him to go downstairs, but yes, he could certainly have done so. And if he saw such a dreadful thing . . ."

Now came the hard part, the idea that could save Manuel or end his life. How much courage did Maria Elena have? "This murderer"—it was hard to speak—"can be stampeded into action. Here's what I think we should do . . ."

When I finished, she pressed her hands against her face. I heard a soft murmur. "Mary, Mother of God, help me, please help me."

Finally, her hands fell. Tears streamed down her cheeks. "Manuel," she said brokenly, "it will kill him if they put him in prison. My nephew, William, talked to me of many things, of plea bargains and getting the charge reduced to manslaughter." One hand grasped the silver cross at her throat. "William said they would be kind to Manuel, that he would go to a place for people who are not responsible. But I know that he would wither away and die sitting in a locked room, not understanding, frightened, alone. And he is innocent!" Anger blazed now in those tear-filled eyes. She struck one hand against the chair arm. "He is innocent. This should not happen. It must not happen. But"— and now her voice quavered—"how can we keep him safe?"

fourteen

RICK hunched over the little writing table, his lanky legs tucked awkwardly beneath it. He stared at the sheet of paper, then made swift sure strokes with his pen. He tapped the drawing. "Uncle Frank's backyard runs all the way to the River Walk. Uncle Manuel worms his way through the honeysuckle to the walk. Along that part of the walk, there's a concrete embankment. Uncle Manuel likes to sit on the ledge and look down at the water. But in Uncle Frank's backyard, there's also a duck pond ringed by willows. You can't see the pond from the patio, and that's where the party will be. None of the guests would be likely to wander that far. There aren't any lights there." He looked at me somberly. "Everyone in the family knows about the pond. Uncle Manuel loves it. Whenever there's a party, he climbs up in the big magnolia at the edge of the patio to watch the dancing and the mariachis, but eventually he always goes to the pond. He thinks it's his secret place."

Manuel's secret place. "How deep is it?"

"Six feet, maybe. When we were little kids, nobody could play near it without a grown-up along. Mother wanted them to fill it in. Once my little cousin, Rosa, fell in. It was scary—reeds and everything. As for the river, it's only about five feet deep along that stretch. But if somebody pushed Uncle Manuel off the ledge, it's a drop of maybe ten feet. He can't swim and he's phobic about being in water. He'd panic and thrash and flail." He took a deep breath. "It doesn't take too many gulps to drown."

One hard shove, just like the stairs.

I stared at the irregular circle Rick had drawn to represent the pond and the hatch marks for the willows. The pond was far from the lights. Loud music would muffle any cries.

I gripped the edge of the table. "Oh, God, Rick, can we protect him? Can we? What if it isn't the pond? What's if it's the river? What if somebody gets a rope and hangs him?" My mind skittered like a mouse helplessly darting from a cat's paw. "The house is two-story, isn't it? But it wouldn't do to push him down those stairs. The steps wouldn't be metal and he isn't old. And there wouldn't be time—not the way we've planned it—for the murderer to do anything but spur-of-the-moment. There'd be no chance for poison." I looked at him beseechingly. "Even household poisons would be too uncertain. Rick—"

He reached out, gripped my hands. "Don't be frightened. Look, we're smart—"

Were we? Wasn't this a gamble with the devil?

"—what can anybody do without advance planning? Remember, this is going to come as a hell of a shock to the murderer. The pressure's on. The only chance to get Manuel will be at the party, and it will have to look like an accident. There's the river, the pond, maybe a tree and a rope, but you can be damn sure we'll check Uncle Frank's garage, make certain there are no ropes. And nobody carries poison around, especially not stuff that works in minutes. We'll handle it." He gave my hands a final reassuring squeeze, picked up his pen.

But Rick was young, and youth is so certain. Age knows nothing is certain. Except death. I realized I was tired and upset, yet I still knew this was not only our best chance to save Manuel, it was quite likely our only chance.

I took a deep breath, managed a smile. "Okay. Now how are you going to get people in position by the pond and along the shore?"

"Maria Elena and Iris are calling all the family right now. It's going to be a huge party, not just the auction guests. But"—and he jotted down five names: Tom, Rey, Gene, Mike and Izzy—"my cousins. You know Tom. Rey's a marathoner, Gene rock-climbs, Mike scuba dives, and Izzy rodeos. They can handle anything. And," Rick's voice was grim, "tonight they will."

I chose my dress with care—a navy silk, long-sleeved despite the warm evening. I could meld into the darkness. But this evening's action wasn't for me. I was in the gallery. It was hard to accept a passive role, but youth and strength were needed now. All I could do was wait and hope. And pray.

The historic King William district, named for King Wilhelm I of Prussia, reflects the enormous influence of German immigrants in San Antonio. The district runs from East Guenther Street in the shadow of the old Pioneer flour mill to Durango Boulevard and St. Mary's Street. The district is bounded on one side by South Alamo and on the other by the river.

The land titles stretch all the way back to 1793, when the area surrounding the Alamo was deeded away from the mission. In the late 1870s, prominent

German immigrant businessmen built substantial and showy homes reflecting many different influences—Greek Revival, Neoclassical, Victorian, Colonial Revival. As with older housing areas in many cities, the district lost favor in later years and many of the homes became shabby. Beginning in the sixties, appreciation for the old architecture spurred renovations, and today houses in the King William district are extremely expensive and beautifully maintained. Mimosas, magnolias, cedars, sycamores, and willows flourish. Houses along a portion of King William Street have back lawns that reach to the River Walk.

At a few minutes before eight, I parked along King William Street a half block from the Garza house. The street was already filling with cars. The two-story home of dressed limestone blazed with lights. Strings of red and green lights sparkled in the massive sycamores and the luminarias that I always associate with Christmas bordered a winding walk that branched from the main entryway to an arbor. More lights glistened over the treetops. The ebullient off-beat rhythm of "El Maracumbe" added pulse and pace to the night. I've always loved mariachi music, the combination of violins, trumpets, and guitars. The two stringed instruments unique to this music, the crisp, clear vihuela and the bass guitarrón, provide a sound unlike any other. But to tell the truth, my heart belongs to the trumpets, their cascade of golden notes as captivating as fireworks. Cheerful voices rose as guests strolled toward the arbor. I was a few feet behind several middle-aged couples.

Frank and Isabel welcomed the guests as they came through the rose-covered arbor to a fairy-tale backyard—more imposing sycamores, two enormous magnolias, a long swimming pool whose cool blue waters shimmered from lights angling up from below the surface. Frank's face was much livelier than usual and flushed almost as bright a red as his crimson shirt. He shook hands with the men, hugged the women, had a special word for each person. Isabel was in her element, her honey-blond hair bright as spun gold, her heart-shaped face radiating sheer delight in herself, the night, and her home. The Garzas even, after an instant of blankness, managed to greet me with more civility than I expected. Or, from their perspective, deserved. But I didn't get a hug from Frank. And Isabel's sideways glance was sharp and puzzled.

I moved past and veered a little to my left, taking my place in the shadow of one of the magnolias. No wonder the Garzas were pleased. If they loved a party, this one was zinging: the music fast and good, the guests smiling and animated, and a line already forming near the buffet. The tables were bright with red, white, and green tablecloths, the colors of Mexico.

The tables filled a broad swath of patio on the far side of the pool. The near side, to the arbor, had been marked off with garlands of red and white carnations, providing ample space for a dance performance. The mariachis stood to one side of the dance floor. There were eight members in this group. The musicians wore the distinctive charro costume—black jacket, white shirt, tasseled tie, tight black pants with the distinctive silver ornaments on the exterior sides of the trousers, and black sombreros also decorated with silver. The mariachis would play until dinner was over and then the dancers would perform, viewed across the sparkling pool. The mariachis swung into "Las Costenas," an ebullient polka.

Iris was slim and lovely in a ruffled white blouse and red-and-green swirling skirt. She hurried toward me with a beaming smile. I hoped that only I could see how strained and unnatural it was. We embraced and she murmured, "Rick said to tell you everyone's ready. And he said not to worry." She slipped her arm through mine, drawing me toward the buffet. "Rick said we should act as if we were having a good time. Maria Elena will speak just before the dances."

That was good timing, cutting even shorter the time the murderer would have to react. Dance programs at big parties usually last a half hour. I remembered so clearly the magnificent dances at the farewell fiesta for Richard and me when we left Mexico City so many years ago. I would never forget the swirling white dresses and all-white shirts and trousers of the dancers in "La Bamba." This dance from the state of Veracruz ends with the courting couple tying a bow with their dancing feet, a lovely way to signify "I love you."

But this evening, I couldn't welcome the force and power of the dances. I eyed the marked-off space for the dancing on the concrete patio. The sound of the dancers' footwork would be magnified by the hard surface. Loud music, staccato steps, so much sound to hide a startled cry in the night.

Iris and I took our place in the slow-moving buffet line. She introduced me to another cousin, Petra, with the familiar beautiful glossy black hair, smooth creamy complexion, and bright dark eyes. Her face alight with excitement, Petra launched into a rhapsodic report of a recent Gloria Estefan concert.

We picked up plates, again bright in red and green and white, and moved along the buffet. My stomach was a hard knot of nerves, but I was tired and with the beginning quivers of a headache. Food would help and this was glorious food: nachos with shrimp and black beans, pineapple salsa and cheese, guacamole, chalupas topped with a meat-and-corn mixture, salsa, sour cream and scallions, beef empanadas, fried bass in cornmeal, chili shrimp quiche, chili roja, spare ribs in a chili-and-cream sauce, chilis rellenos, rice and beans. No one could leave this feast hungry. I even paused by the desserts: roasted cornmeal pudding, fried cinnamon crisps, and burned milk candy, and chose the candy, the pecans and sugar would surely fill me with energy.

"Let's go this way, Iris." I led the girls to a table far in the back, just a few feet away from the largest magnolia. As we settled at the table, waiters came by with trays of margaritas, iced tea, and white wine. I chose the tea. Petra was describing the concert's first set to an abstracted Iris whose eyes darted from me to the tree above us, where a slender form was tucked in the crook of two huge branches. Most of Manuel's body was obscured by the thick, glossy leaves that rustled in the mild breeze.

Iris listened patiently to Petra, but every so often her gaze slid toward me and her eyes were dark with questions and with fear. Once I reached out, patted her arm. Once I half-turned and looked up. Manuel held a magnolia leaf to his cheek. He watched the musicians, his smile curving as softly as a sweep of cloud high in a summer sky.

The chair beside me was empty, so I could focus on the patio as I ate, spotting familiar faces.

Near the arbor, Wiley Harrison looked more than ever like a giraffe or perhaps a courtly stork as he bent low over the hand of an elderly woman. Jolene, bobbing beside him in a lacy white dress, could have subbed for a Tiffany Christmas tree, festooned all in golden baubles—a double necklace of coins, a half dozen coin bracelets on each arm, oversize medallion earrings, even double gold bands perched in her tightly coiled black hair.

Joshua Chandler leaned negligently against the ladder to the diving platform, his eyes aloof, his ruddy skin bright in the lights of the patio. Susana Garza gestured to him, her red-tipped nails flashing, her eyes brilliant, her thin face flushed with excitement.

Talking over the mariachis without effort, Bud Morgan clapped his hands in satisfaction, obviously concluding a story he found extremely funny. Cara Kendall's tight face squeaked into an appreciative smile and she tilted her head coquettishly. I doubted, however, that her exertion of charm mattered a whit to Morgan, who must be the object of attention by lots of lonely ladies.

Celestina Garza stood by herself near the dance floor, one small foot tapping in rhythm to the mariachis, her little face happier than I'd ever seen it.

But two faces I couldn't find, no matter how long and carefully I looked. Neither Tony Garza nor Kenny King were present. I felt a cold uneasiness. Where were they? I hoped King was on the road to California. But where was Tony? I pushed away a piece of fried bass. Damn, damn, damn. Should I find Rick? Certainly there was no point in Maria Elena's announcement if Tony wasn't here.

I was pushing back my chair, every nerve jangling, when Tony strolled through the rose arbor. A heavy gold chain glittered against his fine mesh navy polo shirt. The breeze ruffled his dark curly hair. He was indeed handsome, his big full face, bright dark eyes, bold nose, and blunt chin perfect for a rollicking brigand, and I'd no doubt he'd won his way to many a woman's bed with that vivid smile. But his eyes weren't smiling. He clapped his brother on the shoulder, gave Isabel a touch, then moved on to survey the patio, even louder now as the diners ate and talked and the mariachis strummed "El Tirador."

I knew he was trouble, standing there, rocking back a little on his heels, his eyes checking the tables, scanning the clumps of revelers still visiting and not yet dining. It took him a moment to find me, our table was so remote. His look was as stiff and harsh as a blow. He would have struck me had he been nearer. His face flushed an ugly red, his eyes glinted, his hands tightened to fists.

I knew as clearly as if he'd shouted: Kenny King had demanded the return of his money. In fact, I was willing to bet Kenny King's gray Jaguar was humming on the highway to El Paso right this moment. I suspected King wanted the hell to be out of Texas as fast as possible. But not without his money.

Tony Garza started across the patio, skirting the end of the pool. He was coming to me, moving swiftly.

I stood. Iris started to rise, but I shook my head. "It will be all right." I said so, but I wasn't sure what I believed. I'd not figured on this, not at all. I didn't know what to do or where to go. And Maria Elena had yet to speak. But I couldn't avoid Tony, I was sure of that. I hesitated for an instant, then walked to meet him.

We came face-to-face beside the stairs to the diving platform. The mariachis were singing, their voices loud and strong, repeating the second verse, "Soy tirador que à las aves les tiro en la loma . . ."

The blue metal stairs and platform base screened us from direct view of most of the guests. I don't think Tony cared at this point. He scowled down at me. "You think you've got away with the gold. You better think again. Kenny said you turned it into the cops. You didn't."

Unease rippled through every nerve end. "What makes you think that?"

"I don't think, I know." He leaned close. I smelled the soft scent of hair cream, saw the muscles ridge in his jaw. "I've got two cousins in the burglary division. Anything like that showing up, everybody would know. Everybody. Where is it, Mrs. Collins?"

I tried to step back but the blunt steps of the ladder punched into my back. "Why should I tell you?"

"Because you don't have any choice." There was a hard pleasure in his tone. "You're going to cooperate with me or the cops will get a little word to the wise. And they'll find the gold. They'll search anybody and everybody you've ever known. You can't pull it off. So," and the tension began to ease out of him, he was so certain he had the upper hand, "we're going to make a deal."

The sheer audacity of his offer stunned me. And confused me. A deal? This was a man who killed to get his way. But, of course, that didn't mean I'd have a long life span if he ever got his hands on the gold.

His full mouth spread in a satisfied smile. He looked like a wolf eyeing a succulent lamb. "Kenny's still in the market. Not, damn you, for quite as much. But he'll buy. I'll give you a third. Now, that's a hell of a deal, isn't it?" There was an odd, almost admiring quirk to his mouth. Tony obviously had decided I was no threat, that I'd scammed the gold away from Kenny King and held on to it, and was therefore no more or less a crook than he, an adventurer in common.

I was startled at the mesmerizing quality of his dark eyes, the appeal of his sideways grin. This was a dangerous man, especially to women. I stared into his dark, compelling eyes. Our gazes locked for a long moment. I needed to be careful. Whatever I did, I must not alert him to our impending trap, not by a look or glance or tone. "I'll think about it, Tony."

The momentary flash of good humor fell away. The predatory glare returned like a carcass revealed by drifting leaves. He stepped even closer, his hands gripping the railings of the ladder, capturing me against the metal, crowding me, his breath warm on my face. "Think fast. Tomorrow will be your last chance."

I slipped sideways, ducked under his arm and moved quickly away. I didn't think he'd follow, but I was trembling by the time I gained the shadows beneath the big magnolia.

Tony still stood at the diving platform, staring after me.

My heart thudded. I tried to keep my breathing even.

A trumpet played an arpeggio.

I looked toward the mariachis and the flower bordered stage.

In the sudden hush, Maria Elena, head high, shoulders back, moved regally to the center of the waiting spotlight, her metallic silver dress swirling. Tonight she wore her lustrous hair with its shimmering touches of silver in coronet braids. Silver filigree butterfly pins accented the braids. Silver filigree earrings ended in dangling crosses with malachite inlays. Her long rosary contained filigree silver beads and coral, ending with a delicate filigree cross. Her smooth, creamy complexion was perhaps a little pale, but her gaze was firm, her mouth resolute. As she held up her hand, silence fell across the brightly lit patio like twilight dropping across water.

"Bienvenidos. As all of you can tell, we are having a special"—just for an instant her voice wavered and

I felt an ache in my chest—"gathering tonight." She did not say celebration. How could she say it when she knew heartbreak awaited her when this night ended? "Not only are we welcoming our special auction guests this evening, I have also called the family to join us this evening. Many of you have been with us these last few days since the dreadful violence Monday night at Tesoros. You know how shocked we have been to have our dear and gentle Manuel suspected of an act beyond his scope, beyond his thought, alien to his nature. But"—she clapped her hands together, held them clasped before her and the silver bracelets on her arms and rings on her fingers glistened—"I have wonderful news." She was a large woman and suddenly she seemed even larger, imposing as any monolithic sculpture, indestructible, unrelenting, unquenchable. Her voice deepened, her hands fell to her sides, loose and open. "Manuel will be safe." No trumpet ever sounded clearer, brighter, sharper. "It has turned out to be much simpler than first we thought. We know now that Manuel was on his balcony Monday night looking down at the River Walk—"

At the ladder, Tony Garza's entire body was suddenly rigid, as immovable as the steel railings to which he clung. His handsome face was smooth and hard and unreadable as a Lucifer mask.

"—and we believe Manuel clearly saw the man who was killed and his companion as they entered Tesoros." She lifted one slender hand and pointed, as if standing on Manuel's balcony, the opening door to Tesoros below her. "Manuel, of course, was quite startled. No one, especially not strangers, should have entered Tesoros at night. This drew Manuel downstairs. He came down to find the dead man and in his simple way Manuel felt he must clean the stains from Teso-

ros. The murderer, of course, had fled. But now that
we know that the murderer was seen by Manuel, we
believe the entire case can easily be solved. The police
detective, Mr. Borroel, has contacted a psychologist in
Houston, Dr. Wilson Abernathy, who specializes in
dealing with persons such as Manuel who cannot
speak but who are very aware of what they have seen.
Dr. Abernathy will arrive tomorrow morning to consult with Manuel. So"—Maria Elena looked calmly
about the patio—"I wanted to share the truth with all
of you so that you understand why we are here tonight.
If Dr. Abernathy succeeds tomorrow, the police will
have a description of the man who committed that brutal murder. With that description, they can solve the
crime and Tesoros will be free of this tragedy."

It was a magnificent performance, a public avowal
that the murder had nothing to do with Tesoros, that
the murderer accompanied his victim and soon all
would be made clear.

A shadow from the diving platform sliced across
Tony's face, obscuring one cheek and his mouth. His
eyes glittered in the soft red flare from the tree lights.
He stared across the pool. I followed his gaze.

Susana stood on a step leading to the terrace behind
the back of the house. She too was utterly still, one
hand tight on the heavy gold necklace that hung almost
to her waist. But her eyes seemed to burn through the
night, bright and terrible as Blake's vision, as she
stared at her husband. Her haggard face accused him.

Susana knew. There was no question in my mind.
She knew. I was shocked and shaken. But it made all
kinds of sense. Perhaps she had followed Tony downstairs to the showroom Monday night, wondering why
he was going there. Perhaps she overheard a phone
call from Ed Schmidt to Tony. No doubt Susana was

often interested in the phone conversations of her philandering husband. Schmidt called, insisted he was coming. He was angry and suspicious. He didn't trust Tony. He wanted to know if it was all a lie, this story of a girl running away with the gold. And Schmidt was drunk. He came to Tesoros. Schmidt and Tony quarreled. Schmidt knew Tony well. He knew that above all Tony must keep his involvement in the scheme from Maria Elena. Did Schmidt threaten to expose Tony to Maria Elena?

There was no doubt how Maria Elena would respond. She was an honorable woman. She would never accept dishonor, not in her life, not in her store which she'd built from nothing to magnificence, not in her family which she had loved and cherished.

If Schmidt threatened to storm upstairs and rouse Maria Elena, Tony had to stop him. If Schmidt ever reached Maria Elena, Tony was ruined. Schmidt knew the store, he knew the family quarters upstairs. I imagined him pushing past Tony, heading for the back doorway and the circular steps. As he plunged through the showroom, Tony grabbed up the pottery bank and struck.

Was Susana watching from the shadows? Whatever happened, I was certain now that she knew the truth. And, in her haggard face, Tony could see that knowledge. Was Susana now in danger from Tony as well as Manuel?

The trumpets blared.

Maria Elena clapped her hands. "And now, let the dancing begin." She gave a small bow and moved out of the lights, melding into the shadows. Two couples ran lightly to the center of the flower-bordered dance floor. The mariachis blazed the national dance of Mexico, "Jarabe Tapatío," the effervescent Mexican hat dance. Suddenly all the lights dimmed, with only two bright spots focused on the dancers. The beaded white blouses of the women sparkled and their embroidered green satin skirts swirled. The silver beading of the charros' trousers glittered. A swift bow, flashing smiles, and the courting dance began. The men's shoes clattered against the cement, recreating the ride of a horse across cobblestones and the vigorous knock on the beloved's door.

In the sudden pall of darkness, the lights in the trees illuminated the leaves and the branches but left the ground below and the tables and audience in shadow. The only light played on the dancers, even the pool was dark.

One moment I was watching Tony, the next I dimly glimpsed the dark bulk of the diving platform. I looked up into the magnolia, seeking Manuel. Surely, surely, he was there, tucked into the big crotch of the tree. I stood on tiptoe, reached up, ran my hand along the limb. The feel of the bark was cool and hard and nothing more.

I whirled, bent down, whispered to Iris. "Where's Manuel? When did he leave? Did you see him go?"

Iris's face was a pale blur. I heard the catch of her breath. "I was watching you and Tony. I was frightened. He looked so angry." She reached up, gripped my arm. "I didn't see Manuel leave. Henrie O, should I have seen him?" There was the beginning of panic in her voice.

"Shh." I shook free of her touch. "It's all right. That's what we expected." But when I stepped back, I felt a brush of fear. We'd expected Manuel to watch the dancing or at least to stay in the tree through the first dance. That's what Rick said he usually did. Why had he come down from the tree sooner than usual?

Would the watchers hidden near the pond and the river see Manuel if he came early? What if Manuel wandered off the path, approached the pond through the trees? Would they see him? Would they be prepared to save him when death came stealing along behind?

The music battered my mind, the echoing steps of the dancers obliterating all other sound. But this was what had to happen—Manuel sliding down from the tree, wandering on the dark path down to the pond or out to the river, alone. This was the only way to trap Tony.

I moved away from the tree, found the path that curved away around a stand of cane. I couldn't follow that path. Whatever happened now, Rick and his cousins must be the eyes and the ears, the sentinels to save Manuel.

The staccato of dancing feet rattled the night. Trumpets blared.

My eyes were adjusting to the darkness. I looked for Maria Elena. I knew that she, too, must be straining to see beyond the trees, waiting helplessly, terror plucking at her mind. I scanned the terrace. She'd moved in that direction. The windows of the house that overlooked the terrace were shuttered, but light seeped from around the edges, not enough light to detract from the dancers, but enough for me to see a man walk swiftly past.

I don't know what attracted my attention, held me suddenly breathless, staring at that scarcely seen form, a dark movement in the night. But when he reached the terrace room, there was a brief slice of light as the door opened and Tony Garza stepped inside. The door closed.

Years ago on a safari in Kenya, I saw a panther stalk a gazelle, the graceful cat sinewy, lithe, a predator in-

tent upon the kill. There was that same intensity and
danger and purpose in Tony Garza's swift movements.
I knew with the shock of horror that I was watching
another predator close in on a creature as helpless as
that gazelle.

For an instant, I stood frozen, my mind buffeted
with shock. I looked toward the dark path. That way
lay help, that way awaited the men confident they
could protect Manuel.

But Tony Garza was inside the house. There could
only be one reason, and there was no one, no one at
all within the house, to protect Manuel. I plunged behind the tables, stumbling on the uneven ground. The
dancers pounded in their intricate steps around the
beautiful sombreros, their faces flushed, their eyes
bright. I reached the terrace, ran to the door, pulled it
open, stepped inside. My harsh breaths seemed even
louder in the sudden quiet of a deserted family room,
easy chairs, a large-screen television, a wall of stereo
equipment, two bookcases.

I closed the door and now the music was a distant
pounding. There was no movement, no sound in the
family room. Not too far away dishes clattered and
voices rumbled. That would be the caterers in the
kitchen, a homely sound that should have been reassuring but did nothing to ease the tightness of my
throat.

I eased across the room to an archway that opened
into the main hall. I jerked back behind the wall. Tony
Garza was waiting, too, on the landing of the main
stairs. Head lifted, he gazed upward. The lights from
a glittering chandelier in the central hallway blazed
down on his face, revealing a hunter's gaze, wary,
measuring, implacable. His skin had a faintly oily
sheen. His face jutted forward, hollowing his cheeks,

sharpening his chin, a vulpine mask of danger. Tony moved, one step, several, and then he was out of sight.

Upstairs, how could I get upstairs? I didn't even try to think what I could do. But I had to get there in time. I dashed down the hall, pushed through a swinging door into the kitchen.

A muscular man heaved a plastic tray of dishes onto a countertop.

I skidded to a stop. "The back stairs! Where are they?" This was an old, old house.

A plump woman with her hands deep in suds looked up. She nodded toward an old brown wooden door. "That way, ma'am. But—"

I hurried past the man, his eyes wide, mouth in an O, and yanked open the door, moving up the steep, rubber-capped treads. Dark now, not a trace of light. I couldn't hear over the rush of blood in my ears. I slipped my hand along the banister. My right knee gave a sudden sharp twinge as I raced up the steep, steep steps. At the top, I fumbled in the darkness, found a metal knob slick with age and use. I twisted it and didn't breathe again until I felt the knob turn, the door yield. I edged the door open, found myself at the end of a dim hallway.

His back to the hallway, Tony Garza stood in a flood of light in a doorway midway up the hall. A large man, he filled the doorway. I was certain that inside the room, he appeared overweeningly powerful—broad taut shoulders, big hands hanging loosely by his side, forward-thrust torso balanced on strong legs. Big and strong, utterly still, poised to leap, gathering force to strike.

I opened my mouth to scream. They would hear me in the kitchen. They had to hear me in the kitchen.

"Stop." Tony's voice was deep and guttural, a cry

of pain and despair. His big hands reached out, clung to the doorjambs. "You told me Manuel hit him." His voice rose, quivered. "You told me Manuel killed him." The words were wrenched from deep within. He took one step, another, through the doorway.

I moved down the hall, edged close to the doorway, looked inside at an elegant bedroom in blue with silver accents, the blue draperies drawn for the night. But I didn't even glance at the bed or furnishings. My eyes were riveted on the bubbling surface of the in-floor hot tub just within the huge oversize bath and on Manuel's legs, the trousers sodden and rippling against the force of the water jets.

Susana knelt by Manuel's limp body, her crimson-tipped nails talon tight on his shoulders.

Manuel's head rested on the apron of the hot tub, his chin up, his mouth open, his jaw slack. His eyes were closed, the dark brush of long feathery lashes resting on his face. Despite the silvery streaks in his hair, he looked like a sleeping child, untouched, untroubled, undefiled.

Susana's burning eyes dominated a face ravaged by fear. Her once lovely features twisted in pain and despair until she was almost unrecognizable, her eyes deep and tortured in their sockets, her cheeks a blazing red, her mouth agape and ugly, her breath coming in short bursts.

"Manuel fell. He hit his head." Her voice was thin and high like a keen. Her fingers still gripped Manuel's shoulders. She began to push. The water swirled higher, reaching his chest.

Tony stumbled across the room, his hands outstretched. He fell to his knees, grabbed his brother's limp arm.

"Tony!" Her cry was a piercing wail, sharp as the

scream of a steam engine. "He fell and slipped. They'll find him drowned and then it will all be over. I'll be safe."

Tony pulled Manuel half out of the water, held him tight. He stared at Susana and his face was that of a man beholding horror, a pit of writhing snakes, hell's fire dancing at a witches' midnight.

Susana stared at the brothers. "Damn you, Tony." Her eyes blazed, her voice shook, her shoulders heaved. "I had to kill Ed. I had to do it for you." Now she loosed her grip on Manuel, her hands reached out, fastened on Tony's bare arm, tight enough, sharp enough, to bring blood. "Ed was going upstairs. He was drunk and he was going to tell Maria Elena everything, how you and he planned the biggest theft in the world and how you got away with it. He was going to tell her, Tony!"

Tony pushed away her hands. He slipped one arm behind Manuel, pillowed his head.

Susana knelt by the edge of the floor pool. She leaned forward, stretching out her hands in a plea.

The welts on Tony's arm oozed blood.

"Tony," her voice was low, feverish, "listen to me. It will be all right. They'll think it's an accident. Everybody knows how Manuel loves to look at water. He fell and hurt his head. He'll drown and everything will be all right."

Tony was on his knees now too. He slipped his arms around his brother, slowly picked him up. Straining, he came to his feet, Manuel cradled in his arms. Tony never looked at me as he walked through the doorway into the hall, toward the stairs.

Susana scrambled to her feet. She bent forward, her hands reaching out. "Tony, Tony . . ." She began to scream.

epilogue

I went back to San Antonio for Rick and Iris's wedding. My reunion with Gina was wonderful. We stood by Tom Garza as the couple ran between the cheering guests, a shower of birdseed spangling the soft October air. Iris's face glowed. She held her long train. The creamy satin dress was a glorious foil for her raven dark hair and creamy complexion. Rick's arm curved proudly around her shoulders. He laughed aloud as a young cousin held the door to the car. White shoe polish marked the windows, Newlyweds, Happy, Happy Day. As the car pulled away, I read the legend on the rear window: "Mexico City or Bust."

I stayed another day, had dinner with Maria Elena and Manuel. We spoke of happiness, not sorrow. But, when I was taking my leave, she reached out, took my hands in hers. "Tesoros will be in good hands with Rick and Iris."

We didn't speak of Tony. It was Tom Garza who told me Tony was living in Hawaii, running a parasailing business. Susana's trial was pending, but there was very little evidence. She'd never admitted anything. There was no mention of the gold. Rumor had it she intended to claim self-defense, that a drunken Ed Schmidt demanded entrance, claiming that Tesoros had stolen something of his, that he was unreasonable and threatened her. A lawyer cousin predicted a plea bargain to manslaughter for Ed Schmidt's death. Julian Worth was still accounted an accidental death, but I knew Susana had pushed him to his death.

I couldn't feel the scales of justice balanced, but capital murder demands proof and the District Attorney had no proof.

The next morning, I took a last walk by the river and stopped to say hello to Manuel. When I smiled at my reflection in his shiny, shiny windows, I knew that innocence had been saved and that was what mattered the most.

The end of the story? I was in my Missouri home two days later when the phone rang, a long-distance call from Mexico City. The line crackled and hissed with static.

"Henrie O?" Rick's young voice was jubilant.

"Yes." I held tight to the receiver.

"We had a great trip. Whipped right through customs."

I breathed deeply, happily.

"And we thought you'd be interested in a big news story down here. You know the gold that was stolen from the National Museum last August—"

Yes, oh yes, indeed, I knew that gold, remembered the soft buttery feel on my fingers, the sense of awe and amazement.

"—it turned up at the museum yesterday. Somebody left it there in an attaché case . . ."

We hope you have enjoyed this Avon mystery. Mysteries fascinate and intrigue with the worlds they create. And what better way to capture your interest than this glimpse into the world of a select group of Avon authors.

Tamar Myers reveals the deadly side of the antique business. The bed-and-breakfast industry becomes lethal in the hands of Mary Daheim. A walk along San Antonio's famed River Walk with Carolyn Hart reveals a fascinating and mysterious place. Nevada Barr encounters danger on Ellis Island. Deborah Woodworth's Sister Rose Callahan discovers something sinister is afoot in her Kentucky Shaker village. Jill Churchill steps back in time to the 1930s along the Hudson River and creates a weekend of intrigue. And Anne George's Southern Sisters find that making money is a motive for murder.

So turn the page for a sneak peek into worlds filled with mystery and murder. And if you like what you read, head to your nearest bookstore. It's the only way to figure out whodunnit . . .

December

Abigail Timberlake, the heroine of Tamar Myers' delightful Den of Antiquity series, is smart, quirky, and strong-minded. She has to be—running your own antique business is a struggle, even on the cultured streets of Charlotte, North Carolina, and her mean-spirited divorce lawyer of an ex-husband's caused her a lot of trouble over the years. She also has a "delicate" relationship with her proper Southern mama.

The difficulties in Abby's personal life are nothing, though, to the trouble that erupts when she buys a "faux" Van Gogh at auction...

ESTATE OF MIND

by Tamar Myers

YOU already know that my name is Abigail Timberlake, but you might not know that I was married to a beast of a man for just over twenty years. Buford Timberlake—or Timbersnake, as I call him—is one of Charlotte, North Carolina's most prominent divorce lawyers. Therefore, he knew exactly what he was doing when he traded me in for his secretary. Of course, Tweetie Bird is half my age—although parts of her are even much younger than that. The woman is 20 percent silicone, for crying out loud, although admittedly it balances rather nicely with the 20 percent that was sucked away from her hips.

In retrospect, however, there are worse things than having your husband dump you for a man-made woman. It hurt like the dickens at the time, but it would have hurt even more had he traded me in for a brainier model. I can buy most of what Tweetie has (her height excepted), but she will forever be afraid to flush the toilet lest she drown the Ty-D-Bol man.

And as for Buford, he got what he deserved. Our daughter, Susan, was nineteen at the time and in college, but our son, Charlie, was seventeen, and a high school junior. In the penultimate miscarriage of justice, Buford got custody of Charlie, our house, and even the dog Scruffles. I must point out that Buford got custody of our friends as well. Sure, they didn't legally belong to him, but where would you rather stake your loyalty? To a good old boy with more connections than the White House switchboard, or to a housewife whose biggest accomplishment, besides giving birth, was a pie crust that didn't shatter when you touched it with your fork? But like I said, Buford got what he deserved and today—it actually pains me to say this—neither of our children will speak to their father.

Now I own a four bedroom, three bath home not far from my shop. My antique shop is the Den of Antiquity. I paid for this house, mind you—not one farthing came from Buford. At any rate, I share this peaceful, if somewhat lonely, abode with a very hairy male who is young enough to be my son.

When I got home from the auction, I was in need of a little comfort, so I fixed myself a cup of tea with milk and sugar—never mind that it was summer—and curled up on the white cotton couch in the den. My other hand held a copy of Anne Grant's *Smoke Screen*, a mystery novel set in Charlotte and surrounding environs. I hadn't finished more than a page of this exciting read when my roommate rudely pushed it aside and climbed into my lap.

"Dmitri," I said, stroking his large orange head, "that 'Starry Night' painting is so ugly, if Van Gogh saw it, he'd cut off his other ear."

Some folks think that just because I'm in business for myself, I can set my own hours. That's true as long as I keep my shop open forty hours a week during prime business hours and spend another eight or ten hours attending sales. Not to mention the hours spent cleaning and organizing any subsequent purchases. I know what they mean, though. If I'm late to the shop, I may lose a valued customer, but I won't lose my job—at least not in one fell swoop.

I didn't think I'd ever get to sleep Wednesday night, and I didn't. It was well into the wee hours of Thursday morning when I stopped counting green thistles and drifted off. When my alarm beeped, I managed to turn it off in my sleep. Either that or in my excitement, I had forgotten to set it. At any rate, the telephone woke me up at 9:30, a half hour later than the time I usually open my shop.

"*Muoyo webe*," Mama said cheerily.

"What?" I pushed Dmitri off my chest and sat up.

"Life to you, Abby. That's how they say 'good morning' in Tshiluba."

I glanced at the clock. "Oh, shoot! Mama, I've got to run."

"I know, dear. I tried the shop first and got the machine. Abby, you really should consider getting a professional to record your message. Someone who sounds . . . well, more cultured."

"Like Rob?" I remembered the painting. "Mama, sorry, but I really can't talk now."

"Fine," Mama said, her cheeriness deserting her. "I guess, like they say, bad news can wait."

I sighed. Mama baits her hooks with an expertise to be envied by the best fly fishermen.

"Sock it to me, Mama. But make it quick."

"Are you sitting down, Abby?"

"Mama, I'm still in bed!"

"Abby, I'm afraid I have some horrible news to tell you about one of your former boyfriends."

"Greg?" I managed to gasp after a few seconds. "Did something happen to Greg?"

"No, dear, it's Gilbert Sweeny. He's dead."

I wanted to reach through the phone line and shake Mama until her pearls rattled. "Gilbert Sweeny was never my boyfriend!"

January

From nationally-bestselling author Mary Daheim, who creates a world inside a Seattle bed-and-breakfast that is impossible to resist, comes Creeps Suzette, *the newest addition to this delightful series . . .*

Judith McMonigle Flynn, the consummate hostess of Hillside Manor, fairly flies out the door in the dead of winter when her cousin Renie requests her company. As long as Judith's ornery mother, her ferocious feline, and her newly retired husband aren't joining them, Judith couldn't care less where they're going. That is until they arrive at the spooky vine-covered mansion, Creepers, in which an elderly woman lives in fear that someone is trying to kill her. And it's up to the cousins to determine which dark, drafty corner houses a cold-blooded killer before a permanent hush falls over them all . . .

CREEPS SUZETTE

by Mary Daheim

"AS you wish, ma'am," said Kenyon, and creaked out of the parlor.

"Food," Renie sighed. "I'm glad I'm back."

"With a vengeance," Judith murmured. "You know," she went on, "when I saw those stuffed animal heads in the game room, I had to wonder if Kenneth wasn't reacting to them. His grandfather or great-grandfather must have hunted. Maybe he grew up feeling sorry for the lions and tigers and bears, oh, my!"

"I could eat a bear," Renie said.

Climbing the tower staircase, the cousins could feel the wind. "Not well-insulated in this part of the house," Judith noted as they entered Kenneth's room.

"It's a tower," Renie said. "What would you expect?"

Judith really hadn't expected to see Roscoe the raccoon, but there he was, standing on his hind legs in a commodious cage. The bandit eyes gazed soulfully at the cousins.

"Hey," Renie said, kneeling down, "from the looks of that food dish, you've eaten more than we have this evening. You'll have to wait for dessert."

Judith, meanwhile, was studying the small fireplace, peeking into drawers, looking under the bed. "Nothing," she said, opening the door to the nursery. "Just the kind of things you'd expect Kenneth to keep on hand for his frequent visits to Creepers."

Renie said good-bye to Roscoe and followed Judith into the nursery. "How long," Renie mused, "do you suppose it's been since any kids played in here?"

Judith calculated. "Fifteen years, maybe more?"

"Do you think they're keeping it for grandchildren?" Renie asked in a wistful tone.

Judith gave her cousin a sympathetic glance. So far, none of the three grown Jones offspring had acquired mates or produced children. "That's possible," Judith said. "You shouldn't give up hope, especially these days when kids marry so late."

Renie didn't respond. Instead, she contemplated the train set. "This is the same vintage as the one I had.

It's a Marx, like mine. I don't think they make them any more."

"Some of these dolls are much older," Judith said. "They're porcelain and bisque. These toys run the gamut. From hand-carved wooden soldiers to plastic Barbies. And look at this dollhouse. The furniture is all the same style as many of the pieces in this house."

"Hey," Renie said, joining Judith at the shelf where the dollhouse was displayed, "this looks like a cutaway replica of Creepers itself. There's even a tower room on this one side and it's . . ." Renie blanched and let out a little gasp.

"What's wrong, coz? Are you okay?" Judith asked in alarm.

A gust of wind blew the door to the nursery shut, making both cousins jump. "Yeah, right, I'm just fine," Renie said in a startled voice. "But look at this. How creepy can Creepers get?"

Judith followed Renie's finger. In the top floor of the half-version of the tower was a bed, a chair, a table, and a tiny doll in a long dark dress. The doll was lying facedown on the floor in what looked like a pool of blood.

The lights in the nursery went out.

February

*Carolyn Hart is the multiple Agatha, Anthony, and Macavity
Award-winning author of the "Death on Demand" series as well
as the highly praised Henrie O series. In* Death on the River
Walk, *sixtysomething retired journalist Henrietta O'Dwyer
Collins must turn her carefully-honed sleuthing skills to a truly
perplexing crime that's taken place at the luxurious gift shop
Tesoros on the fabled River Walk of San Antonio, Texas. See
why the* Los Angeles Times *said, "If I were teaching a course
on how to write a mystery, I would make Carolyn Hart required
reading . . . Superb."*

DEATH ON THE RIVER WALK

by Carolyn Hart

SIRENS squalled. When the police arrived, this area
would be closed to all of us. Us. Funny. Was I
aligning myself with the Garza clan? Not exactly,
though I was charmed by Maria Elena, and I liked—
or wanted to like—her grandson Rick. But I wasn't
kidding myself that the death of the blond man
wouldn't cause trouble for Iris. Whatever she'd found
in the wardrobe, it had to be connected to this murder.
And I wanted a look inside Tesoros before Rick had
a chance to grab Iris's backpack should it be there.

That was why I'd told Rick to make the call to the police from La Mariposa.

The central light was on. That was the golden pool that spread through the open door. The small recessed spots above the limestone display islands were dark, so the rest of the store was dim and shadowy.

I followed alongside the path revealed by Manuel's mop. It was beginning to dry at the farther reach, but there was still enough moisture to tell the story I was sure the police would understand. The body had been moved along this path, leaving a trail of bloodstains. That's what Manuel had mopped up.

The sirens were louder, nearer.

The trail ended in the middle of the store near an island with a charming display of pottery banks—a lion, a bull, a big-cheeked balding man, a donkey, a rounded head with bright red cheeks. Arranged in a semicircle, each was equidistant from its neighbor. One was missing.

I used my pocket flashlight, snaked the beam high and low. I didn't find the missing bank. Or Iris's back-pack.

The sirens choked in mid-wail.

I hurried, moving back and forth across the store, swinging the beam of my flashlight. No pottery bank, no backpack. Nothing else appeared out of order or disturbed in any way. The only oddity was the rapidly drying area of freshly mopped floor, a three-foot swath leading from the paperweight-display island to the front door.

I reached the front entrance and stepped outside. In trying to stay clear of the mopped area, I almost stumbled into the pail and mop. I leaned down, wrinkled my nose against the sour smell of ammonia, and pointed the flashlight beam into the faintly discolored water, no longer foamy with suds. The water's brownish tinge didn't obscure the round pink snout of a pottery pig bank.

Swift, heavy footsteps sounded on the steps leading down from La Mariposa. I moved quickly to stand by the bench. Iris looked with wide and frightened eyes at the policemen following Rick and his Uncle Frank into the brightness spilling out from Tesoros. I supposed Rick had wakened his uncle to tell him of the murder.

Iris reached out, grabbed my hand. Rick stopped a few feet from the body, pointed at it, then at the open door. Frank Garza peered around the shoulder of a short policeman with sandy hair and thick glasses. Rick was pale and strained. He spoke in short, jerky sentences to a burly policeman with ink-black hair, an expressionless face, and one capable hand resting on the butt of his pistol. Frank patted his hair, disarranged from sleep, stuffed his misbuttoned shirt into his trousers.

When Rick stopped, the policeman turned and looked toward the bench. Iris's fingers tightened on mine, but I knew the policeman wasn't looking at us. He was looking at Manuel, sitting quietly with his usual excellent posture, back straight, feet apart, hands loose in his lap.

Manuel slowly realized that everyone was looking at him. He blinked, looked at us eagerly, slowly lifted his hands, and began to clap.

March

.

Nevada Barr's brilliant series featuring Park Ranger Anna Pigeon takes this remarkable heroine to the scene of heinous crimes at the feet of a national shrine—the Statue of Liberty. While bunking with friends on Liberty Island, Anna finds solitude in the majestically decayed remains of hospitals, medical wards, and staff quarters of Ellis Island. When a tumble through a crumbling staircase temporarily halts her ramblings, Anna is willing to write off the episode as an accident. But then a young girl falls—or is pushed—to her death while exploring the Statue of Liberty, and it's up to Anna to uncover the deadly secrets of Lady Liberty's treasured island.

LIBERTY FALLING

by Nevada Barr

HELD aloft by the fingers of her right hand, Anna dangled over the ruined stairwell. Between dust and night there was no way of knowing what lay beneath. Soon either her fingers would uncurl from the rail or the rail would pull out from the wall. Faint protests of aging screws in softening plaster foretold the collapse. No superhuman feats of strength struck Anna as doable. What fragment of energy remained in her arm was fast burning away on the pain. With a kick and a twist, she managed to grab hold of the rail with her other hand as well. Much of the pressure was taken off her shoulder, but she was left face to the wall. There was the vague possibility that she could scoot one hand width at a time up the railing, then swing her legs onto what might or might not be stable footing at the top of the stairs. Two shuffles nixed that plan. Old stairwells didn't fall away all in a heap like guillotined heads. Between her and the upper floor were the ragged remains, shards of wood and rusted metal. In the black dark she envisioned the route upward with the same jaundice a hay bale might view a pitchfork.

What the hell, she thought. *How far can it be?* And she let go.

With no visual reference, the fall, though in reality not more than five or six feet, jarred every bone in her body. Unaided by eyes and brain, her legs had no way of compensating. Knees buckled on impact and her chin smacked into them as her forehead met some immovable object. The good news was, the whole thing was over in the blink of a blind eye and she didn't think she'd sustained any lasting damage.

Wisdom dictated she lie still, take stock of her body and surroundings, but this decaying dark was so filthy she couldn't bear the thought of it. Stink rose from the litter: pigeon shit, damp and rot. Though she'd seen none, it was easy to imagine spiders of evil temperament and immoderate size. Easing up on feet and hands, she picked her way over rubble she could not see, heading for the faint smudge of gray that would lead her to the out-of-doors.

Free of the damage she'd wreaked, Anna quickly found her way out of the tangle of inner passages and escaped Island III through the back door of the ward.

The sun had set. The world was bathed in gentle peach-colored light. A breeze, damp but cooling with the coming night, blew off the water. Sucking it in, she coughed another colony of spores from her lungs. With safety, the delayed reaction hit. Wobbly, she sat down on the steps and put her head between her knees.

Because she'd been messing around where she probably shouldn't have been in the first place, she'd been instrumental in the destruction of an irreplaceable historic structure. Sitting on the stoop, smeared with dirt and reeking of bygone pigeons, she contemplated whether to report the disaster or just slink away and let the monument's curators write it off to natural causes. She was within a heartbeat of deciding to do the honorable thing when the decision was taken from her.

The sound of boots on hard-packed earth followed by a voice saying: "Patsy thought it might be you," brought her head up. A lovely young man, resplendent in the uniform of the Park Police, was walking down the row of buildings toward her.

"Why?" Anna asked stupidly.

"One of the boat captains radioed that somebody was over here." The policeman sat down next to her. He was no more than twenty-two or -three, fit and handsome and oozing boyish charm. "Have you been crawling around or what?"

Anna took a look at herself. Her khaki shorts were streaked with black, her red tank top untucked and smeared with vile-smelling mixtures. A gash ran along her thigh from the hem of her shorts to her kneecap. It was bleeding, but not profusely. Given the amount of rust and offal in this adventure, she would have to clean it thoroughly and it wouldn't hurt to check when she'd last had a tetanus shot.

"Sort of," she said, and told him about the stairs. "Should we check it out? Surely we'll have to make a report. You'll have to write a report," she amended. "I'm just a hapless tourist."

The policeman looked over his shoulder. The doorway behind them was cloaked in early night. "Maybe in the morning," he said, and Anna could have sworn he was afraid. There was something in this strong man's voice that told her, were it a hundred years earlier, he would have made a sign against the evil eye.

April

Sister Rose Callahan, eldress of the Depression-era community of Believers at the Kentucky Shaker village of North Homage, knows that evil does not merely exist in the Bible. Sometimes it comes very close to home indeed.

"A complete and very charming portrait of a world, its ways, and the beliefs of its people, and an excellent mystery to draw you along."
Anne Perry

In the next pages, Sister Rose confronts danger in the form of an old religious cult seeking new members among the peaceful Shakers.

A SIMPLE SHAKER MURDER

by Deborah Woodworth

AT first, Rose saw nothing alarming, only rows of strictly pruned apple trees, now barren of fruit and most of their leaves. The group ran through the apple trees and into the more neglected east side of the orchard, where the remains of touchier fruit trees lived out their years with little human attention. The pounding feet ahead of her stopped, and panting bodies piled behind one another, still trying to keep some semblance of separation between the brethren and the sisters.

The now-silent onlookers stared at an aged plum tree. From a sturdy branch hung the limp figure of a man, his feet dangling above the ground. His eyes were closed and his head slumped forward, almost hiding the rope that gouged into his neck. The man wore loose clothes that were neither Shaker nor of the world, and Rose sensed he was gone even before Josie reached for his wrist and shook her head.

Two brethren moved forward to cut the man down.

"Nay, don't, not yet," Rose said, hurrying forward.

Josie's eyebrows shot up. "Surely you don't think this is anything but the tragedy of a man choosing to end his own life?" She nodded past the man's torso to a delicate chair laying on its side in the grass. It was a Shaker design, not meant for such rough treatment. Dirt scuffed the woven red-and-white tape of the seat. Scratches marred the smooth slats that formed its ladder back.

"What's going on here? Has Mother Ann appeared and declared today a holiday from labor?" The powerful voice snapped startled heads backwards, to where Elder Wilhelm emerged from the trees, stern jaw set for disapproval.

No one answered. Everyone watched Wilhelm's ruddy face blanche as he came in view of the dead man.

"Dear God," he whispered. "Is he . . . ?"

"Yea," said Josie.

"Then cut him down instantly," Wilhelm said. His voice had regained its authority, but he ran a shaking hand through his thick white hair.

Eyes turned to Rose. "I believe we should leave him for now, Wilhelm," she said. A flush spread across

Wilhelm's cheeks, and Rose knew she was in for a public tongue thrashing, so she explained quickly. "Though all the signs point to suicide, still it is a sudden and brutal death, and I believe we should alert the Sheriff. He'll want things left just as we found them."

"Sheriff Brock . . ." Wilhelm said with a snort of derision. "He will relish the opportunity to find us culpable."

"Please, for the sake of pity, cut him down." A man stepped forward, hat in hand in the presence of death. His thinning blond hair lifted in the wind. His peculiar loose work clothes seemed too generous for his slight body. "I'm Gilbert Owen Griffiths," he said, nodding to Rose. "And this is my compatriot, Earl Weston," he added, indicating a broad-shouldered, dark-haired young man. "I am privileged to be guiding a little group of folks who are hoping to rekindle the flame of the great social reformer, Robert Owen. That poor unfortunate man," he said, with a glance at the dead man, "was Hugh—Hugh Griffiths—and he was one of us. We don't mind having the Sheriff come take a look, but we are all like a family, and it is far too painful for us to leave poor Hugh hanging."

"It's an outrage, leaving him there like that," Earl said. "What if Celia should come along?"

"Celia is poor Hugh's wife," Gilbert explained. "I'll have to break the news to her soon. I beg of you, cut him down and cover him before she shows up."

Wilhelm assented with a curt nod. "I will inform the Sheriff," he said as several brethren cut the man down and lay him on the ground. The morbid fascination had worn off, and most of the crowd was backing away.

There was nothing to do but wait. Rose gathered up the sisters and New-Owenite women who had not already made their escape. Leaving Andrew to watch

over the ghastly scene until the Sheriff arrived, she
sent the women on ahead to breakfast, for which she
herself had no appetite. The men followed behind.

On impulse Rose glanced back to see Andrew's tall
figure hunched against a tree near the body. He
watched the crowd's departure with a forlorn expression. As she raised her arm to send him an encouraging
wave, a move distracted her. She squinted through the
tangle of unpruned branches behind Andrew to locate
the source. *Probably just a squirrel*, she thought, but
her eyes kept searching nonetheless. There it was
again—a flash of brown almost indistinguishable from
tree bark. Several rows of trees back from where Andrew stood, something was moving among the
branches of an old pear tree—something much bigger
than a squirrel.

May

Once upon a time Lily and Robert were the pampered offspring of a rich New York family. But the crash of '29 left them virtually penniless until a distant relative offered them a Grace and Favor house on the Hudson.

The catch is they must live at this house for ten years and not return to their beloved Manhattan. In the Still of the Night Lily and Robert invite paying guests from the city to stay with them for a cultural weekend. But then something goes wildly askew.

IN THE STILL OF THE NIGHT

by Jill Churchill

"I realized that Mrs. Ethridge wasn't at breakfast and she hasn't come to lunch either. I kept an eye out for her so I could nip in and tidy her room while she was out and about and she hasn't been."

"She's not in the dining room?" Lily said. "No, I guess not. There were two empty chairs."

"She might be sick, miss."

"Have you knocked on her door?"

"A couple times, miss."

"I'll go see what's become of her," Lily said.

Robert, who had been ringing up the operator, hung

up the phone. "I think it would be better for me to check on her."

"But Robert . . ." Lily saw his serious expression and paused. "Very well. But I'll come with you."

They went up to the second floor and Robert tapped lightly on the door. "Mrs. Ethridge? Are you all right?" When there was no response, he tapped more firmly and repeated himself loudly.

They stood there, brother and sister, remembering another incident last fall, and staring at each other. "I'll look. You stay out here," Robert said.

He opened the door and almost immediately closed it in Lily's face. She heard the snick of the inside lock. There was complete silence for a long moment, then Robert unlocked and re-opened the door. "Lily, she's dead."

Lily gasped. "Are you sure?"

"Quite sure."

"Oh, why did she have to die *here*?" Lily said, then caught herself. "What a selfish thing to say. I'm sorry."

"No need to be. I thought the same thing. It's not as if she's a good friend, or even someone we willingly invited."

"What do we do now?"

"You go back to the dining room and act like nothing's wrong while I call the police and the coroner."

"The police? Why the police?"

"I think you have to call them for an unexplained death. Besides, if we don't, what do we *do* with her? Somebody has to take her away to be buried."

June

Patricia Anne is a sedate suburban housewife living in Birmingham, Alabama, but thanks to her outrageous sister, Mary Alice, she's always in the thick of some controversy, often with murderous overtones. In Murder Shoots the Bull, *Anne George's seventh novel in the Southern Sisters series, the sisters are involved in an investment club with next door neighbor Mitzi. But no sooner have they started the club than strange things start happening to the members...*

MURDER SHOOTS THE BULL

by Anne George

I fixed coffee, microwaved some oatmeal, and handed Fred a can of Healthy Request chicken noodle soup for his lunch as he went out the door. Wifely duties done, I settled down with my second cup of coffee and the *Birmingham News*.

I usually glance over the front page, read "People are Talking" on the second, and then turn to the Metro section. Which is what I did this morning. I was reading about a local judge who claimed he couldn't help it if he kept dozing off in court because of narcolepsy when Mitzi, my next door neighbor, knocked on the back door.

"Have you seen it?" She pointed to the paper in my hand when I opened the door.

"Seen what?" I was so startled at her appearance, it took me a moment to answer. Mitzi looked rough. She had on a pink chenille bathrobe which had seen better days and she was barefooted. No comb had touched her hair. It was totally un-Mitzi-like. I might run across the yards looking like this, but not Mitzi. She's the neatest person in the world.

"About the death."

"What death?" I don't know why I asked. I knew, of course. I moved aside and she came into the kitchen.

"Sophie Sawyer's poisoning."

Mitzi walked to the kitchen table and sat down as if her legs wouldn't hold her up anymore.

"Sophie Sawyer was poisoned?"

"Arthur said you were there yesterday."

"I was." I sat down across from Mitzi, my heart thumping faster. "She was poisoned?"

"Second page. Crime reports." Mitzi propped her elbows on the table, leaned forward and put a hand over each ear as if she didn't want to hear my reaction.

I turned to the second page. The first crime report, one short paragraph, had the words—SUSPECTED POISONING DEATH—as its heading. Sophie Vaughn Sawyer, 64, had been pronounced dead the day before after being rushed to University Hospital from a nearby restaurant. Preliminary autopsy reports indicated that she was the victim of poisoning. Police were investigating.

Goosebumps skittered up my arms and across my shoulders. Sophie Sawyer murdered? Someone had killed the lovely woman I had seen at lunch the day before? I read the paragraph again. Since it was so brief, the news of the death must have barely made the paper's deadline.

"God, Mitzi, I can't believe this. It's awful. Who was she? One of Arthur's clients?"

Mitzi's head bent to the table. Her hands slid around and clasped behind her neck.

"His first wife."

"His what?" Surely I hadn't heard right. Her voice was muffled against the table.

But she looked up and repeated, "His first wife."